DARKER THAN LOVE

ANNA ZAIRES

CHARMAINE PAULS

GREY EAGLE
PUBLICATIONS

Copyright © 2020 Anna Zaires and Charmaine Pauls
All rights reserved.

Published by Grey Eagle Publications
www.greyeaglepublications.com

Cover by Najla Qamber Designs
www.najlaqamberdesigns.com

ISBN: 978-1-64366-071-4
Print ISBN: 978-1-64366-142-1

"*M*ommy." The little girl tugs on her mother's sleeve from the backseat. "Mommy, can I have a cookie?"

She's bored and hungry. It's getting dark, and all she can see through the car window are trees and snow. They're taking the scenic route, Daddy said, a pretty route. But it's a longer route, and she doesn't find it all that pretty. She'd much rather they took the train to Grandma Hanna's place, like always.

"No, my darling. We'll be having dinner soon." Her mother turns around in the passenger seat to glance at her. The corners of her blue eyes crinkle with a warm smile, her white-blond hair waving softly around her face as she says, "Just wait a little longer, okay?"

"Okay." The girl sighs and looks out the window. Trees, snow, trees. The black ribbon of the asphalt winding through the forest. All boring, boring, boring.

But she's a good girl, and she knows better than to whine.

Proper meals are important. Listening to parents is important. And if her mother says there will be dinner soon, she trusts that it is so.

She's zoning out, half-dozing, when her father suddenly slams on the brakes, bad words she's only heard on TV flying from his mouth. Her small body jerks forward, kept in place only by the seatbelt cutting into her as the car screeches to a halt.

"Ow!" She rubs her forehead where it hit the hard cushion of the back seat. "Daddy, that hurt!"

"Hush, Mina." Her father's voice is strangely tight as he stares straight ahead. "Just be quiet, okay, sweetheart?"

Blinking, the little girl lowers her hand and follows his gaze. Two men are standing in front of the car. Where did they come from? Were they just standing on the road like that?

Is that why Daddy hit the brakes so hard?

One man approaches and knocks on the driver's window with something hard and pointy.

Her stomach swoops down like a bird, and she suddenly feels cold and dizzy. Because the hard, pointy thing is a gun. And the other man, the one in front of the car, is also aiming a gun at the windshield. Both weapons are black and dangerous-looking, like the ones they show in movies, not bright blue like the toy gun Daddy got her for playing soldiers-and-captives with the neighborhood boys. She's really good at those types of games, fast and strong despite her tiny build. She can beat all the boys, but she doesn't have her blue gun with her. And these aren't boys.

She can hear her father's breathing. It's fast and ragged as he presses the button to lower the window. The stranger leans down, and her mother chokes back a sob as he presses the gun—the scary-looking black gun—to her father's temple.

"Get out." The stranger's voice is low and mean. "We need the fucking car."

"P-please." Her mother's voice is thin and high, as shaky as her breathing. "Please, don't do this. W-we have a daughter."

The stranger's eyes cut to the girl in the backseat, his cold, cruel stare slicing through her like a knife before he returns his attention to her father. "I said, get the fuck out."

"Okay, okay. Just a sec." Her father sounds out of breath as he unlatches his seatbelt. "Come on, honey. Let's just... let's go."

He opens the door and the man yanks him out of the car, causing him to sprawl on the asphalt. Crying audibly, the girl's mother scrambles out of the car on her own and jerks open the back door, reaching for her daughter's seatbelt.

The little girl is also crying. She's never been so scared. It's freezing outside, and the icy wind bites into her as her mother pulls her out, then reaches back in to grab her coat. She doesn't understand what's happening, why these bad men are allowed to do this.

Why Daddy doesn't have a gun of his own so he can stop them. If she had hers, she'd try, even though it's bright blue and doesn't look dangerous at all.

The other man, the one in front of the car, comes toward them. Up close, he's even more terrifying than his partner, his face unshaven and his darting eyes filled with a kind of madness.

"Stop dicking around," he hisses, his gaze bouncing from his buddy to the girl's crying mother, who's putting the coat on the girl with shaking hands, to the girl's father, who's hurrying around the car toward his wife and daughter. "We need to *go*."

The cold-eyed man gets behind the wheel. "Then let's go. Get in." He slams the door shut.

The terrifying man's gaze darts to him, then again to the girl's parents—who are now in front of her, shielding her with their bodies.

"Please." Her father's voice quavers as he pushes the little girl farther behind him. "Please, you have the car now. Please, go. We won't tell, I swear. Just… go."

The terrifying man smiles, the madness in his eyes glowing brighter. "Sorry, no witnesses allowed." And he lifts the gun.

Pop! Pop!

The gunshots punch the girl's ears like a blow. Dazed, she stumbles back as her parents crumple in front of her and a sharp, burning smell fills the air, mixing with something coppery and metallic.

"What the fuck?" The other man sticks his head out the window. "That wasn't the plan!"

4

"Wait," the killer says, taking aim at the little girl, but she's already running. She might be small, but she's fast, so fast she darts behind the trees before the next shot rings out. Behind her, she can hear the hijackers arguing, but she keeps running, her heart beating like a hummingbird's wings.

She doesn't run far into the forest. Instead, she finds a clump of above-ground roots and hides there, all the while telling herself it's just a game she's playing. The tears freezing on her face and the tremors wracking her tiny body belie that story, but she ignores them.

She's strong and fast. She can beat all the boys. Even the adult ones with black, scary-looking guns that make her ears hurt. So what if she's hungry and so cold she can barely feel her nose and toes? She's going to wait for the bad men to leave, then go back and find her parents. And they'll hug her and tell her what a good girl she is. Then they'll all go and have dinner.

So she waits and waits, shivering in the coat her mother put on her. By the time she climbs out of her hiding place, it's completely dark, with only the full moon lighting her way, and she's afraid something will jump out at her from the trees. A wolf or a bear or a monster. At six, she's still young enough to believe in monsters of the non-human kind.

Choking down her fear, she retraces her steps, like she would in a game of soldiers-and-captives. The car and the bad men are gone, but her parents are there, lying by the side of the road in the exact same way as when they fell: her mother on her side, white-blond hair covering her face, and her father on his back, his face turned the other way.

The girl's heart skips a beat, then starts racing so fast it hurts. She feels dizzy again, and cold. But it's not her nose or hands or toes that are freezing now; it's something deep inside her. Trembling, she kneels by her mother and tugs on her sleeve. "Mommy. Mommy, please. Let's go."

There's no response, and when she looks down at her hand, she sees a smear of red on her fingers. And on her jeans.

She's kneeling in a puddle of blood.

Her stomach turns over, and she feels like she might vomit. Backing up on all fours, she bumps into her father's side. "Daddy!" She grabs his hand and squeezes it with all her strength. "Daddy, wake up!"

But he doesn't answer either. His hand is stiff and icy in her grip, and when she turns his face toward her, his eyes are open, as if he's staring at the full moon above.

Only there's no expression in his eyes. They're blank, unseeing. And in the middle of his forehead is a hole.

Trembling all over, the little girl rises to her feet. She doesn't feel hungry anymore, but she's cold. So very, very cold. It's as if the snow is inside her, filling her stomach and chest. It feels good in a way, numbing. The painful, hummingbird-like fluttering of her heart seems to quiet down, edged out by the iciness that fills her lungs with every breath she takes.

1

MINA

BUDAPEST, 15 MONTHS EARLIER

A wave of dizziness washes over me, and the tray I'm carrying wobbles in my hands, causing the beer bottles to topple over, spilling the foaming liquid.

Dammit. When is this going to end?

Gritting my teeth, I sink to one knee behind the column and set the tray on the sticky floor, pretending to tie the shoelaces on my Doc Martens while I wait for the dizziness to pass and my hands to stop shaking.

Thirty seconds pass. Then a minute. And my stupid hands are still shaking.

Cursing under my breath, I mop at the spilled beer with a rag. That much I can manage. Lifting the tray itself, though, is beyond me. It weighs only a couple of kilos, but I'm so weak it might as well be a hundred. And this is only the start of my shift. I have no idea how I'm going to last until the bar closes tonight.

Maybe Hanna was right. Maybe this is too soon, and I should—

"—pop that fucker right in the head." The words, spoken in Russian in a gruff male voice, jolt me like a gunshot. Instinctively, I freeze in place, my military training kicking in as I scan my surroundings, searching for the threat.

There. Two o'clock, a round table behind the column, in Ella's section. The column is hiding most of the table from my view, but I can tell there are two men sitting there.

"One shot, that's all we're likely getting, Sokolov said," the speaker continues. "And since the target's likely to be wearing a vest—"

"I know," the other man interrupts, his deep voice smooth despite the hint of annoyance in his tone. "Aim for the head."

A chill skitters through my veins. I didn't misunderstand. These are indeed professionals discussing an upcoming hit—and I'm crouching right there, less than two meters away from them.

The same column that's blocking them from my view is hiding me and has been for the past couple of minutes, which must be why they're talking so freely. Though the bar is fairly crowded, they're in a nook of sorts, shielded by the column, and with the noise level in the room, nobody at the other tables can hear them.

I can, though.

And if I get up from where I'm crouching, they'll realize that, and I may not walk out of here alive.

A year ago, I wouldn't have blinked twice, confident in my ability to handle whatever comes my way. But in my current state, I'm no match for an aggressive rat, much less two men who specialize in killing.

Men who are as dangerous as I am.

Quickly, I assess my options. I can stay here and hope no one sees me until the Russians leave, but odds are, Ella will come upon me at any moment.

The other alternative—and the one I'm leaning toward—is to get up and feign total ignorance. After all, it's entirely possible that I don't speak Russian well enough to understand what they said. It's highly likely, in fact, as most Hungarians of my generation learn English in school instead.

Yes, that's it. I'm just going to play dumb. And to do that, I have to expose myself rather than wait to be exposed.

The surge of adrenaline steadies my hands. Picking up the tray, I rise to my feet, loudly muttering curses in Hungarian. Because that's what an innocent, ignorant waitress would do if she spilled beer all over her tray and had no idea she was within grabbing distance of two killers.

"Mina, are you okay?" Ella asks, passing by with her own tray of drinks, and I give her a reassuring grin.

"Yep, just clumsy today." I'm purposefully not looking in the direction of the table, but I can feel the men's eyes on me as I step behind the column and head back to the bar to swap out the beer bottles.

As I walk, my heart hammers in my chest, and a

trickle of cold sweat runs down my spine. I can sense their stares following me, but I keep the smile on my face as I swing behind the bar, throw the bottles in the recycling bin, and start cleaning off the tray.

See? I'm just doing my job. That's what I'm hoping my casual actions say. *I'm an innocent waitress, that's all.*

When my tray is clean, I load it up with more bottles and sashay over to my section, still avoiding looking in the direction of the column. My pulse is much too fast, but the expression on my face is bright and cheerful, as befits someone working for tips.

Fifteen minutes pass. Twenty. After a half hour, I risk a glance behind the column as I deliver cocktails to a group of college girls.

Shit.

The two men are still there, and they're still looking at me.

I quickly look away, but not before I register their appearance. One is huge, both tall and broad, like a linebacker in American football. His head is shaved, and his skull is decorated with tattoos, emphasizing his strong, almost brutish features. He's dressed casually, in a pair of jeans and a black hoodie over a dark T-shirt. The other one is of the same height but a leaner build, and is wearing a stylish pair of dress slacks with a white button-up shirt, as if he's just come from a business meeting or an interview. His hair is dark brown, but his eyes are light and striking, though I can't tell the exact color from this distance.

In general, everything about the leaner man is

striking, from the strong, chiseled lines of his darkly handsome face to the power and self-assurance evident in his deceptively indolent pose.

Instinctively, I know he's the one I need to fear.

He's the one who'll decide if I get home alive.

To my shock, my heartbeat jacks up, and a frisson of heat blooms between my legs as I picture myself fighting him. My body clearly didn't get the memo that danger—something I've always been drawn to—is a bad thing for me right now. Even worse, my brain seems to be interpreting the effects of adrenaline as sexual arousal... as attraction to the man who's likely considering whether he needs to slice my throat or not.

This is not good.

Not good at all.

I can feel his gaze following me as I move about my work. The other man is looking at me too, but it's the dangerous stranger's stare I feel most viscerally, as if he's already touching me. Electricity skates over my skin, and more heat floods my core as I imagine him *actually* touching me, and not with the sharp edge of his blade.

Fuck. I have no idea why my libido has chosen this moment to come out of its prolonged hibernation, but I don't like it.

Sex, especially with a Russian killer, is the last thing I need.

Another wave of dizziness hits me, and I almost welcome it this time. My arousal fizzles out, replaced by the faint nausea that often accompanies these episodes of extreme weakness. Dragging in a breath, I focus on staying upright and not dropping the tray I'm carrying. I can't afford to give in to the urge to rest, to act in any way that would sharpen the Russians' suspicions. I have to look like an ordinary waitress doing her job, nothing more.

The dizziness passes after a few moments, and I continue with my shift, resisting the temptation to look at the men's table and see if the dangerous stranger is still watching me.

An hour later, I finally allow myself another glance.

The two men are gone, and a group of girls is sitting there instead, laughing and flipping their long hair over their slim shoulders. They're as harmless as can be, and the knot of tension inside me eases slightly.

Maybe the Russians believed my innocent act, and I'll never see them again.

It should be a relief—and it is—but there's an illogical disappointment mixed in, too. As inappropriate as my attraction to the dangerous stranger was, it was the first time in years I felt *something*, and feeling anything is better than feeling nothing.

Oh, well. He and his companion are gone, and it's for the best.

Now I can focus on my work without the temptation of staring at him.

As the night wears on, I continue with my shift, battling waves of dizziness and growing exhaustion, and by the time the last patrons leave, I'm on the verge of collapse.

"Here, let me." Ella grabs the dirty glasses out of my unsteady hands, and I let her have them.

If I drop them, it's more work for everyone.

Finally, everything is done, and I'm still somehow upright. With the last drops of my strength, I trudge over to the back room, throw on my puffy winter jacket, and stumble out into the freezing alley outside, my mind hazy from exhaustion.

I'm so tired I almost forget about the two Russians, and by the time I hear the footsteps, it's too late.

They're upon me.

2

YAN

I grab the girl while Ilya keeps an eye on the bar exit, making sure no one sees me drag my captive into an even smaller alley on the side of the bar. Despite the bulky jacket swaddling her petite frame, she's incredibly light, as if her very bones are made of air. Keeping one hand over her mouth, I half-carry, half-drag her with my free arm—an easy feat, as she puts up hardly any struggle.

A frightened kitten would've been harder to restrain.

The place we're staying at is only a couple of blocks from here, so we head directly there, keeping to the shadows to avoid being seen by the one or two drunk tourists still stumbling around the dimly lit streets. It's risky, snatching her like this—as fugitives, we don't want to draw any attention—but the alternative was to follow her home, and who knows what or who might've been there.

She might've had a boyfriend waiting in her bed.

An unfamiliar feeling stirs in me at the thought, something dark and ugly. I don't understand it, any more than I fully comprehend why I'm doing this. The threat posed by the girl is minimal. Even if she overheard us and understood what we were talking about, it doesn't matter, as we're supposed to leave Budapest tomorrow. In the worst case, we would've had to forego sleep and accelerate our departure to avoid the authorities.

But no. Instead of sensibly forgetting about the girl, I told Ilya we have to keep her with us until tomorrow morning, in case she decided to blab about what she'd heard, and my brother agreed readily... probably for the same reason I couldn't stop watching the girl for two hours straight.

Because she's the hottest little thing we've come across.

At first, I didn't think so, seeing only a pale, skinny chick dressed like a punk-rock wannabe in her oversized sweater, ripped black jeans, and ugly boots. But the more I watched her, the more I found myself unable to look away. I've always preferred long hair on women, but her platinum-blond strands—shorter than mine and styled in spikes on top of her shapely head— emphasized the delicate prettiness of her elfin features in a way that a more feminine cut wouldn't have, drawing attention to her thickly lashed blue eyes and soft, pouty lips. And what I initially thought was a shapeless, boyish figure turned out to be all subtle curves and tantalizing hints of muscle, as if she'd once been a dancer or a gymnast. Even the excessive piercings in her left ear and the small tattoo on the side of her graceful neck grew on me, morphing from off-putting to sexy once I realized the grungy decorations only highlighted the creaminess of her translucent skin. What captivated me the most, though, was the way she moved around the bar, with a quiet confidence and fluid deliberateness that belied her supposed clumsiness earlier, when she'd emerged from her hiding spot behind the column with the beer spilled all over her tray.

I wondered briefly if she'd spied on us on purpose, but concluded it was unlikely. If she'd had any idea who we are, the bar would've been swarming with Interpol. Still, her sudden appearance made Ilya and me uneasy enough to pay attention to her, and the longer we watched her, the more we both wanted her.

I could see the same lust I was feeling painted across my brother's face.

Normally, it wouldn't have bothered me. For whatever reason, Ilya and I are often drawn to the same women, and as neither of us is the jealous type, we don't mind sharing with each other—and on occasion, indulging the woman's fantasy of a ménage à trois with twins.

We don't look that much alike, but we *are* genetically identical.

This time, though, the idea of my brother coming

anywhere near this girl makes me want to break his steroid-thickened jaw. I know what he's thinking—that once we have her at our place, we'll calm her down and do our best to seduce her together. But he's wrong. He's not touching her tonight.

The pretty waitress is mine and mine alone.

I like the way she feels against me, all small and helpless as I lift her higher and carry her up the crumbling stairs to our second-floor apartment. Her scent, something sweet like honeysuckle and fresh like lemon, teases my nostrils, and my cock hardens as dark anticipation floods my veins. I've always enjoyed tall women, finding them to be a better match in bed, but something about this girl's petiteness appeals to me on a deeply primitive level.

I can do anything I want to her, and the things I want to do are dark and twisted, as wrong as kidnapping her in the first place.

"You can set her down now," Ilya says, stepping through the door behind me and turning the lock. "She's not going anywhere."

Reluctantly, I release her, and she immediately stumbles back, putting as much distance between us as the narrow hallway in this shitty apartment allows. She's clearly terrified, her blue eyes wide and her body shaking as she presses her back against the wall. Yet there's a peculiar gleam in her gaze too, something that doesn't seem to fit the situation.

Something almost like curiosity.

"We're not going to hurt you," Ilya says to her in Hungarian. "You don't need to be afraid, *malyshka*. We brought you here because we want to talk."

I remain silent, letting him do all the reassuring. He's better at it—not that we make a practice of kidnapping the women we're attracted to.

She's the first one, in fact.

Her gaze flits between us, and I see the exact moment she decides Ilya is more trustworthy—a conclusion nearly everyone reaches, despite my brother's intimidating bulk and all those tattoos. Somehow, people can sense that about us.

They can tell which of us retained his humanity.

"I don't understand," she tells Ilya, her voice panicked. "Who are you? What do you want from me?"

Her words, her posture, her tone—all of it screams of the kind of fear any woman would feel when stolen off the street by two strangers, yet I'm still picking up that peculiar vibe from her. Curiosity isn't quite the word for it, though.

Excitement, maybe?

Intrigued, I step closer, and she shrinks back—a proper reaction. But I still don't buy it. There's something almost... calculated about it, as if she's making herself act afraid.

I take another step forward, until I'm looming over her small frame. Placing my palm on the wall next to her head, I lean in, effectively trapping her with my body. "What's your name?" With the other hand, I gently nudge up her chin—which is quivering with appropriate drama, as if she's about to cry.

"M-mina." The word comes out on a breathless, fearful stutter, and I can feel my brother tense behind me. He doesn't like this; we're supposed to be calming her, not terrifying her out of her wits.

He clearly doesn't see what I see.

He thinks the girl is ordinary.

Ignoring him, I focus on the pretty mystery before me. "Okay, Mina," I murmur, stroking the delicate line of her jaw. Her skin is soft, even softer than I imagined, making me wonder how it'll feel farther down, underneath that puffy jacket and big sweater. "Here's what's going to happen tonight. Are you listening to me?"

A terrified blink and a small, jerky nod. Such a good actress. Too bad I've always had a sixth sense for what lies under the surface, and with this girl, fear is not it.

Not all of it, at least.

"We're going to spend the night here, the three of us," I continue, watching her closely as I drop my hand to her shoulder, squeezing it lightly through her jacket. The tattoo on the left side of her neck is a hummingbird, I realize—small but rendered in exquisite detail. "We've got a few beers and snacks in the fridge, some music on our phones. A little house party to celebrate the end of your shift. What do you say? How does that sound?"

Tears fill her big blue eyes. "Please. I just want to go home. I'm... I'm really, really tired."

I frown. The tears are also part of the act, I'm sure, but this close up, I can see the thick layer of makeup under her eyes, meant to hide the dark shadows imprinted on her creamy skin. She's not lying about the tired part; if anything, she looks like she hasn't slept in days.

Fuck. I was really looking forward to having her. I'm pretty sure at least part of what I'm sensing from her is attraction, the same kind of dark, potent pull I'm feeling toward her. If she's this tired, though, she might not be up for a hookup, and I don't force women.

A heavy hand lands on my shoulder, pulling me back before I can say anything. "If you're tired, you can sleep on the couch here," my brother says, all but shoving me aside to stand in front of her. "We just need you to stay until the morning, okay?"

I barely resist the urge to shove him back, the way I would've when we were children. Back then, we'd fight all the time, with bloody noses and split lips as our constant companions. These days, however, our arguments rarely get physical, as with our skill set, things could quickly turn deadly.

We deal violence to others, not each other.

Still, my hand curls into a fist at my side as Mina asks tremulously, "But why? What do you want from me?"

Fucking Ilya. I want her looking up at *me* with those fake-scared eyes, not him.

"You might've heard some things you weren't supposed to," my brother answers with all the subtlety of a wild elephant. "So we just want to keep an eye on you until we leave town."

"Oh." Her eyes grow round. "But I didn't… I don't speak Russian."

"Is that right?" I don't bother to mask the skepticism in my tone as her gaze swings toward me. "Not even enough to recognize a few words? Or a name?"

Specifically, the name Ilya carelessly mentioned, that of our team leader, Peter Sokolov—who's on every Most Wanted list worldwide.

She blinks up at us, the very picture of innocence. "What name?"

My brother glances at me, uncertain, and I give a minute shake of my head. He's not a good judge of whether someone's lying, and he knows it, which is why in situations like this, I always take charge.

"Let's kill her right now," I say to him in Russian, watching the girl as I speak. "We can dump her body in the river before sunrise."

Her expression doesn't change, but I'm not fooled.

She understood exactly what I said.

Ilya's jaw tightens, and he turns to the girl. "How about we talk about this over a couple of beers?" he says in Hungarian, his tone gentle. "We're really not going to hurt you, I promise."

She hesitates, her gaze darting from my brother to me and back. Finally, she gives an uncertain nod. "Okay, I—I guess. But could I have water or tea instead, please? I'm too tired to have alcohol."

"One tea coming up," I say with a mocking salute

and head into the kitchen. My cooking is shit, but boiling water is within my capabilities.

Maybe if I get some caffeine into her system, she won't fall asleep before I can coax her into my bed.

3

MINA

"So, how long have you worked at the bar?" the guy with the skull tattoos—the seemingly kinder one—asks when I remove my winter jacket and we sit down in the living room. With its Soviet-style orange wallpaper and brown drapes, this place looks like it hasn't been renovated since the eighties, but the ratty couch we're sitting on is surprisingly comfortable. Maybe I *will* take him up on his offer to sleep here. That is, if they don't kill me and dump my body in the river before sunrise.

I think my captor was just testing my language skills with that proposal, but I can't be sure.

"Mina?" the man prompts, and I realize I zoned out instead of answering his question. Now that some of the adrenaline is fading, the extreme exhaustion is back, muddling my thoughts and slowing my reactions. I want nothing more than to stretch out on this couch and fall asleep, but I might not wake up if I do.

The Russians might decide that what I heard merits killing me rather than just keeping me captive overnight.

"I've worked there for a few months," I answer, my voice shaking. It's easy to sound terrified, because I am.

I'm with two men who may want to kill me, and I'm in no state to defend myself.

The only thing that gives me hope is that they haven't already done so. They could've easily murdered me in the alley; they didn't need to bring me here for that. Of course, there's another possibility, one that every woman must consider.

They might be planning to rape me before killing me, in which case bringing me here makes perfect sense.

The thought makes my stomach churn, the old memories threatening to crowd in, but underneath the fear and disgust is something darker, infinitely more fucked up. The brief sizzle of arousal I'd experienced at the bar was nothing compared to how it had felt when the dangerous stranger caged me against the wall, caressing my face with that cruel gentleness. My body —the weak, ruined body I've spent the past year hating —had come to life with such force, it was as if fireworks had ignited under my skin, liquifying my core and burning away my inhibitions.

Was he able to sense it?

Did he know how badly I wanted him to keep touching me?

I think he did. And more than that, I think he

wanted to. His eyes—a hard, gem-like green—had watched me with the dark intensity of a predator, taking in every twitch of my lashes, every hitch of my breath. If we'd been alone, he might've kissed me… or killed me on the spot.

It's hard to tell with him.

"Do you like it? Working at the bar, I mean?" the tattooed man asks, bringing my attention back to him. Now *he* is easy to read. There's unmistakable male interest in the way he looks at me, an obvious gleam in his green eyes.

Wait a sec. *Green eyes?*

"Are you two brothers?" I blurt out, then silently curse myself. I'm so tired I'm not thinking straight. The last thing I need is for these two to imagine I'm gathering information on them, or—

"We are." A smile lights up his broad face, softening his harsh features. "Twins, in fact."

Shit. I did *not* need to know that. The next thing I know, he'll be telling me his—

"I'm Ilya, by the way," he says, extending one big paw toward me. "And my brother's name is Yan."

Oh, fuck. I'm so screwed. They *are* going to kill me. "Nice to meet you," I say weakly, shaking his hand on autopilot. My grip is as limp as my voice, but that's okay. I'm playing a damsel in distress, and the more convincing I am, the better.

Too bad the act is mostly real these days.

Ilya squeezes my hand gingerly, as if afraid of inadvertently crushing my bones, and hope nibbles at me. He wouldn't be so careful with me if they were planning to brutally rape and kill me, would he?

As if reading my thoughts, he gives me another smile, an even kinder one this time, and says gruffly, "I'm sorry about my brother. He's used to seeing enemies around every corner. You *will* walk away from this unharmed, I promise you, *malyshka*. We need to keep you overnight as a precaution, that's all."

Strangely, I believe him. Or at least I believe that *he* intends me no harm. The jury is still out on his brother—who chooses that exact moment to walk in, carrying a cup of tea in one hand and two beers in the other.

My breath catches in my throat as he—Yan—sets the drinks on the coffee table in front of us and sits down between me and Ilya, unapologetically wedging himself into the too-small space. Instinctively, I scoot to the side, as far as the couch allows, but that's only about six centimeters, and my leg ends up pressed against his, the heat of his body burning me even through the layers of our clothing.

He's shed the suede winter jacket he was wearing earlier, and is now dressed like he was at the bar, in the stylish dress pants and button-up shirt. Except his sleeves are rolled up, exposing muscular forearms lightly dusted with dark hair.

He's strong, this ruthless captor of mine. Strong and superbly fit, his body a deadly weapon under those perfectly tailored clothes.

"Tea," he says in that smooth, deep voice of his, so

Pulling her into the room, I shut the door behind us, and turn the lock for good measure.

Then I face her.

Her pale face is flushed with a delicate peach color, her lips parted as she stares up at me. "Are you..." She moistens her lower lip. "Are you going to kill me? Afterward?"

A dark smile tugs at my lips. "What do you think?"

She swallows. "I'm not sure."

"Yet you're here. Why?"

She doesn't reply, but her color heightens, answering me as clearly as if she'd spoken the words.

She's here because she wants me.

Because she feels this hunger, too.

I've been hard from the moment I laid my hand on her knee and saw her pupils dilate in response, but the need that's pounding through me now is almost violent in nature, savage and uncontrolled. I like pretty things, and she's pretty all right, but this is so much more. I've never wanted a woman this much, have never known a craving so consuming. I was going to toy with her, to prolong the delicious anticipation of this moment, but my hands reach for her of their own accord, pulling her toward me as I bend my head and claim her lips in a deep, darkly carnal kiss.

A tiny gasp escapes her throat, a sound half of protest, half of surprise, but instead of pushing me away, her small hands reach up to clasp my head, her fingers sliding into my hair as she presses against me in unabashed desire. She tastes like honey-flavored tea, her mouth sleek and warm as her tongue tangles with mine, her teeth sinking aggressively into my bottom lip.

Whatever self-control I still possessed evaporates at the tiny hint of pain. With a low growl, I back her against the bed, yanking the sweater over her head and throwing it aside as she falls backward onto the blanket. Underneath, she's wearing a white tank top with no bra, and the sight of her erect nipples under the thin fabric sends more blood surging to my groin. Vision turning hazy with lust, I climb onto the bed and straddle her narrow hips. Her torso is slender, almost too much so, but her breasts are deliciously round, surprisingly full for her tiny build. My hands ache to touch them, to mold them in my palms as I drive deep into her body, and I give in to the craving, roughly palming the soft globes as I bend to kiss her ravenously again.

She responds with a matching aggression, her tongue pushing against mine and her hands tearing at the buttons of my shirt. A couple of buttons go flying, and I hear them skitter on the floor, but I couldn't care less about the destruction of my clothing. My own hands are already ripping at her tank top, tearing it off her body as I keep devouring her mouth, unable to get enough of the addictive honey taste.

The rest of our clothes come off in a frenzy, my Italian slacks tangling with her ripped jeans on the corner of the bed, and then I have her naked and squirming underneath me, her nails raking down my back as I rain biting kisses down her neck, her collarbone, her gorgeous breasts. Her taut nipple pops into my mouth, and I suck on it, reveling in her gasping moans as my hand travels down her body, skating over her narrow ribcage and flat stomach before reaching the smooth columns of her thighs and the heated slickness of her sex.

She has a bellybutton ring, I note with a still-functioning corner of my mind, and a few lines of writing tattooed on her left side. I want to explore it all in detail, to slow down and look over her sleek body, committing it to memory, but the lust beating at me is too strong to be denied. Pushing her thighs apart, I move down, my mouth watering at the thought of tasting that warm wetness.

Her pussy is as pretty as the rest of her, pink and smooth, completely shaven, and I dive right into my feast, my tongue lapping at her soaked slit before moving up her folds. "Oh, fuck," she moans, her hips rising convulsively as I reach my target, and her hands bunch in my hair, squeezing tightly as I suck, then rhythmically lick her clit, letting my teeth graze it in between. She's salty sweet, as delicious as I expected, and my cock throbs with a desperate need to be inside her, my balls drawing tight against my body as I up the tempo, craving her orgasm as much as I do my own.

Her moans grow in volume, her hips pumping up and down with rising urgency as I continue, and I feel the exact moment it happens for her. With a cry, she arches against me, her eyes scrunched shut and her whole body shaking as more richly flavored wetness coats my lips and tongue. I wait a couple of seconds for her spasms to ease, and then I move up, covering her with my body.

"Wait," she gasps, her eyes popping open as I wedge my knee between her thighs, spreading them apart. Her pupils are dilated, her face pink and glowing with a hint of perspiration. "I'm not on the… I don't have—"

"I've got it," I growl, unable to believe I almost forgot something so basic. Holding myself up with one hand, I reach into the tangle of clothing in the corner and fish out a foil packet I always carry in my wallet. My teeth make quick work of the wrapper, and I roll the condom onto my cock before guiding it to her slick folds.

Then I press in, blood pounding in my temples.

5

MINA

I tense, my breath seizing in my lungs as he pushes in, his thick cock penetrating me slowly but inexorably. I'm wetter than I recall ever being, but even with my body primed for his possession, I feel a stinging stretch. He's big, and it's been far too long for me.

He must feel the difficulty I'm having because he pauses, his jaw locked tight and his green eyes fiercely narrowed on my face. "Am I hurting you?" His voice is rough, hoarse with lust, his powerful shoulders tense above me. There's no trace of his urbane veneer now, no hint of the smooth sophisticate from the bar. Without his tailored clothes, he looks like the savage predator he is, his large, hard-muscled body as lethal as it is perfectly proportioned.

"No, it's…" My voice shakes. "I'm fine." It's a lie, but I don't want him to stop. It might be twisted, but now that we're here, I feel like I deserve this, both the pain and the pleasure. This man, this killer, he's my punishment *and* my reward, a dark gift to myself for making it this far.

His nostrils flare, his eyes narrowing further, and I feel the last shreds of his self-control disintegrate. With a guttural sound deep in his throat, he catches my wrists, pinning them above my head, and surges into me, penetrating me all the way in one hard thrust.

I gasp, my insides burning from the ruthless stretch, yet my body arches against him, my legs wrapping around his hips to take him even deeper. It hurts, but underneath is a perverse kind of comfort, a reassurance that I'm here, that I'm alive to feel this way.

He doesn't let me catch my breath this time. Dipping his head, he claims my lips in another deep, devouring kiss and begins to move, the power of his thrusts pushing me into the mattress. His mouth is hot and rough, flavored with my slickness and a hint of beer, and I find myself kissing him back with the same aggressive hunger as the pain morphs into wild, primal pleasure. I've never come more than once during sex, but my body draws taut again, the tension in my core growing and coiling tighter. Feverish heat pulses through my veins, and my heart races as if trying to escape my chest.

The release that hits me feels like a volcano going off inside my body, incinerating everything within. My vision goes white, my panting breaths deafeningly loud to my ears as every nerve ending I possess sparks to life. With a shattered cry, I arch against him, my inner muscles spasming around his invading cock. It's too much, too overwhelming, yet somehow, I live through it, and as I'm coming down from the high, he groans hoarsely in my ear as his cock throbs deep inside me in his own release.

I MUST'VE PASSED OUT FROM SHEER EXHAUSTION immediately afterward because all I recall when I wake up is a cool, wet towel between my legs, cleaning and soothing the tender flesh. I don't remember him withdrawing from me or disposing of the condom, or even letting go of my wrists. I do, however, have a vague recollection of being held against a large, warm male body and feeling oddly peaceful and secure.

Battling residual grogginess, I sit up and look around. Light is seeping through the heavy shades, so it must be morning. Also, I'm alone. However, I can hear the rumble of male voices through the door.

They're still here, and I'm still their captive.

On the plus side, I've obviously made it through the night. Nobody's offed me in my sleep, which gives me hope that maybe they'll keep their word and actually let me go.

Quietly, I swing my legs to the floor and stand up, suppressing a wince at the soreness I feel everywhere, but especially between my thighs. I'm also a little weak and dizzy, but that's nothing new. I feel that way most mornings, though it's slowly getting better.

Moving as silently as I can, I gather my clothes, minus the torn tank top, and get dressed, then tiptoe to press my ear to the door. The voices outside are getting louder, angrier.

The brothers are arguing about something.

"—not yours," Ilya growls in Russian. "You can't just keep her like a stray cat, doing whatever you fucking please—"

"Fuck you." Yan's voice is equally hard. "You're just pissed she chose me last night, and I didn't share."

"Don't fucking delude yourself. You never gave her the option to refuse. She probably figured it's fuck you or die—"

A loud crash cuts off the rest of the sentence, and I back away from the door, my heart hammering.

This is bad, really bad. If I understood it right, Yan is planning to keep me captive longer, something his brother is objecting to. Not only does that lessen my chances of getting out of this alive—the longer I'm around these killers, the more likely I'm to overhear implicating information—but it also means I won't be able to do my job.

My real job, not the waitressing that's my cover.

And if the prospect of pissing off my clients weren't worrisome enough, Ilya mentioned something about wanting to keep an eye on me until they leave town. Which, considering that the brothers were going to let me go this morning, must be today.

Does this mean Yan wants to take me with him?

To steal me away from here?

More crashing sounds, mixed with Russian curses, reach my ears. The brothers are still fighting, but unless one of them kills the other, they're likely to stop soon. Which means I have to act now.

My searching gaze lands on the window shades, and I rush over, yanking them apart. Bright sunlight hits my eyes, blinding me for a moment, but then I see we're on the second floor.

Not an optimal location, but one that I can work with.

Luckily, the window is as old as the rest of this building, consisting of two separate wood-framed panes that open outward, like French doors. The lock in the middle is rusted and painted over, but when I put all my strength into it, the paint seal breaks, and I'm able to twist the lock and push the panes open.

The effort, minor though it was, exhausts me, but there's no time to rest. The street outside is narrow and deserted. If I were to call for help, nobody would hear me—not that I was counting on some magic rescue.

Hurrying over to the bed, I strip off the top and bottom sheets and tie them together. Then I knot the makeshift rope around the leg of the bed and go back to the window, holding the other end.

It won't extend more than a meter out the window, but anything that brings me closer to the ground is a good thing.

My hands are shaking and I'm sweating as I climb onto the windowsill, gripping the sheet tightly. A year ago, I could've jumped from this height and easily walked away, but now, I'm out of shape, my bones weak and brittle. The ground appears dangerously far, the cracked asphalt looming below me like a death sentence.

For a moment, I entertain the idea of staying, of going with the flow and seeing what happens. After all, would it be so bad to be Yan's captive? To get those mind-shattering orgasms and sleep in his arms every night? Maybe he'd grow attached to me after a while, as much as a man like that can, and wouldn't kill me even if I learned more about them. In fact, we could even partner up and—

I shut the door on that thought before it goes any further. The sex hormones must still be muddling my mind for me to even entertain an idea that insane. If I stayed, I'd be nothing more than Yan's sex toy, I'm sure of that. Besides, even if I were willing to take this kind of risk, it's not all about me.

Hanna needs me.

The thought of my grandmother steadies me, as always. I can't afford to give in to this whim, to let attraction to a handsome killer distract me from my responsibility to the woman who raised me. She'd cared for me my whole life, and now it's my turn to do the same for her.

"Goodbye, Yan," I mouth silently, and tightening my grip on the sheet, I jump down.

PART II

YAN

COLOMBIA, PRESENT DAY

*A*s is my habit lately, I pull out my phone to check my email. With all the shit that's gone down in recent months, getting information in a timely fashion is key.

"Where's Kent?" Julian Esguerra asks when Peter Sokolov—our former team leader and the reason for our current predicament—walks in, joining me, my brother, and our teammate, Anton Rezov, in Esguerra's office.

"How should I know?" Peter retorts, taking a seat next to me at the oval table. I'm only peripherally aware of his presence, or that Ilya is crunching on a cookie Esguerra's housekeeper brought in earlier. All my attention is on my inbox, where a message from our hackers has just landed.

"Isn't he staying in the house with you?" Peter continues as I open the email.

"He was making the rounds with the guards this

morning," Esguerra says. "Looks like we'll have to fill him in later. I have a call coming up." A beat, then: "Any word from Henderson?"

"No, and I wouldn't expect to hear from him anytime soon. We're still"—Peter pauses, as if to check the time—"about an hour from the start of the deadline. I'm guessing we'll have to make good on our threat with at least a few bodies before he realizes we're serious."

"All right," Esguerra says as I skim the message. "I've already given our men the instructions on which hostages are to be killed first. Any word from your hackers?"

I look up from my phone. "Actually, yes. They've just tracked down the sniper for us—the one who shot the agent during Peter's arrest."

Peter visibly tenses. "Who is he?"

"*He* is apparently a *she*," I say, reading more of the email. "Goes by the name of Mink and is from the Czech Republic. Hold on—the picture is loading now."

"What about our doppelgängers?" Anton asks. "Any word on those fuckers?"

His words reach me as if through a wall of water, the roar of my heartbeat thunderously loud in my ears as shock and fury twist my guts. I've always prided myself on maintaining a cool head, the tight leash I keep on my emotions often fooling people into believing I don't have any. But there's no reining in the volcanic rage building inside me.

On my phone is a face I never thought I'd see again

—a pale, pretty face framed by short, spiky white-blond hair. The photographer caught it in partial profile, and if there were any doubts in my mind about the woman's identity, the tattoo of the hummingbird on the side of her neck and the piercings studding her delicate ear would've dispelled them.

The sniper who shot a SWAT agent during Peter's arrest, setting off the firefight that resulted in the deaths of his in-laws, is none other than Mina, my pretty waitress from Budapest.

The girl for whom I'd obsessively searched for days after she ran off.

"What is it?" Ilya demands, and I tear my gaze from the screen to find my twin frowning at me.

If I try to speak, I'll explode. So I just hand the phone to him, letting him see.

His harsh face freezes. "Her?" He looks up, jaw flexing. "*She* is Mink?"

Peter grabs the phone from Ilya and examines the picture with a confused frown. Of course, he doesn't see what Ilya and I see.

He's never met the deceitful little bitch, nor come dozens of times to the memory of fucking her.

"Who is she?" he asks, looking up at me and my brother. "How do you know her?"

I force the words past the knot of rage in my throat. "It doesn't matter." I snatch the phone back from Peter, fighting the urge to break his fingers in the process. "I'm sending men to capture her. She may know where Henderson is."

"It does matter," Esguerra says as I furiously type an email to those of our men who are in Europe, scouring it for traces of Henderson, the former US general who's Peter's—and now our—greatest enemy. I send them the hacker's file on Mink/Mina and direct them to capture her alive.

We not only need to question her about Henderson, who's apparently her employer, but I have an interrogation of my own to conduct.

"Who the fuck is she?" Esguerra demands when no one replies to Peter.

"We met her in Budapest," my brother explains grimly as I send off the email and look up. "She works as a waitress in a bar."

Anton, the fucker, is staring at me with dawning recognition. "Did you sleep with her a while back?" he blurts out. "Is she the one Ilya was pouting about when we were in Poland?"

I almost plant my fist into his bearded face. Only a lifetime of self-discipline keeps me still, my fingers squeezing the phone so hard it's bound to leave bruises on my palm.

My brother can't control himself nearly as well. "I wasn't pouting," he growls back, murder in his eyes. "But yes, *he*"—he jerks his thumb at me—"fucked her."

My vision speckles with red, the rage inside me boiling out of control. Pivoting to face Ilya, I slam the phone on the table. "Shut your fucking mouth."

Face reddening with fury, he jumps to his feet, sending his chair crashing to the floor, and I follow his example, ready to pound his thick skull into the table. *Fuck self-control.* Bloodlust sings in my veins, dark and toxic, spurred by anger and the harsh sting of betrayal.

Mina is Mink.

She lied to me, played me for a fool.

And my brother, *ublyudok* that he is, is still mad I didn't fucking share.

My fist is already balling up, about to fly toward his face, when Lucas Kent bursts in, his square-jawed face tense and his T-shirt drenched with sweat.

"It's Sara," he says, panting like he's sprinted all the way across the compound. "Peter, you need to come with me right away."

Sokolov is already moving, the mere mention of his wife enough to make him forget everything under the sun. A moment later, he and Kent are gone, and with them, some of the fury that had blinded me.

Taking a breath to calm myself, I sit back down, and Ilya does the same, even as Anton and Esguerra eye us like we're a pipe bomb ready to explode. But they don't have to worry. I'm back to being in control.

My brother is not the enemy here.

She is.

And when I get my hands on her pretty little neck, she'll pay for every bit of her deception.

7

MINA

I wake up to a splitting pain in my skull and a dull ache in my ribs. My mouth tastes like stale copper, and my arms are numb, my wrists painfully restrained above my head as I lie stretched out on some hard surface. It's hot and humid, and I can smell my own sweat mixed with old wood and mustiness. For a moment, I can't make sense of any of it, but then my memory returns, flooding my body with adrenaline. It takes all my training to remain still, with my eyes closed and my breathing unchanged, as images of what happened invade my mind.

Attacked.

Captured.

I was heading to a bartending gig in Budapest when four men surrounded me in a dark alley, their eyes as cold as the weapons in their hands. I managed to disarm one and injure another, but there were too many of them.

Even strong and healthy, I was no match for all of them.

My memories after that are a blur. They either drugged me or knocked me out. I vaguely recall a sense of motion—a car, most likely—followed by a loud roar that reminded me of a plane's engines. Did they fly me somewhere?

If so, why?

Fear presses in, the metallic tang of it bitter in my mouth, but I push it aside, forcing myself to concentrate. *Think, Mina. Focus and think.* I rake through the blurry recollections, looking for anything that might explain this situation.

Who would want to capture me and why?

A conversation comes to me, dim and hazy, as if from a dream. Amid the roar of the engines, men were talking—a mixture of English, Russian, and Spanish, if I'm not mistaken. What was it they said? There was some mention of someone named Esguerra, and also something about a captain or a general…

Oh, fuck.

My stomach tightens as it comes to me, the realization of what this is about. I should've known the clusterfuck in Chicago would blow back on me.

It's the one time in my life I didn't listen to my instincts.

The one time I took a job that didn't sit right with me.

The sound of footsteps yanks me out of my thoughts.

Someone's coming toward me.

My heartbeat jacks up, but I don't let it show, doing my best to appear passed out. The newcomer is not fooled. He stops next to me—somehow, I know it's a *he* —and sinks to his haunches, watching me with malevolent amusement. I feel the weight of that stare, sense the darkness in it, and an uncanny sense of familiarity washes over me as the subtle, masculine scent of sandalwood and pepper teases my nostrils. He laughs then, the sound low and cruel, and as his fingers tenderly graze my lips, a chill roughens my skin at the impossible realization.

"If it isn't my little Mina," Yan says in Hungarian, his smooth, deep voice straight out of my darkest dreams. "Or should I call you *Mink*?"

8

MINA

*L*ungs seizing with a mixture of shock and perverse excitement, I stare at the man I've tried—and failed—to forget over the past fifteen months. He's as dangerously attractive as I remember, his hard features as symmetric as if they'd been carved by a sculptor and his blue button-up shirt perfectly tailored to his muscled frame. His mouth—the same talented mouth that had lapped at my sex with startling hunger—is curved in a cold smile, and his green eyes are filled with the promise of hell.

Fuck. He *is* connected to all this.

The possibility had occurred to me when Walton Henderson III, a former US general, reached out to me with the assignment. He wanted me to interfere during the arrest of a Russian assassin in the Chicago suburbs, a man who went by the name of Peter Garin.

The goal was to make sure Garin didn't get taken alive.

The assignment sounded simple and straightforward, but the Russian assassin bit gave me pause. I wondered if the men who'd kidnapped me that night were somehow involved—if it could have anything to do with Yan and Ilya. But the picture of the target looked nothing like the twins, and after some deliberation, I took the job.

Henderson made my skin crawl, but he paid well and Hanna's bills were due.

There was no way Garin was connected to Yan and Ilya, I told myself as I flew to Chicago with the US passport Henderson gave me. Russia is a huge country, one where criminals of all sorts abound. That my target shared a nationality and a dark calling with the man I'd slept with was a coincidence, nothing more.

Later on, when the clusterfuck happened and my target's face and name—his real name of Peter Sokolov —were all over the news, I remembered Ilya mentioning someone named Sokolov at the bar. But it was too late by then, and besides, it could've still been a coincidence.

Sokolov is a fairly common Russian surname.

But clearly, it wasn't a coincidence, and now I'm Yan's captive again, in some wooden shed someplace warm.

"Where am I?" I ask in Hungarian, my voice cool and steady as I quickly survey my surroundings. He now knows what I am, so there's no need for the fainting damsel act. As I speak, I become aware of a stinging pain in my lower lip and a dull throbbing in my jaw—likely from when I fought during my capture.

"Colombia." Yan's smile turns darker as I shift slightly, trying to relieve the pressure on my bound wrists. "Julian Esguerra's compound in the Amazon." He says it in Russian, mocking the lie I told on the night he'd taken me.

I stare at him unblinkingly. The name "Esguerra" means nothing to me, though the fact that I was brought halfway across the world is more than a little worrisome. I switch over to Russian. "Why am I here? What do you want from me?"

"Right now, answers. After that, we'll see."

Despite the pain in my battered body, my insides contract, a dark heat sizzling over my skin. Ignoring the sensation, I ask as calmly as I can manage, "And what do I get if I give you these answers?"

"Your life," someone answers in Russian. It's a different, rougher voice speaking, and I tear my gaze away from Yan to see his brother approaching, the dim light in the shed making his skull tattoos look like a patchy buzz cut.

"Hi, Ilya." I give him my brightest smile—something I immediately regret, as the movement reopens my split lip. Still, it's worth it. Ilya looks taken aback at my enthusiastic greeting, and some of the dark amusement on Yan's face fades.

He doesn't like it that I'm happy to see his brother.

It's probably unwise to piss off Yan, but I don't believe I'm going to get out of this alive. Not this time.

With the Henderson job, I messed up in more ways than one. Not only did I accept a job that I had doubts about, but the SWAT agents *didn't* kill Sokolov when I took a shot at one of them from a nearby roof. Somehow, the bastard managed to survive a firestorm of epic proportions and go on the run with his wife.

And if he's the twins' friend or boss or whatever, the best I can hope for is a quick death.

"Mina." Ilya crouches next to his brother, his expression tight as he gazes down at me. "I guess you were never a waitress, were you?"

"I was—I am. I waitress and bartend part-time." I need a source of legitimate income for things like renting an apartment and keeping my grandmother in the dark.

"Right." Yan's tone is mocking. "And the rest of the time, you do what? Kill SWAT agents for fun?"

"Not for fun," I say evenly. "For money. Same as you two. I was trained as a sniper in the Hungarian Special Forces, but things didn't work out for me there. So when an opportunity to make some extra cash came up, I figured I'd put my skills to use."

There. I've said it. It feels strangely liberating to admit the truth, to drop the mask that I've been wearing for the past few years. No one except my trainer knows about this side of me, and if they did, they'd be shocked and horrified.

The two men in front of me don't look shocked or horrified. They look like they're contemplating killing me, which is still somehow better than moralizing disapproval.

Yan reaches out and strokes my lip again, his touch deceptively tender on my wound. "Where's your employer?"

I lick my lips, tasting blood as he takes his hand away, his fingers smeared with red. "I don't have an employer. I freelance."

"He's talking about Henderson," Ilya says harshly, and when I look up at him, he's glaring at his brother for some reason. Focusing back on me, he growls, "Where is he?"

"I have no idea. I only met him in person once, when he gave me the assignment. The rest of the time, he communicated with me through encrypted emails." There's no point in denying my involvement. Even if I somehow managed to convince them that this is all a misunderstanding, they're not going to apologize and fly me back to Budapest.

I'm a dead woman walking—or lying flat, as the matter may be.

"And what exactly was your assignment?" Yan's voice is silky soft. "Was sleeping with me part of it?"

Ilya visibly tenses at the question, and my face heats despite my resolution to keep my cool. "Of course not. You kidnapped me off the street and dragged me to your place, remember? I had no idea who you were that night, and in any case, I only met Henderson a couple of months ago."

"Really?" Yan drawls, his eyes gleaming. "So you weren't spying on us at the bar?"

"Not on purpose. If you didn't want to be overheard, you shouldn't have been discussing your business in public. I was working at that bar, that's all."

"Bullshit." Yan's tone doesn't change, but the temperature in the shed drops as he touches the side of my neck, his blood-smeared fingers rubbing against my tattoo. "They couldn't locate you in their system, and you never came back—not even to pick up your measly paycheck. There was no Mina with a hummingbird tattoo on social media, either."

I try to ignore the effect his touch is having on my body. "So you did look for me." I feared he might, so when I miraculously didn't break anything during my escape, I went back to the bar and erased my personnel file in the computer. The owner never paid much attention to his part-time staff, and I wasn't close to any of my coworkers, so I figured they were unlikely to know my address or full name off the top of their heads. Looks like I was right—just as I was right to always avoid social media.

Even before I embraced my criminal tendencies, I believed in keeping as much of my life off the internet as possible.

"Oh, I looked for you." Yan's gaze darkens, his hand moving lower to trail over my collarbone. "After all, your pussy—"

"What did he hire you to do?" Ilya cuts in rudely as more color floods my face. His brother's possessive touches and crude references to our night together seem to bother the big Russian nearly as much as they do me. Is it because, as Yan said that day, Ilya is upset his brother didn't share?

Do these two share women often?

Pushing away the X-rated images in my mind, I say steadily, "You already know. I was to shoot one of the arresting agents, prompting them to fire on Sokolov. Except at the time, I thought his name was Garin."

If I'd known my target's real name, I would've remembered Ilya mentioning it at the bar, and I wouldn't have taken the job. I'd been in desperate need of funds, but not desperate enough to cross someone as dangerous as Yan.

"Is that all?" His fingers are now streaking fire over my ear, gently playing with every piercing I have there. "Think carefully before you lie to me, Minochka." The diminutive Russian version of my name—something you'd call a child or a loved one—sounds cruelly mocking on his lips, especially when he smiles and adds softly, "Peter Sokolov is very good at extracting information."

Despite myself, I swallow, my empty stomach roiling. I've been trying not to think about that, about what would happen if I can't give them the answers they're after. I don't fear death that much—with Henderson's payment sitting in my account, Hanna should inherit enough to cover her expenses for a good long while—but I can't deny that the possibility of torture chills me.

"There is one more thing," I say, deciding to just give them everything. Maybe if I'm cooperative enough, they won't feel the need to resort to Sokolov's methods of *extracting information.* "Henderson also needed men who'd be skilled in certain matters… and up for anything."

Yan's gaze sharpens with interest. "Do tell."

"There's a team I've worked with on a few jobs in the past." Or rather, Gergo has—but I'm not about to drag my mentor and trainer into this. "I gave their names to Henderson. I don't know what he needed them for"—though after watching the news, I have an awful suspicion—"or where they are right now, but I can tell you who they are. Maybe if you find them, they'll know where Henderson is."

"Go ahead," Yan says as Ilya pulls out his phone to take notes. "Tell us."

I rattle off all the names in the file I handed over to Henderson. I've actually only met those men once and hated them on sight, so I don't feel particularly bad that I'm betraying them. Gergo might be upset to lose them, but he'll get over it. After all, it's his fault I'm in this predicament.

He's the one who sent Henderson my way.

"Did you get all that?" Yan asks, glancing at his brother, and Ilya nods.

"Got it."

"All right." Yan rises to his feet. "We'll see what we can pull up."

"Wait," I say as he turns to leave. "I need to pee.

Please." I'm not lying; my bladder is uncomfortably full. But I also need them to take me out of this shed, so I can assess my surroundings and figure out what my chances of escape are.

They're most likely zero, but I have to try.

Yan's lips curl in a cruel smile. "Really? Then go here."

Ilya rounds on him, massive fists curling. "I'll take her out. In fact—"

"I've got it." Yan's voice takes on a lethal tension, one mimicked in the stiffness pervading his tall, muscled frame. "You can get started on the names."

Ilya visibly bristles at the order, and so much testosterone fills the air I can practically smell it.

Are they about to come to blows? Over who takes me out to pee, no less?

At the last second, however, Ilya turns on his heel and stomps out of the shed, slamming the door, and I'm left with Yan.

My captor.

The man I fear and desire in equal measures.

9

MINA

*Y*an's gem-green eyes glitter coldly as he sweeps his gaze over my face, lingering for a second on my lips before fixing his attention on the pulsing vein in my neck. My heart starts beating even faster. His proximity both frightens and excites me, the danger that he represents perversely heightening the attraction. As warped as it is, my body reacts to him exactly as it did in Budapest, and when he grabs my wrists to work on the knot of the rope, the touch elicits an involuntary response, like the zap of an electric shock.

He unties me with the smooth efficiency of a killer who knows his way around ropes. Flipping me around, he forces my arms behind my back. My muscles protest at the violent change, my arms aching as the blood circulation reverses. Keeping me flat on the bench with a knee pressed on my lower back, he easily grips both of my wrists in one hand and uses the same rope to tie them back together, winding it around several times before knotting it a little too tightly.

Roughly, he pulls me to my feet. With my hands tied behind my back and after having been immobile for so long, my balance is off, and I stumble. He catches me with a strong arm around my waist. A flash of recognition goes off in my brain, a memory of warm arms and a strange feeling of security, but before I have time to digest the response, he yanks me back against his hard chest with one arm squeezing around my stomach and his free hand finding purchase in my hair.

Pulling my head to the side by the short strands, he exposes my neck and growls in my ear, "Don't try anything. It'll be fun for me. Not so much for you."

I don't doubt that for a second.

When he moves me forward, I trip again, but he effortlessly keeps me upright, maneuvering me as if I'm nothing but a puppet on strings. I suppress an ingrained urge to fight back. Without a weapon, I don't stand a chance, not against Yan. He's too skilled. None of my hand-to-hand combat moves will catch him by surprise. If I'm to escape, I have to use my head.

We move through the semi-darkness toward a poorly insulated door. It's fitted with a deadbolt as well as a chain and lock, and daylight shines through the cracks between the frame and the wooden walls. When Yan pushes it open, the outside air doesn't bring relief. The hot humidity is worse than the somber shade inside. I blink a few times for my eyes to adjust to the brightness.

Two guards turn when we exit, and I catalogue them swiftly. Black combat gear. AK-47s. Male, with Hispanic features and bronze complexions. Their dark eyes fix on my face before skipping down to my white tank top. My body is soaked with sweat, and the thin cotton isn't enough protection against their invasive gazes. With both of my arms drawn back, my breasts are on display, and there's nothing I can do about it.

Groping hands and fists that won't stop. Jeering voices. Helpless fury.

Fuck, no. Suppressing the old memory, I narrow my eyes at the men visually dissecting my body, but that only invites their smirks.

"*Que pasa?*" the tallest one asks.

"Get lost," Yan snaps in English. He must speak several languages, same as I do.

"We have orders," the other guard replies with a strong Spanish accent.

"Then I hope you can execute them blind," Yan says in a tone so boldly sadistic it makes me shudder, "because you're about to have your eyes ripped out."

I have no doubt he means the threat in the most literal sense. Neither do the guards, because the tall one looks away and tilts his head toward a compound in the distance before addressing his friend.

"*Vamonos.*"

The one who speaks English averts his eyes.

Together they walk toward the white buildings, not looking at me as they pass.

I take stock of the environment. We're surrounded by lush vegetation. Most of the plants are unfamiliar to me, but I recognize the toucan beak flowers and Yopo trees with their beaded seed pods from pictures I've seen. A good distance away from the compound, a guard tower is visible above the treetops on the left. Two more are on my right. And if there are watchtowers, the property will be fenced.

My spirits sink. Escape seems more unlikely by the second.

A buzzing noise sounds overhead, and I look up.

A drone.

Dammit, we're being watched as well. Even if I get away, I won't get far.

Yan turns me in the direction of the jungle and gives me a little shove. "Walk, princess." He's back to speaking Russian.

I stumble a step before managing to right myself. Walking to where Yan is pushing me, I squint up at the scorching sun. My lips are parched, but I force myself not to think about my thirst.

Tracing the cut on my throbbing lower lip with my tongue, I ask, "What time is it?"

"Does it matter?" he asks with a note of cynical humor.

"Just wondering for how long I've been out."

He chuckles, not buying my nonchalance, but surprisingly, he answers. "It's past two."

I make a rough calculation of where north should be by using the position of the sun.

After crossing the small clearing that runs around the shed, we enter the dense flora. The drone hovers at the fringe, unable to follow. Yan steers me deeper into the shady jungle until we're completely out of the drone's scope of visibility.

Twirling me around, he pushes me against a tree. My back hits the trunk with a thump, the rough bark pressing into my palms as he stares down at me with that new chill in his eyes. I'm the enemy now. He hates me. He believes I lied to him. And I did, but only about not understanding Russian, and he knew I was lying about that. No, the quiet fury emanating from him is evidence that he still thinks I was spying on him, and nothing I say will convince him otherwise.

He reaches for the button of my jeans, and I swallow. My throat feels like sandpaper. I could ask him to untie me, but it would be a waste of words. That will never happen. The button pops free, and the zipper makes a scratching sound as he slowly pulls it down, all the while holding my gaze.

Those other men, the guards, they frightened me. I've seen what men at war can do to a woman. If not for Gergo, I would've been infinitely more familiar with those sinister intentions. Yet I'm not frightened of Yan. Not like that. I'm terrified he'll kill me, but not that he'll force me. He kidnapped me in Budapest and carried me off to his place. If he wanted to, he could've done anything to me. But despite the twisted situation back then, I felt safe in his bed. Secure. A rare feeling for me to have with a man.

He hooks his thumbs into the waistband of my jeans and slips them under the elastic of my cotton panties. My face heats like I'm an inexperienced teenager, not only at the intimacy of our situation, but also at the memory of how he devoured me, and how I devoured him back.

His lips curve with the self-assurance of a man who knows the effect he has on a woman, but his eyes remain as frosty as the northern lights, mocking me, despising me, as he pushes my jeans and underwear over my hips and thighs to my knees. Goosebumps break out over my skin, following the path of his touch. He straightens slowly, trailing the tips of his calloused fingers up the outside of my naked legs and over the indents of my glutes on the sides.

The heat in my cheeks intensifies when he finally drops his gaze, looking at the triangle between my legs as if it's his right. It's nothing he hasn't seen before, but this is different. I'm bound and naked, exposed with my hands tied and my jeans around my knees. Whereas he's cool, collected, and fully clothed. As he stares at me, a heavy assault of vulnerability hits me in the gut. It's humiliating, and judging by his relentless smile, humiliation is what he's aiming for.

Angry punishment. Cold-hearted revenge.

Despite it all, the underlying current of danger sends a spark of exhilaration to my belly. I can help it as little as I can help my attraction to this dangerous man. My body craves his touch. Just one more time to remember how good it was. A taste to remind me how it feels to be alive. He has an effect on me like no other. Before him, I thought I'd never be able to tolerate a man's touch again without the accompanying repulsion.

But there it is. An untimely, yet undeniable reaction. My core heats. My sex swells. The bundle of nerves between my folds tingles. It takes all the self-control I possess not to tilt my hips toward the cradle of his thighs. I'm lucid enough to admit it's more than physical, that there's a psychological element to my desire to feel his arms around me. I'm not stupid. I know I'm not walking away from here alive, though I do intend to try. Either way, I suddenly crave the soothing security I found in his embrace in Budapest. I don't care that it will be a lie. I just want to feel it one more time, and I refuse to judge myself for that.

It's only natural. Nobody wants to die alone.

I focus on where his hands are resting lightly on my naked hips, those incredibly male hands with long, masculine fingers and perfectly manicured nails. Hands that can inflict pain in a myriad of ways. I pull in a ragged breath, on the verge of begging him to make the end sweet and quick when he steps away and turns his back on me.

"Get a move on." His voice is even, emotionless. "You have ten seconds."

I crouch down and quickly do my business. Having

lived in close quarters with men in all kinds of tactical situations, I don't suffer from stage fright.

I count in my head. He gives me exactly ten seconds before he turns. I'm up already. He makes quick work of dragging my underwear and jeans over my hips and fastening the zipper and button. He's rushed all of a sudden.

Grabbing my arm, he manhandles me back to the shed and forces me into a chair that stands in the middle of the room—for interrogation purposes, no doubt. My insides go cold at the implication of what's in store for me. Yan lifts my bound arms over the chair back so I'm not crushing them with the weight of my body, a strange reprieve when an interrogation is a foregone conclusion and torture a most likely possibility. Then he gets more rope, spreads my legs, and ties my ankles to the feet of the chair.

And that's how he leaves me, tied up in the dark.

I'VE BEEN TRAINED TO ENDURE DISCOMFORT AND PAIN. I slip into a space in my mind where the sensory impressions of hunger, thirst, and aching limbs are nothing but signals to my brain. It's called a mental override. If not for this technique, I'd go crazy.

It doesn't take long before the door opens once more, and a tall, powerfully built man enters. With the sunlight at his back, he's mostly a silhouette. I don't need to be a clairvoyant to know this man's aura drips with the same kind of danger as Yan's.

Two men step in behind him. The twins. Their faces are in the shadows, but I'd recognize Ilya's bulky shape and Yan's distinct, panther-like stride anywhere.

A light flicks on, a naked bulb casting a circle of light around me.

"We've just gotten the files on the men whose names she gave us," Ilya says in Russian, holding out his phone. "Our doppelgängers have quite a resume. All four are former Delta Force, same unit."

Their doppelgängers? What the hell?

Ilya glances at me. "They and a few of their buddies got court-martialed fifteen years ago for gang-raping a sixteen-year-old girl in Pakistan."

What? Every hair on my body bristles at the information. I was right to have had a bad feeling about them. Does Gergo know? No, impossible. Considering my history, he wouldn't have worked with them. I'm glad I gave up their names. I hope the Russians catch them. I hope they make them suffer.

"Six of them got arrested," Ilya continues, "but the others broke them out and they all went on the lam. Since then, they've been doing random jobs here and there, everything from minor assassinations to planting bombs for terrorist organizations."

The man takes the phone as Ilya speaks, his thumb sliding over the screen, presumably checking photos of the men in question, men I recommended to Henderson. A rivulet of sweat runs down my back.

Then the newcomer turns, holding the phone at such an angle that I can clearly see the faces as he flicks back and forth, and I go stone cold.

Holy mother of all clusterfucks.

On the phone are the familiar faces of the Delta Force men, but underneath, matched to each one, are grainy images that must've come from a security camera, photos that show different men entirely. One of them looks like the man holding the phone in front of me, while another is a tough-looking guy with a dark beard. But it's the last two that make my stomach twist.

The twins.

It's Yan and Ilya, and yet it's not. I recognize the Delta Force men's features underneath the skillfully applied disguises.

Is that what Ilya meant by "our doppelgängers?" Was the FBI bombing in Chicago—the terrorist act Sokolov was to be arrested for—a frame job by Henderson? Did the general use the Delta Force team I gave him to carry out the bombing and then pin the blame on Sokolov and his team? A team that includes Yan and his brother?

I want to throw up at the thought.

I don't watch the news much, but even *I* couldn't miss that story—especially since my target, the man I was supposed to get killed during his arrest, was the main suspect behind the bombing. His and his wife's faces were all over the news. I watched the coverage at first, but after a couple of days, I'd had enough.

It was repetitive, and I didn't need constant reminders of how much I fucked up by getting involved in this mess.

Now, though, I have to wonder if that was yet another mistake of mine. Were Yan and Ilya's faces—or rather, those of their doppelgängers—eventually broadcast as well?

If I'd kept watching, would I have known of their involvement?

Wait, those disguises... I catch another glimpse of the photos on the phone, and my mouth goes painfully dry.

Those disguises, they carry a signature trademark, one I know well. I know the style, because I used it myself on many occasions. It's a style the master himself had taught me.

Only one person in the world could've created that effect.

A man known as The Chameleon.

Gergo Nagy.

My mentor, savior, and friend. The man I owe my life, and more.

He, too, must've been involved in this. Which makes sense. Gergo's worked with the Delta Force men before. Many times. And he's the one who gave my name to Henderson.

I start shivering in the tropical heat. If this comes to light, Gergo is dead.

I know what the man with Yan and Ilya is going to ask even before he turns back to me and says, "Who did their makeup and disguises?"

The light of the phone screen illuminates his harsh features, and I recognize him from the pictures on the news.

It's Peter Sokolov, the Russian assassin I was hired to indirectly kill—and apparently, the twins' teammate.

This can't end well for me.

He walks into the circle of light and stops right in front of me, staring down at my face with cold calculation. "It looks like it was someone very skilled."

Yan and Ilya follow on his heel, Yan a little too closely. The twins' faces are stark and forbidding as they scrutinize me, but it's Yan's stare I feel viscerally, as if he's cutting me open and looking right inside.

I dampen my dry lips. I can't betray Gergo. Everything I am, I owe to him. I won't repay him by ratting him out. Anyway, I'm dead. We all know it, all four of us in this room. There's only one solution with a dreadful implication, something that intensifies the nausea in my empty stomach.

The men regard me silently. They're not going to let the question about the disguises go unanswered. They want whoever has done it too badly. Eventually, they will find out. There's no other way.

A part of me dies even before I gather the words and form the lie. It's Sokolov who poses the biggest threat, hovering over me like the brutal killer I sense him to be, but it's on Yan's face I focus as I say softly, "Me. I did it."

The declaration is huge. I've just admitted to framing Yan and his team in the dirtiest way possible.

The mere idea burns like a ball of fire in my stomach, and it's not even the truth. Yet there's no reaction in Yan's frosty gaze. Nothing in his expression. Not even a twitch.

Whatever magic we so unconventionally shared in the dark hours of the night is as dead as his flat, green eyes.

10

YAN

*I*t feels as if flocks of vultures are at war in my chest, picking the meat clean off my bones, but on the outside, I show nothing. I won't give the pretty little bitch that pleasure. She framed me. As a terrorist, no less.

What we shared meant less than shit to her.

I don't pause to dissect why that thought guts me. It just does. Perhaps because while I searched the streets for her like a crazed lunatic, she didn't give a damn. While the delirious intimacy we've shared has been playing in a loop in my memory, she's easily forgotten all about me, maybe the very second she escaped from my room.

No matter. I'm planning on reminding her. Thoroughly.

Sokolov regards her skeptically. "Is that right?" He seems to have a hard time believing she's done the disguises.

The nostrils of her dainty nose flare, as if his doubt insults her honesty when we've already established her honesty is questionable at best.

"Why would I lie?" The anger that shows on her elfin face carries on her voice, but it doesn't make it less musical. "I've already given you all those names. What's one more in the grand scheme of things?"

An idea settles in my frayed mind. Call it hope. Call it stupidity. Call it raving fucking madness. "This will be easy to verify." Not liking how close Sokolov stands to her, I impose myself in his space. If what she says is true—and that stupid part of me I can't fully suppress still hopes she's lying—I'll be doling out the punishment she deserves. It's my right, and mine alone. "She can show off her skill on me tonight."

"And on me," Ilya adds like an insolent child.

Like hell. Nobody touches her but me. She had a choice. She chose *my* bed. It's me she fucked over when she gave me everything and nothing at all.

Sokolov asks more questions. She answers them all. During the exchange, I watch Sokolov closely. Because of Mina—or rather, my deceiving little Mink—Sokolov's in-laws are dead. I know my former team leader well enough. He's not going to let it slide. Even as he stands there, regarding her with a stony expression, I see what's brewing in his mind. Mina's execution is a given. The petite sniper isn't walking away from here. Her tongue will never tangle in a kiss again, her pussy never stretching for a cock like it did for mine, as if it was the most perfect fit. A lie will never leave her lush lips again.

The cut on that lip bothers me. It doesn't fit there. Neither do the bruises on her translucent, perfect skin. It's a good thing the guys who delivered her are already gone, or they'd be leaving in body bags. Liar or not, they had no right to rough her up. I should've said to take her unharmed, not just alive.

Sokolov is playing her, letting her believe her cooperation will win her freedom, but I see the knowledge in her startling blue eyes. Mina is cleverer than that. She's not some civilian girl we snatched off the street. She tells him what he wants to hear, but says she only met Henderson in person once, and she doesn't know where our impersonators are, though she's worked with them in the past.

When Sokolov finally leaves, I relax my guard enough to look Mina over properly. She's holding up well. My chest swells with pride. Unwanted pride, but I can help it as little as I can help how my cock takes interest in her nearness. Despite the anger, there's a warped sense of excitement inside me, joy that I finally have her back. The little traitor still fascinates me to no end.

That fascination won't last much longer if she doesn't drink and eat soon. We've stretched it out as long as we could.

Our thoughts are often in tune, Ilya's and mine, and just as I'm about to offer her what would seem to any captive like a reward for cooperation, Ilya asks, "Are you hungry?"

She gives him a smile that's way too friendly for my liking. "I won't say no to water."

His tone is gruff. "We'll get you something to eat and drink."

Bristling, I turn to him. "Good idea. Why don't you run to the compound and get us a meal and some water?"

His face contorts with an expression I know well from our childhood, when we'd argue over chores. "Why me?"

I cross my arms. "You're the one who offered her a meal."

"You go get it."

"Fine." I turn to my pretty captive. "Sorry, but it seems room service isn't operating today."

Ilya curses under his breath, calling me colorful Russian names. I laugh at his back when he goes for the door like a fuming bull. When he's gone and I look back at Mina, she's studying me.

"Do the two of you always share women?"

I shrug like it doesn't matter—which it hasn't, until her. "We don't mind."

"At the same time, or do you always go first?" There's a bite to her question.

Grabbing the armrests of the chair, I get into her personal space. "Both, actually." I smile. "Jealous?"

She cranes her neck to accommodate my proximity. "You didn't share me."

Just hearing it makes the hair at my nape stand on end. "Did you want us to share?" I drag my fingers through the silky strands of her short hair, the platinum color streaked with dirt. She watches me warily, cleverly not trusting the gentle touch. "Is that your fetish, *malyshka?*" I pointedly use my brother's ridiculously sweet nickname for her. *Little one*, it means in Russian.

"No," she replies heatedly, almost as if offended.

The answer calms me enough to release her and take a step back. She's so pretty, even soaked with sweat and covered in dirt. It makes me want to rip off my shirt and get a different kind of sweaty look on her. No woman has ever affected me like this. Yesterday, I might've adored her for it. Today, I hate her.

Turning on my heel, I march to the door. Like the professional killer she is, she doesn't ask where I'm going or what I'm planning. She knows she won't get an answer.

The guards are back. Just in case, I secure the chain, and lock the door from the outside. Then I go to our sleeping quarters at the compound in search of a bucket and soap. Once there, I grab a clean shirt and a new disposable toothbrush from my bag. A quick walk past the kitchen confirms Ilya is angrily slapping a sandwich together. I leave before he sees me. He'll only launch into another gripe session.

Back at the shed, I fill the bucket with water from the outside tap and lock the door behind me again.

Mina's expression doesn't change, but the quick rise of her chest gives away her fear.

She probably thinks I'm going to waterboard her.

I untie her legs and make quick work of removing her boots, socks, pants, and underwear before tying her ankles back to the chair. I don't bother with removing the top and bra. Those I tear off. They're dirty and blood-soaked beyond saving. On second thought, the pants and everything else can go into the trashcan, too. I'm not doing the little traitor's laundry.

I wasn't going to look at her, not like that, but she's no longer an image from a favorite memory in my mind. She's right here, naked and spread. On display. I can't help it. I start at her narrow ankles and slide my gaze up her shapely calves to the soft flesh of her inner thighs. Between them lies my prize, the prettiest pussy I've ever laid eyes on. I extend my exploration to her toned stomach and the navel piercing, a gold ring. Then the tattooed scribbling on her side. Her ribs are like the bones of a bird. With her arms stretched back, I can count each one.

The blue and black shades on her pearly-white skin are evidence that she's taken a few punches in the gut. I ball my fists in rage. Seeing her marred like this does something to me, something that makes me want to kill.

To throw a bucket of paint on the Mona Lisa would be a sacrilege. This is no different. It's a sin to spoil something so utterly perfect. After having lived in filthy, stinking conditions for all my childhood and most of my adolescent life, I've cultivated a taste for beauty and everything aesthetically appealing to the eye. I prefer dress shirts to casual wear, designer brands over no-name labels. And I can't stomach seeing a priceless portrait vandalized.

Tearing my gaze away from the disturbing sight of her injured midriff, I go higher and am rewarded with those plump breasts. Her nipples are pink and delicate, like icing on a cake. The memory of how they tasted makes my mouth water.

I drag my gaze back to her face. She watches me quietly, accepting the inevitable law of our kind even as a fresh layer of sweat shines on her forehead. Most captives are tortured naked. Not only does it make it easier to access all the body parts, but it also adds an element of psychological vulnerability.

Dunking a sponge in the bucket, I soap it well. Her lips part slightly as I crouch down in front of her and bring the wet sponge to her foot. She jerks at the first contact, then gasps. The water is cold, but it'll be a welcome relief once she gets used to it. It's as hot as a furnace in here.

"What are you doing, Yan?"

Fuck. The way she says my name makes me harder than I already am. As strange as it is, touching her feels like a homecoming—not that I'd know what that feels like. I've never had a home, at least not in the safe, comfortable sense. "What does it look like?"

"*Why* are you doing it, then?" Her voice is soft, as

soft as her smooth skin under the palm I glide up her calf.

Why indeed? Because she's a Mona Lisa, and I'm fascinated with this strange woman who's smaller than most, but does the job of big, merciless men like me. Because she's pretty, and I can't stop looking at her. Because maybe, just maybe, I still want to believe in her. Something about her touches a nerve of humanity I didn't know I still had. Or maybe it's because seeing her dirty brings back unwelcome, deep-buried memories of being filthy and hungry. I can still taste that misery. It tastes too much like stale bread and despair.

"Because I want to lay your body out in your coffin like the piece of art you are." I say the last part like an insult, but honestly, she deserves a glass coffin like Snow White, so everyone can admire her as much in death as in life.

Her throat moves as she swallows, but I can't make myself regret my cruel words.

The pain of her betrayal is too fresh, too raw.

"How are you going to do it?" she asks hoarsely.

"Do what?"

"Kill me."

I imagine her lifeless body on the ground. Not by knife. Too messy for her paper-white skin. Not by strangling. It'll leave bruises on her slender neck. Poison, maybe. A cruel death, but it would leave her unmarred.

"Cooperate," I say, "and we may consider letting you go."

Empty words. Meaningless. And her silence says she knows that.

Meticulously, I sponge her down, working my way down from her waist. I wash away the sweat and dirt. I wash away the smell of the men who captured her, even if said smell is only a concept in my mind. I trail the soapy sponge up the inside of her thigh, watching her face as I drag it over the delicate petals of her sex.

Memories of how hard her pussy worked to take my cock, of how beautifully she stretched for me and how tightly she gripped me when she climaxed, work me into a frenzy. Her lips part, the swollen bottom one stirring something fiercely protective in my chest. She squirms in the chair as I part her folds with two fingers and drag the sponge down her slit. Her chest rises and falls faster. I circle her clit twice before I stop the cruel teasing and move to her other leg.

I wash her stomach and sides, trailing my hands extra gently over the bruised skin to assess the damage to her ribs. Nothing seems to be broken, but she sucks in a breath as I poke around her flesh. Finally, I have a chance to study her tattoo. Tilting my head, I read the script.

In aeternum vivi. Adéla & Johan.

I'm mostly self-educated, which means I've taught myself all sorts of nonstandard stuff—like basic Latin. So I know what her tattoo says.

Forever alive.

What's that about? I'll have to ask her about it later.

Dipping the sponge in the bucket, I soak up a good deal of water and dribble it between her breasts. Mesmerized, I watch the rivulets run into the hollow of her navel, over the belly ring and her mound, and between her folds. Her nipples tighten, and I pay them extra attention with the sponge, as well as the under-curves of her breasts.

When I'm done playing with her breasts, I move to her neck. The arch of that column is elegant, delicate like the intricate detail of the hummingbird tattooed there. I looked it up after that night in Budapest. The pretty little bird is a symbol of life. A strange symbol for a killer to wear.

My attention moves to her beautiful face. My palm would easily cover all four of the senses situated there. If I stretch my hand just so, I could seal her eyes, nose, mouth, and block her ears with my fingers. Such a delicate thing. Maybe smothering would be the perfect way for her to go.

I carefully wash the dried blood from her split lip and confirm it's the only cut on her body. The blood on her top isn't from any other injury. Then I move to her hair, working water and soap through the short strands until they're a pure platinum blond and none of the filth from the long journey or the dirty bench is left. Smoothing her wet hair back over her shapely head, I step back to admire my work.

There. She's all shiny again. Except for the cut and bruises, but those will fade.

She's staring up at me, her whole body covered in goosebumps and her nipples contracted. She's confused. Probably wondering why I'm not dunking her head in the bucket instead. And we'll come to that, but not like she thinks.

My cock is already hard from touching her, from seeing and smelling her, from feeling her warm breath on my face. I'm tempted to free it and sink into her, right here in the chair, but not like this.

A loud thud on the door yanks me from the moment. Ilya's voice filters through the wood. "Open up."

In his dreams. "Leave the food by the door."

"What the fuck?"

"Do you have a hearing problem?"

He calls me every lowlife name he can think up. When he finally runs out of insults, there's a sound of clinking cutlery, and then the angry stomping of receding footsteps.

I wait a good few seconds before I go to the door and peer through the crack. The guards have their backs turned to the door. No sign of Ilya. I open the door and retrieve the tray before locking it again. Mina gives me another one of those wary looks as I carry the tray over and leave it on the floor.

"Hungry?" I know the answer, but she hasn't said a word to me since she brought up the killing bit and I have a craving to hear the sweet, birdlike sound of her voice.

"Thirsty," she says on a croak.

Twisting the cap off the bottle of water, I tip it against her lips. She drinks greedily, taking everything she can get. In her position, there's no knowing if another such mercy will be granted.

A quarter way through the bottle, I move it away to indicate she should go slower. She'll vomit it all up if she drinks too fast. Understanding, she takes smaller sips. When half of the water is gone, I put the bottle aside and reach for the sandwich. I turn the bread sideways to check the filling. Ham and cheese.

Fucking Ilya. Couldn't he have come up with something a little more interesting?

Stepping between her legs, I offer her the bread. She opens her lips a little too wide, like the starving kitten she is. Her cut splits anew, but that doesn't stop her from biting off a huge chunk of the corner.

"Small bites," I remind her.

She chews and swallows, watching me as she eats, probably wondering if there's poison in the food. I don't bring the bread back to her lips. This time, I stand and wait. She leans toward me without taking her eyes away from mine, carefully taking the bite from my hand. It's like winning the trust of a small, wild animal, teaching it to eat from your palm. I like it way too much. Then again, I can't forget that wild animals, no matter how cute, won't hesitate to bite the hand that feeds them. It's in their nature.

The cut on her lip is bleeding again from all the stretching to accommodate the sandwich. Visions of those lips around the tormenting hardness of my cock assault me, but I push them away. I won't allow my hope to grow until she's passed—or rather failed—the test of disguising me.

Breaking off small pieces of the bread, I feed it to her to spare her further discomfort from the reopened wound. I alternate it with sips of water until she's finished everything, except the last bit of water. I give her that to rinse her mouth after I've brushed her teeth and tell her to spit on the ground.

She looks infinitely better after eating, although still weak. There's even a bit of color in her cheeks, the same peachy glow she had when I rocked my cock into her. Before she regains her strength and decides to put up a fight, I untie her, dress her in my shirt, and tie her up in the chair again.

Her gaze follows the path of my hands as I fasten the buttons. "It's yours."

Like I'd dress her in another man's clothes. I swallow down a vicious laugh.

"Why are you doing this?" she asks.

"You prefer I leave you naked?"

She shuts her mouth at that.

The hem reaches her thighs, but her naked pussy is only an arm's reach away. I straighten and ask brusquely, "What do you need for the disguise?"

Her answer is tentative, as if she's reluctant to do this. "The usual. A wig. Beard. Stage makeup."

I glare down at her. "What were you hoping to achieve the night you let me take you?" I can't let it go. I can't wipe it out of my head. "Information, perhaps?"

You never know. Some information is a valuable commodity.

"I told you. Nothing."

I laugh. "You expect me to believe that?"

She glares right back at me. "What about you, Yan? What were *you* hoping to achieve? I heard you and Ilya. I heard what you said about keeping me."

"Is that why you ran?"

She looks away.

I grip her chin and turn her face back to me. "Answer me."

"There's that, and..." For a second, she looks guilty. "And who I am."

"Ah. A killer, you mean. I wouldn't have judged you for that, princess, but framing me as a terrorist? Now that's a different story."

"It wasn't personal," she whispers.

My smile is mean. "Is that so?"

"It was a job."

A job. I was a job.

Fuck me if I know why the knowledge slices me up ten different ways inside. Maybe because she's not the waitress she pretended to be, and what she is makes her all the more perfect for me.

Under different circumstances, we may have had something, she and I. But as it stands now, we're enemies.

And her life is mine.

11

MINA

*I*t's been a while since Yan left, taking my dirty clothes with him, but the scent of musky sandalwood and spicy pepper lingers in the space. Contrary to his overpowering personality, his signature cologne is subtle and airy, but it still dominates the shed, enough to mask the musty smell of the wood in my nostrils. It clings to his shirt, the one I'm wearing. Why did he bathe, feed, and dress me in something clean? Is this some psychological tactic, a way of softening me before breaking me? If so, it will be most effective. If he's going to be physically cruel to me later, these kindnesses will make it seem worse.

Bars of shadows from the thin gaps between the wall planks stretch over the floor and finally disappear. Crickets start to chirp. There's one somewhere in the corner of the shed, trapped inside, like I am. His song is out of tune with the chorus of the free ones outside. I distract myself by trying to spot my little companion, but the glow of the light Yan left on doesn't bleed into the corners. It falls around me in a white pool, failing to reach the dark corners of my heart where fear beats out of tune.

It's completely black outside when the door opens and Yan steps into the shed carrying two metal cases. They're generic cases, the types that can be used for weapons or instruments of torture. The knot in my stomach tightens as I look from the cases to his face. His angular features are set in a hard expression, and the masculine beauty of his face somehow makes it look more dangerous, more calculated. He locks the door and crosses the floor. With every step he takes, my insides wind tighter together.

He drops the cases at my feet. "How are you doing, my little waitress?"

The accusation is bitter. To reply to it would only add to his wrath. And I can't fault him for feeling this way. I understand how it looks from his perspective. One night, we meet and have sex, and fifteen months later, he finds out I'm the sniper who tried to get his friend/boss killed. What is he supposed to think? The only logical conclusion is that I was spying on him that night at the bar. To top it off, because I lied to protect Gergo, he believes I helped frame not only Sokolov but him and his brother by putting their faces on the team that committed a terrible act of terrorism. He doesn't know that I had no idea what Henderson would do with the Delta Force men whose files I gave him, nor that I never would've taken the Sokolov job if I'd had any clue he was connected to Yan. And I can't tell Yan the truth.

In his eyes, I'm a heartless monster, and I have to remain that way for as long as they let me live.

"We're going to do this in reverse," Yan says. "You're going to disguise me to look like one of the Delta Force assholes." Leaning over, he grips the armrests and adds in a soft, menacing voice, "For your sake, I hope you fail."

I swallow. I already failed when I took responsibility for the job.

His full lips tilt in one corner, but there's nothing friendly about the gesture. "Ready, princess?"

I nod.

His mouth ghosts over mine. "If you try anything, I'll make you wish you were dead. Understand?"

I shiver more at the cold deliverance than the threat itself.

"Good," he says, taking my silence for the correct answer. In this game, I don't have a choice.

I study him as he crouches down to untie my feet. He's wearing a fitted dress shirt and pants, and he's not carrying any weapons, at least none I can see. Not that he needs any. His hands are strong enough to inflict lethal damage. And coming unarmed is wise. It eliminates the chance of me disarming him and using his own weapon against him.

He walks around me to work on my wrists. "Need to pee?"

"Yes."

I hiss when the ropes fall free and he moves my arms to my sides. After hours of being in the same position, even the slight movement hurts. He rubs his big, warm palms over my arms, aiding the circulation. When most of the pins and needles are gone, he pulls me to my feet by my upper arm and guides me outside.

There's no light around the shed, but I can make out two guards, different ones, in the moonlight. One of them is holding a dog on a leash. The animal bares its teeth when we pass. This is more than a sniffer dog. It's trained to attack.

"You don't want them to get their hands on you," Yan says softly against my ear.

I understand what he means and he's right. I don't. I also understand why he brought me out here. It's to make sure I understand what waits for me if I do somehow manage to overpower him.

He takes me to the same tree, but this time, he doesn't turn away as I relieve myself. Despite my training, my cheeks turn hot. The tail ends of his shirt hide my private parts, but he stares at me as if he can see right through the shirt. When I'm done, he takes a travel-sized packet of wet wipes from his pocket and hands it to me. I quickly clean myself before wiping my hands, appreciating the small hygienic luxury. Not knowing what to do with the used wipes, I ball them in my fist.

He grabs my arm and steers me back to the shed.

The exercise, however minute, is welcome. Some of the ache in my back dissipates.

Back inside, he locks us in and drops the key into the front pocket of his pants. Then he pulls me roughly to the chair.

Indicating the cases, he says, "Open them."

There's a bin next to the chair, maybe for blood or vomit when they torture their enemies. I dispose of the wipes in the bin.

"Now, *Mink*. I don't have all night."

Ignoring the accusation in the way he said my code name, I crouch down in front of the cases, flick open the clasps, and flip up the lids. One is filled with an assortment of wigs, moustaches, combs, and glue, and the other with makeup and brushes. How did he get these so fast? One look is enough to tell me these products are on the high end of the scale.

"Pick one," he says.

I turn my attention back to him. "What?"

"Pick a guy." His tone is mocking, but I don't miss the anger running underneath. "Who are you going to turn me into?"

"I don't remember them by heart. I'll have to see their faces again."

He gives me a piercing look as he fishes his phone from his pocket and flicks over the screen without breaking eye contact. Sweat forms on my forehead from the intensity of his stare. If I really disguised those men, I should be able to remember their features. I hold my breath, praying he won't call me out on it.

He glances briefly at the screen before holding it up to my face.

I let out a silent breath of relief. Looking at him for permission, I lift a hand. He nods. I swipe a finger over the screen, running through the photos of the Delta Force men. I pause on the one with the beard and bushy eyebrows.

He turns the phone back to look at the image. "Ugly bastard." Leaving the phone well out of my reach on the bench, he turns back to me with crossed arms. "What are you waiting for?"

"You'll have to sit down." He's too tall for me to reach his face.

A little shock runs through me when he grips my hips. His gaze sharpens, as if he knows. He moves us around, reversing our positions, and lowers himself into the chair. Spreading his legs wide with a lazy movement, he pulls me between them.

"Do me, *malyshka*."

I jerk inwardly at the nuanced meaning. Memories of us *doing each other* naked in his bed assault my mind, and a faint pulse of arousal starts beating in my belly.

Slowly leaning back with a predatory gleam in his eyes, Yan releases me to rest his arms in a deceptively casual pose on the armrests. I do the wise thing. I jump to create distance between us, rummaging through the contents of the makeup case. Grabbing a tray of cream-based foundations, I study them in the stark glow of the naked bulb.

"I need better light."

"This is all you get."

I select a color that corresponds to the darker skin tone of the bearded man and take a wedged sponge from its package. To reach his face, I have to step closer, my thighs brushing the insides of his legs. My body tightens with an uninvited sensation, one that sends heat to my core. I busy myself by dragging the sponge through the foundation, soaking up just enough of the cosmetic to spread it evenly over his cheek without creating a caked effect.

At the first swipe over the hollow of his cheek that emphasizes the stark lines of his high cheekbone and strong nose, my hand starts to shake. I have to lean closer to reach. Tilting back his head, he holds my gaze with the piercing interest of a lover, or maybe an animal on the hunt, as he offers his face like a canvas. It's not the unconventional beauty of the canvas I focus on, but that he's offering me anything at all. Men like Yan give nothing easily. Emotions? Never. I can forget about counting on his compassion to escape alive.

I scoop up more foundation, dabbing it onto the rough skin of his jaw. He shaved. By the smell of soap still clinging to him, he showered, too. I take a deep breath, but it's useless. I can't keep my hand steady. I freeze when he closes his legs the tiniest bit, squeezing my hips softly. My lower body starts to hum, and more heat pools in my abdomen. The notion of pending death only adds to the sensations, making my body feel more alive than ever. Every bolt of awareness that runs through me is amplified. When you're hungry, food tastes extra good. When death is so real you can taste it in the back of your mouth, physical awareness is stronger. I'm powerless to control these impulses. As before, my body responds to him. My flesh doesn't recognize that the man who gave it life is the same one who'll take it away forever.

"Nervous?" he drawls.

Another nuanced question. He knows the answer. He can feel it in the unsteadiness of my hands. With his fine-tuned killer senses, he can probably hear the minute change of my breathing as my pulse quickens.

There's no point in denying the truth. Biting my lip, I nod.

For some reason, my answer pleases him. He likes to make me nervous.

Keeping my gaze, he places his hands on my thighs, just below the hem of his shirt. His broad, calloused palms are abrasive on my skin, making my flesh contract. Measuring my reaction with his piercing, all-noticing stare, he slowly glides his hands up under the shirt until they rest on my naked ass.

My shiver is visible. Electric shocks run down my spine and up my legs to collide in the center. Like an invisible charge, the current explodes in my clit, making it swell with an instant ache. Watching me, reading me, he rubs his hands down the back of my thighs and up my inner legs. I pinch my knees together, trying to hide his effect on me, but he pushes them apart with little effort. At the seam of my folds, he stops. I hold my breath.

The lazy casualness of earlier is gone. The hunger in his eyes is blade sharp. More dangerous. Edgier. For one, two seconds, we freeze, me in a desire to deny my body's reaction—I don't want him to know how much power he wields over me—and him with the unmistakable intent of examining that reaction. Then he moves his hands back to my ass with a gentle sweep. Tightening his fingers on my globes, he yanks me to him, hard. I collide with his body and grab his shoulders to steady myself. His hard-on is trapped between us, pressing at the seam of my opening. I try to push away, but the harder I fight to escape, the tighter he holds me. All I'm accomplishing with my squirming is rubbing myself over his erection.

I stop.

He grunts. "Come here."

I can't come any closer. I'm practically on his lap. And that's exactly where I want to be, whatever happens after be damned. If I'm going to die anyway—

"Mina," he says more harshly.

I focus on his eyes, on the jade-green color that shines so coldly.

He drags his palms up my back and over my shoulders until his big hands frame my face. "Do you want this?"

There are many reasons why I shouldn't, but the truth is an easy answer. It's one-worded and uncomplicated, devoid of who we are and what that means for the short future I have left. It only knows the undeniable pull that brings our lips closer.

He takes the last step, crushing our mouths together. The makeup sponge drops to the ground, but not before I've painted a streak of bronze over the collar of his shirt. I manage a feeble whimper, a weak sound of surrender, but it's lost in the turbulent kiss that takes my reason. The whimper grows into a moan, its meaning quite different. It says how much I want him, this dangerous Russian killer.

The moment that needy sound slips into his mouth, he turns even wilder. He opens my lips impatiently with his tongue, taking as if I belong to him. The roughness of his kiss is matched only by the gentleness with which he cradles my head. He drags his hands down to my neck, one big palm fastening around my nape while the other folds around the front in a possessive hold. He keeps me in place while conquering my mouth, making sure I have nowhere to go but where he wants me.

My knees grow weak. As if sensing that little sign of submission, he grips the back of my thighs and lifts me onto his lap. My legs are stretched uncomfortably wide over the armrests as I straddle him, but I don't care. I only care for more of him. Our chests press together, the warmth of his body seeping into me. His heartbeat reaches me through flesh, skin, and clothes. The strong, erratic beat simultaneously soothes and excites me further, the knowledge that he wants me adding to the burning heat inside me.

Impatiently pushing me away without breaking the kiss, he unbuttons my shirt. When it falls open, he takes a moment to look at me, then lowers his head and closes his mouth around my nipple. The wet, hot flick of his tongue over the unbearably sensitive tip makes me arch my back, giving him more. He closes his teeth around the tip and does that wicked thing with his tongue again. Another moan escapes my throat, louder this time.

The wet heat around my nipple disappears, and he presses a finger on my lips. "Shh." He must not want the guards to hear.

Pulling back, he stares at my body with satisfaction and hungry lust. My nipple is hard and extended, a telltale sign of my arousal. So is the wetness between my legs. He drags a finger over my other nipple, inviting a similar reaction, then down between my breasts and over the ring in my navel, coming to a stop at the top of my slit. His gaze finds mine. I want to watch his hand, to look at the devastating work of his finger, but I'm helpless against the pull of those green pools.

Slowly, he parts my folds, reading my face. I gasp when he sweeps the pad of his thumb over my clit. Approval tightens his features as he discovers my wetness. All gentleness vanishes. He flips his hand palm up and drives a finger into my core. At the same time, he slams a hand over my mouth. My involuntary gasp as the heel of his hand slaps against my sex is caught behind his palm. With his thumb, he draws circles over my clit. I'm caught in the vise of his hand, his shirt slipping down my arms as I writhe in exquisite pleasure. Balancing me on his lap, he thrusts that one finger into me, taking me away from the harshness of my reality with a different kind of harshness. I embrace it greedily, letting him finger-fuck me in whatever way he pleases.

"That's it," he says with tender appraisal. "Show me how you come."

And I do. My inner walls clench with a delicious pressure. It's sweet freedom. Shockwaves weave through me, sending lethargic impulses to my brain. I sag in his arms, dragging in air through my nose to try and settle my ragged breathing. Dropping his hand from my mouth, he presses his lips against mine in a soft kiss.

I want to feel his skin on mine. When I reach for the buttons of his shirt, he doesn't stop me. I unbutton them and brush the edges apart. Leaning forward, I push our chests together. I absorb as much heat as I can, letting it sink into my skin before pulling away to trace the grooves of his lean muscles. It's a shape imprinted in my mind. The slab of his ridged abdomen is hard like marble, his skin velvety warm. The trail of hair that disappears under the waistband of his pants draws my hands. I glide my palms over his erection, tracing the outline through his pants. When I reach for his belt, he doesn't stop me either. He lets me undo the buckle and unbutton his pants, then unzip his fly.

I've never trembled with anticipation, but I do as I slip my hands into the elastic of his briefs. That's when he stops me, locking his fingers around my wrist. "Not yet."

He pulls me up until I'm standing on my knees, my legs on either side of his thighs on the chair. When he slides down in the seat to put his head on level with my sex, I understand his intention. I tense in anticipation.

His voice is commanding. "Not a sound."

Yes, I'll swallow them for him. Anything to have his mouth on me.

This time, he doesn't watch my face. All his attention is focused between my legs. My face heats as he opens me with two fingers, exposing my clit.

"Such a pretty little flower."

My cheeks grow even hotter at his sweet, roughly murmured words. No one has ever been sweet with me.

At the first sweep of his tongue, I forget everything. I forget why I'm here and that I'm not going anywhere. I give up on the control I always fight for so hard. I simply feel. And it's amazing. He bites down softly on my clit while flicking his tongue over the engorged flesh. My toes curl from the pleasure when he dips his tongue inside, fucking me with shallow strokes. I cling to his shoulders and whisper his name, not daring to scream it. When he sucks hard on my clit, sparks sizzle in my lower body, and another orgasm starts to build. It's not going to be slow-detonating like the first one. This one is going to wreck me. My legs start to shake.

His fingers tighten on my waist, and he holds me up when the pleasure explodes, eating me out throughout my climax as I bite down on my lip to keep in the sounds. I'm both depleted and strangely energized when he finally lets me go. Folding my arms around his neck to keep my balance, I sit back on my heels and watch, transfixed, as he frees his cock. He's as big as I remember. The skin is smooth like velvet and embossed with masculine veins. Tracing a finger along the slit, I catch a drop of pre-cum. His cock twitches.

He watches me, waiting.

He's giving me a choice. I take it gladly, climbing from the chair and kneeling between his legs. I fold my hand around him and angle the shaft toward my lips. When I lick the head, he hisses. I like the sound. I like knowing I have power, too. I want more.

A gruff sound of pleasure tears from his chest as I close my lips around his cock. I can't take all of him—he's too big—but I trace his length and girth until I've covered every inch with my tongue. His hands rest in my hair, guiding my tempo as I fold my lips over the thick head and take him as deep as I can.

"Enough," he finally grits out, forcing me back to take a condom from the front pocket of his pants.

He tears the packet open with his teeth and makes quick work of fitting the condom, then helps me to my feet. Turning me to face away from him, he pulls me into his lap. I tense a little, remembering how hard it was to take him.

He kisses my neck. "Just relax."

Whispering encouraging words in my ear, he lifts me higher and positions his cock at my entrance.

Slowly, he starts lowering me. I grip the armrests for support. Even wet and with my muscles supple from two orgasms, I still battle to take his size. He's patient, working himself deeper little by little.

It feels like forever until he's fully seated. It burns, but I embrace it. The discomfort rekindles the fire, making my need climb again.

He presses a question against my ear. "Still good?"

"Mm-mm." I barely manage a nod.

He takes me with shallow strokes until I've adjusted enough to take more. Then he shoves a little harder, making me whimper.

Oh, God. I'm going to come again.

His movements turn more urgent. I try to match his pace, bearing down when he slams up, but he curls an arm around my waist and holds me still. The rhythm becomes demanding. I hold on to his arm, my nails digging into his skin as I swallow a scream. Just as I'm about to float away from reality again, a hard voice calls through the door.

"Open up, Yan. Peter wants to see her work."

Ilya.

"Fuck," Yan mumbles, not breaking his pace.

"Mina?" Ilya says. "Are you all right?"

"We're not done," Yan calls back, the irritation evident in his voice.

My cheeks flame. Ilya must know what we're doing. I try to push away, but Yan holds me tighter.

"Ignore him." He gently bites the skin where my neck and shoulder meet. "Finish with me."

"Open the fucking door, Yan."

"Go the fuck away, Ilya."

"Fuck you."

It's impossible. The moment is gone. "Yan."

He uses his free hand to rub my clit. "Just one more time."

"I can't."

"You will."

He gets rougher, moving faster and pivoting his hips harder until I'm at the limits of what I can take. Despite my self-consciousness, the need Yan creates continues to climb. It rises inside me like a tide, until I'm trapped in the foaming waves of a violent ocean, and the drumming of my heart in my ears washes out the persistent tapping on the door.

My pleasure explodes. I let out a raw sound. Yan goes rigid. His cock grows thicker inside me, and then his whole body jerks.

"*Mater' Bozh'ya*," he grunts.

We come together. In a dirty shed with witnesses outside, I find release in the arms of my soon-to-be killer. I don't reflect on how ironic that is. I barely have time to find my breath before Yan pulls out, leaving me strangely empty and cold. Lifting me to my feet, he tests my balance before letting go. In an instant, he's gone from hot to cold, his face a stoic mask as he removes the condom and discards it in the bin.

"Yan," Ilya calls from outside, "I'll break down this door. I'm not joking, motherfucker."

Yan calmly adjusts his clothes, looking at me with stony eyes. "Cover yourself up."

I glance down at the open shirt. There are smudges of foundation over the front. Yan's collar carries the same marks. My hands tremble as I fasten the buttons. Yan waits until I've finished, then trails his gaze over me. He frowns. Bending down, he brushes the dirt from my knees. I stand there like a puppet, for the first time in my life uncertain how to act.

When he straightens, there's ice in his tone. It's as if the heat we've created not seconds ago has frozen over. "Time to get back to work."

He walks to the door, takes the key from his pocket, and unlocks it.

Ilya all but falls through it. The bulkier of the twins looks between Yan and me, and back at Yan. Accusation burns in his eyes. "What's going on in here?"

"Nothing," Yan says with much irritation. He locks the door and comes back to the chair, lowering his big frame without a hint of emotion. "You heard me, princess. Show us what you're worth."

I glance at Ilya, who stands there with balled fists and flaring nostrils.

"Don't mind him," Yan says. "Now, where were we?"

Yes, where were we? I was about to demonstrate my guilt with the swipe of a makeup brush.

"I go first," Ilya says with an obstinate lift of his chin.

Yan fixes him with a look. "You go nowhere."

"What's your fucking problem?"

"Now's a good time to shut up."

"Fuck you."

"So you've said."

I clear my throat. "Cut it out, you two."

"You," Yan says flatly, "don't get to tell us what to do."

Fine. Let them tear into each other. What do I care? A small voice says I do, but it's a silly notion. Nothing I care about matters now, anyway.

With a brooding Ilya watching, I get to work. I use the skills Gergo taught me, transforming Yan into a different man. When I'm done, I step back to evaluate the result.

"Fuck," Ilya says behind me.

Yan's instruction is harsh. "Give me a mirror."

I hand him the one from the makeup case.

If it was possible for the glittery gemstone color of his eyes to turn dull, they would've. "Well," he says, turning his face from side to side, "at least this is one thing you didn't lie about."

There can be no bigger lie between us. How's that for irony?

"We better go tell Peter," Ilya says in a surly tone.

"Yes." Yan gets to his feet, retrieving his phone from the bench. "We better."

"Yan." I take his arm. "I'm sorry it's like this."

He shakes off my touch. "I'm sure you are." He brings his face close to mine. "You're going to be much sorrier before this is over."

With those prophetic words, he steers me back to the bench, makes me lie down, and ties my arms to a hook on the wall above my head. Then he and his brother leave, this time flicking off the light when they go.

Darkness prevails.

In some lone corner, a cricket chirps out of tune.

12

YAN

*A*ll I want is to get rid of the disguise. It goes deeper than washing the makeup from my face. I want to scrub the proof of Mina's betrayal from my skin.

I'm walking back from the main house to our sleeping quarters after showing Sokolov Mina's work when Ilya catches up with me.

He cuts me off. "Give me the key to the shed."

I laugh.

His face turns red. "Who appointed you as her jail keeper?"

"She chose me." I stab a thumb at my chest.

"You didn't give her a choice."

Like hell. "She made the decision."

Maybe not for the right reason. Maybe she only fucked me that night in Budapest to distract me from killing her or to win time so she could escape later, but she chose *me*. It's my hand she took. It's me she followed to the bedroom.

Still, a nasty kernel of doubt sprouts in my mind. If Ilya had been sitting next to her on the couch and I'd been the one making the sandwich, would she have gone with Ilya? But no. She had her chance when I was making the princess her tea.

"She'll want me," Ilya says. "Give me the key and I'll prove it."

"Sorry, brother." I move around him and say over my shoulder, "Not this time."

He runs to keep up with my long strides. "Why do only you get to have her? Why can't we share?"

I see bright fucking red. "It's me she fucked over. The revenge is mine."

"I was there."

I chuckle. "You made the sandwich." When it comes to revenge, a fuck weighs a lot more than a wasted sandwich.

He grabs hold of my arm, stopping me. "Sokolov is going to kill her. You know that, right?"

I pull free. "What do you take me for? An idiot?"

"Is that what this is about?" He lowers his voice and glances at the sky, probably scanning the air for nosy drones. "You want to be the one to swing the blade?"

"That's exactly it," I grit out.

He scoffs. "You think that's your right?"

He better believe it. "Everything concerning that little traitor is my right."

111

"Explain to me how one fuck makes her your property."

I put my face in his. "Why? Because you want to fuck her before I kill her?"

His features tighten. "You're overreacting. It's her job. Anyone would've done the same. Put yourself in her shoes. You fuck her once, by random coincidence, and by frightening the hell out of her. Then someone comes along—say, Sokolov—and shows you a picture of Mina. He offers you money to disguise another woman to look like her. It's how you make your living, so you do it. Would you have asked questions? Would you have wanted to know why he needed to make another woman look like Mina?"

Yes. I would've asked questions. And no, I wouldn't have done it. I wouldn't have set up the woman I'd had in my bed only once but have craved every day after. Maybe that's what makes my anger blaze so hot.

"Don't justify her behavior," I say. "What's done is done."

He changes tactics, going for a softer tone. "Let me take her some food, maybe some wine. Let me at least make it better for her."

I grin. "So you can break her free, or force your advances?"

Just like that, his anger is back. "It won't be forced."

"I'm tired of giving you the same answer. I'm telling you one last time. No."

"You're a bastard," he yells after me as I continue on the path. "She doesn't deserve this and you know it."

The first part? True. The second? False.

She deserves everything she's going to get.

I leave my brother standing in the jungle like the idiot he is, and continue to our room, where I rip off the eyebrows and beard before having a shower. Then I change and go to the kitchen to rummage through the fridge. I fix a sandwich and swallow it down with a beer, then make another and grab a bottle of water.

It's late, and the guards who changed shifts have gone to bed. I sneak out quietly—not because I care who knows where I'm going, but to avoid Ilya—and make my way to the shed. I acknowledge the guards with a nod, unlock the door, and make sure I lock it again behind me.

She's awake. I don't need the light to know that. I can hear it from her uneven breathing. Moonlight enters through the cracks in the walls. The strips of light fall over her body, illuminating her in patches. A swatch of her pretty face, the swell of her breast, her flat stomach, a naked thigh, a delicate ankle. It's different, looking at her like this. Subtle hints. I can focus on small portions of her, one at a time.

Leaving the light off, I advance on her. She goes rigid. Every visit from me brings the opportunity of death. I know it. She knows it. And I know what the knowledge does to a person. Even frail and small like a kitten, tied up and helpless, she doesn't panic when her enemy looms over her. Oh, she's scared. Terrified. But brave. I admire her courage. In fact, I admire it too much. It makes me hate her more, but it doesn't make me want her less.

My cock jumps to life at the notion. I can have her like this, spread out like a sacrifice.

I put the food and water on the ground, and trail a hand over her leg. Her skin is soft. She watches me as I grip the hem of her shirt and drag it higher with the path of my fingers. I trail my fingertips over her thigh, ribs, and the side of her breast, exposing her slowly until she lies naked in front of me with shards of light falling diagonally over her pearly skin. The light catches one pink nipple that rises and falls with her breaths. The patch between her legs is in the dark.

Lightly, I slide my knuckles down the valley between her plump breasts. Despite the heat, her nipples harden. Her stomach flutters under my touch, and she gasps softly when I reach her sex. I keep the exploration light as I run the back of my fingers over her folds to where the curves of her ass press on the bench. Gently, I cup her pussy. She's damp and warm, and I nearly groan as her slickness coats my palm.

She wants me.

Staring down at her face, I curl my middle finger and sink it into her heat. She's tight. Perfect. Her lips part with a soft sigh, and her back arches. She's showing me pleasure, but Ilya's words harp at the back of my mind.

You didn't give her a choice.

"You want this, *Mina*?" Her name is delicious, a soft sound on my tongue, a forbidden word I swore I wouldn't utter again. But it's a word made just for me. How can I not swallow it like honey?

"Yes," she whispers.

"Why?"

"Do I need a reason?"

I give her a slow smile. "No."

She whimpers when I withdraw my hand and leave a wet trail on her inner leg. I don't need a reason for taking off my clothes, for getting hard for her, either. I take my time folding my pants and shirt, and placing everything neatly on the chair. I want to drag this out, but I already know I'm not going to last.

When I stop naked next to her, she swallows. There's always this bit of nervousness in her eyes before I take her, as if every time is the first, every time new. I take a few moments to study her. The more I look, the more her unconventional beauty seeps under my skin. From the moment I noticed the femininity hidden under layers of baggy clothes, I wanted her. I wanted to see and feel every inch of her. Getting her naked once didn't appease that desire. It only whetted my appetite. Her prettiness hits me harder each time I remove her clothes.

I trail my gaze over her short length. She's so small and light, her body merely the narrow width of the bench. I could easily crush her with my bigger frame.

So breakable. So utterly at my mercy.

With no mattress to absorb my weight, I straddle the bench and pull her thighs over mine. In this position, I have the full advantage of the view, and I

ANNA ZAIRES & CHARMAINE PAULS

intend to make the most of it. I push her thighs wider and tilt my hips to find the right angle. When my cock nudges her entrance, she stiffens. I always hurt her a little. I can feel it from the way she tenses, but she doesn't tell me to stop, and I can't make myself.

I part her pussy lips with just the head of my cock, then pause, giving her time to adjust. Those delicate pink lips are like the petals of a flower. They stretch wide around me, straining to take it all. I sink in another inch while she breathes heavily through her nose and strains in the ropes binding her arms. Open like this, her clit is a pretty treasure for the taking. I press my thumb on the little nub, massaging lightly to help ease my way into her body.

Slowly, I work into her, pressing deeper when her inner muscles give until I'm fully lodged. It's not easy to be patient. The urge to break loose and hammer into her is a powerful temptation, a painful need, but I focus on Mina's body and what she can take until her tight grip on my cock relaxes marginally. Only then do I start moving.

She moans when I do, and the sound spurs me on. I clench my teeth with the strain of holding back as sweat beads over my forehead. The power she holds over me is frightening. As with the time before, and our night in Budapest, I'm about to lose myself in her, forgetting everything for the few blissful moments while we're physically connected. It's not something I've experienced before or something I pause to examine, because violent pleasure is overtaking every cell in my body.

With the speed the climax is building, I'm going to erupt soon. I double my assault, rolling her clit under my thumb. The effort earns me a loud whimper. I lean over and seal her lips with mine to muffle the sound, mimicking the pace of my cock with my tongue, taking her in every way I can.

My rhythm is grueling, but she doesn't ask me to slow down. She gasps into my mouth when I hit the barrier of her cervix. When I let her take a breath, a scream tears from her throat. I barely have time to clamp a hand over her mouth. Screaming will attract the attention of the guards, and there are too many cracks in the wall through which to peep.

Mina is my show, no one else's.

She shakes her head, trying to tell me something, but I'm beyond listening. Nothing matters but getting us both over the line to the only place that will soothe this goddamn insane ache.

Keeping one hand over her mouth, I sit back and rub her clit harder. Her inner muscles tighten with her orgasm, triggering my own release.

The blast of pleasure is beyond intense, but I don't stop moving. Not yet. My fingers dig into the soft flesh of her thigh as I pump myself dry. The high doesn't let me go, not even when my cock starts going soft. My breathing is heavy, my head spinning.

This woman. She's fucking dangerous.

I release her mouth, keeping the connection between our bodies.

"Yan," she says on a hoarse whisper, her eyes wide.

I can't help the heat in my voice, not after what we've shared. "What?"

"You didn't use a condom."

I freeze.

Fuck.

Fuck, fuck, fuck.

This never happened before. Wait, no. It almost happened in Budapest. With her. She warned me then too, in time. I look down to where her milky white lap is draped over mine, her pussy still stuffed full of my cock. I jerk out. My release leaks from her slit, dribbling down her ass. I should feel a lot of things at the sight, but not the perverted satisfaction that feeds an animalistic part of me.

What have I done?

Yes, she is fucking dangerous, and not because of what she does for a living.

Moving out from under her, I get to my feet.

"Yan?"

I ignore the tremble in her voice as I go for my clothes.

Why the fuck didn't she stop me? Because I had my hand pressed over her mouth.

I shake inside as I pull on my pants, socks, and shoes, not meeting Mina's eyes. I only look at her again when I use my shirt to wipe up the spillage between her legs. She says nothing. I pull the shirt down over her body to cover her, then loosen the rope tied to the wall just enough to let her sit up.

I feed her the sandwich with lettuce and tomato to get some vegetables into her body, a need that seemed crucial at the time I made it and insubstantial in light of the current situation. When she's done, I make her drink the water, and then I get the hell out of there, stumbling into the night.

13

MINA

*I*t's a long night. With the loosened rope, I can turn on my sides on the bench, relieving the cramps in my muscles. The ache between my legs is something entirely different. There's no remedy to take that away. Nothing can undo what Yan has done.

I'm not on birth control. It may be difficult for me to conceive, but not impossible.

Why did he do it? Why did he come inside me?

Because it doesn't matter. He's going to kill me anyway. I guess some men aren't sentimental about things like that, about the possibility of wiping out their gestating seed along with the woman who carries it.

When dawn breaks, Yan returns with a breakfast of bread and water. Afterward, he takes me outside to pee before tying me up in the chair.

Nothing is said of last night.

He comes back sometime during midmorning.

Unscrewing the cap of a bottle of water, he comes to stand in front of me. "Open your mouth."

My lips are halfway parted when he takes a pill from his pocket. I slam my mouth shut, panic rushing through me. Pills can have detrimental effects. Lethal. I know with sudden insight that's the method he'd use. A blade is too messy. Drowning will get water on his fancy clothes. A bullet is too quick, too easy for a traitor, and when you strangle someone, you have to look into her eyes.

"What is it?" I ask.

His features are tight. "The morning-after pill."

That takes me by surprise. I guess this particular killer is sensitive to wiping out his spawn after all.

"Open," he says again, this time with impatience.

When I open my mouth, he puts the pill on my tongue and tips back the bottle for me to swallow. I take a few sips. He catches a drop that runs from the corner of my lips with his thumb.

"I'm assuming there's no pharmacy on site," I say. "How did you get it so fast?"

"You'd be surprised by the kind of resources money can buy." He gives me a cold smile. "Then again, maybe not."

"When are you going to do it?"

"Do what?"

"Kill me."

He studies me for a moment. "Did I say I was going to kill you?"

"You didn't say you weren't."

"And clever girls know the unsaid is more important than what's said."

"Something like that."

He smirks.

I lick my cracked lip. "Can I ask you something?"

"You're not in a position to ask anything."

"Will you make it quick?"

His eyes flare. At first, he looks taken aback, but then anger replaces his surprise. "You're asking for mercy?" He shakes his head slowly, giving me a disapproving tsk of his tongue. "The question you should be asking is if you deserve mercy."

And with that, he leaves me.

ILYA IS WITH HIM WHEN YAN COMES BACK WITH LUNCH, and by the look of it, Yan isn't happy about it. This time, Yan leaves the door of the shed open. Heat and sunlight filter in, and my face warms. The smell of sex still hangs in the air, or maybe it's clinging to my body.

Ilya leans against the wall as Yan feeds me pasta. "How are you holding up?"

Yan shoots him a look.

"What?" Ilya pulls his shoulders up to his ears.

Yan brings another forkful to my mouth. "Don't ask stupid questions."

"Hey," Ilya says, "I'm just trying to be nice."

Despite the situation, I smile. He's sweet. "I'm good."

Now I'm at the receiving end of Yan's hostile glare.

"Can I get you anything?" Ilya glances at the bottle of water on the ground. "Tea? You like tea, right?"

Yan feeds me the last bite and wipes my mouth on a paper napkin. "This isn't a hotel."

"If you need a bath, I could—" Ilya starts, but Yan cuts him short.

"She doesn't need a fucking bath." His voice is clipped. "She doesn't need anything."

"Are you going to tell her or must I?"

I look between them. "Tell me what?"

Yan glowers at Ilya before turning his attention to me. "Sokolov needs a disguise. You're doing it tonight."

"Why?"

"He's going after Henderson," Ilya replies.

"Shut up," Yan says.

"What difference does it make if she knows?"

My chest shrinks. "Are you going with him?"

"Yes," Yan says. "Ilya and Anton, too." Mockingly, he adds, "Why? Are you worried?"

The scary part is that I am. Henderson is sly. Dangerous men work for him. What if my kidnappers don't come back? What if *Yan* doesn't come back?

"Stop taunting her," Ilya says. "Don't worry. You won't die of starvation tied up in here. We'll be back."

Yan walks over and smacks him upside the head. "Fucking idiot."

"Hey! What was that for?"

Yan turns to me. "We'll see you tonight." He grips Ilya's arm and pulls him out of the shed.

The door slams, and the rattle of the chain sounds.

AS PROMISED, THEY RETURN LATER WITH PETER Sokolov. Yan unties me while Ilya opens the cases with the props and makeup. I do Sokolov's disguise. When I hand him the mirror, he gives a satisfied nod, though tension is rolling off the men. What they're doing is dangerous. Despite Ilya's promise, there's a very good chance they may not come back. The guards outside will finish me off, but I prefer that it be Yan. *Please let him return.* I don't dare look too deeply at my motivations. Not all of them are selfish.

Sokolov leaves first. Yan takes me out for a bathroom break before tying me back up on the bench and hastily feeding me an empanada. Ilya gathers the makeup. I want to tell Yan to be careful, but I swallow the words. They'd be unwanted.

"Good night, Mina." Ilya's smile is guilty. He feels bad about killing me, even if he believes I framed him. Of the two brothers, he's the one with the heart. Why couldn't I be attracted to *him*? "We'll be back before you know it."

God, I hope he's right.

The men make their way to the door. In the frame, Yan turns. He gives me a long look. I want to say many useless things, like tell him not to go. I want to tell him

I hope he gets Henderson. Even I have to admit what Henderson did with the bombing was a low blow. I want to tell him the night in Budapest was real. This shed, what we did here, was real, too. But just as I open my mouth, he steps through the door, and he's gone.

I TOSS AND TURN ON THE BENCH, AS MUCH AS MY restraints allow. To say I'm going out of my mind with worry is an understatement. Not even mind control helps to steer my thoughts away from Yan and what's happening with Henderson right now. Escape is still at the forefront of my thoughts, but I simply don't see a way. Will I get an opportunity when, or if, Yan returns?

The sun rises. One of the black-clad guards comes inside to feed me bread and weak tea. He hardly looks at me. I'm acutely aware of my nakedness under the shirt and relieved when he leaves quickly, omitting the bathroom break.

The sun moves to a position directly above the shed. I can glimpse it through one of the cracks. Hunger sets in. I got used to being fed. My bladder is full. A long time later, I don't have a choice but to move over the edge of the bench and relieve myself on the ground.

The same guard comes back with more bread and water for lunch. He leaves as soon as he's shoved the last bite into my mouth.

I count in my head. The minutes drag on until it's dark once again.

Still, no one.

No dinner.

More anxiety sets in. I don't know how I get through another night. It's hell. I can move a bit, but not enough to get the circulation in my arms going. I can't feel them anymore, which is a strange kind of relief. The worst is the fear. It's killing me. I just want it to be over. I practice every mental skill I know for disconnection from reality, but it's no longer enough.

By the time the sun rises again, I start wishing Yan had killed me before he'd left. I've barely slept in all the time they've kept me here, and sleep deprivation is cruel on the mind and body. I've seen big men broken with that kind of torture. Even if it wasn't my captors' intention, it's taking its toll. I ease back on the bench, trying to relax my muscles, when I hear it.

A footstep.

I still, not daring to so much as breathe.

There. Another.

I turn my head toward the sound. It's coming from the side of the shed. A voice filters through the wall, speaking softly in Russian.

"She no longer serves a purpose."

Sokolov. I go rigid, my heart pumping hard.

A smooth, deep voice replies, "I'll take care of it."

Yan.

My first reaction is overwhelming relief. Joy, even. He's alive. Then the terror sets in. Like the joy, it's a natural response. It happens unguarded, before I have time to put up defenses around my emotions.

The words run in repeat through my mind. *I'll take care of it.* They chill my body and freeze my heart. Cold shivers set in.

It's time. Yan is going to kill me.

I've been trained to deal with death, to expect it as part of the outcome of every mission, but nobody's trained me to cope with having feelings for my killer. I'm not even sure what I feel for Yan, only that his words fill me with immense grief. But what did I expect? I know who he is, what we both are. There's no other way this could've gone. Still, it's as if the dagger is already twisting in my heart, the damage far more painful than if it were for real.

I strain my ears, but the voices are gone, their footsteps ominously quiet.

Where is he? Why doesn't Yan come inside? Why doesn't he just do it already?

I'm sweating and shivering. My teeth are chattering. All biological reactions to a specific mental knowledge. I've accepted my fate, but my body doesn't comply. As long as I'm breathing, my body will keep on fighting to survive.

I think of Hanna. For what it's worth, I say a prayer for her. I think of my parents, of the last time I saw their faces. It's a hurtful memory I don't often revisit.

When the chain on the door finally rattles, I'm ready. Yan's big body fills the frame. He's carrying a tray. For a moment, we just look at each other. I drink him in, how alive he seems, how strong.

I'm glad it's him. I'm glad he's my executioner.

He leaves the tray on the chair and flicks on the light before locking the door.

I don't speak. I wait for him to say it.

He crosses the floor and stops next to me. His handsome face is clean shaven, and he smells good. Fresh, with that understated hint of sandalwood and pepper. He looks refreshed too, as if he's slept ten hours or more. There's not a trace of tiredness on his features, only dark determination and cold calculation.

"Henderson is dead," he says.

I battle to swallow past the dryness in my throat. "What happened?"

His smile is mocking. "Do you really want to know?"

What he's asking is if I care. I nod.

"He attacked the house."

What? "Here?" This shed must be far from the main house for me not to have heard any gunshots.

Yan nods. "The guards took him and his team out."

I take a wild guess. "The Delta Force men?"

"They got what they deserved."

The words are measured. They carry a message, a promise, but it's the ice in his eyes that makes me tremble harder than I already do. It throws me off balance, that frostiness, not because he hates me, but because his hate hurts.

He loosens the rope, giving it more stretch, and

helps me to sit up. I stare at him. What is he doing? He fetches the tray and sits down next to me, balancing it on his lap. There's a plate covered with a silver lid and a glass of white wine. It's a beautiful glass with a skillful cut and long stem. Drops of condensation run down the glass. I don't understand. But then I take in the ornate knife and fork, and I get it. I grasp the meaning of the pretty crystal and expensive cutlery.

This is a last meal.

My conclusion is confirmed when he lifts the silver lid to reveal a scrumptious-looking dish of chicken on rice, complete with a sprig of parsley as garnish. The rich aroma fills my nostrils. Under different circumstances, my mouth would've watered, but my empty stomach only churns.

"*Pollo con chocolate*," he announces. "I've been told it's one of the best Latin American dishes."

"Who made it?"

"Esguerra's cook." He scoops up a forkful and brings it to my mouth. "Open."

"Is it poisoned?"

He chuckles. "No."

He has no reason to lie. He can easily force it down my throat if I refuse to eat. I part my lips not because I'm hungry, but because I don't have a choice. If this is my last meal, I should try to make the most of it.

When he carefully pushes the fork into my mouth, the flavors burst on my tongue. The dish is creamy with a savory, peanut-flavored sauce and a hint of cacao that complements the chicken surprisingly well. The bite of chili that registers after I've chewed is mild.

"Like it?" he asks when I've swallowed.

"It's delicious," I say honestly. "Have you tried it?"

"Not yet."

He offers me a sip of wine. It's crisp, tangy, and refreshingly cold. It somehow enhances the flavors of the food that linger on my tongue. With my arms stretched tightly above my head, I sit dead still while he feeds me. I watch his eyes while he watches my lips. He seems to home in on every bite and swallow. He's meticulous in feeding me, offering small enough bites so I can chew comfortably. When the fork leaves a trace of sauce on my lip, he wipes it away with a linen napkin before giving me another bite. In this manner, he alternates between the food and the wine until half of the food on the plate is gone and I'm buzzing.

I shake my head. "I can't eat another morsel."

He frowns. "You haven't eaten much."

"It was a big portion."

"At least finish the wine."

I'm pathetically grateful for his kindness, for numbing my senses with alcohol for what lies ahead. When he tilts the glass, I gulp down what's left. He puts the glass back on the tray and leaves it on the ground. I start to tremble in earnest when he stands.

This is the moment.

The shaking gets worse when he lifts a hand to my face.

"Shh." He traces my bottom lip with his thumb, dragging it ever so gently over the healing cut.

His gaze follows the action, all his concentration focused on the task. I bite down hard on my back teeth to stop the involuntary quiver of my jaw that betrays my body's severe state of stress. He trails a finger along the line of my quaking jaw and gently cups my face. Then he kisses me sweetly, invading my mouth with leisurely strokes of his tongue until I melt and the uncontrollable chattering stops. My eyes flutter closed. He tastes of mint and coffee.

"That's better," he breathes against my lips.

When I open my eyes, I catch him staring at me with searing heat. My face is slack from his kiss, but my body still trembles. He smoothes his hands over my arms, rubbing softly, and I don't resist when he pushes me down slowly until my back hits the bench. I let him stroke me all over. I let him feel me under the shirt, brush his palms over my nipples and stomach. I let him feel between my legs where my wetness betrays me.

No meaningless words are said when he unzips his fly and takes out his cock. I open my legs and allow the touch of his hands to chase away the shivers of my body and the chill of my heart. He stretches out over me, supporting his weight on a hand next to my head. He fists the other around the root of his cock and aligns it with my opening. I sigh when he sinks into me, embracing the feelings he offers. The rocking of his hips makes me forget. I go with the ebb and flow, surrendering my fear. The shivering stops as my back scrapes over the rough wood of the bench and my arms pull at the ropes. I give over to the gentle pace of this strange, soft coupling, knowing everything from here on is out of my control.

He doesn't kiss me again. He watches me as he touches my clit and brings me closer to the edge. He's kind after all, this ruthless killer, giving me pleasure as a distraction. My need climbs. My back arches. In that split second before everything unravels, panic hits. Claustrophobia strangles me. I toss in my constraints, frantic with helplessness. I need to hold on to him.

"Shh." He kisses my lips. "I've got you."

I desperately need to hold on to something, so I cling to his gaze. He lets me. He doesn't close his eyes or hide his pleasure. He gives it to me truthfully. He shows me the rawness that reflects in my body.

True to his word, he's there for me when my body bows and the climax tears me apart. I turn warm inside. He fills me up with his release, pumping as if he's set on making me take every drop. I'm drowning in his heat, his smell, and the angry undercurrent that's always present between us, especially during his release. I'm high on endorphins, floating in a euphoric space. Vaguely, I'm aware of him taking something from his pocket and pushing it against my neck. The sharp prick of a needle registers too late.

My vision swims, and I start to drift away. Straining my neck, I force my head up and desperately try to claw my way through the haze. I try to hold on to that ice-green stare with all my might, but it slips out of my reach.

His words are soft, spoken in Russian. "Let go, Minochka."

The beautiful sound of his mother tongue strokes over my senses, as does the term of endearment.

Poisonous words.

Poison seems fitting.

He catches my head when my neck fails to support the weight.

He's still inside me when I drag in a final, laborious breath. The last word I speak when I blow out that breath is his name.

PART III

14

MINA

The nightmare is horrendous. I'm back in the car with my parents, seconds before we take the bend in the road. I ask for a cookie. My mother smiles back at me. Her hair is loose and soft around her face. My father takes her hand. She tells me I have to wait a little bit longer. We'll have dinner soon. My body jerks forward as my father slams on the brakes. The man taps on his window with a gun, his lips pulled back over his gums in a grin.

I scream and scream.

"Mina!"

Shaking. Somebody shakes the car with me still inside. My brain sloshes in my skull. My head hurts. *Mommy. Daddy.* Their eyes are open, but they're not replying. "No!"

More shaking. "Mina." A hard voice, speaking in Russian. "Wake up."

That voice. The rough timbre is familiar. There's a

memory of strong hands cradling my head, a gentle voice urging me to let go. I want to heed it, to sink back into the darkness where dreams don't exist, but the shaking won't let me. A warning pierces through the daze, and that too won't let me go.

Yan.

It's like a knife jabbed into my chest.

Gasping, I jerk into a sitting position.

"Easy." The strong hands from my memory push me down.

My back hits a soft surface. I blink, battling to focus. The light makes the pain in my head worse.

"Drink this."

A hand folds under my nape and lifts my head. My gaze collides with an ice-green one. Yan stares at me soberly.

He slips a pill onto my tongue and brings a bottle of water to my lips. "For the headache."

I'm alive. "You didn't kill me," I mutter, battling to make sense of anything.

"I gave you a sedative."

"But the dinner…"

He arches a brow, waiting for me to finish.

"The fancy crockery, the wine," I continue hoarsely, "it was a last meal."

"You needed to stock up on energy for the long trip."

I lick my dry lips. "How long have I been out for?"

He checks his watch. "Twenty hours."

I look around in panic. The room is small but

modern. The white walls are adorned with framed photographs. They're black-and-white landscapes. "Where am I?"

"Prague."

I try to sit up again. "What?"

He prevents me. "You're at my place. Keep still. The sedative was strong. It needs to work itself out of your system."

"Ah." Ilya's bulky frame appears in the door. "You're awake."

Yan tenses. "Barely. Give her a moment."

Ilya's expression turns sour, but he leaves.

Yan puts the water on the nightstand. "You should drink as much as you can. Your body needs fluids. It'll help with the pain. Much of the headache is due to dehydration."

"You didn't kill me," I say again, posing the phrase as a question.

He smiles, but it's not friendly.

Immense relief flows through me, and then the anger hits. "You let me believe you were going to kill me."

He gives me a strange look. "I'd never kill you."

"I don't understand."

"What don't you get?"

"Why am I here?"

"Rest for now," he says tersely. "We'll talk about that later."

"Why don't you tell me now?"

He pats my hand that lies on top of the covers. "Get

your strength back." His voice drops an octave. "You're going to need it."

"Wait," I say when he turns for the door, but he leaves and closes it behind him.

Rigid, I prick up my ears for the turn of a key. Nothing. He didn't lock me in.

I take better stock of my surroundings. I'm lying in a big bed. The pillow smells of him, Yan. That deliciously airy, sensual scent. The sheets are silky and the blanket soft. High-thread Egyptian cotton. From the weight of the comforter resting on top of the blanket, it's the goose feather variety. He has luxurious taste.

Sitting up, I lift the covers and peek underneath. I'm still wearing Yan's shirt and nothing else. I throw the heavy comforter aside and swing my legs from the bed. The hardwood floor is warm. Under-floor heating. It seems like an excessive luxury. It's only late summer.

I pad to the window and push away the curtain. We're on the third floor. The ornate bars in front of the window prevent me from climbing through. The street below is quiet, and the building on the opposite side looks similar to this one. It's a white block with square windows. They all have differently colored curtains.

Apartments. It's a residential area.

I go back to inspecting the room. There's a dresser and a closet. I feel the drawers. They're locked. A door off to the side gives access to a bathroom. Like the room, it's small, but the accessories are fancy. The shower is fitted with a high-tech nozzle. I shut the door, turn the lock, and open the tap. While the water runs warm, I pull off the shirt. It's smelly. Wrinkling my nose, I dump it in the laundry basket.

Getting under the spray of water is like heaven. I make quick work of cleaning myself, using the forest-scented shower gel and shampoo. Grabbing a towel from the rack, I wrap it around my body. The fabric is warm. It must be a heating rack. I don't need a brush for my short hair. My fingers work well enough.

I regard my face in the mirror. There are faint bruises in shades of yellow. They'll be gone in a couple of days. My lip is healing well, too.

A new toothbrush still in its plastic wrapping lies on the basin. I use it to brush my teeth and look around for clothes, but there's nothing.

The pill must be kicking in. The headache is almost gone and I feel more like a human being than I've felt during the past four days. It gives me hope. I'm alive. I have another shot at escaping.

Tiptoeing to the closed door, I put my ear against it. Male voices come from the other side, talking in Russian.

"We need to lure Dimitrov out of his fortress and away from his guards," Yan says. "The order was clear. No other casualties."

Ilya's louder voice booms through the space. "Why can't we just pop him in public?"

"The risks are too high," a voice I don't recognize says. "He's always surrounded by his bodyguards."

Ilya again. "What about when he's at the casinos?"

"Same," Yan replies. "We'll never get a clear shot."

"I say we use the fact that he's an art collector," the unfamiliar voice says. "We can fake an invitation to an event."

"He's too clever," Yan says. "His personal buyers will check the authenticity of any event. Besides, his art dealings are shady. They mostly happen secretly behind closed doors."

If they're talking about who I think, they're referring to Casmir Dimitrov, a powerful Balkan crime group leader who runs a chain of casinos as a guise for drug smuggling. He also collects stolen art. These criminals open businesses in the Czech Republic to gain residency, and then use the well-developed road and air infrastructure to transport their drugs. If Yan and his friends are planning a hit on Casmir, they've got a hell of a job on their hands. The man is the best-guarded criminal in Prague.

"Shouldn't your waitress be up by now?" the stranger asks.

I lean away from the door as a chair scrapes over the floor.

Before one of them can come looking for me and discover me eavesdropping, I grip the handle and open the door. Barging in on them looks less suspicious.

Ilya and a man who looks vaguely familiar sit at a table in the corner of an open-plan kitchen-lounge. Yan is on his feet. The men pause at my entrance, three sets of eyes trailing over me.

"Well, hello, little waitress," the stranger says. "Right

on time." There's nothing friendly about his dark eyes. If anything, they're malicious. His thick black beard is neatly trimmed, and his shoulder-length hair is tied into a ponytail. He's dressed in black from head to toe, and is sporting a Glock and some impressive knives in his gun and knife holsters.

Another dangerous man. Handsome, in a vicious sort of way, but very dangerous.

Yan clenches his jaw. "Go back to the room, Mina."

"I don't have clothes to wear," I say in Russian.

Yan narrows his eyes. "Which part of go to the room didn't you understand? Do you need me to say it in Hungarian?"

The stranger chuckles.

Yan turns on him. "Something funny, Anton?"

"No." Anton lifts his hands. "Nothing."

Yan's voice is icy. "Good."

Of course. That's where I recognize him from. Anton Rezov is part of their team. One of the Delta Force men was disguised to look like him.

"Are you hungry?" Ilya asks me.

"Get in there." Yan points at the door behind me. "Now. We'll sort out the food when you're dressed." His tone takes on a challenge. "Or must I carry you?"

Anton whistles through his teeth. "Territorial much?"

Before my entry can cause a fight, I go back to the room and shut the door. Clutching the towel at my chest, I sit down on the bed. It doesn't take long for Yan to come find me.

143

The door bangs in the frame as he shuts it. "You don't walk around naked in front of the men again. Understood?"

His outburst unsettles me. I give a nervous nod.

He grabs my wrist and pulls me up. "Come."

The towel drops to the bed. I reach for it, but we're already at the door. "Wait."

He looks back at me, his gaze heating as he drags it over my naked body. "You'll do like this."

"What? I thought you said—"

"The others are out."

"Out?"

"Picking up provisions."

He opens the door and pulls me through it. I'm overly conscious of my unclad body, something new to me. Why does he have this effect on me?

Pushing me down on one of the chairs by the table, he orders, "Stay."

I don't move. Instead, I watch with a pounding heart as he takes a container from the fridge and dumps it in the microwave. Then he fills a glass with milk and puts it down in front of me. When the microwave pings, he serves the food onto a plate and hands it to me with a fork.

"Eat." He stands over me, watching.

"I'm not hungry."

"It's the aftereffect of the drugs. You need to eat. Must I feed you?"

At that, I bring the fork to my lips. It's shepherd's pie, the commercial kind.

He makes me finish everything on the plate and drink all the milk before he asks, "How's your head?"

"Fine."

"Good." He puts the dirty dishes in the sink and takes my hand. "Come. It's time we have that chat about why you're here."

My throat goes dry.

He leads me to the bedroom where he takes a key from his pocket and unlocks the dresser. Grabbing a T-shirt from a drawer, he throws it at me. I catch it in mid-air. It's big. It must be his. I pull it hastily over my head.

He comes to stand in front of me, his much taller frame intimidating as his green eyes glint at me coolly. "You were right. I *was* supposed to kill you."

The news is cold coffee, as Hanna likes to say, but it still rattles me. "But you didn't."

"No." His lazy smile is filled with familiar frost. "I didn't. What does that mean?"

That my life is his. This is how it works in our world. "What are you going to do with me?"

"Whatever I please."

"I'll only be a burden, a mouth to feed, a prisoner you'll constantly have to prevent from escaping."

His eyes tighten. "Do you have a death wish?"

"I'm only stating the facts."

His cool smile returns. "You won't be a burden. Far from it. I can think of many ways to make you useful. And you won't escape."

There's more to the last declaration. My stomach tight, I wait for him to continue.

"While you were out cold," he says, "I planted a tracker in you."

The strength leaves my legs. I sink down onto the edge of the bed. Lifting my arms, I inspect them for cuts.

"It's at the back of your neck," he says, studying me with his frosty eyes.

I lift my fingers to my nape. Sure as hell, there's a small scab. The bump under my skin is merely the size of a rice grain. It doesn't hurt. That's why I didn't notice it when I took my shower.

"Should you ever be foolish enough to run, you won't get far," he says, "but I advise you not to test me."

"All of this because I framed you?" I ask, breathless with disbelief.

A part of me knows otherwise. Already back in Budapest, before he knew who I was, he was planning this. The fact that he's capable of taking and keeping a person for no reason other than wanting to says a lot about this man I hardly know.

"What about Sokolov?" I ask when he doesn't reply. "What if he finds out you didn't kill me?"

"How do you know he wanted you dead?"

"I overheard you talking outside the shed."

"As long as you stay out of Sokolov's way, it won't be a problem. He's busy enough picking up the pieces of his life."

I don't ask about that. The less I know, the better.

The front door opens to a duo of laughter. Ilya and Anton step through the frame, carrying shopping bags. They fall silent when they spot us inside the bedroom. Anton stares at me narrowly as he dumps the bags on the kitchen counter and starts unpacking groceries.

Ilya comes into the bedroom with a boutique bag. Smiling, he hands it to me. "I hope it's your size. I think it'll fit."

"Thank you," I say gratefully. Walking around in Yan's T-shirt makes me feel vulnerable, especially around Anton.

When Ilya leaves, Anton is still glaring at me.

Yan's order is brusque. "Get dressed."

Slipping into the bathroom, I pull on the clothes. The underwear is pink lace. The brand-name jeans and T-shirt are a little too big, but the socks and sneakers fit.

I step out to find the bedroom door still open. Anton is sitting on the couch, watching television and eating peanuts. Ilya is playing solitaire at the table, and Yan is working on his laptop. Uncertainly, I hover in the frame. How is this supposed to work? What am I supposed to do? Hide in the bedroom?

Anton throws a peanut in the air and catches it with his mouth. "Why don't you get us each a beer instead of standing there?"

Yan lifts a glacial gaze over his laptop. "Get it yourself. She's not your servant."

"Isn't she supposed to be a waitress?" Anton asks with his mouth full.

The accusation is silent. I get it. In their eyes, I betrayed them.

Walking to the fridge, I pull it open and take out a beer. When I pass the table on the way to the couch, Yan grabs my wrist. His grip is painful. He says nothing, but he takes the beer from my hand, pops the can, takes a sip, and puts it down next to him. Then he goes back to work.

Anton snickers. "She may as well fix dinner. What else is she going to do?"

"Enough." Yan's tone is even.

"He's right, you know." I cross my arms. "What *am* I going to do?"

This time, Yan doesn't stop me when I go through the cupboards and take out ingredients from the fridge. I'd rather keep busy than sit around doing nothing and going out of my mind. I chop up onions and carrots for a goulash, peel the potatoes, and fry the meat. This is easy for me. Hanna is old school. She believes the way to a man's heart is through his stomach, and she insisted on teaching me to cook. She still hopes I'll find a man and settle down.

While the stew cooks, I tidy up the mess I made of the kitchen.

It's too early for dinner when the food is ready, but the men keep on sniffing the air with hungry looks. Yan packs away his laptop and Ilya sets plates on the counter while Anton cuts the bread. They dish up big portions. When they're seated at the table, I serve myself and grab a fork. I prefer eating at the kitchen counter. I don't want to strain the air with my presence at the table. Yan glances at me, but says nothing.

Soon, the men are so absorbed in the meal, they almost forget about my presence. The hearty food makes them jovial. They laugh and chat in Russian, letting me see a very private side of them.

Before long, they take seconds, scraping the bottom of the pot, and the conversation turns to Casmir Dimitrov. Yan must've been serious about never letting me go, or they wouldn't speak so openly. They're weighing pros and cons, deciding how to best separate him from his guards. Anton suggests kidnapping his wife. Ilya says it's better to take his dog. Apparently, he paid a fortune for the Samoyed, and gossip is he loves the animal far more than his trophy wife.

"If you take something from him," I say, "you'll cause a war. It's better to offer him something he doesn't have."

The men stop talking and turn in their seats to look at me.

Anton regards me as if he's pondering whether I'm worth a response. After a beat, he says, "The man has everything."

"Not the Salvator Mundi," I say as an idea comes into my head. A dangerous one, but if it works…

"What's the Salvator Mundi?" Ilya asks.

"A painting by Leonardo da Vinci," Yan replies. "It made big news when it was sold for four hundred and fifty million dollars to a Saudi prince in 2017. Two weeks before the unveiling at the Louvre Abu Dhabi, the painting mysteriously disappeared. To this day, nobody knows where it is."

"No one's going to offer him the Salvator Mundi," Anton says.

I smile. "Natasha Petrova will."

"Who's Natasha Petrova?" Ilya asks.

Yan leans back in his chair. "The most notorious stolen arts dealer."

"He won't fall for it." Anton pushes away his plate. "He'll want to speak to her in person."

"Exactly," I say. "I could disguise myself to look like her."

Anton smiles with contempt. "Why would you help us?"

I shrug. "Debt repayment." And more. I have my reasons, but I keep my face carefully blank.

Anton snorts.

"Look," I say, "take it or don't. I'm trying to be nice, but I don't owe you anything. The job with Henderson wasn't personal."

At the mention of Henderson's name, Anton's face darkens with anger.

"Mina," Yan says with a warning in his tone, "if we want your opinion, we'll ask for it."

"No," Ilya says, "she's got a point. Anyway, it's not like we have a better idea."

Yan turns on his brother with a cutting look. "Dimitrov will see right through her. She's not even the same build or height as Natasha Petrova."

Ilya frowns. "How do you know what Petrova looks like?"

"She's been in the news enough." Yan gets up and takes a bottle of vodka from the freezer. "Remarkably, there's never enough evidence to warrant an arrest, which means ties in high places, such as the government."

"Some say she's the president's mistress," Anton adds.

Ilya leans forward, his curiosity piqued. "Which president?"

Yan fills their glasses with a shot of vodka. "Some say Russian, some say American, and others say both."

Ilya whistles. "If the chick is that famous, it will be tough imitating her. Unless the meeting takes place on a video call."

Yan takes a sip of his vodka. "Then what, wiseass?"

"I offer him a deal," I say. "Private viewing. Just the two of us. His guards stay outside. Not an unreasonable request, considering how fragile the painting is. Even the carbon dioxide we exhale has a damaging effect on something so old. In the meantime, you'll be in position."

"He's not stupid," Yan says. "He'll let you go inside first. The location will be monitored."

"I can wear body pads and heels. By the time he realizes I'm not Natasha, it'll be too late."

Yan toys with his glass. "What about the painting? He'd want to see it before he agrees to a meeting."

"I have a friend." I shift my weight. "She makes

151

excellent replicas. It will look real enough on a photo or video. We can fake the authenticity certificate."

"This can work," Anton muses.

"No," Yan says harshly. "It's too dangerous."

"For who?" Anton's tone turns snide. "For your waitress?"

Yes, there is a risk, but only if Casmir smells a rat. "I can pull it off."

"She pulled off the Henderson job," Ilya reminds them.

Anton downs his vodka and slams the empty glass down on the table. "I'm in."

"Me too," Ilya says.

"Looks like you're outvoted," Anton says to Yan.

Yan crumples his napkin in his fist. "This isn't a fucking democracy. I'm the leader." He jabs a thumb at his chest. "I'll decide."

"Will you?" Anton's lips quirk. "In whose best interest? Ours or hers?" He gives me a dirty look.

Yan looks at me from under his lashes, his jaw bunching. After a moment, he says, "Fine, but I do the risk control."

"I can live with that," Anton says.

Ilya smiles at me. "You're in, Mina."

Not moving his eyes away from me, Yan says in a measured tone, "Don't think for a second this makes you part of the team."

"I'd never be so presumptuous."

He lets it go, but I feel his gaze burn into the back of my head when I turn to scrub the pot.

After dinner, Ilya and Anton play a game of cards while I rinse the dishes and Yan packs the dishwasher. My mind is working at full speed. This will indeed be dangerous, but it beats being nothing more than Yan's new toy. More importantly, this might give me a chance to let Hanna know I'm all right. I hate to make her worry. I also have to warn Gergo. The Delta Force men are dead, but the threat is far from over. If Yan digs a little deeper, he'll discover my secret. And if he knows Gergo trained me, he'll ask questions. If I'm to get a message to Hanna and Gergo, I need a measure of freedom—freedom the job with Casmir will win me. Plus, I could always use the money to pay for Hanna's care.

Drying my hands on the dishcloth, I turn to Yan. "How soon do you want to make a move? With Casmir, I mean."

He regards me suspiciously. "Soon."

"My friend will need time to make a high-quality replica. A month, at least."

"She has three weeks."

"Impossible."

He gives me a dark look. "Three weeks."

"I know where to get quality material for the disguise. If we're going to make it work, we need the best."

"Let me know where, and I'll pick it up."

"My supplier won't trust you. He's right here in Prague. It won't take me long. I can already meet with him tomorrow."

I give a start when he yanks the dishcloth from my hand and grabs my wrist. Ilya and Anton look on quietly as he pulls me behind him to the room. The door has barely slammed when he pushes me up against the wall, my wrist still clamped in his iron grip.

Planting a palm next to my face, he leans in. "I'm many things, but I'm not a fool." His voice is brutally soft, his look dangerous. "Don't ever make that mistake."

An internal shiver runs through me.

"You can lie to Anton, but not to me. Never to me. Understand?" He emphasizes the order with a hard squeeze of my wrist. "Now, tell me again. Why are you willing to help us?"

I meet his eyes squarely, giving him a small portion of the truth. "I need money."

"You want me to pay you?"

"Will you let me go back to my waitressing job?"

He laughs. "In your dreams."

My gaze flits to the bed. "You'd rather I earn it in a different way?"

He curls the fingers of his free hand around my neck. "If I wanted a whore, I'd get one."

"Explain to me how this is different."

The look in his eyes turns cruel. "Whores deserve more respect than you. At least they're honest about why they fuck."

The jab drives deep, hurling me back into the past where a chorus of *whore, whore, whore* taunts me as the circle of men plant their boots in my stomach.

Violently, I shove the mental image away and force myself back to the present that somehow, on a deeper level, hurts worse than the memory over which my mind has painted a big, red keep-out sign.

I want to hit Yan, hurt him. With my neck and one arm pinned against the wall, the best I can do is plant a fist in his side. He doesn't even grunt. He taunts me with his eyes, mocking my smaller and weaker body as he holds me still. I try to kick, but he hooks a leg around my thigh. Silently, he laughs at me, challenging me to do my best, all so he can demonstrate his superior male strength.

I hate him.

I hate that he can restrain me with his hands and hurt me with his words.

I hate that despite it all, my body heats where his erection grows against my stomach.

I'm out of defenses. He took them all. I have nothing left but the dirtiest insult of all. Sucking in a deep breath, I spit in his face.

He flinches. Both of us freeze. There's a moment of shock in his unmovable demeanor, but it vanishes as quickly as it appeared, his gaze turning into pure ice.

Fuck. I regretted it the moment I did it, but it's too late to take it back.

Letting go of my neck, he slowly wipes the back of his hand over his face. The promise of retribution in his expression is unmistakable. I utter a shriek when he grabs my face in his big hand, digging his fingers into my cheeks. Before I can make another sound, he crashes his mouth into mine. The kiss is hard and punishing. He doesn't spare me, not even when I taste blood on my tongue. He swallows my breaths, kissing me so viciously my jaw aches.

Something inside me gives, and the helpless anger transforms into lust. I channel all the emotional pain into desire. His roughness ignites a fire that burns up my legs and gathers in my core. It should frighten me. It should repulse me. Instead, I moan in agreement when he yanks my arms up and pulls the T-shirt over my head. I reach for the buttons of his shirt, but he swats my hands away, lifting them back up over my head. He pops the button of my jeans, pulls down the zipper, and shoves them over my hips. Grabbing my waist, he spins us around. My feet leave the ground as he flings me through the air. I land with a thump in the middle of the bed. He strips as he advances—shirt, shoes, pants, briefs, and socks. His erection is big, proud, angry.

"Stay," he growls when I instinctively start to scoot back.

I pause. He grabs my ankles and drags me to the edge of the bed, then yanks off my sneakers and socks. He almost rips the panties as he pulls them off with the jeans. Bending my knees, he positions his cock and drives the head through my folds. I gasp at the sudden invasion. I'm wet, but he's too big.

He's impatient. He takes me with a few shallow strokes until my inner muscles relax. I push myself up on my elbows to watch. When my inner muscles turn softer around him, he drives home with a hard thrust. My arms give out. Swallowing a scream, I collapse onto my back.

Leaning over me, he whispers against my swollen lips, "Do you want this?"

Always the same question. Always the same answer.

He teases me with a steady rhythm, making it feel so good I almost lose my reason.

I grab his forearms, digging my nails into his skin. "Wait."

He stops.

"Condom," I say breathlessly. I don't want to repeat our mistake.

"I gave you a birth control shot."

"You did what?"

He doesn't elaborate, doesn't explain. He takes my body like he took my life, without making excuses. The physical possession is more than fucking. It's a statement, proof that his power over me stretches further than defeating me with strength or words.

When I'm close to coming, he climbs onto the bed and pulls me on top of him. Gripping my ass, he sets the pace, keeping release just out of my reach. Sadistically, he watches the agony on my face as he cups my breasts over the lace of the bra and denies me relief. It's a lesson, a demonstration of who holds the power.

Sweat covers my body. My skin is slick. I'm raw inside. "Yan."

He slaps my ass, grabbing a handful of flesh. "Who owns your life?"

I don't want to say it, don't want to admit it. Stubbornly, I bite my cheek.

His fingers tighten on my thighs as he increases his assault, bringing me so close I want to cry with frustration. I need just a little more. When I reach for my clit, he grabs my arms and bends them behind my back.

"All you have to do is say it." He slows his movements to a leisurely roll of his hips.

I grit my teeth so I won't beg.

"One word, Mina."

I can't take it anymore. I break. "You."

He lets go of my arms to grip my hips. Bracing me, he gives me what I want, what I've earned with a word.

He slams up and orders, "Touch yourself."

I drag circles with my finger around my clit. He watches with concentration, learning what pleases me. When the orgasm hits, I don't have enough strength left to remain upright. I fall over his chest even as he picks up his rhythm to find his own release. He comes shortly after, his seed bathing my body with more proof of what I've become.

Depleted, I lie sprawled out over him.

Beaten.

In his bed, I lost the war I started against the wall.

15

YAN

The woman lying on my chest doesn't cry, but she wants to. I know what vanquishment looks like. Wrapping my arms around her, I hold her close and give her what I can, whatever I'm capable of. I hate her for what she's done, but I own her. That gives me a responsibility toward her.

My anger is gone. It burned out with the wild sex, vanished when my cock softened and slipped out of her body with my seed. What's left in the wake of our fire is a wet spot on the sheets and the cold ashes of reason. With that comes a tinge of regret. Ilya was right. Mina fucked me with her own, justified motivations. I had no right to see more into it.

Whatever the case, she's here now, and she's staying.

Rubbing her back, I ask, "What do you need the money for?" Because I said things and I feel guilty. A strange sentiment for me.

It takes her a moment to answer. "A girl has to live."

"Taking care of you is my job now."

"Am I not allowed to be proud?"

I admire that. It pisses me off that I find it endearing. Unnecessary, but cute. Still, my voice is harder than intended when I ask, "And exactly how much were you hoping to earn?"

She intertwines her fingers on my chest and rests her chin on her hands. "How much is the hit worth?"

I smile. Nice try.

She shrugs when I don't bite. "A million."

I raise my brow.

She huffs. "Five hundred thousand?"

She looks so hopeful with her big, doll-like blue eyes I can't help but drag my fingers through her hair. Fine. What is giving her a little pride when I've taken her freedom?

"Tell me what you're going to do with the money."

She bends her legs and crosses her ankles. "Shoes, handbags, jewelry."

Why does the thought of her splurging on the things women like send a jolt of heat straight to my chest? I've never wanted to play house, but imagining her wearing pretty things, dresses to look good just for me, has an unexpected appeal. She's joking a little. Her half-smile says so, but I suddenly want that: the shoes, handbags, and jewelry. The illusion.

I tangle my fingers in her hair. "You know what will happen if you let the information slip, right, princess?"

Despite all the sweetness she makes me feel, I can't go soft.

"Yes." She doesn't wince or blink. She gets me. She understands how it works because she's part of my world.

"Good."

She pulls on my chest hair. "Does that mean it's a yes? Five hundred?"

I catch her hand. "We'll see."

She presses her cheek to my chest, but not before I glimpse her smile. "Who ordered the hit?"

Whether I like it or not, she's in on this. She's in on my life, because I'm never letting her out of my sight again. "Government."

"Czech?"

"Yes. Dimitrov is a thorn under their skin."

"And they can't arrest him without starting a crime war."

"Exactly."

"I need my phone and laptop."

"You don't."

"People will start asking questions if I don't reply to my messages."

"What people? You don't have any friends." I checked, especially to make sure there weren't any boyfriends.

"I have employers. Bar gigs."

"Taken care of."

She lifts her head. "What?"

"My hacker set up an auto-reply."

Her pretty features tighten. "With what excuse?" She looks like an angry little kitten.

"You're traveling around Europe."

"I can't be on holiday indefinitely."

"You needed a break. You'll earn your way as you go, like a backpacker. The profile suits you, no?"

"What about my apartment? I have to pay the rent."

"You moved."

"What?" she cries out, pushing on my chest. "What about my clothes and furniture?"

I press on her back to prevent her from rising. I like her where she is. "Don't fret. I put everything in storage."

"You can't do that!"

I pin her with a look. "I can do whatever I want." My words aren't warm, and the message even less so. I pull her face to the crook of my neck. "Get some rest. Tomorrow we contact your friends."

Her sigh is exaggerated, rebellious. I grin.

I should shower and change the sheets, but I can't make myself leave the bed. Not when I'm holding her like this. It gives me a feeling of warmth, of something I've never had. She must be tired, because seconds later, her soft, even breaths fill the room.

HER STIRRING SOMETIME IN THE MIDDLE OF THE NIGHT

jostles me awake. She's a restless sleeper. I know that from our first night together. I turn us on our sides and drag her body against mine. It settled her that night in Budapest, but not tonight. Her muscles tense. She mumbles something, then repeats it.

"No."

I shake her gently. "Mina."

"No!"

"Mina, wake up. You're dreaming."

Her lashes lift. I watch her face in the moonlight. There's terror in her eyes.

"Nightmare?" I know all about those.

She rolls onto her back and throws an arm over her forehead. "Sorry I woke you."

"Was it the same one as this morning?"

Dropping her arm to her side, she stares at the ceiling. "What does it matter?"

"Tell me about it."

Her gaze meets mine. "It's nothing."

"It's not nothing."

She tries to turn away, but I catch her waist. "Tell me."

"Why? What do you care?"

"It helps."

She scoffs. "Does it help you?"

I don't give her an answer she already knows. "Maybe talking will make it better for you."

She smiles sadly. For a moment, her eyes soften as she cups my cheek, but then she pulls away.

I'm not letting this go. Once, yes. But having the same nightmare twice? I want to know what this is about. Mina is no angel. She's not unfamiliar with sights and deeds that would make grown men spill their guts. Whatever the dream is about, it's bad.

"Don't make me drag it out of you," I say.

She sighs. "A car hijacking. There. Happy?"

I push up on an elbow. "When did it happen?"

"A long time ago."

"How old were you?"

"Six."

And it still haunts her? "Who was driving?"

"My father." She swallows. "Both my parents were in the car."

"What happened?"

"Two armed men forced us to get out."

I rub her arm. I didn't think I had compassion left in me, but my heart clenches because I know even before I ask, "Were you injured?"

"Not me. They shot my parents."

Fuck. Just like that, she switches off, her expression going blank. I grip her shoulder. "I'm sorry."

"As I said, it was a long time ago." She turns on her side and folds her hands under the pillow.

I spoon her from behind and throw an arm around her waist, holding her close until she falls asleep again. Me, I'm battling to wrap my mind around the information she shared. I try to picture a six-year-old Mina with a tiny body and big blue eyes standing next to the corpses of her parents.

Other than Ilya, I don't have family—unless you count the abusive uncle who raised us until we turned fifteen. The only feeling I had for that alcoholic pig was hatred. My mother was a village girl who died in childbirth. My father is unknown. It's hard for me to imagine what it must feel like to lose your parents. All I know is it would rip me apart if anything were to happen to Ilya, even if he can sometimes be an ass. Physically speaking, my brother is a little bigger and stronger, but I was the one who took responsibility for us. I took care of him like he was my younger brother, not my twin. I wanted to save him from the horrors I couldn't save myself from.

Looking at the sleeping form of the small woman who fits perfectly in the curve of my body, I make a mental note to find out more about her past. No, not more. Everything. I want to know all of it.

With that resolution, I finally fall asleep.

It's early when I wake. I try not to disturb Mina, but her eyes open when I stir. She stretches and flinches.

My body heats at the recollection of why her muscles are sore. I want to do that to her again. And again. But I restrain myself. I can at least give her until tonight to recover. Besides, I have a hit to focus on. I shouldn't be spending hours in bed, behaving like a sex addict.

I sit up. "Can I get you something? A painkiller?"

"I just need a shower."

She throws off the covers and swings her legs over the bed. I lean back against the headboard, intent on enjoying the show, but when she gets up and flashes me with a view of her ass, I still, the heat in my veins turning cold.

Her beautiful, pale skin is marred with bruises. On her sides, her ass, her thighs. Everywhere I fucking touched her. Self-directed anger combusts in my chest. I hate those marks on her. I hate spoiling her flawless skin. I hate knowing I hurt her like that.

She looks at me from over her shoulder. "What?"

Her gaze follows mine, slipping down to her ass and legs. Her face turns paper white, her delicate skin even more translucent than normal.

"Mina." I grate out the words. "I didn't realize I was so rough."

She plasters on a smile. "It's nothing."

I jump from the bed, walking to her with long strides. "It's not." Gripping her shoulders, I turn her to face me. "I want you to tell me if I hurt you."

"You didn't hurt me."

"I'll be more careful."

She pulls away. "It'll fade."

When she tries to escape to the bathroom, I go after her. I don't know who's more upset, her or me. She has more reason, that's for sure.

I can't stop beating myself up as I get into the

shower with her and take the shampoo from her hand. I wash her tiny scalp, so small I can crack it like a nut. So fragile, and I ruined her.

I try to make it up to her by being extra gentle as I wash her. To smooth over my error by kissing her gently while massaging her shoulders under the running water. I've never taken responsibility for a woman before, and I'm already fucking it up.

She dresses while I shave. After, I take her to the kitchen for breakfast.

Anton is drinking coffee by the counter. Ilya is sitting at the table with a stack of toast in front of him.

Seeing us, my brother jumps up and pulls out a chair. "Sit here, Mina."

I didn't like that she ate like a servant in the kitchen last night, so I overlook Ilya's eagerness to make her comfortable.

"Want some toast?" he asks. "Here. I'll butter it."

I grab a piece from his plate and take a bite on my way to the kitchen. "It's cold. I'll make fresh ones."

Mina smiles at Ilya. "You're sweet."

"Sweet?" He tries to make a mean face, but the idiot is grinning like a cartoon cat.

"Like a teddy bear," she says.

Anton snort-laughs.

"I like teddy bears," Ilya throws back over his shoulder at Anton.

I pop bread in the toaster and pour two cups of coffee.

"We've got a site for the meeting with Dimitrov in mind," Anton says.

I drop a cube of sugar in each cup. "Where?"

"Hotel Paris," he says. "It's one of Natasha Petrova's favorite hangouts. She often dines at the Sarah Bernhardt restaurant." He grins. "And what's more appropriate than setting up a meeting to sell a stolen masterpiece in the Gustave Klimt suite?"

I rub a hand over my chin. "Security will be top notch."

Anton nods. "Ilya and I want to go check it out this morning."

"If the government puts pressure on the hotel manager to play along, security shouldn't be a problem," Ilya says. "We'll only have to worry about Dimitrov's guards."

"We better be sure we can trust the manager." Many high-end professionals here are in cahoots with the crime groups. "I'll get our hackers on the case to see what background information they can find. Meet us in the bar before lunch. I'd like to get a feel for the place."

"Thanks," Mina says when I hand her a warm slice of toast and a cup of coffee.

By the time Mina and I are done eating, Anton and Ilya are on their way.

"Need anything from town, Mina?" Ilya asks. "I didn't get too many clothes. I wasn't sure about the size."

"No, thanks," I say flatly. "We'll shop on the way."

Ilya grabs his jacket from the chair back and stomps after Anton. When the door closes, Mina gets up and starts clearing the table. I study her closely. She's been quiet. The marks on her body bother her. She says otherwise, but the frown on her pretty forehead hasn't smoothed out since she saw the bruises.

"Come here," I say.

She walks to my chair like an obedient girl.

I hand her the phone that the guys who delivered her to us had taken off her. I made sure it's charged and not bugged. "Call your friends." When she unlocks the screen, I grab her hand. "On speakerphone."

She calls and explains what she needs. We negotiate a price, and all is set. The disguises guy, a man called Simon, agrees to meet us at his shop before noon.

Pocketing her phone, I offer her a hand. "I'll take you on a tour of the apartment." Or rather, the small part she hasn't seen yet. She's going to live here now, after all.

I show her the room and en-suite bathroom Ilya and Anton are sharing. The space isn't big, but it's ample by Prague's standards.

"I'm sure you have enough money to afford a mansion," she says when the quick tour is over.

"I'm sure you do, too."

She avoids my eyes. "What's the point? I'm not home—wasn't home—very often."

"Neither am I."

She's hiding something. My well-developed sixth sense is never wrong.

On the way downstairs, I text our hackers and instruct them to get information on Mina Belan, a.k.a. Mink.

We get into a car Anton rented for the duration of our stay in Prague and drive to a boutique that stocks the kind of clothing Mina fancies, at least from what I've seen at the bar. Sure enough, she goes straight for the ripped jeans and badass T-shirts. While she's trying on a pair of combat boots, I flip through a rack of dresses. I take out a crocheted one. It's nude-pink. Cute.

I throw it in her lap. "Go try that on."

She stills in the middle of pulling off one of the boots, and looks at the heap of fabric in her lap before gaping at me. "Are you kidding?"

I raise a brow. Do I ever? Arms crossed, I wait.

Sparks detonate in her eyes. My little assassin doesn't like to be told what to do, or what to wear, for that matter. I grin at her, which only makes the anger in her pretty eyes burn hotter.

She grabs the dress and checks the label. "It'll fit."

"If you say so."

The shop assistant comes over. "Can I help you with anything?"

I motion at the dress in Mina's hand. "We need shoes to go with that."

"Of course," the lady says. "Size?"

"Thirty-six," Mina answers, her spitfire eyes still trained on me.

"What about a bag to round off the outfit?" the woman asks.

"Sure," I say.

When the woman walks away, Mina says bitingly, "That's not Petrova's style."

Leaning over her, I place my hands on either side of her body, caging her in on the pouf. I bring my lips to her ear, over the delicate shell with the multiple piercings that are simultaneously rebellious and hot, strangely feminine. "This isn't about a disguise." I rub my lips over her skin. "Far from it."

She leans so far back to escape my touch her abdominal muscles must be straining. "No? What is it about?"

I give her a slow smile. "Me."

A woman clears her throat. I straighten. The shop assistant stands there with a pair of nude-pink heels and a matching bag.

"How about these shoes, ma'am? Would you like to try them on?"

"No," Mina says like a defiant child.

"It's her size," I remark dryly, taking the items from the woman to go pay.

Armed with five shopping bags, we get into the rental and drive to the address Mina gives me. Simon operates from an antique store in the old town. He seems legit. I had him checked out.

When we arrive, he puts a closed sign on the door and guides us to the back of the shop. Unlocking another door, he takes us into a vault room. I keep a hand on the gun in the back of my waistband under my jacket. The guy is eighty years old, but you never know. Mina hates me enough to set a trap. Caged beings never stop fighting for freedom. I can never let my guard down around her.

The old man shows me to a sofa. While he and Mina go through an arsenal of disguises, pulling items off shelves, I check my email for a message from our hackers, and keep one eye on Mina and Simon as I scan through the information.

Mina was born in the Czech Republic. Shortly after, her parents moved to Budapest, Hungary, where her grandmother is originally from. The grandmother, Hanna, raised her after her parents' murder. Even as a child, Mina showed exceptional endurance, excellent sports skills, and an aptitude for languages, along with above-average intelligence. Psychological reports state a lack of empathy. The speculated reason is the trauma from the murders. Treatment was interrupted after a few years of unsuccessful results. The diagnosis is incomplete. The Hungarian Special Forces recruited her in her final year of school.

I lower the phone to stare at her, this beautiful, strange, gifted girl with the complex history. Of course the Special Forces snapped her up. She makes the perfect soldier. And paired with that body and face, an even better spy. Who wouldn't fall for her in a wink? I realized how dangerous she was, but I haven't appreciated the full force of it until now. Yet there's something vulnerable about her too, something that awakens my protective side. I can't put my finger on it. I only know that it makes me want to lock her up in a glass cage in a very high tower, out of reach of everyone but me.

My stomach tightens when I think about how she may have used her skills in the line of duty. Not the fighting kind of skills, but the pretty little flower between her legs, the perfectly rounded breasts.

But no. Since we captured her, she hasn't used her body to manipulate me. When we fuck, it's raw. Pure. That kind of honesty can't be faked.

Irrational jealousy somewhat abated, I return my attention to the report. She stayed with the Special Forces for six years and took up a job as a waitress when she resigned at the age of twenty-four. For the past five years, she's been working on and off at several bars in Budapest. The part-time bar gigs obviously offered flexibility, as well as a means of staying legal. During that time, she made frequent trips abroad, claiming vacationing on her visas as the reason for the visits. There's nothing that links Mina to Mink. She's been careful.

With regards to Mink, our hackers couldn't dig up much. Her name came up here and there, mostly in outsourced government assassinations, but there's nothing concrete. Her jobs must've been strictly by word of mouth.

"I'm ready," my little assassin says.

I look up, studying her with new admiration. What she accomplished isn't easy. No one understands what it takes better than I do. Not for the first time, I wish things could've been different between us. The logical part of me knows loyalty doesn't exist for our kind— we're ruled by money—but the unreasonable part of me doesn't care. It only cares that I meant little enough for her to frame me.

Sometimes, things just are what they are.

I get to my feet. "Let's go."

Taking the heavy case from her, I lock it in the trunk and drive us to the Hotel Paris. On the outside, the building looks like a Bohemian castle, but it only dates back to 1904.

We walk inside like we own the place. When in Rome and all that. That's how you attract the least attention. The foyer shows the appropriate amount of luxury. I count the ceiling cameras and number of security personnel on the floor. Then I check the emergency exit and staff entrance while Mina takes what will appear to be tourist photos with my phone.

Approaching the concierge, I query the availability of the Gustave Klimt suite without asking for the price, and tip the guy. Not so outrageously as to be remembered. Just enough to sink away in the sea of the norm in his memory. Then we make our way to the bar.

We sit down at a table in the back, and I order two beers while we wait for Ilya and Anton. I use the time to send further instructions to our hackers, asking for whereabouts of Natasha Petrova, as well as her future schedule. She's a social butterfly. It should be fairly easy to pin her down at any given time.

Mina sits quietly next to me. She hasn't touched her beer. It's a warm day, nice weather outside. Yet despite the sunshine, she looks pale.

I drag my beer closer. "Not thirsty?" Taking a sip, I study her carefully over the rim of my glass.

She looks at me quickly, as if she's forgotten about my presence. No, she'll never forget why she's here or who she's with. She was somewhere else, somewhere deep in her mind.

She forces a smile. "Just tired."

The tension in my chest gives a fraction at the reasonable explanation. "It's the drugs." They should've been out of her system by now, but she's tiny. The effect will last longer.

I order a smorgasbord and push it toward her when it arrives. At my insistence, she nibbles unenthusiastically on a tiny lox sandwich.

Just before one, Anton and Ilya walk in. They join us at our table and order beers. By the time they've filled me in on their observations, they've cleaned the plate I ordered, so I get the bar lunch next. Mina has to eat.

A brunette enters and sits down at the bar counter. She's classically beautiful. Expensive dress. She leans over and says something to the bartender. Drumming her red fingernails on the countertop, she turns on her seat to scan the room. I pay attention, because it's my job. Paying attention means the difference between life and death. This isn't death. I know her type. Her gaze lands on me. She makes direct eye contact and smiles.

Draping my arm over the back of Mina's chair, I lift a finger to caress her ear. I trace every silver hoop pierced through the shell before dropping my hand to her neck to stroke the outline of the hummingbird tattoo.

At the rejection, the woman turns her attention to Ilya. It doesn't take him long to catch on.

"Excuse me." He pushes back his chair and saunters to the bar.

They strike up a conversation as her drink arrives. By the time her glass is empty, Ilya's arm is around her shoulder. It's a pose I know well. We've played the game together enough times. They order a round of shooters. And another. My brother glances at me, and the brunette follows his gaze. He says something, and she gets up.

Anton stops talking when she comes over to our table and takes Ilya's seat.

Placing a hand on my leg, she smiles brightly. "Hi, handsome. I hear I'm up for double the fun."

I remove her hand. "You heard wrong."

She pouts. "And here I was getting all excited. Your brother over there is paying for the room. You may as well"—her voice drops an octave—"take advantage."

Next to me, Mina goes rigid.

"What's wrong?" Anton mocks. "You can't disappoint the lady's fantasy. Go if you like. I'll keep our guest occupied." At *guest*, he looks at Mina.

Fucking Ilya. I'm going to kill him. And then Anton, too.

In a few strides, I'm at the bar and in my brother's face. "What the fuck are you doing?"

"What we always do. Why does that surprise you?"

"You're acting like a moron."

"I'm not behaving differently than normal. You are."

The shooters must've gone to his thick head. "That"—I point at the brunette who's still sitting at our table—"was unwarranted."

His gaze narrows. "You're fucking exclusively now?"

"How I fuck is none of your business."

"Are you trying to push me away? Is that it?"

"What?" I stare at him in disbelief. "This has nothing to do with you."

"No." His tone is bitter. "It doesn't. That's the whole point."

"What the fuck?" Did my brother smoke something? "What are you talking about?"

"You know what? Stuff it. I'm taking her upstairs and fucking her. Join us if you want, or don't. I don't care. At least I was willing to share."

"What is this? You give me something so I have to give something back?" I grab his arm. "Nothing you do will ever convince me to share Mina, so get it out of your dense skull once and for all."

He jerks out of my hold. "Fuck you. What happened to all that talk about brothers watching out for one another?"

"Ilya," I warn, "don't let this come between us."

He sneers. "Too late."

"Yan," Anton says urgently but softly, walking fast toward me. He tilts his head in the direction of the door.

I spin around just in time to see Mina disappear through the frame.

16

MINA

With my nose pinched shut, I run through the lobby toward the bathroom, slam a palm on the door, and rush to the vanity. When I let go, blood splatters on the white marble of the basin.

No.

Fuck.

I grab a paper towel from the dispenser and, tilting back my head, press it under my nose until the trickling stops.

Bracing my hands on the countertop, I look at my face in the mirror.

Not this.

On the outside, I'm like a granite statue. Inside, I'm shaking.

The bruises scared me this morning, but I hoped. I hoped they were remnants of our rough sex. Shock and disappointment fill my chest until my heart drowns in despondency. All I want to do is scream, but I slam a fist on the counter instead. The blow hurts, the pain sharp and sobering as shame overcomes me.

Don't be pathetic, Mina. Pull yourself together.

I don't know anything. Not yet.

Sniffing, I stare at the mess that's my face. This won't do. This won't do at all. Straightening my spine, I wet a paper towel and clean the blood off my skin. I've barely dumped the bloodstained towel in the trash when a loud tap sounds on the door.

"Mina!"

Yan.

"In here," I call out. "I'll be out in a minute."

The door bangs against the wall. My keeper storms through it, his green eyes like wild, poisonous ivy.

"What are you doing?" He looks around the empty bathroom as if he expects to see someone else—or as if he thought he'd catch me climbing through a window.

Can't blame him. I've done it once, and I would've done it again if he hadn't tagged me like a dog.

"Jeez." I turn and lean on the vanity, all cool, casual mockery. "Can't a girl pee in peace?"

He regards me closely, searching for the lie. "You're not any girl."

No, I'm not. I give a wry laugh. "So what? Do I have to ask permission to use the bathroom?"

His answer is curt. "Yes."

"Fuck, Yan." My turmoil spills into anger. "I think we've established I don't have a fucking chance at escaping. You can cut me some slack."

His beautiful eyes harden. "Watch your mouth."

"Or what?"

"Want to lose more freedom? I have no problem keeping you locked up in my flat."

I shut my mouth. The very point of helping him with this job is gaining freedom. I need that now more than ever.

He smiles coldly. "Glad you understand."

My body sags, the fight leaving me abruptly. All I feel now is tired, and it scares the hell out of me.

Closing the distance, Yan puts his hands on my shoulders. "It wasn't what it looked like back there."

The unwelcome image of him in bed with Ilya and the brunette slips into my mind. Like earlier in the bar, the idea constricts my chest. I don't know why it bothers me so much, but it does. It hurts like the continuous prick of a tattoo needle.

I stare up at his face, taking in the hard lines of his handsome features. He doesn't belong to me, I know that. Or I should. "What you do is none of my business."

"I'm not going to have sex with someone else while I'm fucking you bareback."

My snort is as crude as his words. "That's most considerate. Thanks for not giving me STDs."

He catches my head between his broad palms. "Drop the sarcasm. It's not about diseases. Using a condom with someone else will solve that risk easily enough."

The *someone else* cuts into my heart. "Then why bother to abstain? Go ahead. Fuck her."

His hand fists in my hair. "You don't tell me what to do. In case you're slow in figuring it out, it's the other way around."

"Oh, I've figured it out."

His jaw flexes. "Then what's your problem?"

"I don't get it," I say honestly. "I don't understand you."

"What don't you understand?"

"If it's not about diseases, then what's it about?"

"Principle."

I laugh. "Are you telling me you actually have some?"

His gaze turns sharp, the green of his irises cooling further. "Careful, princess. You're skating on thin ice."

He's right. I'm risking his anger and for what? A warped sense of jealousy? I still. Fuck. I can*not* be jealous. I didn't ask for this. I didn't choose this situation, this very wrong situation. Yet a little voice deep inside says I keep on telling him "yes" every time he asks me if I want sex.

"While we're on the topic"—he releases my hair and drags his fingers over my scalp, as if soothing the sting he's inflicted—"it works both ways. You don't sleep with someone else. You don't even look at another man."

I blink up at him. "Like who?"

"Ilya."

Ah, twin rivalry. Is that what this is about? "You were happy enough to share before."

His eyes darken. "You're different."

"How?"

"No one has ever belonged to me."

It's not a compliment, nor a sweet declaration of feelings. It's a warning, a reminder of who we are, of what I am to him. An object. A toy. A convenient fuck to keep his bed warm. An enemy to lock up while he lives his life freely.

Someone to kill once he's done with me.

I push the knowledge away because I can't look at it too closely. It hurts too much.

He tilts back my head, forcing me to meet his eyes. "Do you understand?"

"I'm not stupid," I say softly.

His gaze skims over my lips. "Stupid is the last thing I'd take you for."

"Then you didn't have to barge in here chasing me. You know I won't run."

"Just making sure you get how this works." His words are full of a dark promise.

"You've been crystal clear."

He nods. It's a small peace offering. "Let's get out of here before someone needs the bathroom."

Anton is waiting outside when we exit. He informs us Ilya and the woman have gone upstairs.

"Don't worry," he says to Yan. "Ilya signed in under a false name."

"Great," Yan says. "In that case, you get to stay here to make sure Ilya doesn't do something foolish in a fit of drunken rage—like paying with a credit card." And ignoring the long string of cusswords flying out of Anton's mouth, he drags me off.

AT YAN'S PLACE, I UNPACK MY NEW CLOTHES. HE MAKES space for me in his closet, and I hang the dress next to the dry-cleaning bags with his pressed shirts and pants. It seems wrong there, out of place, but I have bigger worries on my mind.

After arranging the disguise material on the bed, I wrap each item in the provided tissue paper and seal it in a plastic bag. I make sure nothing is squashed or creased when I pack it back into the case and store it on the top shelf of the closet where it'll stay dry and cool. Even that simple task exhausts me.

I need energy. I need to eat, but the mere thought of food makes me queasy.

Wearily, I take off the clothes I've been wearing since yesterday, dress in a new T-shirt and sweatpants, and go in search of Yan. I find him working on his laptop on the couch.

He looks up when I lean on the doorframe, and trails his gaze over me in a slow evaluation that ends in a frown. "Why don't you take a nap?"

He's observant. And as dangerous and cruel as he can be, he's not always unkind. Sometimes, like now, he seems almost considerate.

I walk over and sit down next to him, folding one leg under myself. "How did you get into this business?" At his raised eyebrows, I clarify, "Killing people."

He smiles. "How did you?"

"I told you in Colombia."

"Tell me more."

He's not going to give me anything unless I give him something first. "When I left the military, I needed money. An old comrade told me about a job that involved taking out a drug dealer. I didn't pull the trigger, but I was part of the operation. It kind of set the ball rolling."

His lips twitch. "It kind of set the ball rolling, huh? As simple as that?"

"Something like that."

"Who was your first kill?"

I tell him honestly, "The men who murdered my parents. They were never convicted. Lack of evidence. Shortly after I joined the military, I tracked them down and popped them."

He regards me curiously. "And how did it feel?"

"Fantastic." When he says nothing, my defensive hackles rise. "Do you think less of me now?" *Horrible. Evil. Sociopathic.* That's what society would call me. *Emotionally dysfunctional* would be a more suitable term. Not that what he thinks matters.

His lips curve in a peculiarly warm smile. "No, not at all, princess." His gaze shifts to my side. "Is that who they are, Adéla and Johan? Your parents?"

My ribcage tightens, constricting my lungs. It's a relief to be honest with someone for once, but my parents are off limits. I can't even talk about them to Hanna.

"*In aeternum vivi*," he says when I don't reply. "Forever alive."

I blink at him, briefly startled out of my memory-induced funk. "You know Latin?"

"Some phrases."

He doesn't seem inclined to elaborate, so I decide to change the subject. "I told you about my first. It's only fair you do the same."

He stares at me, then says evenly, "The man who killed my uncle."

My breath catches, a dark curiosity gnawing at me. "How did you do it?"

"Knife. I was sixteen. I didn't have enough money for a gun—not that I would've wasted a bullet on that scum."

Of course. Admiration, dark and perverse, rises within me. I know normal people would deem it wrong, utterly deviant, to cheer on a sixteen-year-old in his quest for bloody vengeance, but I'm not normal, haven't been since I was six. I'm proud of Yan for doing this, even as something inside me squeezes at the pain he must've felt at the loss of his family—pain that I'm only too intimately familiar with. "Were you and your uncle close?"

To my surprise, he chuckles. "Not remotely. He was a drunk and an abusive bastard."

"Then why avenge him?"

"He was family." He says it like it makes perfect sense, and it does.

Even bad blood runs thicker than water.

I want to know more, want to hear all the gruesome details about that first hit of his, but that can wait. There are other things I'm more curious about.

He's turned his attention back to his laptop, so I nudge him with a touch of my knee. "Your turn."

He looks up. "For what?"

"For telling me how you got into the business."

He hesitates, then closes the laptop. "We enlisted in the army, then were recruited into Spetsnaz."

"You and Ilya?"

"Yes."

"How old were you when you enlisted?"

"Seventeen. We lied about our age."

So a year after his uncle's murder. I study him, cataloguing his thick dark hair and the hard, symmetrical lines of his face. "How old are you now?"

He smirks. "Does it matter?"

"Just curious."

"Too much for your own good."

"I'd say…" I can't help my grin. "About forty-five? Fifty?"

He gives me a narrow-eyed look. "Thirty-three."

"Ah. Who could've guessed?" I fake surprise, but he doesn't smile at my joke. "How did you end up working with Sokolov?"

"He headed the anti-terrorism unit of Spetsnaz,

which we joined later. When he went rogue after his wife and son were killed in a bombing, we followed."

"I'm assuming you're no longer a team." Not after Yan disobeyed Peter's order to kill me.

"I'm the leader now." His voice hardens a little. "Peter's out."

"Does that bother him?"

"He left the team of his own volition, so I assume not. But even if he wanted back in, it's too late. It's my team now. *My* business."

Tilting my head, I study him. "It sounds as if you didn't get on."

"We had our philosophical differences, but it had nothing to do with *not getting on*. I've just never been good at taking orders."

"Then why did you follow him in the first place?"

He gives me a level look. "Why do you think?"

"Money."

Yes, of course. Everyone needs money. Some love it. Some love it more than others, splurging on flashy cars or designer houses. Yan has under-floor heating—which he uses even in the summer, so his feet won't be cold walking from his bed to his bathroom—and Egyptian cotton. He doesn't use his money to show off with a Porsche or a flashy house, but to buy the luxury of comfort. As adults, we tend to compensate for what we didn't have as children.

"What about your other family?" I ask.

"What about them?"

I can't help but throw a jab. "Am I not going to meet

them?" Under normal circumstances, if I'd moved in, he would've introduced me to his mother by now.

"You've met him."

"Ilya? There's no one else?"

"No."

Short and sweet. He doesn't like to talk about it. "Why did you lie about your age to join Spetsnaz?"

His features harden. "We were living on the streets."

My heart lurches. I've been to Russia a few times. I've seen their winters, have walked some of their streets. And picturing sixteen-year-old Yan and his brother there, freezing, hungry, and alone... "I'm sorry. I shouldn't have pried."

"I have nothing to be ashamed about," he says harshly.

"Of course not." I look at my hands.

"What happened to your grandmother?"

I lift my head quickly, my pulse jumping. "How do you know about my grandmother?"

"Do you really have to ask me that?"

Fuck. It makes sense that he would've done a background check on me, but I've kept communication with my grandmother private. I never speak about her to anyone. Caring about someone is a liability in our business.

His green gaze sharpens. "I asked you a question, Mina."

He's going to find out soon. It's better I tell him than make him think I'm hiding something—because I *am* hiding something, and I can't afford for him to go sniffing around. "She's in a private clinic. She suffers from Parkinson's."

He studies me closely. "A private clinic where?"

"Budapest."

"Private clinics are expensive."

"So?"

His voice takes on a quiet tone. "Is that why you need the money?"

I shrug, as if it doesn't matter. "She took care of me. Now it's my turn. She's a good woman."

His gaze warms a fraction. "I don't doubt that." He pauses, then says with a peculiar deliberateness, "You'll have to introduce us."

I give him a startled look. "You're joking, right?"

"Why would I joke about it?"

Fuck. This is the last thing I need. "As far as Hanna is concerned, I'm a waitress, nothing more." Not that I'll have any recourse if he blurts out my secret to my grandmother.

His eyes gleam brighter. "My lips are sealed. Who am I to disillusion an old woman?"

Dammit. He's really set on this. "How do I explain who you are?"

"Don't worry, my little waitress." His smile is calculating. "I'm sure I can come up with something."

Hanna isn't a subject I want to discuss either. It's bad enough he knows about her existence. I motion at his laptop. "I want the five hundred thousand upfront."

The corner of his mouth lifts. "Is that so?"

"A deal's a deal."

"Fifty percent upfront. The rest you get when Dimitrov is dead."

"You don't trust me."

"Should I?"

Probably not. "I'll give you the account number."

His smile is lazy. My bluntness amuses him. He looks at me like an owner may look at a pet. His permissive expression lets me know he's only allowing me to get away with this because he wants to, because he can. In a twisted way, even this—indulging me—is a display of his power.

After logging on, he types in the offshore bank account number I rattle off. When the transfer is done, he turns the screen toward me.

"Thank you," I say.

"You better earn it."

I'm full of sass, but it's all acting. "I'll do my best."

He cups my chin, wiping his thumb over my lips. "We're not so different, you and I."

The touch throws me off kilter. It's simultaneously gentle and threatening. I want to both lean into his palm and pull away. "You mean we both kill for money."

"You don't let anyone get close to you." His voice is soft, filled with an understanding I don't want him to possess. "You don't get close to anyone."

It takes everything I have and more to stay put instead of jerking away. "You're close to Ilya."

"You're close to your grandmother. That's family. I'm talking about lovers. Friends."

There is one person, the only friend I have, and Yan can never know about him. Breaking the disconcerting contact, I get to my feet. "I'll have that nap after all."

His clever eyes see through me. He knows I'm running. Hiding. "Go ahead. I put clean sheets on the bed."

I don't let him tell me twice.

I run and hide.

17

MINA

*W*hen I wake up in a cold sweat from my nightmare, it's dark. I've slept for a few hours, but I don't feel rested. Pulling the comforter up to my chin, I stay curled up under the warm covers. I don't get up for dinner. I don't have a shower. The mattress dips next to me as Yan gets into bed, but I don't even have the strength to pretend I'm sleeping.

He pulls me close. "Mina." When I don't respond, he orders harshly, "Look at me."

I wearily turn to face him.

"You skipped dinner," he says. "I can make you a snack."

"I'm not hungry."

"You barely touched your lunch. You have to eat."

"Later, okay?"

He sighs. "Rest. Tomorrow you'll be better."

"Yes." My reply is meek, because I don't believe him. I know what's happening, what's in store for me.

As he traces the tattooed script on my side, the unspoken questions hang thick in the air, but he doesn't talk. He lets me rest. Even if his erection presses against my ass, he doesn't ask or take.

As exhausted as I am, my brain refuses to shut off. I lie in his arms in the dark and scheme.

I have to see Hanna, and soon.

COME MORNING, YAN'S SIDE OF THE BED IS EMPTY. To my surprise, I do feel a little better. Some of my strength has returned.

After showering and dressing in baggy sweatpants with a vintage punk emblem and a black hoodie T-shirt, I go to the lounge. A guilty-looking Ilya sips coffee at the table. His eyes are bloodshot and his skin looks ashy.

"Morning." I leave out the *good*. It doesn't seem fitting. "Where's Yan?"

"He and Anton left."

"Where did they go?"

"They're meeting our government connection in Ostrava about putting pressure on the Hotel Paris manager."

"Ostrava? When will they be back?"

"Tomorrow. I'm supposed to take care of you." As if suddenly remembering an important task, he asks, "Can I make you breakfast? Eggs? You didn't eat much yesterday."

I shoot him a grateful smile. "Thanks, but I can take care of myself." I grab a cup of coffee and take a seat next to him. "Rough night?"

He barely meets my eyes. "Listen, I owe you an apology."

"What for?"

"I didn't mean to hurt your feelings yesterday. I didn't know you and Yan were, uh, exclusive."

Neither did I. It doesn't make sense, but I do breathe easier knowing Yan won't fuck anyone else while he's fucking me. The hurt at seeing the brunette's hand on his leg lifted after his declaration in the bathroom.

Not wanting to examine the reason behind that muddle of feelings, I brush the thought away. "You don't owe me anything. What you do with your life is hardly my business."

Yan's twin drags a hand over his shaven head. "The thing is, you see, you *are* our business now."

My laugh is uncomfortable. "I can see you're a decent guy, Ilya. Surely, you don't agree with what Yan is doing." To me, that is. Nobody here has any problems with the assassination part of the business, myself included.

Ilya's expression turns apologetic. "I may not agree, but I can't let you go."

Right. That's why Ilya didn't go with Yan and Anton. He stayed to babysit. Knowing how jealous Yan is of him, it can only mean Yan didn't leave Anton with me because he can't trust his bearded teammate not to hurt me.

I suppose I should be grateful for that.

I fake nonchalance. "I'm not going anywhere. This says so." I point at the back of my neck.

Ilya flushes. "The tracker is for your safety."

"Right."

He shifts in his chair. "This doesn't have to be bad for you. We'll take good care of you."

"Until Yan grows tired of me?" He didn't bring me here to grow old with him.

Ilya's eyes, as green as his brother's, flare. "He won't hurt you."

"So when he no longer has a use for me, he's just going to let me go?"

Conviction hardens his face. "I won't let him kill you."

"That's sweet." But an empty promise. I doubt Ilya is able to change any course of action once Yan's mind is set.

The Russian cocks his head, regarding me with a peculiar expression. "How do you feel about my brother?"

I stare at him, taken aback. "How do you mean?"

"That night in Budapest, did you really choose him? Willingly, I mean."

My cheeks turn warm. "I can't deny that there was an attraction."

"Was?"

The heat seeps down to my neck. "Is." I can't lie

196

about this, no matter what this twisted attraction says about me.

"What about me?" Ilya asks hopefully.

I shake my head, giving him an apologetic smile.

His face drops. "Ah."

"I don't mean to hurt you. I can't help how it is."

He stares at his coffee. "I'm good. I get it."

"Do you always share women with Yan?" I ask hesitantly, trying to understand this big, scary-looking man with the easily woundable heart.

Ilya shrugs. "There are, or rather were, exceptions. For the most part, we're attracted to the same kind of women, and we don't mind sharing with each other. On the rare occasion, it turns into a threesome."

I clear my throat. "Doesn't that feel weird? Sorry if it seems like I'm prying, but I have a hard time picturing the two of you together in bed."

He grins. "You'd be surprised how many women have a twin fantasy."

"Oh." Not my cup of tea, but I can imagine how the two of them could turn a woman on. Resting my chin in my hand, I study him. He's handsome, even if he doesn't look that much like his twin. Yan is attractive in a sleek, dangerous way, while Ilya has a different appeal, more of a rougher, biker-type look. And there's a reassuring side to him too, a certain humanity that Yan is lacking. I clear my throat again. "May I ask you something?"

"Shoot."

"Why do you do it? Is it just to please the women, or

197

do you get a kick from it, too?" His face tightens minutely, and I hastily add, "If the question is too personal, you don't have to answer."

He takes a breath and lets it out slowly. "I don't know. I suppose… it makes me feel closer to Yan."

My heart clenches. Behind the honesty, there's an unspoken need for acceptance, approval. Both are basic human needs, the pillars of a healthy self-esteem. We get those fundamental pillars from our parents. If our parents fail to meet those needs, we search for them elsewhere. Ilya is looking for them in his twin. In sex.

"I don't know if you've noticed, but Yan isn't very good with emotions," Ilya continues gruffly. "My brother, he… well, he usually only gives affection during sex. I don't mean that he touches me—he doesn't—but he's less shielded. Freer, if that makes sense."

I stare at him, the ache in my chest intensifying. I can feel the pain behind his words, the longing that he can't quite hide. Like Yan, he's never had a normal family, and whereas Yan has been able to manage his emotions by largely denying them, Ilya has latched on to his brother as the one constant in his life, channeling at him all the love that should've belonged to their parents.

A love that Yan can't reciprocate outside of sex.

My stomach feels strangely tight at the thought, so I force it away, push it deep down where it can't hurt me. Turning in my seat, I fold my arms around Ilya's big frame. I'm not good with emotions either, but I can give him this, try to make him feel better at least for this one short moment.

His big frame is tense at first, but then he relaxes, the air escaping his lungs in a sigh as he lays his head on my shoulder. Awkwardly, I pat his back, then pull away, releasing him.

"You're a nice guy, Ilya," I say softly when his green eyes meet mine. "I like you. I really do."

"But not like that?"

"No, not like that."

He sighs and rubs the tattoo above his right ear. "If that changes, let me know."

I punch him playfully. "Don't hold your breath."

"Hey." He gives me a mock-frown. "I appreciate your honesty, but you could hold back just a little. Rejection stings."

Despite his words, his tone is light, so I grin at him. "You're a big man. You can handle it."

He grins back. "Maybe, but I don't get why Yan is so selfish when it comes to you. He's never behaved like this with a woman."

My smile fades. Discussing Yan makes me edgy, as does thinking about the reasons for his possessive behavior.

Like Ilya just said, Yan doesn't give affection easily, so whatever's between us can't be more than just hot sex.

Thankfully, Ilya seems oblivious to my change in mood. "Are you sure I can't fix you breakfast?" he asks, still grinning. "It's no trouble, I promise."

I think fast. This is an opportunity I can't waste. I may not get another chance. Pasting on a smile, I say, "If you don't mind, I'd rather go out for breakfast. I'm developing cabin fever."

Understanding flashes in his eyes. "Is that why you've been acting so under the weather?" He stands and grabs his jacket from the back of the chair. "There's a place nearby that makes mean pastries."

Laying a hand on his arm, I say quietly, "Alone."

He stills with a bewildered look.

"I need some time on my own. It's hard to process everything that's happened."

He frowns. "Look, I know you have a lot on your plate, but—"

"Where am I going to go with a tracker embedded in my neck?"

The manipulation works. Guilt splashes over his features, stark and remorseful. I feel bad for deceiving him, but what choice do I have?

Slowly, he lowers the jacket. "Yan won't like it."

"He doesn't have to know."

Guilt transforms into doubt. "I don't know."

"Please, Ilya." I get to my feet and grip his hand, staring at him with all the begging I can muster. "I'm not going to run." At least, not for long.

After a moment's hesitation, his shoulders sag. "Fine, but you come back here. Don't make me call Yan in the middle of his meeting."

"I'll come back." It's a given, a part of my life I no

longer have control over. Awkwardly, I add, "I'll need some money."

"Oh. Of course." He reaches for the wallet in his back pocket and takes out a few bills, enough for ten generous breakfasts. "Here you go."

Rising on tiptoes, I kiss his cheek. "Thank you."

His smile is uncertain.

Before he can change his mind, I pull on a sweater and rush outside. I force myself to walk normally in case he's looking through the window.

The minute I round the corner, I run.

18

YAN

*I*t doesn't take long to convince the government agent to cooperate. He's not in favor of involving a prominent civilian, but he knows getting the Hotel Paris manager to work with us is our best bet.

We go through our plan with him. Mina, disguised as Natasha Petrova, will arrive with the fake da Vinci in a crate in case Dimitrov has the hotel watched, which I expect him to do. He'd be a fool not to, and the crime lord didn't get to the top of the drug business by being a fool. Anton will accompany Mina, as Dimitrov will expect her to have a bodyguard. The hotel manager will let Petrova and her entourage—which will include Anton, Ilya, and me—use a private entrance to walk in unnoticed, something else Dimitrov will expect. A famous socialite like Petrova will demand privacy, and the hotel will happily oblige. She's a frequent client, after all. The secrecy will

202

reassure Dimitrov that the sale of the art will remain discreet.

Ilya and I will be disguised as transporters. Our job will be to carry the crate and open it in the Klimt suite. We could've gotten real transporters, but I want to make sure Mina gets in safely and that nothing is out of place. Once that's done, Ilya and I will leave, making sure our exit is caught on camera. Timing is of the utmost importance. We'll enter the elevator in which there is no security camera. Two hotel guards disguised as us will be already inside. We'll exchange clothes, our company overalls for their suits, and hand over the keys for the delivery van.

They'll get out on the ground floor and leave in the van in which we arrived. Dimitrov will have men outside watching. They will inform him of the transporters' departure, and Ilya and I will exit on the rooftop, where we'll have stored a rope and detachable sniper rifles. We'll set up the rifles and use the rope to climb down to the balcony of the Klimt suite. It will be a tricky descent, but we've done more dangerous stunts. Then we'll get into position and wait.

In the meantime, Dimitrov and his team will arrive. Dimitrov's guards will be heavily armed. They'll sweep the suite before allowing Dimitrov inside to ensure there's no one besides Mina—a.k.a. Natasha—and her bodyguard, no hidden weapons or planted bugs, and, of course, that the painting is there. They'll search Mina and Anton for weapons or wires. The deal is that Mina, Dimitrov, and his art expert meet alone, as per Mina's demands. Anton and Dimitrov's guards will leave, letting Dimitrov and his expert into the room with Mina after Anton has searched them. No weapons inside the room. Only Dimitrov's smartphone on which he'll make the transfer after confirming the painting is authentic. Mina will offer Dimitrov champagne while the expert studies the painting. Pretending to get the champagne, she'll slip into the bathroom and lock the door.

A couple of attractive hotel waitresses will serve snacks and vodka to distract the guards waiting in the hallway. While they're eating and drinking, Anton will excuse himself to take a piss and disappear. As soon as Mina is out of sight, Ilya will hit the expert with a dart, and I'll shoot Dimitrov. The idea is to sedate the expert to immobilize him and prevent him from alarming the guards. With the silencer, the guards outside won't know what's going on until it's too late. Mina will get onto the balcony. Ilya will climb up, and we'll lift her with the rope to the roof. Then I'll join them, and the three of us will make our way outside, where Anton will be waiting with our getaway car.

It's a good plan. It's as good as foolproof. But something can always go wrong. I don't like that Mina will be involved. Risking her life has a strange effect on me. It makes the thought of locking her up in that tower all the more appealing. Admittedly, she's a crucial part of the plan. Without Natasha Petrova, there is no plan.

This morning, before Anton and I had left, I told Ilya about my reservations.

"I don't like it," I said, "that Mina's life will be at risk."

Ilya tried to reassure me. "She's not just any woman. She's one of us. She can handle herself."

True. She's not just any woman. I said so myself yesterday in the bathroom when I cornered her. I meant it differently, though. She means something to me, something I can't name. It's not the feeling I have for Ilya. It's more than responsibility and brotherly love. It's a sense of belonging, of having found the female version of my soul.

Yes, a soulmate. That would've been a fitting description if I hadn't captured her like a bird in a cage. Mina may not be a willing yang to my yin, but she's mine. I claimed her that night in the alley when I pressed her up against the wall, and I'm keeping her.

No matter what it takes.

"Then we agree?" Anton asks, pulling me back from my thoughts.

"This girl," the agent says. "She better be as good at disguising as you say, or your plan will blow up in your faces. If Dimitrov suspects for one second—"

"She's good." I finish my espresso. "You can take my word for it."

Mina will have to disguise the two hotel staff members posing as us, as well as herself. We'll have to do it in a different location. Maybe an apartment nearby. Ilya is already looking into it.

"What's the timeline?" the agent asks.

Rising, I adjust my jacket. "Three weeks."

He gets to his feet and shakes my hand. "Text me the date and time. Everything will be ready."

Anton sees him out. When he gets back to the lounge of the hotel suite we rented for the meeting, I'm reading the email from our hackers about Petrova's whereabouts. She has a charity ball scheduled in Austria in two weeks' time. Then the opening of a new art gallery in Vienna. After that, she's planning a vacation in Spain to work on her tan. It looks like Natasha Petrova will be making a deviation in her traveling plans. She can definitely work in a secret visit to Prague before hitting Puerto Banús.

By the time the paparazzi catches her on camera, sipping champagne with Antonio Banderas and Nicole Kimpel on their luxury yacht in the glamorous port, Dimitrov will already be dead.

19

MINA

*E*very second counts. I give Ilya about an hour before he realizes I'm not coming back. That means I have a one-hour head start. Ostrava is more than a three-hour drive away. That gives me four hours before Yan gets back to Prague. By then, I'll be well on my way. As long as I'm on the move, I'll maintain a four-hour advantage.

When we drove to the old town, I paid attention to our surroundings, so now I go straight to the electronics store and buy a cheap burner phone. In a quiet alcove, I dial a secure number.

Gergo picks up immediately. "Mink?" He only uses my professional name in the unlikely event that the secure line, a number only the two of us use, is compromised.

"My grandmother would like to invite you for tea," I say.

"A visit is long overdue. When is a good time?"

"Can you come over at five-thirty?"

"Shall I bring some Earl Grey?" That's code for weapons. "I've recently been to Russia. I stocked up. I know your grandmother doesn't like the British kind."

"That's considerate but not necessary. See you there."

I cut the call and dump the phone in a trashcan before flagging down a taxi.

"The train station, please," I tell the driver.

In less than thirty minutes, I'm on the train and on my way to Budapest, the last of Ilya's money spent on a ticket.

Sick with nerves, I put out of my mind what Yan will do to me when he finds me and focus on my plan.

Get to Budapest. Take care of my grandmother's future. Warn Gergo.

It would've been a piece of cake to slip into a restaurant, nick a steak knife, and cut out the tracker in the bathroom, but I need the money Yan promised me for the job. I need to provide for Hanna, to make sure her needs will be met when I'm no longer around.

At least that's what I tell myself. I'm not reluctant to leave Yan. I can't be. That wouldn't make any sense.

At every station, my stomach grows tighter. At every stop, I expect Yan to hop onto the train and drag me away, even if it's unlikely unless he charters a helicopter. But just over seven hours later, the train pulls into Budapest without any incidents.

With no money left, I go to the nearest boutique bank office and tell the private banker my handbag was stolen on the train, all my cards and passport gone, and that I'm on my way to make a declaration at the police station. After verifying my identity with a fingerprint scanner, I make a small withdrawal. At the pharmacy next door, I buy foundation and lipstick, and apply a thick coat of each to conceal the faint bruises and almost-healed cut on my lip.

A taxi drops me off at the private clinic in District 11.

The receptionist knows me well. She smiles when I enter. "Miss Belan. It's been a while."

"I've been traveling. How is she?"

Her look is sympathetic. "She has her days." Her face brightens. "Seeing you will definitely cheer her up."

"Can I go through?"

"Of course." She picks up the phone. "I'll let the nurse know you're on your way."

I make my way through the long hallway, my sneakers squeaking on the shiny floor. Natural light filters through the skylights and contemporary art brightens the clean white of the walls, while floor-to-ceiling windows encase the spacious lounge, giving a magnificent view of the city. A staircase takes me to the first floor. At the end of the hall, I pause to gather myself. Carefully schooling my features, I knock and enter.

Right away, overwhelming emotions clog up my throat, and it takes all I have to suppress the tears stinging my eyes. My grandmother is the only person who can make me feel like this, who can get through the icy walls that have encased my heart after my parents' deaths. With her, I'm again that little girl running through the woods, and as much as I hate the feeling, I could never give it up.

I could never give her up.

She—Hanna—is sitting in her wheelchair on the balcony, her soft, white hair forming a halo around her weathered face in the late afternoon light. A nurse is feeding her tea.

Making my way over, I take the cup from the nurse. "I'll take over."

The woman nods and takes her leave.

A smile splits Hanna's face. "Mina, darling. It's been so long."

I take a seat and bring the cup to her lips. It breaks my heart to see how hard the simple task of closing her lips around the rim is. "I've been busy at work. It was hard to get away."

Hanna gives me a chiding look. "You shouldn't waste your free time on an old woman. You should take a holiday, go away." Her eyes sharpen. "Meet people."

Meet a man, she means. If only she knew. I push away the thought. My time with her is short, and I'm not going to spoil it by dragging the reality of my twisted relationship with Yan into the moment.

"There's no one I'd rather spend time with than you," I tell her, bringing the cup to her lips again.

Through sips of tea, she watches me with observant eyes. "You're pale."

I use the napkin to wipe away a dribble of tea that has spilled down her chin. "I haven't gotten out much."

"I hate how your job makes you a vampire."

That makes me laugh. "I'm hardly a vampire."

"You sleep in the day and work all night. Look how white you are. If you carry on like this, you'll develop an intolerance to the sun."

"I'm sitting in the sun now, and I'm not turning into ashes," I tease.

Frowning, she peers at me. "Is that a bruise under your eye?"

"Just dark rings from a lack of sleep."

She sighs and shakes her head. "From how thin you are, you're not eating either."

"Don't worry, Grandma. I'm not drinking blood."

"Hmpf. Are you cooking?"

"Yes."

"What?" A challenge.

"Goulash."

She relaxes somewhat. "Good. The greasy food they serve in that bar where you work will give you heart disease, not to mention pimples."

If only. I'd kill for some acne and high cholesterol right now. Taking a cookie from the plate, I hold it for her to take a bite. I don't miss how much her hands are shaking in her lap, and my heart cracks all over again. "Are they taking good care of you?"

It takes her a while to chew. "Oh, yes. The nurses

are very kind." She tilts her head toward the plate. "Have one. They're healthy. Oats and honey."

To appease her, I take a cookie. "How's the food? Still good?"

"Everything is great. As always. Why are you so concerned about all of this today?"

"Just making sure you're happy."

"How about you? Are you happy, Mina?"

It's hard to look her in the eyes. "Very. Are you tired? Would you like to have a nap before dinner?"

"Are you staying?"

"Yes."

She smiles. "Then I'd like a little nap."

I push her back into the room and take her arm to help her stand. Her frail form shakes so badly it takes a full minute to cross the short distance to the bed.

When she's comfortable, I kiss her cheek. "I'm going to see Lena. I'll be back after your nap."

She reaches for my hand and gives it a tremulous squeeze. "I'm happy you're here."

"Me too." Emotions tighten my chest. "I'm sorry it's been so long."

"Don't be silly. You're young. You have a life to live." She squeezes once more and lets go. "Go see Lena. She'll be happy to see you, too."

I FIND THE DOCTOR AND CLINIC DIRECTOR IN HER OFFICE. She's soft and curvy, her gray-streaked dark hair twisted into a French roll. She was my mother's best friend, and she's fiercely loyal to Hanna. It was because of her that Hanna could get into this clinic despite a five-year waiting list. We're not close—I keep too many secrets to get close to anyone—but with this, I can trust her.

She looks up and smiles when I enter. "Mina!" Rising, she rounds her desk and kisses my cheeks. "It's been too long."

"Yes, it has." I close the door. "Do you have a minute?"

She looks from the closed door to my face, her smile fading. "Of course. What is the matter?"

"Hanna's stay here, up to when is it covered?"

"You're paid up for the next several months. Why?"

"I'd like to transfer a large sum, enough to cover her stay for life. Can it be done?"

She gives me a startled look. "Yes, of course, but why would you want to do that?"

"I want to be sure she's looked after, no matter what."

"A large enough donation will ensure your grandmother's expenses and medical treatments for life."

"How much?"

"Two million."

"I can pay most of it now." I have the money from Henderson's job in my offshore account, plus the fifty percent that Yan has already deposited. "I should have the shortfall in a few weeks' time."

"What's going on, Mina?" She searches my eyes. "Is there something I should know?"

"I need you to run tests."

"Shit." She grips my shoulder. "What are your symptoms?"

I shrug as if the answer is inconsequential, as if the signs mean nothing. "Bruises. A nosebleed. The bruises could just be rough sex. The nosebleed could be purely coincidental."

"Shit," she says again. "You've hardly recovered. How long has it been?"

"Sixteen months."

"Why don't you go to your regular doctor? Are you in some kind of trouble?"

"Yes, and you can't ask me what it is."

She nods. She doesn't know the full extent of my job, but she's aware I've been involved in secret government operations, and she suspects I do something besides waitressing to cover the bills here.

"All right," she says. "Come with me."

She leads me to the lab and takes a blood sample. While she's handing it over for analysis with an instruction to move it to the top of the list and email the results to her immediately—a perk of running one of the most prestigious clinics in the country—I make use of a private computer booth in the visitor's lounge to transfer whatever money I have left to the clinic.

When I'm done, I have five minutes to spare before meeting Gergo. I visit the bathroom and pinch my cheeks to make them look less pale before going outside to the gardens. He'd notice, and I don't want Gergo to know about my situation. He may get it into his head to try to save me. And that would be a problem. Not only is my life not worth saving, but I don't want anything to happen to Yan. Why exactly that is, I don't know, but my chest tightens inexplicably at the mere thought of him getting hurt.

Gergo is sitting on the usual bench in a secluded corner hidden from view. Meeting at my grandmother's has become our way of discreetly making contact. He disguises himself as some patient's family member and signs in at the gate under a false name.

Today, he's wearing a black wig and thick-rimmed glasses. He has more laugh lines around his eyes, as if he's fifty years old instead of thirty-five. There's a big mole on his left cheek, complete with a long hair growing out of it. Great disguise. The student in me can't help but admire the teacher.

His greeting is a soft exclamation. "Mink. Thank fuck." He pats the spot next to him and throws an arm around my shoulders when I sit down. "I was going out of my mind with worry when I saw the shootout between Sokolov and the feds on the news. That fucker, Henderson. He must've known the Russians would come after you."

I pick at the skin around my nails. "He couldn't have known Sokolov would get away."

"If I'd known what his plans were, I would've never given him your name."

"It wasn't your fault. I should've trusted my instincts."

He squeezes and puts a little distance between us when I stiffen. "I had no idea when I did the disguises that he was planning on framing the Russians."

"That's why I needed to see you." I meet his gaze. "Sokolov was looking for the person who'd done the disguises."

His eyes tighten. "How do you know?"

"The Russians sent a team. They picked me up here in Budapest."

His face twists into an expression of hatred mixed with compassion. "Where did they take you?"

"To a place in Colombia owned by a certain Julian Esguerra."

"Those motherfuckers." His fingers clench on my shoulder. "How did you get away?"

"It doesn't matter. What matters is that Sokolov was looking for you."

"Why?"

"He was hoping he'd be able to track Henderson through you."

Gergo visibly relaxes. "Ah. Well, Henderson is dead. It was all over the news."

"Sokolov may still come after you. You framed his team, after all."

He stills, his face hardening. "They tortured you and you broke? You gave up my name? Is that what you came to tell me?"

"They didn't have to torture me. I gave them the

Delta Force men's names willingly. As you said, together with Henderson, they fucked me over. But I didn't give up your name."

"What did you tell him then?"

"I told him it was me."

He stares at me. "You?"

"I said I did the disguises."

"And he believed you?"

"Only after I demonstrated my skill."

"Mink." He squeezes my shoulder, his expression softening. "Why would you do that? You shouldn't have taken the fall for me."

"I owe you my life. I owe you—" I stop, unable to say it.

"Hey." He pulls me tight. "You owe me nothing, sweetheart."

I pull away, uncomfortable with his friendly embrace. "Look, Henderson may be dead, but if the Russians start asking questions, they may discover our connection. You have to be careful."

"You came to warn me," he says with disbelief.

"You're my friend." Perhaps the only one I'll ever have.

He shakes his head. "You're unbelievable, you know that?"

"I didn't do anything you haven't done for me first."

"It's not the same."

I grab his wrist to check the time on his watch. "I have to get back inside. Hanna will be up for dinner soon."

"Wait. What are your plans now?"

"To lie low." If I were going to come clean about Yan, this would be my chance, but I can't bring myself to do it.

"Tell me where you're going. Don't make me worry."

"It's better like this." I stand. "I'm going off the radar for a while. So should you."

"Let me help you. I got you into this."

"I'll be fine. Just take care of yourself."

He gets to his feet. "Why does this sound like a goodbye?"

I try to make light of it. "Because it is?"

His expression remains serious. "You know what I mean. Talk to me. What's going on?"

"Nothing. If I'm not back within the next five minutes, Hanna is going to send out a search party of nurses."

I turn, but he grabs my elbow.

"I'll walk you back."

I glance toward the security cameras fixed around the building. "It's too dangerous."

"No one will recognize me."

He's right. I let it be, soaking up the last few moments with the person who taught me everything I know about disguises, weapons, and how to use the skills I've acquired in the military in highly profitable ways. We walk together quietly, side by side.

At the entrance, he turns me to face him. "What about after?"

"After what?"

"After lying low."

"We'll see."

Normally, he wouldn't let my vagueness go, but this isn't normal circumstances. If our secret comes out, his life is at risk.

Wrapping my arms around him, I give him a quick hug. Besides Hanna, he's the closest person I have to family.

"Take care," he says when I pull away.

I rush up the steps and don't look back. I go forward, like I always do.

Fetching Hanna, I take her down to the dining room. We have dinner against the backdrop of the view. I feed her, my heart aching when I remember the strong, proud woman who'd cooked for me in her kitchen. I miss those times, but this is the present, and this is who we've become. I imprint every detail in my mind. I inhale her perfume. *Anais Anais.* I make a new memory as I sit next to her and hold her hand while we talk about old times.

When it's time for Hanna's medication, the nurse tells me Lena would like to say goodbye before I go. My heart breaks a little more with every step I take away from the small, wrinkled woman who raised me, but I keep my shoulders straight. Turning in the doorway, I wave cheerfully, giving Hanna my happiest face. Then I round the corner and she's gone, lost from my view. The loss is so profound I have to brace myself with a hand on the wall.

A nurse walks by. "Is everything all right, ma'am?"

"Yes." I straighten. "Perfectly."

Swallowing my tears, I go to Lena's office.

Her face is grim. "Sit down, Mina."

My chest shrinks as I sink down into the chair facing her desk. "Is it bad?"

"I'm afraid so." She leans over and takes my hand where it rests on the desktop. "I'm sorry. The leukemia is back."

Even if I expected it, the news comes as a blow.

"There's a new treatment," Lena says. "It's still experimental, but—"

"No." The previous treatment was hell. "No more treatment."

She gives me a sympathetic look. "Are you sure?"

"Yes." I get to my feet. "Thank you for running the tests."

"You're welcome."

"Will you take care of Hanna?"

"You can count on me."

"I'll transfer the rest of the money soon."

"Take care of yourself, and call me if you change your mind about the treatment."

With the reassurance that Hanna's every need will be catered to, I catch a taxi to the train station where I buy a ticket to Prague. While I wait, I order a cup of tea in the cafeteria. The brew is strong and bitter.

It tastes like goodbyes and regret.

20

YAN

*S*omething's up. Ilya wouldn't call me otherwise. The hair on my nape stands on end as I hold up a palm to silence Anton in the middle of his sentence and take the call.

"What's wrong?"

Ilya clears his throat. "It's Mina."

I'm on my feet. "What did you do?" I'll kill the fucker if he touched her.

"It may be nothing." He hesitates. "I didn't want to take a chance."

Grabbing my jacket, I motion for Anton to follow. "You're wasting time. Spit it out."

"She went out for breakfast and—"

"She what?"

"She said she needed time alone to deal with all the shit happening in her life."

Motherfucker. Rushing out the door, I take the stairs two by two. "How long ago?"

"Just over an hour."

"You let her go on her fucking own?"

"She said she'd be back."

"And you fucking believed her?"

"I felt bad, okay? What you're doing, Yan, it's not right."

He thinks now's the time for a moral lecture? "Where did she go?"

"She didn't say."

"Tell me you didn't give her money."

"Of course I did."

My brother is a goddamn pushover, a fucking pussy when it comes to that little spitfire of a woman. I'll deal with him later. The priority is finding Mina. "Where are you now?"

"At the apartment. Should I go look for her?"

"Stay the fuck put and call me if she shows up."

I cut the call and activate the tracker app. We're running the two blocks to where the rental is parked.

Throwing the keys to Anton, I say, "Drive."

As always, he's fast and efficient. Cool and collected. He unlocks the doors and takes the wheel. "What's going on?"

I slide into the passenger side, nearly choking on my relief as the tracker appears on the app. "Mina ran."

"Fuck."

Mina didn't get rid of the tracker. The microscopic electrodes are picking up her pulse. The elevated reading shows she's stressed. Otherwise, her vitals are normal. She could've easily cut out the tracker, something I wouldn't put past her, but the red dot blinks reassuringly on the screen.

I pull up the coordinates as Anton steers the car into the heavy traffic. By the speed at which she's moving, I'm guessing she's on a train. She's roughly four hours ahead of us. Opening a railway plan, I study the lines. If my assumption is correct, she's on her way to Hungary.

"Where to?" Anton asks tightly as we near the first exit.

"Budapest."

He doesn't ask questions. He programs the GPS and does as he's told. Unlike Ilya. When I get my hands on my brother, he'll pay for not following the one, simple fucking order I gave.

According to the GPS, it will take us eleven hours to get there with the current traffic. That's if Budapest is indeed Mina's destination. What the hell is she doing? If she thinks she can run from me, she'll be sadly disappointed. I'll catch her.

Again and again.

Anton shoots me a sidelong glance. "What about flights?"

"It's better to follow her on land. Easier to change direction if needed." Our own plane is undergoing maintenance, and if we're stuck on a commercial flight, it may take us even longer. There are a lot of overbookings and delays, as it's the end of the summer holiday and the Czech Republic is swamped with tourists.

Time crawls by. We don't stop. Not to eat, not to stretch our legs, not even for a piss. We only take five minutes to refuel. I don't work. I don't check my messages. I do nothing but study the red dot that represents Mina. The farther we advance, the more convinced I become I'm right about her destination.

Six-and-a-half hours later, she stops moving. I look up the location. It's a private clinic in Budapest. I can only imagine why she'd go there. Tapping on the listed number, I dial the clinic. A female voice comes onto the line, asking if she can help me.

"I'd like to speak to Ms. Hanna Belan, please."

"Certainly, sir. Who may I say is calling?"

"I'm having trouble hearing you. I'll call back when I have a better connection."

I cut the call. Just as I thought.

"Family of Mina?" Anton asks.

It's not his business. Nothing concerning Mina is anyone's business but mine. "Pull over at the next gas station."

We swap places. He catches a nap and I drive, keeping an eye on the tracker app. For the moment, Mina is immobile. It's only when I pull into Budapest that she starts moving again.

Changing direction, I drive to the station and park in the drop-off zone.

"Circle around until you hear from me," I tell Anton.

The station is busy. I tuck a Glock into my waistband and pull on my jacket to hide the weapon. I stay vigilant as I walk, following the tracker to the cafeteria. It doesn't take me long to spot Mina's spiky, platinum-blond hair.

She's sitting alone at a table, drinking something. There's a teapot on the table. No food. I take in the details with a practiced eye. The tables around her are all occupied. A single man with black-rimmed glasses, dark hair, and a mole on his cheek sits in the corner. He's attractive, about fifty I'd say. He's the only other person on his own at a table, which is why he stands out. He's reading a newspaper and eating a pastry. Maybe just waiting for his train. Still, I take nothing for granted. I scan over the mothers with children and elderly people with dogs. I check the exits and escalators. Then I glance at the departure screen. The next train for Prague leaves in forty minutes.

When I've committed every detail to my mind and evaluated every escape option and possible danger, I finally allow myself to feel. The emotions hit my chest like arrows. Worry, angst, and white-hot fury. The more I acknowledge the worry, the darker my anger turns. Sensations I didn't know existed bulldoze over me, the biggest of them the fear of loss. I've never feared like this. Not even for my twin. It makes me vulnerable, makes my hands shake.

It makes me something I've never been.

Fucking weak.

I accept it all. Internalize it. What hits me the hardest is the punch of jealousy in my gut as I round the entrance and get a full frontal view of Mina's face. Her lips are crimson, dark like blood. She's so fucking beautiful, so stupidly brave, and all I can think about is that she's never put on makeup for me. Who did she smear that lipstick on her gorgeous lips for?

Standing here, taking in my captive, I hate her as much as I want her. I want to hurt her, to make her pay for what she did, but I can't really blame her. Who wouldn't run in Mina's shoes? This is all Ilya's fault.

My mind is a mess of muddled thoughts as I slowly make my way over.

She's so lost in herself she doesn't notice me until I'm three steps away. When she finally senses the danger and lifts her gaze, her pale cheeks turn even whiter, her blue eyes flaring for a second before acceptance sets in.

She knew I'd come after her. She knew I'd find her.

Pulling out a chair, I sit down opposite her. "Hello, Mina."

She swallows. "I wasn't running."

I look at the drink still left in her cup. The lipstick left a perfect red imprint of her lips on the rim. "Drink your tea."

"Yan, I—"

"I said, finish your tea."

Holding my gaze, she brings the cup to her lips and downs what's left before placing the cup in the saucer. It clinks softly, a sound of gentle finality, but there's nothing gentle about the way I feel.

I hold out my hand. "Ticket."

She fishes a train ticket from her pocket and hands it to me. I glance at the destination. Prague.

"I was coming back," she says.

"Do not speak unless I tell you to. Do not utter as much as a sound." I'm too volatile, too close to losing my shit. I stand and extend a hand. "Get up."

She obeys without arguing, putting her small hand in mine. I drag her closer. With a palm on her back, I press her against my side. She's so tense her body is like a thin bar of steel, but she doesn't resist.

From over her shoulder, I catch the eyes of the man, the one with the mole. He averts his gaze, ashamed I caught him staring. There's something about him, about his smile, that doesn't feel right. But then he folds his newspaper, gets up, and leaves.

With Mina tucked against my side, I walk us out. I'm a cesspool of conflicting emotions. I'm boiling with rage, yet my relief is so huge it makes me shake in the aftermath of my fear, of eleven long hours of the worst torture of my life.

My steps match my fury. Mina battles to keep up with her shorter legs. She's practically running next to me, but I don't slow down. Tightening my fingers on her hip, I fish my phone from my pocket and call Anton to let him know he can drive back to Prague.

"What about you?" he asks.

"We'll catch the next flight."

I enter the nearest hotel—a two-star, rundown place—and pay cash for a room. The wooden stairs creak under my shoes as I drag Mina up the two flights to a room with a bed, chair, and dresser. Nothing more. The wallpaper is orange and flaking. The walls must be paper thin, but I don't care. I pull her with me to the bed, sit down, and drape her face-down over my lap.

She cranes her neck to look back at me. "What are you doing?"

"Didn't I tell you not to speak?"

"Yan."

Gripping the elastic of her sweatpants, I pull it with her panties over her thighs, exposing her tight ass. Perfectly rounded. The skin is pearly, soft. I stroke my palm over the curves because I need to feel her. I need the confirmation that she's here.

"You ran from me, Mina."

"I didn't—"

"Quiet. I didn't tell you to speak."

She shuts up at my tone.

I caress her globes gently, squeezing the toned flesh. "What did I tell you?"

Now she's quiet. Now that I'm asking her a question.

"I'll remind you." I drag my hand down her thigh and between her legs. "I told you not to test me."

Biting her lip, she just looks at me.

I outline her folds with a finger. She's dry. "You're giving me no choice." I have to make good on my word.

When the first slap falls on the underside of her ass, she starts to struggle. I press a hand on her nape, feeling the small lump where the tracker is buried under her skin, knowing it will never be enough. Nothing can ever be enough.

Smack!

She cries out.

I can't lose her again. I fucking hate the feeling.

Smack!

Her back hollows.

Smack!

Another smothered cry.

I don't hit her hard enough to bruise, only to leave a red imprint of my hand. I cover every inch of that snow-white skin until her ass is as pink as a rose. She's not crying, not that I expected her to. She's a killer. A soldier. She's gone through much worse. But I know it hurts. The heat seeps from her red skin into my palm as I rub her globes slowly. She squirms. The caress is painful on her smarting ass. Still, it's not enough to settle the hell she put me through.

Flipping her around, I stand with her in my arms. I'm not gentle when I dump her on the bed. I don't look at her face as I yank her sweater and T-shirt over her head, and rip off her bra. I don't look into her eyes because I don't want to do it. Not like this. But she left me no choice.

I finish undressing her. My command is curt, humiliating, something aimed at a pet, not an equal. "Stay."

She flinches.

Going through the room, I find nothing that can serve as restraints. The threadbare towels will have to do. I twist the biggest one like a rope, lift her arms above her head, and bind her wrists to the headboard. She watches me as I work. She's quiet, but her eyes glint with her own anger.

I test the knot, then spread her legs. "Don't move."

She continues to watch me silently as I undress and climb between her legs.

"This is how you want it?" I position my cock at her entrance. "Like it was in Colombia?"

Her reply is soft. "No."

"If you run, you tell me otherwise."

I don't get her ready. That's not what this is about. I press the head of my cock at the pink flesh between her legs and part those delicate petals. I'm too thick for her, too angry. Yet her pulse quickens, her breasts heaving with her fast little breaths.

"You want this?" As angry as I am, I'll stop if she tells me to. Forcing is a line I won't cross.

Her nod is cryptic.

I grip her hair. "Say it."

"Yes."

"Why?" I need to know. I don't know what I expect her to say, only that I burn to know why she wants this.

"Does it matter?"

It fucking does. Maybe not to her. To me, nothing has mattered more. "Tell me why."

Her gaze takes on the steel-blue hue of a winter sky. "Just do it."

So be it. I do it. I sink into her greedily, selfishly. Violently. Like she asked. As if she's proving there's nothing loving about this. It's savage. It's unquestionable. It's a truth, the rawest truth I've known. She's too tight, her flesh unrelenting as I draw back and slam home again, going as deep as I can.

Tears fill her eyes, drowning the gray, softening the steel. I grip the towel around her wrists. I don't dare sink my fingers into her hips. I'm not leaving marks on her again. Then I move. Savagely. With truth. I take her over and over, thrusting into her body like I'm chasing unobtainable dreams.

Our hips slam together in a rough, punishing rhythm. I don't take care of her pleasure; I come. Harshly, brutally. I empty myself in her body, filling her up. I leave my mark inside her, and when I'm done, I kiss her. I kiss her hard, smearing the red lipstick over her face. I bite her lip and stroke my tongue over the teeth marks. Then I pull out and let go.

My cum leaks out, staining the ugly orange bedspread. When I get up, she closes her legs. Her cheeks are red, and she can't look at me. She turns her face away.

I wet the remaining towel and clean her up before settling down next to her and pulling the sheet over us without untying her.

Draping an arm over her stomach, I press my lips on the shell of her ear. "You could've had it like in Prague. Just remember, this is how you chose it."

She doesn't speak. She accepts the verdict, and I fall into an unfulfilled, haunted sleep.

I wake up early. The sun isn't up yet, but Mina's eyes are already open. Maybe she never slept. My anger has burned out, and regret tastes like cold, stale ashes. It could've been different. I want it to be different.

"Uncomfortable?" I ask.

She nods.

I kick away the sheet and slide down the mattress. She doesn't ask what I'm doing when I bury my head in the soft flesh between her thighs. I lick her pussy, taste her on my tongue. What wouldn't I give her, if only she asked.

"What were you doing in Budapest?"

She shivers when I trace her clit with my tongue. "You know."

"Tell me."

"I went to see my grandmother."

I suck a little harder. When she gasps, I let go. "Why?"

"I didn't want to make her worry."

"If you'd asked me, I would've taken you."

"Would you?"

She says it like she doesn't believe me, but she does. The truth is there in her eyes, in the quick way she blinks before schooling her features. She's good at masking her emotions, but I'm better. I'm better at reading them.

She's lying. She's hiding something.

"Yes," I say. "I would've liked to meet her."

Her cheeks flash an angry pink. They're like peaches on cream. Stunning. Beautiful. "You're not going near her."

I bite down softly, the warning subtle. I don't want to lose my calm again. "I thought you understood who's giving the orders."

She sucks in a breath. "Please, Yan. I don't want to frighten her. She's fragile."

This, I believe. I open her pussy between my thumbs and take a good, leisurely look. It'll never be enough. I can't grow tired of this, of her.

I lift my eyes to meet her gaze, dragging a thumb over her clit. "I told you it didn't have to be like this, but you left me no choice."

Her voice is tremulous. "Like what?"

I close my lips around her clit and draw circles with my tongue.

Delicious. She's my peaches, my cream.

She lifts her hips and moans, but the caution in her eyes doesn't diminish. "Like what, Yan? Are you going to hurt me?"

"I said I wouldn't."

"Then what? Keep me tied up? Locked up?"

I need her for the Dimitrov job as per her own clever design. Locking her up is no longer an option. We've already set the ball rolling with our meeting in Ostrava.

No, keeping her tied up is not how I'll punish her.

"You'll spank me?" she asks bitingly.

My smile matches her tone. "No, princess. The next time you run, I'll slit Hanna's throat."

She blanches. Her shock is fleeting, though, drowned out by anger. "You son of a bitch."

She tries to kick, but I easily grab her ankles. She tosses in the constraint of the towel, trying to move her hips from side to side to shake me off, but her struggles only spur me on. I push her ankles toward her body, bending her knees, and under her hateful glare, I go back to my feast. I trace her pussy lips with my tongue, wedging them apart to taste her clit. She fights, but I don't stop. She's not fighting the pleasure.

She's fighting the threat on her grandmother's life.

She's fighting the surrender.

I don't let her win. I make her need climb slowly. Taking my time to enjoy her womanly taste and the feel of her soft flesh under my teeth, I draw an orgasm from her that makes her tremble. She shakes with aftershocks, quivers with defeat as I give her what I withheld last night.

When her whole body sags, her teary eyes hazy and her battle lost, I untie the towel and lower her arms. I rub them to aid the blood flow and then carry her to the shower. Lowering her onto the chipped tile floor, I study her body to make sure I haven't left new marks.

The setting is wrong. My pretty little flower—a deadly one, no less—doesn't belong in a cracked cubicle with a moldy shower curtain. I turn on the water and wait for it to run warm before pushing her under the spray. I wash her body and hair with the white bar of hotel soap. I'm gentle, giving her comfort after dealing a heavy blow. She'd rather die than let her grandmother suffer. I know, because we're the same. A great deal of what we do is for the only thing we have.

Family.

And now for me, there's also her. Ilya is no longer all I have.

I turn off the water, towel her dry, and tell her to get ready.

While she dresses, I pull on my clothes, make a flight reservation via my phone, and email Anton the details. Afterward, we have breakfast at a street café, but she hardly touches her coffee or croissant. I use the time we have to wait at the airport to send an encrypted message to our government contact, informing him that I need the surveillance camera footage of the Újbuda Clinic. I don't state a reason. He won't ask questions.

All through this, Mina sits quietly. I keep an eye on her while I catch up with my messages, and the footage I've requested arrives in my inbox as we're boarding the plane. I seat Mina by the window and fasten her seatbelt before seeing to mine. She turns her head away, staring out the window, and I tap on the link and start scrolling through the recording. I go fast, not expecting to see much. I'll go through everything in Prague, or better yet, I'll make Ilya go through it, frame by fucking frame.

Halfway in, I freeze with my thumb on the screen.

My heartbeat picks up. There, in black and white, is my little princess, and she's hugging another man.

Jealousy erupts, hot and fierce. In my mind's eye, I see her red lips and the way I rubbed the lipstick over her face last night.

Enlarging the frame, I zoom in on the man.

He has dark-rimmed glasses and a mole on his cheek.

21

MINA

I feel bruised inside.

It's not the cancer or the thought of never seeing Hanna again. It's last night. The threat on Hanna's life damaged something fragile that had started growing between Yan and me. I didn't even realize a kernel of emotion that goes hand in hand with a deep need for his approval had germinated until I crushed it.

I know what Yan is capable of. I expected him to whip or torture me. Instead, his punishment was crueler. He couldn't have hurt me worse than through Hanna. He's a man who keeps his promises. He won't hesitate to slit the throat of an innocent old woman.

I should hate him. Part of me does. Still, an undeniable part of me mourns what we've lost. I can't put a label on that loss. The concept is vague, indefinable, but it doesn't diminish the warped sense of devastation tormenting me. The notion is too twisted

ANNA ZAIRES & CHARMAINE PAULS

to examine fully, so I focus on trying to get some sleep on the plane and eat the airline food to build my strength. I need it. The job with Dimitrov is important. It's vital to Hanna's well-being. That's what I have to focus on now.

Anton waits at the airport when we land. Not Ilya.

We get into the back of the car while Anton drives. Yan is tense. He doesn't speak but keeps our fingers interlaced, placing my hand on his leg. I'm not fooled into seeing the gesture as a sign of affection. It's just another form of restraint. It's less brutal than a cheap hotel towel, but no less impactful.

The message is clear.

I belong to him.

It doesn't matter now, though. This won't last long. Leukemia goes fast. If I'm lucky, I'll have a few months.

When we get to the apartment, I reach for the door handle, but Yan stops me. His instruction to Anton is brusque. "Take Mina for coffee."

I go cold. "Yan." I grab his arm. "It wasn't Ilya's fault."

He shakes me off, gets out, and slams the door.

"Yan!" I push on the button to open the window, but the car is already pulling away.

Anton glares at me in the rearview mirror.

Crossing my arms, I try to dispel the chill that has invaded my body. "What are you looking at?"

"I hope you're happy."

He means about what's going to happen between

Yan and Ilya. I'm not happy. Far from it. Guilt is eating me, but I don't bother telling him what I feel.

He doesn't care, and he won't believe me, anyway.

We go to a café. Anton orders coffee that I don't drink. After an hour, he gets up and flicks his fingers at me. I follow, feeling like a dog. By the time we arrive at Yan's place, my nerves are shattered.

Anton opens the door and all but shoves me inside. Anxiously, I scan the lounge. Yan is in the kitchen, a glass half-full with clear liquid in his hand. A bottle of vodka is standing on the counter, and his dark hair, normally so neatly styled, is disheveled. The top three buttons of his shirt are undone, the sleeves rolled up to his forearms. The small part of his chest that's exposed is chiseled, and his arms are muscular and veined. His body screams power, strength. The last thing I want is for him to unleash that power, and the anger churning underneath, on his brother. But what did I expect? That Yan would let a weakness go?

A toilet flushes, and someone coughs. The bathroom door opens, and Ilya steps out.

Holy shit.

He's sporting a swollen eye and a cut on his lip, and his nose is askew.

Taking a few uncertain steps toward him, I reach for his face. "My God. Let me see."

"Do not touch him." Yan's voice is harsh.

I drop my hand. "This needs ice." I change direction for the kitchen, but Yan's hostile tone stops me again.

"Leave it, Mina."

I shrink back, giving Ilya a regretful look. "I'm sorry."

Ignoring me, Ilya plops onto the couch and switches on the television.

Anton grins as he walks past me.

I stand there awkwardly, not sure what to do.

Yan takes a big swallow of his drink, his eyes never leaving mine. He tilts his head toward the bedroom. "Go work on Petrova's disguise."

With a last look at Ilya, I escape into the room and sit down on the bed, my mind reeling.

Except for Hanna and Gergo, I hardly feel anything for anyone. It's been tough for me to get attached to people after my parents' deaths. It took Gergo a long time to get close to me, and I don't think it would've happened if he hadn't saved me from being gang-raped by my own teammates. But I feel now, and it's horrible.

I feel awful for what Yan did to Ilya because of me.

The fact that I'm experiencing such strong emotions when it comes to the twins shocks me. I'm capable of switching off the human part of me when I'm on a job. When I pull the trigger, I don't feel remorse. I tell myself it's because most of my targets are criminal filth, like the hijackers who murdered my parents, but deep down, I know it's because a part of my soul died in the snow with my parents. Ever since that day, I've been going through life half-frozen, only partially alive.

Until the big, kind teddy bear, Ilya.

Until Yan.

Pinching my eyes shut, I stop the psychoanalysis. What's the point? What matters is the job, the last one I'll do. I think about Hanna as I get the suitcase from the closet and stand in front of the bathroom mirror to start my transformation. My stomach grumbles with hunger by the time I'm satisfied with the results.

The twins are sitting on the couch, Anton squeezed between them, when I come out of the bedroom. They must've been talking, because the television is off. Anton whistles in appreciation of the results. Ilya doesn't look at me, and Yan's expression is tight, bored almost.

"It'll be better when I have the right clothes," I say.

Yan gets up and goes to the laptop that's lying on the table. "Come here."

I walk to his side as he wakes up the screen and activates the camera to test the background. He turns it so it faces the wall and nothing else is visible.

He pulls out a chair for me to sit. "You know what to say."

"I need to listen and watch her a few times." I'm a quick learner. I can pick up accents and intonations like a parrot.

He opens a video file of Natasha Petrova, news and social media clips he must've collected, and pushes on the play button. I pay attention to her mannerisms, the way she flicks her hair and says "darling" a lot, and especially how she tries to conceal her mother tongue by rolling the r's less when she speaks English.

In what language would she address Casmir

Dimitrov? Would she speak to him in Hungarian or English?

No, she'd use his own language to be respectful. She'd choose Albanian.

"Ready?" Yan asks when the clips come to an end. "We'll do a practice run."

He picks up a Hermès scarf from the table and drapes it over my shoulders, gently almost. He arranges the silk just so before he activates a video call to himself.

I fall into the role, right down to the way the arts dealer flirts by batting her eyelashes and pushing out her breasts. I become Natasha Petrova, body and soul.

When I'm done, I look up at Yan for his reaction. His face is unreadable, but the intent way he stares at me is disturbing.

"Fuck," Anton says. "She nailed it. She fucking nailed it to a T."

Even Ilya lifts his unwilling gaze to me.

"I think she's ready," Anton says.

"I don't think it." Yan perches on the corner of the table. "I know it."

"It's too soon," Ilya says in a nasally voice.

"We have three weeks," Yan says. "Dimitrov is a busy man. Petrova wouldn't give him less time to arrange a meeting and clear his schedule if needed."

"Can you do it again?" Anton asks me. "Exactly like that?"

"Yes." I'm certain.

Anton rubs his palms over his thighs. "I say let's seize the moment."

Yan opens a contact list and clicks on Dimitrov's name. "You'll go through a gatekeeper, a secretary or a guard. If you tell them what the call is about, Dimitrov will take it."

The call connects. I take a deep breath, and the show is on.

As predicted, the moment I mention the Salvator Mundi, Dimitrov takes my call. He sits behind a desk—in his office, I presume. Even with the new beard, he's as handsome as in the media photos. He's wearing a white shirt and black waistcoat, and he's in good shape for fifty-six. A woman, maybe his secretary, puts a glass of water on the desk. He waves a hand to dismiss her. When a click sounds as the door closes, he turns his full attention to me.

He's charming, complimenting me—or rather, Natasha—on my appearance and elegance. He says he likes a well-dressed woman who takes care of herself. We talk about the weather and the current shortage of Russian caviar. I say I know he's a busy man so I'll get to the point. When I mention the painting, the change in the atmosphere is palpable.

"Are you sure your line is secure?" he asks, leaning closer to the screen.

"Of course." I'm full of sugar, full of tease. "You can test it."

"How much?"

Yan shows me a number with his fingers. "Two

hundred million."

"Dollars, I assume."

"You assume correctly, darling."

"Miss Petrova, your talents dazzle me. Not only are you beautiful and clever, but also resourceful."

"Thank you," I reply coyly.

"Maybe we should put some of those talents to the test when we meet in person."

I give a coquettish laugh. "I'm sorry, darling, but it'll take more than that."

"Flowers, champagne, an expensive dinner, and extortionately priced jewelry?"

"Throw in a diamond ring, and I may consider."

Yan gives me a hard look.

"You make me regret that I'm married," Dimitrov says with a wink. "I like a woman who knows what she's worth. I could make a different kind of proposition."

"It seems we'll have a lot to talk about when we meet."

"I can't wait."

I tell him I'll be in Prague in three weeks' time and suggest the Klimt suite at the Hotel Paris, claiming the manager is a personal friend who'll respect our need for privacy. We agree on a meeting just before lunch. I hint at extending our business affair into dinner. He likes it when I say we may need the suite afterward.

"How do I contact you if needed?" he asks.

Yan gestures with a pinky on his lips and a thumb at his ear.

"I'll text you a secure number."

We talk about our mutual requirements. No weapons, and only him, his art expert, and me in the room. He states his demands, namely to have the room and me searched before he enters. He recommends a few restaurants to visit while I'm in Prague, and invites me to one of his casinos. Everything on the house. I wish him good luck with his business, and we say goodbye like old friends.

My sultry smile only drops when he cuts the call, no doubt to launch straight into an investigation to find out everything he can about Petrova and the missing painting.

"Good job," Anton says. "He bought it."

Yan straightens. His gaze is dark and his mouth set in a hard line. Unbuttoning his shirt, he says on his way to the bedroom, "I'm going to take a shower."

Anton pats Ilya's knee. "I think I'll go for a run. I've been sitting in a car for the past two days."

He gets up and disappears into their bedroom. Ilya grabs the remote and switches on the television. I give it a moment before I slip into Yan's room to take off the wig and scarf. The false eyelashes will have to stay until Yan has finished his shower and I can use the oil-based dissolvent I stored in the cabinet. I also applied silicon gel under a thick layer of foundation to make my cheekbones appear higher, and a cream that contains a small dose of bee venom to puff out my lips. They sting a little, feeling unnaturally tight, but the effect will soon vanish.

Going through the fridge, I take out ingredients for chicken *paprikash* and start dinner. For once, I'm hungry.

The silence is uncomfortable. When Anton leaves, I dare to approach Ilya, stopping short of the couch.

"Ilya, I owe you an apology."

He ignores me.

"I didn't want to deceive you, but there was no other way. I had to see my grandmother."

He keeps his eyes trained on the television, pretending to be watching the news. "Spare me the excuses. I don't care."

I step between him and the TV. "I didn't lie about coming back. I swear. I was waiting for the train when Yan found me."

He cranes his neck to look around me. "If you say so."

"Let me have a look at your nose. Did you try to set it straight?"

Silence.

"Ilya, please."

He clicks off the television, stands, and goes to the bedroom, shutting the door behind him.

I can only hope he'll come around in time. With a sigh, I go back to preparing dinner. It's weird, this see-saw of energy and appetite. It was the same before, the first time I was diagnosed. The chemo lasted for twelve months. I lost all the hair on my body, including my eyebrows and eyelashes. My hair had barely grown back by the night I overheard Yan and Ilya in the bar.

When they intercepted me in the alley, I had still been so weak. The nausea, the vomiting, it had utterly depleted me. There were days I didn't have enough energy to get out of bed.

Making the most of my spurt of strength, I clean the kitchen and set the table. Dinner is almost ready when Yan comes out of the bedroom freshly showered and dressed in slacks and a tailored shirt.

He looks neat. Classy, like always. I've never seen him in comfy clothes.

"Do you always dress like that?" I ask.

He stalks toward me, caging me against the counter with his arms. "Why? Do you have a problem with it?"

He smells so good. I can't get enough of that clean sandalwood scent with the spicy pepper undertone. "Don't you ever want to relax, just lie around in sweatpants and a T-shirt?"

"No."

"I see."

He drags a thumb over my lip, no doubt smearing my lipstick. "Go wash your face." He almost sounds angry.

"What's wrong?"

"I don't like you as someone else."

I don't know what to say to that. I slip around him and hurry to the room.

"Mina."

I turn in the door.

His frosted gaze is piercing. "You'd tell me if you went to Budapest for a different reason, wouldn't you?"

The air leaves my lungs, my chest deflating. "You know why I went." It takes great effort to keep a poker face with him. With other people, it's second nature, but Yan can cut me open with a single look.

He studies me, missing nothing. "Just checking."

"Was there anything else?"

"No. Go."

Beyond grateful, I close the door on his invasive stare and take a few deep breaths. He doesn't know. It's only his suspicion. He can't know.

Still, my hunger vanishes. Suddenly feeling depleted, I get rid of the disguise, clean everything, and put it back in the case. After washing my face, I go back to the lounge where a brooding Yan and Ilya sit on opposite sides of the table.

Yan pulls out the chair next to him. "Sit."

I walk over and sit down as I'm ordered. Yan gets up and brings the pots from the stove to the table. Ignoring Ilya, he dishes up some for me before helping himself. When Yan digs into his food, Ilya grabs the serving spoon with a grunt. His gaze rests accusingly on his brother as he dumps a portion of rice and chicken on his plate.

Our meal takes place in strained silence. I'm pushing the food around on my plate, managing only a few bites.

"Not hungry?" Yan asks, glancing at my untouched food.

I shift in my seat. "No."

Ilya huffs. "She must've lost her appetite when she

came out of the room and saw you."

Yan turns a steely gaze on Ilya. "Did I ask for your opinion?"

Leaning back, Ilya stretches out his legs. "You're getting it anyway."

"If you know what's good for you," Yan says through tight lips, "you'll put a cork in it."

"If you grow tired of his pretty face, you know where my room is," Ilya says to me.

The crockery rattles as Yan slams a fist on the table. "I'm warning you."

"Please, Ilya." I lean over and touch his arm. "Cut it out."

"You"—Yan's tone is clipped as he glares at me —"don't get to say anything."

Ilya grins. "Touché." He turns to me. "The truth is, I have a bigger dick."

A glass of water falls over as Yan jumps to his feet.

Ilya is up, too. He rounds the table, putting himself in Yan's way. "I took your beating because I deserved it. This time, I won't let you win."

"Yan! Ilya!" I push back my chair, almost stumbling in my rush to stand. "Stop it."

Yan grabs the front of Ilya's T-shirt in a fist. "Go for it, moron. Give it your best shot."

Squeezing myself between the two men, I push on their chests. "Break it up. Focus. We have a fucking job to do."

They still at that, and Yan lets Ilya go with a shove.

I'm responsible for this rift, and I feel awful,

especially after what Ilya confided in me. "I'm sorry, Ilya. Really, I am."

Even so, this fight isn't about me. Not really. It's about Yan's rejection of his brother when he punished him for being nice to me, for trusting me. Ilya is just taking his frustration and the fact that Yan hurt his feelings out in the wrong way—the only way he knows, with his fists.

"Stop fucking apologizing to him," Yan says.

"It doesn't matter," Ilya replies in a bitter tone. "What's done is done." He turns away from me, rejecting me in his own way, and walks to his room. The door slams behind him.

With shaking hands, I pick up the glass and wipe up the water with the napkins. Yan fetches paper towels from the kitchen and dries the spillage on the floor. We're salvaging what's left of the meal when Anton returns.

He watches us with his hands on his hips. "What happened?"

Yan only glances at the closed bedroom door.

Anton's look is accusing as it settles on me.

"Go have a shower," Yan tells me.

"The dishes—"

"Mina." The way he says my name sends chills down my spine. "You're pushing me too far."

Dropping the dirty cutlery I was gathering, I go to the room, bristling. I'm tired of this. Who does he think he is to treat me like this?

I may be his prisoner, but I'm no one's puppet.

I'M READY FOR HIM WHEN HE WALKS INTO THE ROOM. Eyeing me where I stand next to the bed, my arms crossed and every muscle in my body tight, he closes the door with a soft click.

My annoyance boils over. "Is this how it's supposed to work?" Walking up to him, I poke his chest with a finger. "You order me around and tell me what to do?"

He appears amused, his sour mood all but vanishing. "Actually, yes."

"No."

He raises a brow. "Excuse me?"

"It must be difficult for you to understand the word. Don't worry. I get it." I infuse my tone with mock sympathy. "I suppose not many women tell you no."

The corner of his mouth lifts. "Not many, no."

"If you're going to keep me prisoner and I'm to live in your space, we need to lay down some rules." I jab him in the chest to emphasize the part about the rules.

He grabs my finger and moves it away. "Rules, huh?"

"Are you listening?"

"You're cute when you're trying to be bossy."

"I'm serious, Yan. If we're to survive under one roof without killing each other, we both need to compromise."

Holding my hand, he walks me backward. "Are you proposing a relationship? Because that's what it sounds like."

251

"I'm proposing getting along." My back hits the wall. "Or do you prefer we fight all the time?"

He cages me between his arms. "I'm curious. What would such compromises entail?"

"You and Ilya, I'm sick of your fighting."

"You don't have a say, remember?"

"I'm my own person. You can't tell me what to do."

He bends his head down to mine. "Is that so?"

"You might've taken over my life, but you have to give me a small measure of freedom in the mundane decisions."

His voice is low, seductive. "Such as?"

"Such as when to have a shower."

"This is about a shower," he says with disbelief.

"This is about…" Making the most of whatever time I have left. But I don't say it. I can't. Instead, I stare up at him silently, defiant.

"You asked me if I'm listening." He rolls his hips forward, pressing his erection against my stomach. "Now that I am, you don't know what you want to say?"

I flatten myself against the wall, but the spark is already there, my senses waking to the dark magic of his touch. "Just don't treat me like an animal, like I have no say over my body. I'm a grown woman. I think I know when I need to shower or eat. When you order me around like that, it's humiliating."

"An animal. Humiliating." He nuzzles my neck. "You believe you have any power to negotiate?" His breath is warm on my ear. "You think you can say no to me?"

"Yes." My tone is firm despite the pleasurable chills rippling down my arm. "Give me this, and I'll give you what you want."

He pushes his hand under the elastic of my sweatpants and underwear, resting his fingers on my sex. "What is it you believe I want?"

My breath catches when he parts my folds with a finger. I try not to show him what he does to me, but it's hard to keep my voice even. "To get on. To live in peace."

He watches my eyes as he curls the digit, dipping it inside. I grab his wrist to push his hand away, but he's stronger. He doesn't let me. Instead, he pushes the length of his finger inside. My body clenches around him, my arousal spiking. I'm breathing too fast, feeling too much.

"No, princess. You're wrong," he says, studying my face as he starts moving his finger. "I want everything."

The starkness of the confession makes my knees weak. What was I thinking? I should've known with Yan there could never be give and take.

The pleasure climbs as he pushes the pad of his thumb on my clit, massaging in circles. The sensations hit me hard and fast. Instead of trying to push him away, I'm clinging to him.

"Are you really going to say no to me, Minochka?" he asks gently, his gem-green eyes already bright with his victory.

We both know it's a foregone conclusion. I'm so close.

He brushes his lips over mine. The kiss is feather soft, deceivingly caring. "Answer me."

I want this. I want him. Despite everything, I, too, want it all. And maybe in a different life, I could've had it. If I hadn't taken the Henderson job when Gergo recommended me. If my body wasn't as messed up as it is. But this is how it is now, and nothing can be done about it.

"Tell me," he insists, deepening the kiss.

"Yes," I say into his mouth. The word is a sigh. It's surrender. In the bigger scheme of things, time is too short. "Yes."

He picks me up and carries me to the bed. Laying me down gently, he kisses me until I feel dizzy, then undresses me slowly, caressing every part of my body as he does. His gaze is reverent as he watches the path of his hands where they slide over my breasts and down to my stomach, his fingers tracing my belly ring. I want to feel him against me. I need the warmth of his skin. I yank up his shirt, not bothering with the buttons. He lifts his arms to aid me, gets tangled in the sleeves, and finishes the task himself. His shoes, socks, and pants follow.

When he stretches out over me naked, he's tender. He frames my face and kisses my lips softly as he enters me. He pours care into the way he holds me, setting a lazy pace. He makes me come before he does, and even after, he kisses me still. Like Ilya said, he gives me what he can't outside of bed.

He gives me compromise and affection.

22

YAN

*M*ina is sleeping soundly in my arms, her small shape fitting against the curve of my body as though she was made for me. Still, even after the tender lovemaking we just shared, I can't help feeling agitated. The image of the man Mina embraced is burning a hole in my brain. They must've made their way to the station together before splitting up. He didn't look at us because he was gawking at a couple hugging in public. He looked at *me*. He was sizing me up like a rival. The bad feeling I had about him was right.

Are they lovers? Is that why Mina went to the clinic? To see her boyfriend?

The thought of a boyfriend I might've overlooked is like an iron peg hammered into my chest. The image of them together has been driving me insane since I saw it on the video feed. Even while I was making love to

Mina, I saw it in my mind. Thought about it. Obsessed over it.

There's only one thing to do.

Find him.

Deal with him.

Mina is mine. I don't give a fuck about their history. This is the present. This is how it is now. This is how it will be forever. If my bossy little woman lied to me about their rendezvous, it's to protect him.

Too late. He sealed his fate the moment he touched what belongs to me.

Despite my anger, I smile when I think about earlier. I like that she keeps me on my toes. She's right to put me in my place. I need it. Of course, I'm not going to let her know that. I'll just enjoy it quietly, like I'm enjoying her relaxed body in her unconscious state. She's much more pliant like this. With her in my arms, I can forget about the circumstances that landed her here.

I can forget I'm making her stay by holding a figurative gun to her head.

Careful not to wake her, I get up and make sure she's covered. I close the bedroom door and walk into the dark lounge. The apartment is quiet. It's just after three in the morning. I don't switch on the lights. In the kitchen, I use the light from the freezer to pour a shot of vodka into a chilled glass and sit down at the table to boot up my laptop. I've watched it twenty times, but I play the security feed from the clinic again.

The black-and-white image comes to life, the

resolution startlingly clear. The clinic must use high-quality equipment.

Mina enters the building. The feed skips to where she's walking down a hallway and up a flight of stairs. She enters a room, which I've confirmed is her grandmother's. After a while, she goes to an office downstairs. There are no cameras in the rooms or offices. The video jumps to her leaving the office and walking outside. The gardens aren't under surveillance either. She disappears in a blind spot and remains out of view for ten minutes.

The next part is where my heartbeat spikes and fury claws inside my ribcage. A man is with her when she walks back to the entrance. He says something that makes her smile. That smile, it's sad. That's what hurts the worst. She didn't want to say goodbye. She has feelings for him, feelings she doesn't have for me. He hugs her, the motherfucker, and then she goes back inside while he gets into a vehicle in the parking lot.

I freeze the frame and enlarge the license plate, something I've been meaning to do after dealing with my idiot brother and showing Mina to whom she belongs.

I don't watch the rest again. The rest doesn't matter. Mina exited alone but must've met her friend in the street to travel to the station together. I've ordered the station camera feed as well. The recording only shows him entering the cafeteria a few minutes after Mina, taking a table behind her. Maybe they were planning on taking the same train to win more time together.

Maybe I ruined their plan when I showed up. Whatever the case, their plans—past or future—will soon be of no consequence.

Mina's companion signed in at the clinic gates as Izsak Varga fifteen minutes before she arrived. The search for Izsak Varga was fruitless, as Mr. Varga doesn't exist.

After signing in, he headed straight for the gardens, which tells me they had agreed on the place and time of their meeting. Somehow, Mina must've communicated with him. Perhaps via a burner phone. She could've easily bought one and chucked it once she was done. Tracing the call is near impossible. I won't find his number via that route. My best bet is the license plate.

Ignoring the late hour, I type a message to our hackers, asking them to run a search on the vehicle license plate. They never sleep anyway. Two minutes later, a reply comes in. As I expected, the car was a rental. Varga rented it under the same false name.

I'm at a dead end. Not knowing where to go from here, I open Mina's personal file. Somewhere in the vague mass of information that makes up her past must be a clue about Varga's true identity. Thread by thread, I'll pull apart her history until I find him.

An hour later, I'm still none the wiser. I instruct our hackers to dig deeper into Mina's background, especially the years she was in the Special Forces and after—the time Mina turned into a woman old enough to harbor sexual interest in a man.

Rubbing my temples, I fight the first faint pulses of

a headache. I won't be able to go back to sleep. Instead, I quietly grab my running gear from the bedroom, get dressed in the lounge, and hit the streets. I run until sweat pours down my body and endorphins from overexertion expel the headache. My muscles are cramping by the time I get back, but it feels good. I needed the physical outlet for my frustration.

Mina wakes up when I enter the bedroom at sunrise.

Sitting up, she rubs her eyes. "Yan?"

I use the hem of my T-shirt to wipe the sweat from my face. "I'm here."

"Where were you?"

"Out for a run."

The sheet slips to her waist, exposing her breasts. They're pale and round, too full for such a slight body.

I should have a shower. My feet should carry me to the bathroom, not to the edge of the bed.

All traces of sleep vanish from Mina's face as she stares up at me with guarded blue eyes.

Reaching out slowly, I weigh one of those perfect tits in my palm. The tip is candy-sugar nude, a beautifully light shade. I roll her nipple between a forefinger and thumb until it grows hard and her pink areola contracts. I pull gently until it extends, popping out like a bitable cherry. Mina regards me with slightly parted lips and a peachy blush on her cheeks. I like her like this, all flushed and ready to be sucked.

Unable to resist, I lower my mouth to her breast. When she doesn't object, I plump the curve between my fingers and taste that little cherry on my tongue. She gasps as I lick her. I like that, too. I like to hear what I do to her. I suck deeper and swirl my tongue.

Threading her fingers through my hair, she moans. "Yan."

Yes. That's exactly what I want to hear. I want my name on her lips when she comes.

I release her breast, moving my lips to her flat stomach while I drag the sheet away. Catching the gold belly ring between my teeth, I tug gently.

"Yan." She clutches my shoulders. "I haven't brushed my teeth."

"Don't worry. It's not your mouth I'm going to kiss." Gripping her thighs, I yank her to the edge of the bed.

She shrieks. Belatedly, she clamps a hand over her mouth.

I kneel between her legs. "They can't hear." The room is practically soundproof. "And if they do, I don't give a fuck."

I spread her wide and go straight for my prize. I don't ask if she wants this. At this stage, the question is rhetorical. She moans as I alternate between sucking and nipping. Her arousal coats my chin, her wetness saying everything I want to know. I dip my tongue inside her warm pussy and nearly come in my pants when her inner muscles clench around the tip.

I need to make her come. Fast.

Licking her clit, I slide a finger inside. She arches her back. The action lifts her hips and gives me better access. The sounds she makes are sexy as hell, stoking the fire inside me to an unbearable inferno. Just like that, I lose control. I eat her like a maniac. The rhythm of my hand isn't gentle. She grabs a fistful of the sheet and comes. I don't wait for the aftershocks to settle. I'm too far gone. Flipping her around, I pull her up onto all fours.

"Don't move," I growl, watching her pussy contract around nothing as I strip quickly.

She's stunning like this, wide open and poised for my viewing. I position my cock at her entrance and grab hold of her hips. She pushes backward, giving me compliance. The head of my cock stretches her as I slide in slowly. As always, she struggles to accommodate my size, but as soon as the head is sheathed, her muscles adapt. Her flesh turns softer, enticing me to push deeper. I do so inch by inch, watching the progress as I sink into her body, not stopping until I'm buried all the way inside.

Fuck. She's tight. Warm. Made just for me.

I start to move, telling myself to take it easy, but my lust is dark, fueled by jealousy and a bitter need to prove my possession. The faster I go, the more it feels like it's not enough. I'm fucking her hard, too hard, but I can't stop. Her arms give out. She catches her weight on her elbows, her body rocking with my rough rhythm. She takes my brutal thrusts with her cheek pressed on the mattress and her lip caught between her teeth. Her brows are pinched together, her moans loud.

For her sake, I try to get it over with quickly. I go faster. Her knees buckle. She collapses onto her stomach. I climb onto the bed and over her, chasing after her without breaking the pace of my thrusting. Her closed legs add more friction, preventing me from driving to the hilt. With an arm around her waist, I lift her lower body and spread her knees with a thigh. I don't know what comes over me. I only know how enticing her dark entrance looks as the rosebud teases me. I have no idea if she's done this before, but it's as if a demon took hold of my body.

"Stay," I grit out, testing her weight to make sure she'll stay on her knees before I let go.

Gripping her tight globes, I pull them apart. There's no time for better lubrication than my saliva. I spit generously, yank my cock from her pussy, and press the head against the hole I'm about to claim.

"Yan."

She reaches around, trying to grab my wrist, but her movement stills when I plunge forward. The tight ring of muscle gives with a soundless pop, her body yielding under the merciless pressure. She cries out, a frightened sound.

I freeze.

Fuck. What am I doing? She's so tight her ass must be virgin.

"It's all right." My voice is hoarse with the dark need burning inside me, but my touch is gentle as I smooth a palm over her spine. "I'm not going to do anything you don't want."

She relaxes slightly at the promise, and I swear at myself again.

This is no way to initiate anal sex. She needs a warning in advance, lots of preparation. I start to pull out, but she grabs my arm.

"No," she says softly. "I want this."

I clench my jaw, fighting the urge to thrust in, hard. "We should wait."

"I'm done waiting. Life's too short."

Her words jar me. There's something melancholic about them. I want to ask what she means, but she's pushing back, straining against me, and my cock slips an inch deeper.

Goddamn. She's killing me. "Mina." I lock my hands around her waist. "Slow down. I don't want to tear you."

She doesn't listen. She rolls her hips, nearly driving me insane. I fight hard for control, ignoring the violent need boiling inside me. It takes everything I have and more to stretch her slowly with short, gentle thrusts. Every time her tight inner muscles adapt to the intrusion, I give a little more, shoving a bit deeper. The squeeze around my cock is almost unbearable. I grit my teeth as I make slow progress, fighting the urge to come each second I'm inside her.

Tearing my gaze away from where our bodies are connected, I look at Mina's face. Her cheeks are red and her eyes hazy. A droplet of perspiration runs down her temple and drips on the sheet. I drag a hand over her flank up to her breast, caressing her nipple with one hand while slipping the other between her legs. Her ass dilates faster when I play with her clit. By the time I'm buried up to my balls, we're both on the verge of coming. All it takes are a few long strokes and two swipes over her clit. She cries out my name as her ass clenches on my cock and her pussy around the finger I ruthlessly shove inside. Every muscle in her small frame draws tight.

Her orgasm triggers mine. I come the hardest I have in my life, filling her up with hot spurts of cum that don't stop for several seconds. She collapses under me again, and I go down with her, covering her body with mine but making sure to keep my weight on my elbows. Nuzzling her neck, I plant soft kisses on her shoulder and down her spine. I stay inside her as long as she allows me. It's only when she moans that I gently pull out.

Kneeling between her spread legs, I look at my work. It's devastation and reverence all in one, an explosive mix of dark lust and beautiful passion. It may be wrong, unconventional, but that's how it is between us. However twisted, this is who we are when we become one, and I'm already greedy for more. Forever with her won't be enough. And it's not a new notion. With every stolen glimpse and granted touch, the feeling is getting stronger.

Her body is so damn small. My fingers overlap when I circle her waist. Placing a palm between her shoulder blades, I feel her chest expand with breaths, and I soak in the reassurance of her heartbeat. It's a wild rhythm. Even if I tried to take it easy, the sex must've been hard on her tiny frame. I check for blood or signs of bruising and sag in relief when I find none.

Rolling her onto her back, I kiss her gently. I cup her face and caress her like a man who lays himself at a woman's feet. I want to give her this for the gift she's given me. It's inadequate, but it's all I have that truly matters. It's more than money and gifts, but nothing as prosaic as love.

Ours is not a sweet romance. It's larger than love. Darker than love. And it's hers. All hers.

After a long while of kissing, I pull back to look at her face. She's a little pale, but she's smiling.

"I thought you weren't going to kiss my mouth," she says, stretching her arms above her head.

"I lied."

She pouts. "That's not nice."

Her playfulness is enticing, but I'm not biting yet. "How are you feeling?"

"Fine."

"Did I hurt you?"

"A little."

I like her honesty. I much prefer it to her lies. "Does it hurt still?"

"It burns a little."

Getting up, I lift her into my arms and carry her to the bathroom. We shower together. It's tender. It's nice. Just like that, we're back to the way we were, as if Budapest never happened. A gnawing tenseness darkens my mood when I think of the man she met, but I push it aside. I don't want to spoil the moment.

While I pull on my clothes, I watch her dress from under my eyelashes. I drink her in until I feel drunk on the novelty of having her back here, in my space. This is where she'll fucking stay. I don't care if she wants him. I'll give her more, and in time, she'll forget about him.

I'll make it so good for her she won't even remember his face.

ANTON AND ILYA ARE IN THE LOUNGE WHEN WE GO TO the kitchen for breakfast. Our brief exchange is strained, but I don't linger long enough for their sulking faces to sour my spirits. I tell them to clean the apartment—an instruction that elicits much protest—and take Mina clothes shopping for her meeting with Dimitrov.

We drive to an exclusive boutique chain store Petrova frequents. While Mina is browsing the dresses for something in Petrova's style—a task she's better equipped for than I am—I take a seat on the sofa in the waiting area and check the messages on my phone.

There's a new one from our hackers.

Keeping one eye on Mina, I read the message. When I get to the second paragraph, I sit up straighter. My stomach churns, my blood boiling. I read the sentence again. And again.

"Yan?"

Mina's soft voice breaks through the cloud of fury

that threatens to smother me. I look up to see her standing in front of me, a white dress dangling from her fingers and a frown on her face.

"Is everything all right?" she asks warily.

No. Nothing is all right. I want to go on a murdering rampage. In fact, that's exactly what I'll do. "Did you say something?"

"I asked what you think about the dress."

With difficulty, I turn my attention to the garment in her hand. It's sleeveless and short, definitely something Petrova would wear. "Seems fitting for the occasion."

She throws a thumb toward the fitting rooms. "I'm going to try it on."

"Do that, and come show me."

With a roll of her eyes, she walks off. I watch her enter the changing area. I see how dainty and beautiful she is, how fucking perfect, and everything is tainted with red and nothing is all right. I feel like vomiting. I turn back to the text on my phone, to the reason why Mina left the Special Forces, but all I can see is her small body and the ten soldiers who tried to violate it.

All I can see is the photo of my beautiful, perfect Mina, and how broken they left her.

23

MINA

*T*he door of the changing room opens as I'm pulling up the zipper of the dress. *For crying out loud.* Did Yan seriously pick the lock? I get that he doesn't trust me, but where will I go in a cubicle with no windows? I'm in a dead-end changing area. I'm not Houdini, for God's sake.

"You don't have to check up on me in here." I turn with a scowl and freeze.

The man shutting the door behind him and turning the lock isn't Yan. He's blond with brown eyes and about sixty years old. I can easily take him out, which is why I don't. I don't feel threatened, but I'm vigilant.

I point at the door. "Get out."

He puts a finger on his lips and motions for me to be quiet. I may not recognize his face, but I don't miss the smile or the distinct way he carries himself with blatant fearlessness, a trait many mistake for arrogance or vanity.

My heart starts galloping so fiercely I can hear the blood pumping in my ears. "Gergo?"

He smiles.

Fuck, he's good. No wonder they call him The Chameleon. My shock turns into fear. Is he crazy? Yan is sitting a short distance away. He can walk in on us at any minute.

I grab Gergo's arm and whisper urgently, "You have to get out of here."

"No one saw me come in."

"It's not safe."

"I can take care of myself."

"I'm not alone," I grit out.

"I know." He tilts his head toward the door. "Yan Ivanov is babysitting you."

In the mirrors surrounding us, my eyes grow large. "How do you know? How did you find me?" *Please tell me you didn't follow me.*

"I followed you."

Shit. "Why?"

"I'm worried about you. Back in Budapest, you weren't yourself. I wanted to make sure you were all right, and just as well I did."

"Gergo, I'm serious. You have to go. If he finds you here—"

"He looked absorbed in whatever he was doing on his phone. He's not going to come looking for you. We have a few minutes."

"What if he'd seen you coming in here? I can't believe you'd take such a risk."

"I pushed a rail of clothes in front of the entrance to the changing area."

Going on tiptoes, I peer over the door. A rail of clothes shoppers had tried on but not taken does indeed block the view. I look back at my ex-teammate. The judgment on his face makes me cringe. "It's not what you think."

"You're living at his place. He brought you clothes shopping. What must I think?"

"I'm doing a job for him."

"A job? You're working for the Russians now?"

"Kind of."

"They were going to kill you. You said you escaped. What are you hiding?"

"Nothing."

"Fine." He pulls a gun from his waistband. "In that case, I'll just take him out now. He won't even see it coming."

At the sight of the weapon, my heart slams into my ribs. The idea of anything happening to Yan makes my palms sweat and my temples throb with my quickening pulse. I don't stop to analyze these symptoms. If anything, I should encourage Gergo to carry out his threat. Instead, I grab his arm again and whisper-shout, "No."

He stills, but he doesn't put the gun away. "Is he blackmailing you?"

I rub my neck, my fingers playing over the small bump in my nape. "It's complicated. I don't want to get you involved."

"I'm already involved." He lowers his head to put us on eye level. "Talk to me, Mink. I want to help you."

"Gergo, please. I beg you. Just go."

"I'm not going anywhere until you talk to me."

I'm getting increasingly nervous. If Yan decides to check on me, one of them will definitely end up dead. "I can't. Please, Gergo. I just can't."

Hurt spills into his eyes. "Don't you trust me?"

"What? No! You know I do."

"Then what's the issue, sweetheart? Why won't you let me help you?"

Groaning, I spear my fingers through my hair. "You have to go. Now! He'll come looking for me. I've taken too long already."

He tucks the gun back into his belt and grips my shoulders. "Go out, parade for him, then come back in here and tell me what the hell is going on."

"I can handle myself." My harsh tone is meant to chase him away. "I don't need you to save me."

Gergo isn't deterred. He turns me to the door, unlocks it, and all but pushes me out.

It takes a moment to find my bearings and put my mask in place, but I was worried for nothing. When I get back to the waiting area where wealthy men sip vodka on the house while their women spend their money, Yan is still reading something on his phone, his attention definitely elsewhere.

I clear my throat, and he lifts his head. The look in his eyes makes me shiver. It's hateful and cold, nothing like the heat he shows me in bed. It's a view into the part of him that grew up in the streets, committing acts to survive nobody should ever have to. But as he drags his gaze over me, the cold-hearted, cruel gleam disappears, the dangerous, soulless man I glimpsed replaced with my calculated assassin and skilled lover.

The calculated part approves of my look. It says I'll pull off the part of Natasha Petrova. The lover who claims he owns me doesn't like how much skin I'm flaunting. He frowns as he focuses on the low neckline and short hem.

"It's two sizes too big." God, I hope I sound normal. "It'll fit tighter with the body pads."

With his ankle resting on his knee and his thumb playing over his lips, Yan studies me quietly. The seconds tick on. What is going on in his mind? Why is he acting like this? Did whatever it was that distracted him earlier upset him? Maybe it's work. Or has he spotted Gergo? I'm holding my breath, praying the morning won't go down in bloodshed while clinging desperately to my poker face, but as always, he sees right through me.

Even as he speaks with a soft voice, his eyes are like hard, polished jade stone. "What's wrong?"

I laugh with forced casualness. "Nothing."

"Don't fucking lie to me."

"I'm not."

He stands so abruptly I give a start.

In two strides, he's in front of me. Gripping my hip, he brushes his thumb over my hipbone. The caress is gentle but intense. Possessive.

"I asked you a question, Mina."

It's impossible to hide my fear from him. He sees everything he wants to see. He sees the truth. Giving in to the apprehension, I sag in his hold. "You're acting weird."

He considers my answer for a moment, his gaze drilling into mine. "Do I scare you?"

"Sometimes," I whisper.

He nods, his expression softening. "I'm not going to hurt you, not unless you give me a reason."

"A reason?" I swallow. "What would be a reason?"

"Running from me again."

"I'm not going to run again."

"I know it's unpleasant for you, so I won't remind you of the consequences of running."

He's right. I can't bear to think of Hanna getting hurt because of me.

Suddenly, his face goes blank. It's as if a switch flips. Putting a step between us, he drops his hand. "Go change."

I nearly trip in my hurry to get away. Before skirting the rail that still blocks the passage, I glance back, but he's already sitting again, his head bent over his phone.

I slip into the cubicle to find Gergo poised on the bench, his knees pulled up so anyone walking past wouldn't spot his shoes from under the door.

He pulls me deeper inside and turns the lock. "Talk."

Another argument will only waste time. He won't let it go. I hesitate, but then make up my mind. I trust

Gergo with my life. Taking a deep breath, I say, "For some reason, Yan has taken an interest in me."

He turns me around to help with the zipper. His tone is clipped, his voice angry. "He's keeping you against your will."

I glance at him from over my shoulder. "He planted a tracker in my neck."

His gaze flits to my nape. "That son of a bitch. I can cut it out. I'll get you out of the country."

"I would've done it myself if I didn't need this job with him."

"Why do you need it so badly?"

"I need the money for Hanna. Her care is expensive." I wiggle out of the dress and pull on my jeans and T-shirt. Gergo and I are used to being around each other in our underwear. It comes with the job. We often completed missions in cramped spaces.

"I can get you another job or give you a loan."

There won't be enough time. It's running out too fast. "What's the difference? A job is a job."

"When is this job supposed to be done?"

"In three weeks."

"Three weeks? Yan Ivanov is a dangerous man. I don't trust him with your life for a day, never mind three weeks."

"I know what I'm doing," I say, tying my sneakers.

"Goddamn, Mink. Do you know how risky this is?"

"Yes."

"Are you willing to put your life on the line?"

I don't tell him it's already over for me. If he knew

the cancer is back, he'd never let me walk away. I pick up the dress. "I've got to go."

"I'll get you out after your three weeks are up."

I smile at that. "You'd do that for me?"

"I'll organize a private plane. You can assume a new identity and fly to Tahiti. They'll never find you."

"I'm sorry." I squeeze his hand. "I can't do that."

He narrows his eyes. "What is he holding over your head?"

"Hanna."

"That piece of shit. You should let me take him out now and get it over with."

"No," I say quickly. "There are others on his team. They'll make good on his word if he's dead."

Scrutinizing me, Gergo says slowly, "You don't want him to die, do you?"

I avert my eyes.

"Fuck, Mink. Do you have feelings for him?"

I want to deny it, but the lie sticks in my throat. "What I feel doesn't matter. What matters is Hanna and therefore this job."

"And after?"

"I'll take it one day at a time."

"You do understand if you stay with him, we won't be able to see each other. You won't be able to take referrals from me."

I nod. "It'll be safer for you if we don't have contact."

"You're asking me to turn my back on you."

"There's no other way."

"I can move Hanna somewhere safe."

"She's fragile. She won't survive the stress." I glance over the door. "I better go."

"Wait." He catches my wrist. "At least tell me what you're getting yourself into. Tell me what this job entails."

"It's better you don't know."

"Just put my mind at ease. That's all I'm asking. For God's sake, I may never see you again."

Hearing it hurts. It hurts as much as I'm able to feel for someone other than Hanna. And Yan—though I'm not yet comfortable admitting that to myself. "The job is Dimitrov."

His eyes widen. "Casmir?"

"Yes."

"The man's security is unbreachable."

"I'm going to pose as Natasha Petrova under the guise of selling a stolen painting."

"I'm not sure there's any painting he'd find worth the risk."

"He already agreed."

"What? What the hell are you selling?"

"The Salvator Mundi. It's a fake."

He gives me an impressed look. "I can't believe you pulled it off. Where are you doing it?"

"Hotel Paris. Yan has a government connection that put pressure on the manager to work with us."

"The painting was your idea, wasn't it?"

"It was the only way I could think of to get Dimitrov alone."

"Mink, you know what will happen to you if your cover is blown."

"No one will blow my cover. Yan and his team are invested in this job. They're not going to jeopardize their own mission."

"What about the hotel manager? Can you trust him?"

"Yan's government connection does. I think he's safe."

Gergo presses a finger above my heart. "Just make sure *you're* safe."

"It'll be a piece of cake. All I have to do is walk in, say hello, offer Dimitrov a glass of champagne, and that's it. I don't even have to pull the trigger."

"If you have doubts—"

"I don't."

"Are you sure you know what you're doing?"

"One hundred percent."

"If you need me—"

"No. I'm not dragging you into this. Promise me you'll stay away from Yan and his team. I don't want anything to happen to you."

He cups my cheek. "Nothing is going to happen to me. I'm tougher than that."

A loud knock falls on the door. "Mina?"

Fuck. Shit. It's Yan.

The blood drops from my head all the way to my toes. Gergo climbs onto the bench and flattens himself against the wall, his hand going for his gun.

Yan won't hesitate to break down the door if I take

a second too long to let him in. I turn the lock and open the door wide, hiding Gergo behind it. I don't give Yan a chance to step inside. With the dress clutched in my hand, I walk out ahead of him, not looking back to see if he's following. All the way to the register, my heart beats in my throat, but I walk with confidence.

I walk like I have nothing to hide.

At the counter, I hand the dress to the sales lady. It's only when she rings it up that I dare to turn. Yan is right behind me, taking a wad of bills from his wallet. Relief floods me, leaving me lightheaded. From the corner of my eye, I see Gergo cutting across the floor toward the exit. Pretending to watch a mother with a screaming child, I follow Gergo's progress until he steps out onto the pavement. By the time Yan lifts his eyes to the tantrum scene, Gergo has already disappeared around the corner.

My hand shakes slightly when I take the bag from the sales lady.

Yan fixes his attention on the exchange, his eyebrows pulling together. Taking my elbow, he steers me outside. "Everything all right?"

"I'm just a little hungry." It's not a lie. "I get shaky when I don't eat."

He checks his watch. It's close to lunchtime. Reassured by my explanation, he walks me to a fancy restaurant and asks for a table on the terrace. A hostess leads us to the rooftop where I'm surprised to see only one table set among flowering potted plants.

Yan orders *the usual.* The waitress serves champagne, giving him a sultry look. My pulse spikes in protest, a feeling close to jealousy burrowing into my chest.

"You come here often," I say when the woman is gone.

"They have good food."

I lift the glass to my lips and take a sip. The champagne is fizzy and yeasty. "Just the food?"

He doesn't reply, which is an answer in itself.

The expensive liquor turns sour on my tongue. "I'd appreciate it if we went elsewhere in the future."

He cocks a brow. "Is there something wrong with the setting?"

"I don't like to have my face rubbed in your ex-lovers, at least not while you're fucking me."

His gaze drills into mine. "Why does that bother you?"

"It's humiliating."

"Sleeping with me is humiliating?"

"It's humiliating to be paraded in front of your ex-lovers."

A spark of amusement lights up his eyes. "Are you jealous?"

The bastard is pleased I'm feeling like this. "No."

He considers me for a moment, then says, "We'll go somewhere else next time."

"Thank you," I reply grudgingly.

His lips quirk. "You're welcome."

With that genuine almost-smile on his face, he's

even more handsome. His features are hard and uncompromising, but so virile. My body heats in response, my stomach fluttering with an echo of this morning's orgasms when I think of what we've done. The arousal is untimely, the attraction uncontrollable. But recollections of sex with him isn't what warms my chest. It's that fact that he's giving that semblance of a smile to me and no one else.

The exclusivity makes me feel special. It's the same feeling I get when he takes me to bed and showers me with twisted lust and intense passion. When he fucks, he pours everything into the act, as if the woman on the receiving end is his beginning and end. I desperately want to believe it. I want to believe I'm the only one. That's why knowing he fucked the waitress hurts so much. Because I want to be more than just another woman he fucked. I want to be someone special to somebody before it all ends.

No, not just somebody. I want to mean something to *him*.

At the revelation, I give an internal start. Since when does what he thinks matter to me? This is dangerous ground. Something about this man is getting through my shields, penetrating the comforting numbness that has encased me since my parents' deaths. I better be careful. It will be so damn stupid to fall for him. I don't want to die with a broken heart after it's been frozen for so long. It's bad enough I'll be his prisoner until I blow out my last breath.

The waitress arrives with our food. She serves two plates of squid ink risotto with grilled prawns.

"White wine?" she asks Yan.

He looks at me.

"Not for me, thank you." I'm already buzzing from the glass of champagne I've downed.

"Just mineral water, please," he says, barely paying the woman attention.

She scoffs at his aloofness and leaves.

"I hope you like seafood." He picks up his fork and gestures for me to do the same. "I should've asked."

"I'm not a fussy eater." I've survived on bugs and worms on some of the more difficult missions.

He loads his fork, brings it to his mouth, and watches me expectantly. He wants me to like the food. Why, I can't fathom. What does he care? I'm hungry, however, and I know from experience a good appetite isn't something I should take for granted. It'll become worse as the days go by. Eating will become difficult.

Making the most of the favor my body is granting me, I take a bite. The savory flavors explode in my mouth. The risotto is al-dente and the sauce creamy. The shellfish tastes of garlic butter. I can't help but close my eyes as I hum my approval. When I open them again, Yan is regarding me with a pleased expression.

"I'm glad you like it," he says.

A waiter arrives with our water and pours two glasses. I suppose Yan's non-interest offended the waitress. I'm relieved that I get to enjoy my meal without the hurtful reminder of her presence.

I finish every morsel on my plate and even the freshly baked bread roll. When Yan asks if I'd like dessert, I ask for coffee, too.

"You're feeling better," he observes.

There's no way to explain my ups and downs, so I simply shrug.

He lifts the bottle from the ice bucket. "More champagne?"

"No, thanks. I've had enough."

He pours himself another glass as the waiter reappears with strawberry pavlova and our coffee. My mouth waters at the sight of the delicate meringue crust filled with fresh berries drenched in a red fruit reduction.

It tastes every bit as good as it looks. I'm halfway through devouring my portion when I feel Yan's stare on me. Lifting my eyes, I find him studying me with a disconcerting look, his pavlova almost untouched.

I swallow the bite I took and dab my mouth with the napkin. "What's wrong?"

His gaze follows my action. "The cut won't leave a scar."

"Excuse me?"

"The cut on your lip. It's healed. In a few days, the mark will be gone."

"I suppose."

He studies my eyes. "Bruises too. They've all but faded."

"Um, yes." Suddenly feeling self-conscious about my appearance, I touch my hair. I showered, but I haven't made an effort to look presentable. Certainly nothing like the well-groomed waitress with her perfectly styled hair and carefully applied makeup.

"It wasn't supposed to happen," he says.

"What?"

"The mercenaries. They weren't supposed to beat you."

My craving for the sweet treat vanishes. I put down my desert fork. "I fought them."

His smile is flat but not unkind. "Of course, you did."

He didn't want me to get beaten up? What am I supposed to make of that? "What are you trying to say? Are you offering me an apology?"

"Yes." The word is firm, a strong affirmation that surprises me. His next words are spoken harshly, and are even more surprising. "I'm dealing with them."

My mouth drops open. "Dealing with them? How?"

"A connection is repaying the favor."

"You're having them beaten?"

"Seems fitting, no?"

This isn't what I expected from my kidnapper. "Because I'm a woman?"

My hackles rise. If the fight was fair, I would've stood a chance. The mercenaries outnumbered me. I've always been prone to gender discrimination in the military, no matter how many times I proved myself and executed missions better than my male comrades. Which is maybe why they resented me, why they thought a lesson was in order. My mouth tightens involuntarily at the memory, at the ugly pictures invading my mind.

"No," Yan says, leaning back in his chair and spreading his legs. "Not because you're a woman."

"Why then?"

"Because you're *my* woman."

Something in me gives, like a cord snapping, allowing my heavy heart to lift. The possessive pronoun sounds way too good, even though I know I shouldn't read more into it. Of course, I'm his. His belonging. His toy. He claimed me the first night in Budapest. He admitted as much to Ilya in the conversation I overheard.

He scrutinizes me. "Why did you quit the Special Forces?"

The elation evaporates, the delicious food turning into a stone in my stomach. "I already told you. Money."

"You said you needed the money after you left the military." He stirs sugar into my coffee. Leaning over the table, he holds my eyes as he hands me the cup. "So tell me. Why did you leave?"

Something in his gaze says he already knows, and the realization both angers and shames me. It takes everything I have to keep my voice even. "If you know the answer, why do you ask?"

"Tell me what happened."

"Why did you dig so deep?"

He pulls his espresso closer. "It came up."

It couldn't have just come up. That reason was

never stated on my resignation. Only our superior, the guilty men, Gergo, those involved in the investigation and the resulting court case, the medics, and I know what happened. And none of them will ever talk. Of that, I'm sure.

No, Yan must've found out because he's looking into my history. Because he's searching for something. My heart rate jumps. Could he have seen Gergo and me together? It's unlikely. We were careful. Still, the mere possibility pushes a sour burn up my throat. I can't let Yan find out about Gergo. He can never know I took the blame for Gergo's job, or Gergo is as dead as I'll be soon.

"Mina?"

I look at my hands. "I don't like talking about it."

"Tell me."

The burn turns to bile. This is as much as I can take. Pushing up, I make to leave, but he grabs my wrist. His hold is an iron band. He doesn't hurt me, but he makes it clear he's not going to let go. Slowly, he drags me to him. I feel his eyes on my face, but I can't look at him. The memory is too shameful, too devastating. I can't bear for anyone to witness my humiliation, and I especially don't want Yan to see in my eyes the shadow that day still casts over my soul.

When I reach the vise of his legs, he pulls me onto his lap and nuzzles my neck.

His voice is soft and reassuring when he repeats his order. "Tell me."

"Yan, please."

He slides his fingers through my hair, caressing my scalp. "I need to know."

"The past is best left alone."

He kisses my neck, his breath hot on my skin. "Not always."

Turning my face an inch, I finally meet his eyes and give him the most honesty I've given anyone. "It took years to forget. I don't want to relive it."

His lips brush over mine. "You're not going to relive it. Just give me the facts." He tightens his arms around me, his green eyes fiercely intent on my face. "You're not alone anymore, Minochka."

The promise is sweet, but he doesn't know about the nightmares that had haunted my waking and sleeping hours for months and years after the incident. I'm not going to dig that skeleton out of the closet. Besides, the more he goes poking around my past, the more likely he's to stumble onto my friendship with Gergo. "Why are you so set on hearing me repeat the sordid history? What will it change?"

"Everything." His jaw flexes. "I'm going to make them pay."

He can't be serious. Why does he care? I don't get it. No matter how many times Yan and I share an unnaturally intense intimacy, I'm no closer to understanding him, because our intimacy is limited to the bedroom. Or does this count? Does holding me close and offering me retribution count as affection when he's blackmailing me with my grandmother's life?

"Think about it," he urges. "Don't you want this?"

I can't pin a motivation on his offer, but I do think about it. My attackers haven't been convicted. They haven't been expelled or lost their ranks. It was my word against theirs. They claimed my injuries were the result of a bad fall, that I lied about the attack to get them in trouble for coming on to me, like all men under the circumstances would. They labeled me as a slut who paraded naked in front of them, a cock-tease. But that was bullshit. Yes, we shared the same barracks and communal showers, but we were trained to look beyond our nudity and anything else that wasn't part of the mission. We were machines, instruments to obtain a goal, nothing more. I always waited until the bathroom was empty, and I never took off my underwear in front of them.

Yet the senior officers investigating the matter didn't take a stand for me. Circumstances were questionable, to quote my superior. A man will always be a man, he'd said. And I'd felt so betrayed, so utterly brutalized by the attack that all I'd wanted was to put the incident behind me. I told myself I'd get revenge on my attackers later, when I wouldn't be as likely to get arrested for their deaths, but then Hanna's health worsened, and I got my leukemia diagnosis.

As illogical as it was, it felt like the universe was punishing me for something, and I chose to focus on survival in lieu of vengeance, on paying the bills with my deadly skills rather than seeking revenge on those who wronged me.

"I want them to suffer as much as you did," Yan says, bringing me back to the present. "To feel every ounce of what you felt, so they'll never forget."

I want that too, so badly. Maybe that *later* is finally here. But no, Yan sniffing around my former unit is too dangerous for Gergo. As much as I crave vengeance, I need to dissuade Yan from this. "Those men are powerful. Most of them are still in the Special Forces, and the rest joined the government ranks."

He chuckles. "Is that supposed to scare me?"

"You'll be making unwanted enemies."

"With as many as I have, what's a few more?"

Despite the situation, I smile at his light tone. "I wish it were that simple."

"It is." He drags a finger over my lips. "I'm not going to force you to talk, but I'm going after them, with or without your relay of the event. I have a good imagination. I'll put it to use when I decide what dues to dish out. Believe me, it's going to get very creative."

I swallow. "It's not worth it." Or at least that's what Gergo told me after the attack. He convinced me revenge wasn't worth getting arrested or killed over, especially with my grandmother relying on me.

"The fuck it's not. *You're* worth it."

The words hit a bull's eye in my heart. "Take a good, hard look, Yan. I'm not a good person."

"You're *mine*, and I like you fine how you are."

"I'm a killer for hire."

"You're the closest thing to perfect I've seen in this fucked-up world."

Baffled, I stare into his eyes. "You don't mean that."

"Don't tell me what I mean or don't. I don't mince my words."

No, he doesn't. *You're the closest thing to perfect.* If I didn't know better, I'd say Yan cares about me.

He picks up the check. "Let's go." When he helps me to my feet, all traces of his gentleness vanish. "I want to swing by your friend's place to see how she's advancing with our painting." And just like that, he's back to being the dangerous man Gergo warned me about.

24

MINA

*W*e get back to Yan's place in the late afternoon, after he's assured himself our fraudulent painter is on schedule with the Salvator Mundi replica. Ilya is lounging on the couch with a beer. He informs us Anton is picking up the sniper rifles from their supplier. The apartment looks surprisingly clean. Ilya must've been busy. I hope that's why he looks so disgruntled and not because the air between the brothers is far from cleared.

Yan announces he has private business to take care of. While I hang the dress in Yan's closet, I hear him asking Ilya if he'll get it right this time—*it* meaning making sure I don't escape.

Ilya answers with a grumbled, "Fuck you."

Great. So the air isn't cleared, after all.

When Yan is gone, I make myself useful and keep out from under Ilya's feet by doing the laundry and pondering what to cook for dinner. However, I'm too distracted for even such a mundane decision. I can't stop thinking about Gergo's daring appearance and Yan's planned revenge on my assailants. I worry about Hanna, too. I wish I could call her.

After going through the contents of the fridge for a third time, I slam the door with a sigh. It's useless.

"What do you feel like having for dinner?" I ask Ilya.

He crosses his ankles on the coffee table. "Whatever."

"That's not helpful." Sighing again, I tidy the lounge by picking up the old magazines and Ilya's empty beer bottle that's leaving a wet ring on the wooden coffee table top.

"Mina," he exclaims when I straighten.

I give a start. "What?"

Pointing at my face, he jumps to his feet. "Your nose. It's bleeding."

"Shit." I press my free hand under my nose so I don't get blood on Yan's immaculate mohair carpet and rush to the kitchen where I dump the bottle and magazines in the recycle trashcan before grabbing a kitchen paper towel. Tilting my head back, I wait for the bleeding to stop.

"Let me see that," Ilya says, coming up next to me.

"It's nothing. It happens sometimes."

He takes my elbow. "Come sit down."

"No. I don't want to stain the carpet."

"Fuck the carpet." He leads me to the table and pushes me down in a chair. "Do you need ice or something?'

"No. It'll stop in a minute."

"You say it like it happens a lot."

"Sometimes," I say again.

He takes his phone from his pocket. "I'm calling Yan."

"No." I grab his arm.

At the urgency in my tone, he gives me a quick look.

"I don't want to worry him for nothing," I explain.

"It's not nothing."

"It's a nosebleed. It's not like a part of my face has been amputated."

He appears uncertain.

"I don't want to bother him," I insist. "It's a silly thing."

"None of the times my nose bled was silly."

I smile from behind the fumbled kitchen towel. "Because you got hit on the nose?"

"More or less."

"I'm sorry Yan hit you because of me."

He sighs and rubs his neck. "Yan's right. You should stop apologizing."

"I just want you to know I mean it. If I had a choice—"

"Bullshit. You only had to ask. Yan would've taken you to see your grandmother."

"Do you believe yourself?" The dripping stops. I wipe my nose and stare at Ilya's bruised face. "I'm not his girlfriend. This isn't how it works between us."

"He's different with you."

"So you've said, but it doesn't change what we are. Besides, do you honestly think I want my grandmother to meet him?"

He grins. "He's not so bad, you know."

"Maybe you should tell him that sometime."

"Oh, he knows it. He doesn't need a bigger head than what he already has." Ilya ducks his head for a better look at my nose and frowns. "You better rinse that with cold water."

I get to my feet, but he holds me back with a hand on my arm. "Are you sure you're all right?"

My smile is the one I use when I assume a persona. "Absolutely."

"You'd tell me, right?"

"Tell you what?"

"If something was wrong."

Shit. I don't want to lie to him more than I already have. I like him. Really like him. If not for this situation, I think we could've been friends. Maybe even despite the situation. God knows, I could do with a friend, especially now that Gergo is out of the picture. He used to be my go-to when I needed a shoulder.

"Mina?" Ilya stares at me, his rough features pulled into a suspicious expression.

"I'm okay now."

His frown says he disagrees. "Why don't you go wash your face? I'll make you a cup of tea."

I smile at his kindness. "That's sweet, but not necessary."

"I'm having a cup anyway. It's no trouble."

In an impulsive gesture of gratitude, I throw my arms around him and give him a hug. "You're a teddy bear, you know that?"

He splays his fingers over my lower back. "If you change your mind about us..."

"Hey." I move his wandering hand away. "We already had this discussion, remember?"

"I can be more than cute and cuddly."

I grin up at him. "I don't doubt that."

"If you give me a chance—" He stops at the sound of a key being inserted into the front door.

I pull away and whisper urgently, "Don't tell him. Please. He'll fuss over nothing."

Ilya's look is conflicted.

"Please, Ilya."

He gives a tight nod.

By the time the door opens, I'm already escaping to Yan's bathroom. He walks in as I'm drying my face on a towel. Our eyes meet in the mirror.

"What's going on, Mina?"

"Nothing." I turn, gripping the vanity behind me. "Why?"

He closes the distance, staring down at my face as he stops in front of me. "Why were you standing so close to Ilya? When I opened the door, you shot like a bullet from a barrel. Why were you running?"

"I wasn't running."

"He touched you."

"I hugged him."

"You hugged him." The words are dangerously even.

I have to diffuse the situation before it ends in another fight. "Not every touch is sexual. Hugs can be platonic."

"Explain to me why you had to hug him."

"Yan," I say with a huff of frustration, trying to move around him.

Grabbing my face in one big hand, he holds me in place. "Why did you have to hug him?"

"He offered to make me a cup of tea."

"A cup of tea."

"That's what I said."

"That warrants a fucking hug?"

"He's your brother. Don't you ever hug?"

He narrows his eyes. "Not each other."

"Only the women you share?"

"We're *not* back on that subject."

"You started it."

A smoldering look invades his eyes. They turn a shade darker as his gaze runs over me. "You don't hug him for anything, do you hear me? Not even if he offers you a diamond necklace. In fact, you don't take anything from him either."

I blow out a frustrated breath. "Stop it. You're overreacting."

His jaw flexes. "You want tea?"

I shake my head meekly in his hold. "No."

"I'll make you a fucking cup of tea."

"Yan, please."

"Please, what?"

"Cut it out. I don't want to fight."

"We're not fighting, are we?"

"Then what do you call this?" I motion between us.

He reaches for my jeans with his free hand. "Setting boundaries." The button pops free, and he keeps on watching my face as he pulls down the zipper. "Making sure you understand that this"—he yanks me against his erection by the waistband of my jeans—"is exclusive."

Before I can say anything, he slams his lips over mine. He kisses me savagely even as his fingers dip gently into my underwear. I'm already soft, wet. He groans into my mouth as he gathers the slickness and spreads it over my clit. I arch my hips toward the touch, searching for more friction. He nips my tongue and licks my lips, then spears two fingers through my folds and drives them deep inside while rubbing the pad of his thumb over my clit.

The pleasure is instantaneous. My lower body heats, my knees growing weak. I grab his forearms and cling to him as he bends me backward and plunders my mouth. My neck aches from the strain, but I can't think about anything other than how close to the edge his deft fingers are bringing me.

"Mine," he growls, breaking the kiss.

Out of breath, I grip the vanity for support as he kneels and unties my laces. He removes my sneakers and my jeans. My panties follow next. Fastening his hands around my waist, he lifts me onto the counter and yanks off my T-shirt and bra. He doesn't take the time to undress. He's barely unfastened his belt and pulled down his zipper before he's inside me. The intrusion is sudden and absolute, the stretch burning. I welcome it by snaking my arms around his neck, the discomfort reminding me I'm still alive, just like fifteen months ago when he fucked me for the first time. Like then and every time since, my body comes alive for him. He has a singular effect on me.

"It's never been like this," I admit in a moment of heat, wrapping my legs around his hips.

"Mina." He smothers me in kisses and lifts me from the vanity.

Grabbing the back of my thighs, he walks to the bedroom with my body still draped around him and his cock buried inside me. At the edge of the bed, he stops. Instead of lowering us onto the mattress, he pulls out until only the head of his cock is lodged inside, then slowly lowers me back over his length.

"Fuck." He stares into my eyes as he keeps a slow pace. "You feel as good as I knew you would. Better. Better than anything."

Switching positions, he sits down so that I straddle him. "Ride me. Use my body to get off."

The invitation is too tempting to let it pass. Yan likes to be in control. It's not often he gives it away. Sensing his need to watch, I lean back and do exactly what he asked. I use him for my pleasure, moving at the right pace and depth for me. I look at his face when I touch my clit. He grits his teeth and leans back on his arms, giving me his body and permission to do with him as I please.

Giving up this much control requires trust, especially for him. I push up on my knees and sink back down, taking him deeper. His gaze snaps to where we're connected. His eyes are a dark shade of green, his whole body drawn tight. He's close to coming, but he doesn't take over. He lets me ride out our mating dance until my body reflects the tightness of his muscles with an answering spasm. Sweating with the effort of holding back, he curses as my inner muscles clench. It's only when I break that he lets go. When pleasure rips through my body, he follows suit with a low groan, filling me, emptying himself into me.

For a brief moment, I think about the possibility of creating a new life, about the choices and opportunities we'll never have, and acute pain rips through me. Not that children would ever be an option with our lifestyles. Not that I expect this to ever go that far. It's simply the fact that I don't have a say and we'll never get to choose. As illogical as it is, I'm mourning the ending when we've hardly had a beginning. I don't want to admit what these emotions rippling through me signify. I only know I can't let him go. I keep on rocking in his lap and kissing his lips to drag out the moment, willing it not to end. The invitation is long since over, but I still use him, this time not for my body but my soul.

With a palm on my back, he pushes me to his chest. I turn my face to the side and stay like that. His heartbeat is an erratic but strangely soothing sound in the tangle of my thoughts and feelings. Practicalities I haven't considered up until now bombard my mind. The end will be tough. I won't be pretty. What will he do with me? Will he grant me the mercy of a hospice and morphine, or slit my throat once it gets bad? When he realizes I'm no longer of use to him, will he keep me or set me free? I can't imagine he'd want to be by my side when my body is bone thin and my skin sagging.

"Mina." He drags his fingers through my hair. "Why are you so tense?"

I haven't noticed how I've locked my muscles. Making a conscious effort, I release them one by one.

"Wasn't it good?" he asks.

"Perhaps too good."

"That's a bad thing?"

"No," I reply softly. "Definitely not a bad thing."

"Wrap your legs around me." Standing, he pulls up his pants so he doesn't trip over them and carries me to the shower.

Like every time after we've fucked, he washes my body and hair. He towels me dry and plants a soft kiss on my spine. Studying my reflection in the mirror as I finger-comb my hair, he announces, "We're going out for dinner."

"But we've been out for lunch."

"That was hours ago."

"Are we going with Ilya and Anton?"

His expression hardens. He walks back to the room and yanks open the closet. Flipping through his shirts, he says, "We're going alone."

I know better than to question him when his mood shifts like this.

"No," he says when I reach for a pair of jeans. "Put on the dress."

"That's way too fancy."

"It fits the occasion."

"What occasion?"

"We're celebrating."

"We are?"

He takes his phone from the pocket of his discarded pants, punches in his code, and turns the screen toward me.

The photo makes my skin crawl. It's the face of a man whose features are imprinted in my memory forever.

"Recognize him?" Yan asks.

I swallow.

It's one of the men who attacked me.

"Where did you get this?" So fast, I want to add. And more importantly, did he find out anything about Gergo?

He sweeps to the next photo, and I go cold inside.

It's the same man. I know it instinctively, like a soldier would feel the presence of an enemy without relying on sight, even though the man's proud sneer and vain features are unrecognizable.

They're unrecognizable because his face is beaten to a pulp.

25

YAN

I can't tear my gaze away from Mina where she sits opposite me in the restaurant. She's biting her lip as she studies the chef's recommendations. I should do the same, at least pick the wine, but I can't stop staring at her from over the top of my menu.

I meant what I said at lunch. She's the closest thing to perfect. In that nude-pink dress with the matching bag and shoes, she's the prettiest woman I've seen. The crocheted cotton thread of the dress forms a delicate lace pattern that hugs her small body. If she shifts just so, I can glimpse her pink satin underwear. I got her a full bra and boy shorts with the dress in mind, but the modest undergarments don't hide her round breasts or firm ass. The sight makes me hard. I can't help but think about everything I want to do to her later.

With her platinum-blond hair gelled back and the makeup I insisted she wears, she looks like she belongs on the cover of a fashion magazine. The centerfold, if I strip her from that dress. Her blue eyes are even more startling with the smoky eyeshadow and eyeliner, and the pink gloss on her lips accentuates their lusciousness. The piercings and tattoo add an air of rebelliousness, spunk. She's everything I've ever fantasized about rolled into one.

The total package. Feminine. Alluring. Intelligent.

Fucking deadly.

She's everything. The real deal.

Too fucking bad she's also the woman who framed me. I still hate her for the flippant brushoff, but not enough not to take her to my bed. Not enough not to want to keep her there forever. My fixation with her is too absolute. I love her strength and resilience. I love her brightness and sass. I love her touch. A stroke from one of those slender fingers, and I'm ready to go up in flames and fall at her feet in ashes.

She's gotten under my skin and I'm helpless to prevent the pride and protectiveness she brings out in me. I want to keep her safe. I'm proud of how she's handling the Dimitrov job. I'm proud just for having her at my side. It's becoming more difficult to ignore that she didn't choose the position out of free will— that she's not sitting here because she wants to, but because I ordered it. Yet I can't help but adore her. I simply hate her a little more for her lies and deceit. I should never forget that.

Who is the man you met in Budapest, princess?

As if feeling the heaviness of my question, she lifts

her gaze. I lower mine quickly, pretending to read the letters that are floating in front of my eyes. I don't want to give her more power than what she already has.

"Yan?"

Her voice is husky. It makes me want to crawl under the table, spread her legs, and eat her right here.

Get a fucking grip. "Yes?"

"I'm not very hungry."

Concern pushes all my darker thoughts aside. Her appetite is on and off. Is she suffering from depression? The situation she finds herself in certainly merits some serious psychological shit, not that I've bothered with that kind of stuff before.

She shuts her menu. "I'll just have a starter."

Should I make her see a shrink? But what good would that do? If the root of the problem doesn't change, treatment isn't going to make a difference. I'm not keen on pumping her full of drugs, either.

Then again, lies or no lies, adoration or hate, I took responsibility for her when I claimed her, and I take my responsibilities seriously.

"Would you like to see a doctor?" I ask.

She flinches. It's a slight movement, but I miss nothing where she's concerned. "Why would I need a doctor?" Her tone is defensive.

"You've been through a lot." My gaze slips to her legs that are hidden underneath the table. "Your bruises don't seem to be fading as fast as they should." Another observation that's been worrying me.

"You know what?" She opens her menu again. "I'll

have the escargot for a starter and the salmon for the main course."

Nice deflection, but that's not going to work with me. "I'll call someone in the morning."

"You'll be wasting your time. I'm fine."

"No waste of time." I give her my most charming smile.

She answers with a look that's meant to shred me to pieces. "I don't need a physical evaluation."

"I wasn't referring to the physical kind."

Her eyes widen as she catches my drift. "You want me to talk to a psychologist?"

"A psychiatrist." In case she needs anti-depressants or something.

"Fuck you, Yan."

"Careful with the insults. You know where those will get you."

"Draped over your lap?" she asks scathingly.

"I'm glad you're still quick to catch on."

"If I need a head doctor, I'll tell you."

"There's no need to be so defensive. I'm acting in your best interest."

"Says the man who's the reason why I'd need a shrink."

"Mina." I say her name with enough warning to put a wary look on her face. "I want to enjoy this dinner with you."

"Then you shouldn't have brought up a goddamn shrink."

"I thought you didn't want to fight."

"I don't."

"Then what's the problem?"

"You think sitting in a reclining chair and telling a stranger about our fucked-up situation is going to make me feel better?"

Any other man would've felt remorse. Gut-wrenching guilt. But not me. Her resistance only adds to the challenge. "Maybe."

"No, thanks."

"How about pills, then?"

"I'm not the pill-popping type."

"Suit yourself. However, the offer stands."

She narrows her pretty eyes. "How kind."

We fall silent when the waiter comes to take our order. I choose the same as Mina. With all my gawking, I haven't had time to look at the menu, but I don't want to ask for two more minutes because the men at the bar are unabashedly staring at Mina. I'm suddenly eager to take my woman home. It's ironic, considering we're here to escape being home and around Ilya too much. When the guy in the suit gives Mina another long look, I twist in my chair, ready to bash in his face. He catches my eyes and looks away quickly.

Good.

No, fuck that.

I get to my feet.

Mina gives me a startled look. "Where are you going?"

"Stay. I'll be right back."

The guy blanches as I advance on him. I stop in front of him and his friend. "Do I know you?"

"No," he stammers.

"Then what the fuck are you looking at?"

"N-nothing."

"She's beautiful, right?"

He shakes his head. "No."

"Are you saying my woman isn't beautiful?"

"Yes, I mean no. Yes, she's beautiful."

"Is that what you were looking at?"

He lifts his hands. "Look, man, I didn't mean anything. I couldn't help but notice."

"If you value your life, you'll look fucking elsewhere."

His throat bobs with a swallow.

"Got it?" I ask with a cold smile.

"Yes. Yes, I got it."

"Good." I pat him on the shoulder none too softly and go back to our table.

Mina watches me with big eyes as I take my chair. "Was that really necessary?"

Our glasses have been filled. I down half of the wine without tasting the Italian bouquet. "Yes."

Averting her eyes, she rubs a palm over her brow.

"What?" I snap.

She sighs. "Nothing."

"Say it."

"You can't threaten everyone who looks at me."

Just like that, what's left of my good humor slips. "That's where you're wrong." I lean over the table toward her. "Don't let the fact that I'm wining and dining you fool you into seeing this for something it isn't. Your life is mine. I can do whatever the fuck I want with you or anyone who as much as glances at you. Or have you forgotten?"

Hugging herself, she rubs her arms. "No." Her voice is soft. "I haven't forgotten."

Fuck. I feel like banging my head on the table. She does this to me. She drives me insane. I'm fucking jealous because I'm uncertain of her. Insecure. My head says it's not her fault, but my anger is too fierce for reason.

Avoiding my eyes, she picks up her glass and takes a sip. She looks at the table centerpiece, at the paintings on the wall, at the other diners, at anything but me. When she starts rubbing her arms again, I get up, remove my jacket, and drape it around her shoulders.

She tenses, then remains frozen in a strange kind of limbo, not rejecting the jacket but also not truly accepting it by pulling it tighter around her. It annoys me, because she's shivering, though the place is cozy enough. To humor Mina, I've chosen a restaurant I've never been, someplace where I don't have a history with a woman. I wanted this to be nice, but all of my good intentions flew out the window the minute I opened my big mouth. And now the atmosphere is strained, even more so than earlier, when I showed Mina that photo. Her reaction wasn't what I expected. I thought she'd be grateful I took care of one of her assailants. Instead, her face turned as white as the wall, and she clammed up, turning away without a word.

I don't know what about that picture got her so bothered, but if she thought I'd let those fuckers walk around with no cares in the world, she doesn't know me at all. First, they'll suffer. Then, they'll die.

But my thoughts are regressing. We were talking about her not needing a doctor. I was thinking about her frequent lack of appetite. That photo did pop up in my mind, but it wasn't what spoiled her appetite. Yes, the sight of the ugly bastard's mashed-up face wasn't pretty, but she's used to seeing that, and worse. There's something else, something more she's hiding from me.

I never thought I'd need her trust, but I do. I want it like I want her body. I want everything. I can't stand the thought of her keeping anything from me. She wants me. She's wanted me from the start. Baring her body to me has never been an issue. It's baring her heart that's the problem.

The more I think about what she's withholding, the more I lose my own appetite. The silence stretches. I've never wanted her to talk as badly as I do now, but I don't know how to breach this quiet standoff.

When our meal arrives, we both push the food around on our plates. This is unfamiliar terrain. I know how to make a woman's body sing, how to make her scream, but I've never tried to coax one into talking. Fuck, I've never had the urge to listen to any woman before. As much as I hate to admit it, this is where Ilya is better skilled. He'd know how to do it, but I can't fucking ask him for help knowing he still wants to get into Mina's pants.

By the time I get the bill, I'm so wound up with frustration and so torn up about how to handle the situation, I feel like a zip line stretched between two trees. Mina doesn't speak to me in the car. She doesn't talk in the shower or when I fuck her six ways from Sunday in bed. She moans and gasps and makes all the right sounds, but how I'm making her body feel is no longer all I want to know. I don't know when exactly it happened.

I only know it's no longer enough.

26

YAN

*L*ong after Mina has fallen asleep, I'm still lying awake in the dark, beating myself up about how the evening turned out. There's only one remedy for getting rid of pent-up frustration. I have to take it out on someone else.

Another photo waited on my phone when we got back after dinner, the men I've hired carrying out their job promptly.

Two down, nine to go.

I sneak out of our room and close the door so I won't disturb Mina. Then I wake Anton quietly. Ilya's snores remain steady as Anton grabs his pants and follows me into the lounge.

"What's up?" he asks, dragging a hand through his disheveled hair.

"We're going to Hungary."

He gives me a disgruntled look. "Again?"

"You're flying."

I pull on my jacket and head for the door. Anton curses softly, jumping around to fit his pants. He takes his trench coat from the back of the sofa and dons it over the T-shirt he'd been sleeping in.

"Hurry." I want to be back before Mina or Ilya wake up in the morning. Once we're on the landing and the door is locked behind us, I ask, "How fast can you get our plane ready?"

"It's already on standby at the private airfield."

I head for the stairs. "Let's go."

"What's going on?" he asks, running to catch up.

Pulling up the collar of my jacket against the cool bite in the night air, I check the message on my phone as I walk down the street to where the rental is parked. The men I hired are being clear about why they're beating up the scum who served with Mina, and the two who've been beaten would've called their cronies to let them know what's happening. That's good. I want them to know what's coming. Even if they go into hiding, I'll sniff them out.

Not one of them will escape his punishment.

Since Mina was part of the Special Forces when she filed her complaint, her case was handled by court-martial. Her ranking officer, Major General Rafael Tóth, should've protected her. Instead, he claimed what happened was her own fault. I read the report he submitted. I read the half-assed excuses of the men who teamed up against an unarmed woman. I read the military attorney's sad attempt at defense. Now I have a few questions of my own for the asshole who testified against Mina.

Nine to go. Ten if I count Tóth.

These days, he's an advisor to some minor idiot for Veteran Welfare at the Ministry of Defense.

"Yan," Anton says as we reach the car. "What the fuck is going on?"

"I have someone to interrogate."

"With regards to Dimitrov?"

"No."

"What then?"

"Something else."

He shifts into the passenger seat when I unlock the doors. "Are you going to tell me?"

"No."

"*Mudak*," he mutters as I start the engine.

IN LESS THAN AN HOUR, WE LAND AT A SMALL AIRFIELD just outside the eastern border of Budapest. Anton's control tower connection helped to get the takeoff and landing permissions in record time.

The driver I requested before takeoff is waiting next to a car. I've worked with him before. He's reliable and discreet. Once Anton and I are settled in the back and I've given our chauffer the address, he raises the partition to allow us privacy.

I pull up the blueprint of the house on my phone as we pull off.

Anton glances at the screen. "I don't want to meddle in your private war, but that address will come with good security."

"Good, but not top notch."

"What aren't you telling us?"

"Us?"

"Me. Ilya."

"I didn't know this was me against you."

His dark eyes harden. "It's Mina, isn't it?"

"Do not fucking say her name."

"There you go again." He shakes his head. "You've beaten up your own brother over this woman. How far are you going to let this go?"

"Let what go?"

"You're letting her manipulate you."

"Shut your mouth. You have no idea who's manipulating who."

"Do *you*?"

"Anton, I'm fucking warning you."

"Fine." He huffs. "Don't say *I* didn't warn *you*." He looks through the window, then back at me. "Why am I even here? If you're going to be this jumpy, you should've left me on the plane."

"You're here to break into this house."

He looks at the screen again. "You want me to get you in, but you won't say why."

"If you don't want to help me, say so now."

He throws his hands in the air. "I'll fucking help you."

"Good. Was that so hard?"

He shakes his head again, but doesn't answer.

If it had been anyone but Mina, I would've told him. But this isn't his business, and I have no right to share her private matters. Before this whole thing can blow up, these men will be dead. By then, we'll be far away from here, spending the money the hit on Dimitrov will bring in. Someplace warm will be nice.

Maybe a private island off the coast of Mozambique.

Anton and I go through a few checkpoints during the drive. Cutting the alarm and breaking in is easy. The idiot doesn't have a guard or a dog. We enter the spacious house on an isolated property outside of town and make our way to the main bedroom upstairs, where our target's heavy bulk is tenting the covers on the bed. The fucker only wakes up when I press the barrel of my gun against his temple.

The whites of his eyes are wide in the moonlight that shines through the window. Cleverly, he keeps his mouth shut. His wife is asleep next to him.

"Tsk, tsk." I shake my head. "Not very vigilant for an ex-soldier. You're losing your touch."

At the sound of my voice, the woman stirs. She opens her eyes, blinks, and shoots upright.

"Shh." I press my finger to my lips. "You don't want to wake the kids."

"Whatever you want," Tóth says, his sleep-hoarse voice unsteady.

I address his wife. "I'm going to ask your husband a few questions. Stay here, and you won't get hurt."

She swallows as she looks at her husband. At my nod, Anton moves to her side of the bed, making sure she sees his weapon.

"Get up," I tell Tóth. Keeping the gun against his head, I push him into the corridor. "To the garage."

He doesn't argue. He leads me downstairs into the double garage through a door in the kitchen. I lock the door and flick on the lights. He turns to look at me, holding up his hands. He's calm now. Too calm.

"You know why I'm here," I say.

"I heard about the others."

I give him a grim smile. "News travels fast."

"That woman sent you."

"No one sent me."

He appears confused. "Then why are you here?"

"Because of *that woman*." Motherfucker. He doesn't even remember her name. I cast a quick glance around the space. He seems to do a lot of DIY. The shelves are neatly stacked with jars of nails and screws. Hammers and saws hang from hooks on the wall. "Get some cable ties."

The fat slob goes to a drawer and pulls out a bunch of ties.

I kick a workbench closer. "Sit."

"I'll do what you want if you promise not to hurt my kids."

"Sit," I say again, harsher.

He flops down onto the bench, his fringe falling over his face.

"Hands behind your back."

When he complies, I tie his wrists and bind his ankles to the feet of the bench. He's ex-military. If he gets the chance, he'll come at me. Not that I can't take him down, but I have no intention of getting into a fight that will wake his kids. He doesn't need to know that, though.

He stares up at me from under his hair as I round the bench and stop in front of him. His stomach strains in the wife-beater he's wearing and his thighs stretch his boxer shorts. He hasn't been taking care of himself. It seems the cushy job in government made him lax.

"That woman," I say. "What's her name?"

His face scrunches. "What?"

"What is her fucking name?"

"It's been a long time. I hardly remember her face."

"Don't fucking bullshit me." A man doesn't forget something like that. A name maybe, but not what she looked like lying naked and twisted in a puddle of blood and vomit. Not even a hardened soldier forgets that. "Answer me."

"158–14–something."

"I asked for her name."

"I never looked at their names. It's better to think of them as numbers."

I grit my teeth. "Mina. Mina Belan."

"Fine. So what?"

"You took her statement."

"I was the superior in charge."

"What happened?"

"You know what happened."

"I want to hear it from you."

"What is this?"

"What do you think it is?"

"Revenge?" When I don't answer, he asks, "Why wait all these years? Why now?"

"I asked you a question."

"She said the men attacked her in the shower. They beat her and were going to rape her, but a teammate walked in on the scene."

"A teammate?"

"Gergo Nagy."

"Ah, so you remember *his* name."

He gives me a cutting look. "I'd been on missions with Gergo. Ms. Belan hadn't been deployed with any of the teams I supervised in the field."

"Keep talking."

"The men backed off when Gergo pulled a gun. He called the medics."

I walk around him, digesting his factual manner. Apathetic. Like a soldier trained to inflict torture. "What happened to this Gergo guy?"

"He resigned not long after she did. He claimed the attack was too much. They were good friends, Gergo and Belan."

So, Gergo is the only person who helped her, who stood up for her. "Where is he now? What does he do?"

"I have no idea. I didn't keep in touch with the men who served with me."

"What injuries did she sustain?"

The tensing of his shoulders is the first sign of

emotion he shows. Even more significant is his silence. The incident left a mark on him, after all.

"What were her injuries?" I repeat, taking a wide stance in front of him.

He sighs. "Four broken ribs, broken arm, concussion, and internal hemorrhage."

"They punched her in the face." I go deathly cold as I recall the image of her eyes swelled shut, purple and bloody. "Repeatedly."

"Yes." The admission is regretful.

"Until her skull fractured."

"Yes."

My rage mounts. It's a cold fury, the most dangerous kind. "They kicked her while she was down."

"Yes."

"Until her right kidney split like a bean."

"Yes."

"Then they kicked her in the stomach."

He turns his face away.

"Look at me," I grit out. When he obliges, I repeat, "They kicked her in the stomach."

"Yes."

"Until they damaged an ovary."

"Yes. I get it. You can stop this game."

"It may be very hard for her to conceive."

He hangs his head. "Yes."

"Yet you have three beautiful children."

He jerks his gaze back to mine. For the first time, his voice takes on a note of panic. "They're innocent."

"So was Mina." I tilt my head, considering him, considering his part in what should've been justice. "Yet you said otherwise. You claimed she fell down the stairs and then tried to pin her injuries on her teammates."

"I said what was reasonable."

"Is that so?"

"What do you expect when you throw a young, beautiful woman into a room full of men—healthy, virile soldiers—who don't see women for most of the year?"

I think of that photo, that Evidence A, and the long, blond tresses caked with blood. I see Mina in my mind's eye, irreparably broken, the picture ingrained in my brain. I'm unraveling, the edges of my soul tearing, and all I can think about is that bloodstained hair. Why did she cut off such beautiful hair?

"I'd always been against including her in the elite corps," Tóth continues. "I knew it was going to lead to something like that."

Ah. Some truth, at last. "Is that why you let those would-be rapists off the hook with a reprimand?" A fucking reprimand, when Mina fought for her life in a hospital bed for months. The coldness escalates, slowly creeping over every part of my body, hardening my heart.

"You can say what you want, but it's human nature. Of course, they'd go for her. She showered with them. She slept with them. She flaunted her body. And then, when they took her up on the offer, she said no?"

Motherfucker. I want to kill him with my bare hands, but that'll be too easy. "Are you fucking serious?"

"The decision wasn't mine to make. It was the court-martial's ruling."

Right. Sweeping a scandal under the rug. "The special commission the court appointed leaned heavily on your opinion and recommendation."

"As I said, a woman had no place in the elite corps. It was a lesson for our future selection process."

"A lesson in discrimination, you mean."

"Look, I can't take back my decision. Do what you have to. It's not going to change anything."

I lean closer to him. "That's where you're wrong."

He blanches a little. "What do you want from me? Money? Is that why Belan sent you?"

"No." The smile I force hurts my face. "As I've already told you, Belan didn't send me, and I don't want your filthy, measly money."

"What then?"

"Justice." I put my nose an inch from his. "An eye for an eye."

"If you're going to beat me up, get to it."

I shake my head.

"Kill me?" He laughs. "Go for it. I'm not afraid of dying."

"Of course not." I smile snidely. "You've been trained all your life to die. No, dying will be too easy."

He stares at me, his slack mouth parting a fraction.

"You turned a blind eye," I say. "You kept quiet when

you should've spoken up. I'll let you choose. Eyes or tongue?"

His foul breath washes over my face as he cries, "What?"

"Do you want to live the rest of your life blind or mute? Oh, the part you don't get to choose is your dick." I didn't show Mina those pictures, the ones where her assailant had his dick stuffed in his mouth. She looked upset enough that he'd been beaten up.

Tóth shakes his head. Drops of sweat fall around his face.

"What?" I grin. "Didn't the men who warned you tell you about that part? I guess they're too ashamed of what they've been degraded to."

He utters a barely coherent, "No."

"What was that?" I taunt.

"No, please. Just kill me."

I will, but he doesn't need to know that yet. I tsk-tsk chidingly. "And leave your family in the lurch? Some father you are."

"What kind of man will I be if…?" he slobbers.

I grab his hair. "Tongue or eyes? Choose, or I take both your sight and speech."

"God. Fuck."

"Nope. No help coming from that way. I suppose this is what Mina must've felt like when she begged for help."

"I-I… No. Fuck. Kill me. Please. I'll give you money."

I go for the shears on the wall. "Fine. We'll play it your way. I'll start with your eyes."

"Tongue," he cries. "Tongue. Fuck. Jesus."

"As you wish."

The fucker doesn't have an ounce of Mina's courage or strength. He pisses himself when I grip his tongue and pull.

It's a pity he passes out before I chop off his dick.

MINA

*B*eing locked up is slowly driving me insane. I'm not used to being out of action. I thrive on danger and adrenaline, not being cooped up in Yan's place with nothing to do but cook. Sure, there's plenty of danger and adrenaline in my current situation, enough to entice the darkness in me, but I'm a passive participant, unwilling—except for when Yan takes me to bed. But harping on what I can't change will only make it worse, so I ignore the listlessness eating at me and go to bed straight after dinner.

Yan follows shortly after, his arms folding securely around me, anchoring me to him in more than just a physical way. He intrigues me, this dangerous killer. I'm drawn to him as much as I want to escape this maddening imprisonment. It's conflicting. Confusing. It makes me even more restless.

"What's wrong?" he whispers in my ear.

"Nothing."

"You didn't say a word during dinner."

"Is conversation another requirement? In addition to being your sex toy?"

"Mina." There's a warning in his voice, and it's not subtle.

I shut my mouth before I say something that'll only make an already-impossible situation worse. His hand skims over my stomach under the cotton T-shirt I'm wearing, coming to rest on my hip. He's hard already. I know what he wants, but I'm not sure I can shake this strange, listless mood.

"I'm tired," I whisper.

He stills in our spooning position. I wait for him to contest or challenge me, but he only drapes his arm around my waist again and pulls me tighter against him. When he shifts into a comfortable position, like he does before sleeping, I have an inexplicable urge to cry. He didn't try to force or seduce me. He simply accepted that I'm tired, and I'm uncharacteristically torn, both pathetically thankful for his consideration and irrationally sad that I might've hurt his feelings.

I drag in a short, shaky breath. "It's not you."

"Go to sleep," he says in a clipped tone, but the coldness cracks, a hint of warmth seeping through.

Closing my eyes, I block out the disturbing thoughts running on repeat through my mind, and it doesn't take long to fall asleep. I really am tired. But the reprieve of rest doesn't last long before I'm back in the car, snow and trees zipping past as the headlights illuminate the asphalt road.

We round the bend, and my stomach clenches. I'm Mina, the adult, sitting in the back. I look on like an observer when the car skids to a stop. It's Mina, the adult, who gets out with my parents, the adult who's supposed to protect them, but the gun in my hand is shiny and blue. Plastic.

"No!"

A shot goes off. My mother falls, her blond hair covering her face.

Pop!

My father sinks to his knees.

"No!"

I jump on the men, stabbing them in their white, flabby, syringe-bruised arms just enough to immobilize them. Just enough to tie them up and make them look at me, but they don't know Mina the adult. They only know the little girl. And they've long forgotten my parents. They'll die without confessing their sin, because they can't confess a sin they can't even remember.

"Mina!"

The voice of my kidnapper is the voice of my savior in the dream. He jerks me from the claws of the nightmare and pulls me back to reality.

"Wake up."

I open my eyes, knowing I screamed. I always scream at this part. "I'm sorry." My T-shirt is soaked in sweat.

He switches on the lamp on the nightstand and

shifts up, resting his back against the headboard. "Come here."

I scoot up to the crook of his arm, needing the warmth, the comfort.

He kisses the top of my head. "Same dream?"

I nod.

"They're dead, those men," he says. "They paid for what they did."

I drag a finger over the dusting of dark hair on his forearm. "Did they pay if they couldn't even remember?"

"They couldn't?"

"They were high when I shot them. Maybe they were high on the night they..."

"Say it," he urges gently when I trail off.

I know why he's doing this. This sort of thing festers when you seal it up under skin and bone and flesh, when you bury it in your heart.

Yan is still looking at me, waiting, so I take a breath and say with a rush of air, "On the night they killed my parents." My chest deflates from the effort.

He caresses the side of my face with his knuckles. "Tell me."

I want to, but not because I sealed it up. I didn't; I just went numb. Cold, like the snow and ice that night. I haven't had the nightmare for many years, but since Yan took me, it's returned with a vengeance. And I suspect the reason is that Yan is slowly defrosting my heart, making me feel again. Making me vulnerable.

"How did you get away?" he asks softly.

A shiver ripples through me. "I ran. I ran so fast. I hid out in the woods, and waited. I thought my parents would come get me when the bad men were gone, but it took so long and I was so, so cold."

He rubs my arm as if trying to dispel the cold of that night.

I continue, because it does feel better telling him. "Eventually, I went looking for them. At first, I didn't understand. Then I felt the wetness, the blood. I saw my father's eyes, glassy like marbles, before I saw the hole in his head."

"What did you do?"

"Nothing. I just… started walking." I make myself small against his side, hiding in the safety he offers. "I didn't feel the pain, just the cold. I still don't feel it fully. At times, it's almost as if it happened to someone else, as if the girl in my dream is a stranger."

"Detachment," he muses, dragging his chin through my hair. "It's often a coping mechanism in severe trauma cases."

I stare at where my hand is gripping my knee, my knuckles white. "They tried to fix me for a very long time."

"They?"

"Psychiatrists. Therapists. Guidance counselors. They said I was dysfunctional. Not normal. Difficulty making friends and forming new attachments. Lack of empathy and unhealthy fascination with danger. I went to therapy every week for years, unsuccessfully. They finally gave up when I started high school."

Yan's body tenses against me. "They had no right to judge you. Nobody's all sweetness and light, rainbows and puppies. Not deep down, where it matters. We all carry a darkness within ourselves. Some just have the luxury of never knowing it. In any case, *normal* is a vague and tricky concept. What is normal other than a broad generalization based on the standards and values of the majority of people in the world? Just because you're different doesn't mean you're not normal."

My chest glows with warmth, something new for me. No one has ever defended me like this. "I knew I was different from the moment I stood over my parents' bodies. Instinctively, I knew I wasn't going to be like other children. They never understood me, and I never got them. It was simply easier to be alone."

He covers my hand with his. "Friends are overrated, anyway."

Something soft settles inside me. He's not judging me, and it's liberating. It feels a lot like peace. "It did make me an ideal sniper candidate. So there's that, I suppose."

"I bet." He pulls me tighter. "A perfect little killer. Is that what you always had in mind for a career?"

"At first, I wanted to take out the bad guys. Then I realized good and bad are very gray concepts, and that the bad guys could be your own comrades, the very men who took an oath to have your back."

"And that's when you became a freelancer."

"Yes." I look up at him with an ironic smile.

"Though I'm still selective with the jobs I take." When his face darkens, no doubt at the recollection that I allegedly framed him as a terrorist, I quickly change the subject. "How about you? Was it hard the first time?"

"Easier than it should've been." His gaze turns unreadable. "You said it felt fantastic. Me, I felt nothing. I felt the flesh part when I drove the knife into that filthy bastard's side. I felt the warmth as his blood ran over my fingers. But that's as far as it went. Nothing else. No need to spill my guts afterward. No remorse. Just another box on a list to tick off."

Interesting. And he was only sixteen. Does that mean he's even more dysfunctional than I am?

My shrinks would've had a field day with him.

"Why don't you have a professional name?" I ask.

He laughs softly. "I don't need one. That's for fancy assassins like you."

I punch him on the arm.

"Ow," he says, although I know he hardly felt that. When I don't rise to the bait, he drops a kiss on my temple and asks, "Why Mink?"

I inhale deeply. "Just before the hijacking, I asked my mother for a cookie. She said I had to wait for dinner." It was such a mommy thing for her, healthy food first. "I wanted that cookie so badly, but I didn't nag because I was still a good girl back then, right up to the point when I started walking alone down that road." Pushing aside the memory, I continue. "The cookie brand was Mink. Chocolate-chip mint was the flavor. It went off the market a few years ago. Did you know it?"

He shakes his head. "Cookies weren't thick on the ground where I came from. If I'd ever eaten a Mink, I would've remembered."

I fold my arms around his waist, giving him comfort, because all kids deserve cookies.

"What happened after you started walking?" he asks.

"I walked for hours, I think. A car eventually came past. The driver pulled over. She was a kind lady, on her way to visit her family. She gave me a lift to the nearest police station. They contacted my grandmother."

He brushes a thumb over my side. "When did you get the tattoo?"

"The minute I turned eighteen. It's my own version of a memorial stone."

"That's nice. I'm sure they would've approved." He lifts his hand to my neck and traces the tattoo there. "What about the hummingbird?"

It's hard not to stiffen and give myself away. "It symbolizes life."

And what good does it do me now? I got it after my first treatment of chemotherapy as a small token of victory, a symbol of my fight to live. For the majority of that first year after being diagnosed, I hated my body for its defect, for failing me when I ate healthily, worked out religiously, and needed my dangerous job like I needed air and food. And it wasn't only because of the money. The adrenaline of the missions made me feel alive. It was the only thing reminding me I still have a heart.

Until Yan. Now he reminds me of that, too. In so many other ways.

"I like it," he says.

"You do?"

He traces the piercings in my ear with a finger. "Everything."

"Why?" A part of me wants him to admit to liking more than just what he sees on the surface.

"You know why."

"I don't."

"I'm sure you're aware of the effect you have on men."

This time, I'm not quick enough to hide the rigidity that sets into my muscles. Yan isn't a fool, and he's exceptionally clever at reading people. Especially me, it seems.

He grips my chin, his perceptive gaze narrowing. "After Budapest, how many men did you sleep with?"

He means after we fucked like animals in his bed. I give him the truth. "None."

His gaze sharpens further, a tinge of possessive darkness bleeding into the magnificent green depths of his eyes. "And before Budapest?"

That's a truth I'm not prepared to share. I pull away, but he holds tight.

"Answer me, Mina."

"I had a few flings after school. None of them were ever serious."

"That's not what I asked. Before me, when was the last time?"

I bite my lip. "I can't remember."

"I think you can."

"I don't want to talk about it."

His hard features are thoughtful as he considers me. "Was it before or after you left the military?"

I know him well enough to know he's not going to let it go. "Before," I admit softly.

His hold is tight, his question unrelenting. "Why?"

"After the incident, I couldn't let a man touch me."

"Why me, then?"

"Why you what?" I ask, stalling.

"Why did you sleep with me? Was it a diversion to escape? Or did you think I'd kill you otherwise?"

Ilya's accusation comes back to me. He said I slept with Yan because I believed it was fuck him or die. Now Yan wants to know if I only had sex with him to save my own skin. It's tempting to lie to protect myself, but what we shared is too big to let him believe this.

"I slept with you because I wanted to," I admit. "I thought my body was dead for all men, but you broke that spell. You made me come alive."

Satisfaction and pure male possession darken his eyes. In a wink, he turns into the predator who stalks me. I'm pressed down and pinned underneath him before I can drag in a breath.

"I told you we were two of a kind," he says against

my lips. "I haven't fucked another woman since you either, and your hands definitely make my body come alive."

To prove it, he grinds his erection against me, letting me feel my effect on him. And this time, my skin heats in response, my breathing picking up as my body—the one he'd brought back to life in Budapest—comes awake with a rush, the earlier malaise disappearing.

"I want you," he says huskily. "Still tired?"

"No." And spreading my legs, I wrap them around his hips, allowing him to touch me, to make me feel all the beauty and pain of being alive.

WHEN MORNING COMES, I'M WOKEN WITH A TENDER KISS on my shoulder. "Time to get up."

I snuggle deeper under the covers as Yan gets out of bed. What's the point? I have nowhere to be, nothing to do. I'll just stay here until mid-morning, or noon, or evening.

"Ilya is making pancakes," Yan says.

"I'm not hungry."

I pull the sheet over my head, only to shriek when the warm comforter is suddenly jerked from my body and a rush of cool air contracts my skin.

"What the—?"

Yan throws a T-shirt and a pair of shorts at me. "Get up."

I grab the pieces of clothing grudgingly. "What's your problem?"

"We're going jogging."

"What?"

"You need to get out, to exercise. That's why you're so grumpy."

"I'm not grumpy."

"You're depressed."

"I'm not depressed!"

He regards me with his hands propped on his hips, a frown marring his brow. "Denial is the first symptom of depression."

"Fine. Label me however you like. I've been called worse."

He grabs my ankle and yanks me to the edge of the bed.

"What are you doing?" I squeal.

"I'll drag you outside in your T-shirt and panties, or you can get dressed. Your choice."

"Asshole," I mumble, sitting up.

He grins. "Call me that again, and you won't sit for a week."

I shut my mouth, because I don't doubt he'll make good on his threat.

"Now, Mina." He has the audacity to snap his fingers at me on the way to the bathroom.

"Hardheaded mule," I mutter, getting out of bed.

We dress without speaking, me sulking and him in an irritatingly good mood. When we enter the quiet living area, it's clear Anton and Ilya aren't up yet. I give Yan a narrowed glare. He lied about the pancakes.

"Don't fret," he says with a wink. "I'll make you pancakes when we get back."

He drapes an exercise towel around my neck and pushes me to the door. "Let's go."

I suck in the early morning air as we hit the street, and fall into pace next to him as he starts jogging toward the old town. His pace is taxing, but as soon as my body feels the tease of adrenaline, it perks up. My energy returns with a rush. I keep up, and even give him a run for his money. We jog for a good hour before we stop to do some resistance training, using an outdoor exercise area in a park.

I'm sweating by the time we're done, but a lot happier than when we left his apartment. The strenuous workout was exactly what I needed.

"See?" he says, giving me a gentle punch on the shoulder. "I was right."

I roll my eyes. "All men think they're right."

"Admit it," he says, a glint in his eyes.

"Fine. I enjoyed it. Happy?"

"Ecstatic." He gives me a peck on the lips. "I'll race you back."

I'm always up for a dare. And I always win. Of course, he says I only won because he let me.

28

MINA

*T*he days after the morning Yan dragged me outside to exercise are easier. Despite my flagging energy, we run and work out every day. It helps to channel my frustration and chase the depressive feelings away. And that's not the only gift he gives me. He also continues to give me vengeance.

Ten more men.

Yan brings the proof of their torture to me like a cat would proudly show off a mouse to its owner—an undead mouse, one he's cruelly playing with. I'm terrified he'll stumble onto Gergo at any moment, but so far, it seems like he's only focused on the men who assaulted me. I'm also worried the violence will catch up with us and we'll have to flee before we finish the job in Prague, but my ex-teammates aren't talking about their run-ins with Yan's hired team. It's not as if they can press charges. What will they say? They don't want the world to know what they've done—or what was done to them in retaliation. Yan intends to let them suffer for a while; then he'll go back to finish them off. Of course, it takes him time to flush them all out, and by the time there's only one name left on the list, we're two days away from our meeting with Dimitrov.

The stress runs high. The apartment is small, and the men get on one another's nerves. It's a good thing this will soon be over. Not only for the men, but also for me. As the days go by, my strength deteriorates. It's happening faster than before. I can almost feel the defective cells growing inside my body, destroying me little by little.

And as I deteriorate invisibly, our plan progresses.

Dimitrov uses the secure number I gave to ensure our meeting is still on. The painting is dry, thanks to the acrylic paint. The fact that it's not oil will be obvious on closer inspection, but by that time, Dimitrov will already have a bullet in his brain. I try on the dress with the body pads and practice my disguise. I work on my persona. We go back to the hotel and speak to the manager, making sure everything is set. We do a practice run on site. We rent a room in another hotel up the street where I can disguise the two hotel security guards. Yan and Ilya test the weapons. They clean and take the rifles apart for less conspicuous transportation. They test the rope and go abseiling at an indoor training site. All the while, we keep an eye on Casmir Dimitrov and Natasha Petrova in case he behaves suspiciously or she makes a sudden change in her schedule. But everything goes smoothly —which is why we're all extra tense. In our business, it's never a good sign when the sailing is too smooth. Nobody says as much, however, because that will only jinx it.

That evening, we eat a quiet dinner and watch a movie to relax, since everyone is strung out. I'm sitting next to Yan on the couch while Anton takes the chair. Ilya is in the kitchen, making popcorn. It's a stupid horror movie, a film that has us laughing rather than being scared. Yan has his arm around my shoulders. His fingers play with my upper arm, sending delicious chills over my skin. It's a soothing touch. Familiar. I can't believe how quickly he became a part of my life, how much I miss him when he steps out for even a minute.

Over the past three weeks, my captor has somehow become my anchor.

Ilya finally joins us with a bowl of popcorn, stuffing a handful into his mouth as he squeezes in next to me. Predictably, Yan stiffens, and the gentle brushing of his fingers on my arm stops.

I turn my head to look at him. "Not tonight," I whisper-plead, kissing his temple. I don't want them to fight.

He catches my chin before I can turn my face back to the television. Holding my eyes with a smoldering look, he brings his mouth down to mine for a passionate kiss. My cheeks heat a little, knowing Ilya and Anton are watching, but the kiss seems to settle Yan, because he goes back to stroking my arm.

Ilya holds the bowl out to me, and I help myself. The popcorn is warm. It melts with a buttery taste on my tongue. I get engrossed in the silly movie again until Ilya picks up the popcorn I've dropped in my lap.

"Messy eater," he says, nudging me.

Yan shoots him a look. Anton clears his throat.

The woman on the screen leaves the safety of her house to see who's hiding in the woods. We all laugh at that.

"That's so unrealistic," Anton complains.

"Without the dumb moves, there wouldn't be a movie." Ilya pushes his leg against mine. "Tell him, Mina."

Yan tenses again. Since the episode in the restaurant, he's made a big effort to behave less possessively, even with Ilya. It's as if he's trying to make up for his behavior that night, for the hurtful way he reminded me of my place. And I want to believe this, want to trust that the affection he shows me stems from more than a physical attraction, but I know better.

No matter how real this seems, I'm nothing more than his possession.

Sure enough, when Ilya throws his arm along the back of the couch, hugging me from the other side, Yan pushes to his feet.

Jaw tight, he holds out his hand. "Come, Mina. Time for bed."

ANNA ZAIRES & CHARMAINE PAULS

"The movie isn't finished," Ilya protests. "I was going to make hot chocolate."

"Enjoy the rest of the movie with your hot chocolate," Yan says coldly.

My captor doesn't tell me when to shower or eat any longer, but when he orders me to bed, I don't argue. It only pisses him off. Besides, I know when a fight is brewing.

Taking Yan's proffered hand, I let him pull me to my feet. He drags me behind him to the bedroom. To my surprise, Ilya gets up and follows.

Yan stops in the doorway and turns to his brother. "What the fuck are you doing?"

"Mina." Ilya shoves his hands into his pockets. "You don't have to be afraid of Yan's reaction. In fact, pretend he's not here. I want you to tell me honestly. Are you with him because you want to be?"

Yan lurches, going for Ilya, but Ilya jumps back.

"You motherfucker." Yan glares at him, fists clenched. "What's your fucking problem?"

"I think Mina could be attracted to me," Ilya says calmly, "if you'd allow her to look at someone else."

"You know what I think?" Yan asks through thinned lips. "I think you have a death wish."

"Guys." I step between them. "Cut it out."

"No," Anton says, joining the circle. "I want to know." He looks at me. "Tell us, Mina."

Swallowing, I look between the three men. "What is wrong with you? We're going after Dimitrov in two days!"

340

Anton's bearded chin juts out. "Stop using that as an excuse. Tell us the truth now. Do you have feelings for Yan?"

I gape at him, my mouth opening and closing, like a fish out of water. I wait for Yan to tell Anton it's none of his business, but Yan just stands there, staring at me. Waiting.

Fuck.

"That's not fair," I say.

Yan crosses his arms. He's not coming to my rescue.

"What's not fair," Anton continues, "is playing games."

"I'm not playing games!"

Anton widens his stance. "Then answer the question."

Yan glares at him. "Back off."

"We just want her to tell us," Anton says, "since she seems to have you wrapped around her little finger."

I narrow my eyes at him. "What are you saying?"

"I don't know, Mina. That maybe you're using your body as a weapon with Yan."

I lunge and slap him without thinking, my palm connecting with his cheek with a sharp *thwap* before he has a chance to jump back. I've had enough of these false accusations. "I didn't ask for this," I growl as he stares at me in disbelief, his hand cradling his stinging face.

My words are barely out when Yan grabs Anton by the front of his shirt. In a flash, the two men are wrestling. Fists fly everywhere. Ilya ducks just in time as Yan swings an arm past his face and punches Anton on the jaw. The blow makes Anton stumble. His back hits the wall.

"Stop it!" Jumping between them, I try to push them apart, but Yan is too strong.

He easily shoves me away. "Stay out of this, Mina."

Ilya grabs my arm and pulls me aside. "Let them fight it out."

"You started this," I accuse, freeing my arm.

Holding Anton pinned against the wall with an arm pressed against his throat, Yan raises his fist. "Apologize to Mina."

Anton's dark gaze only hardens. "Not before she admits the truth. I'm not apologizing for anything."

A crunching sound reverberates as Yan brings his fist down on Anton's nose, then steps back, breathing heavily as Anton grabs his face with a string of profanities. "You fucking broke my nose," he snarls as blood drips through his fingers.

"Apologize," Yan says through clenched teeth, advancing on him again.

I grab Yan's arm before he can get in another punch. "I don't need his apology. I don't need anything from him."

Anton sneers. "The truth is ugly, isn't it? Not easy to admit, either."

I take a stand in front of him. "You know nothing about me." Turning in a circle, I look at the three men. "You're unbelievable." I'm shivering with indignation and anger. "You better get your act together and your testosterone under control. We have one shot at taking Dimitrov out." I poke Anton's chest with a finger. "Try to focus on that."

Marching into Yan's bedroom, I close the door. Let them fight it out, as Ilya suggested. For all I care, they can kill each other. At least then, I'll be free. And without the shortfall to pay for Hanna's lifelong stay in the clinic.

I walk to the window and peer through the burglar bars, looking at the quiet street below but seeing nothing. I feel like a hamster in a cage. Trapped and beyond frustrated. There's no way out of this for me. I keep on telling myself it doesn't matter. In a few months, I'll be dead. But it does matter. It matters because I don't want it to be this way. I've been lying to myself all these weeks.

I do care. Way too much.

My body isn't the only part of me Yan brought back to life.

The door opens and closes. For a moment, the room is as quiet as if no one has entered, but I can feel him standing there. Yan. I can feel him watching me.

I don't turn to look at him. I don't want him to see the truth in my eyes.

The floor creaks as he advances. He stops close but doesn't touch me. The heat from his body folds around me, offering make-believe comfort, momentary happiness.

"Mina," he says at long last, his voice gentle. "Look at me."

When I don't react, he takes my shoulders and turns me to face him. The expression on his face is as soft as his voice. It holds an apology, but not remorse. He doesn't feel bad about what he's doing. He's not going to let me go.

He studies me for a long time before he speaks again. "Anton and Ilya are jumpy. We're all tense."

"Are you justifying their behavior?"

"Just putting it in perspective."

I suppose it's noble of him to try and patch things up, especially seeing how possessive he is. "Why does he hate me so much? How many times do I have to apologize for the job I did?"

"Anton doesn't hate you. It's me. I'm not behaving like myself. It worries him, especially before a job."

"What do you mean you're not behaving like yourself?"

"I've never been attached to anyone except Ilya. This..." He waves between us. "Anton doesn't understand what's happening. We've worked together for a long time. He knows what I'm like. He believes I'm incapable of caring for anyone who's not family, so he thinks you're leading me around by my dick. We've already had one team leader—Peter—bow out because of a woman; he doesn't want the same thing to happen with me."

It's the caring part I latch on to. "You care for me?"

"Isn't it obvious?"

"I thought you hated me."

He doesn't reply.

My heart shrivels. "So you do hate me."

"I hate what you did."

"It's the same thing."

His gaze homes in on me as if he's drinking in my very thoughts. "There's always been chemistry between us, Mina. We've wanted each other from the start. And I hoped to take a chance with you, to see where it would lead…" He lets me go to drag a hand over his face.

"But you couldn't because I framed you," I finish for him, my chest squeezing agonizingly. I can't believe Yan is telling me this much, letting me glimpse the man under the cool, distant mask he presents to the world.

A man who can be vulnerable. Who can feel.

His mouth twists. "Put yourself in my shoes. Knowing how easily you threw me under the bus, how would you have felt?"

Every part of me aches to come clean, but I can't be honest without risking Gergo's life. There's no choice but to accept the consequences of my lie and live with them. "So you're never going to stop punishing me."

"I'm not punishing you."

"Then let me go."

He stares at me as if I've slapped him. "You want to leave? After everything we've shared, this is how little I mean to you? Just like when you sold me out?"

I clench my jaw in frustration. "No, Yan. That's not what I meant. I don't want to leave. But how can we have anything without freedom and trust?"

"Do I have reason to trust you?"

Tears burn behind my eyes. "I'm not going to run."

Uncertainty plays on his face. He looks at me like he wants to believe but is incapable. "That's what you said before you ran."

"I didn't run. I went to see my grandmother."

"Why?"

"You know why."

My answer disappoints him, I can see that. "Maybe trust isn't in the cards for us."

Defeat makes me weary, the usual tiredness snagging me as the adrenaline from the fight drains out. "Then we have nothing to talk about." I try to move around him, but he grabs my wrist.

"There's more to talk about."

"Not now, okay? I need a shower."

"Now." He's unmovable, his mouth set in a firm line. "You haven't answered Ilya's question. Do you have feelings for me?"

I stare at him, the ache in my chest intensifying. Do I tell him the truth? Do I even dare to admit it to myself? Ever since my parents' deaths, I've felt so little, going through life on autopilot, subsisting on Hanna's love and the adrenaline buzz from my jobs. I thought it was impossible for me to love, to feel anything beyond a mild attraction, but I was wrong.

So very, very wrong.

Stepping up, Yan cups my cheek. "Tell me, Mina. Just give me this one truth."

He regards me as if he needs this truth with every fiber of his being, as if the answer is his alpha and omega. I consider lying to protect my heart and pride, but what's the point? I'm not going anywhere. The war is long lost. And Yan might not have given me his trust, but he's given me vengeance—and as much of himself as he has to give. The man who's incapable of affection outside of sex has opened up to me, letting me see into his icy heart. For that, and for making me feel again, he deserves the truth.

For the short time left, we both deserve the truth.

"Yes. I do have feelings for you." My admittance escapes on a rush of air, defeat weighing me down even before the words are out. "Yan… I'm in love with you."

His expression is a mixture of shock and satisfaction that grows into tender possession. Folding his arms around me, he pulls me against his chest. It's not an exuberant caress that celebrates love. It's a gesture that offers comfort, a Band-Aid on a cut. He holds me close and consoles me for having lost not only my freedom, but also my heart.

"Minochka," he murmurs, "I'll make it good. I promise."

The fact that he doesn't reciprocate my love declaration isn't lost on me. He wants my body. He cares about it like someone cares for a pet, making sure it's fed and healthy to serve its owner's purposes. He may even care about my mind, in his own twisted way, but he'll never love me. The thought hurts, but the clock is ticking and there's not enough time for resentment or pain.

Melting against him, I take what I can get. I accept

the physical affection, the mistrust, and the inevitable blame I'll carry to my grave. I take responsibility for my feelings and lower my defenses, giving him access to both my body and my soul.

Anton was wrong. It's not my body I used as a weapon; it's the walls I'd built around my heart. But now, I have no more weapons left.

I've given Yan the ultimate power over me.

Sensing my surrender, he scoops me into his arms and carries me to the bed. He's lowered me onto this mattress countless times, but never with so much tenderness, such reverence. He holds my gaze as he unbuttons his shirt to expose the chiseled muscles of his chest, then undoes the cuffs and peels the sleeves off his arms. He goes about undressing slowly, creating a memory I'll never forget.

His movements are strong and decisive when he unbuckles his belt and pulls down his zipper. He studies me as he removes his shoes and socks before pushing the pants with his briefs over his hips. I watch everything, taking in every detail, committing it to memory. I imprint the picture of his lithe and powerful body in my mind, reveling in how hard he is for me, how much he wants me.

Climbing onto the bed, he straddles my legs and slips his hands under the hem of my T-shirt. His palms lock around my waist, and he strokes up, bringing the fabric with him and baring my skin. When my upper body is exposed, he lowers his head and kisses a path from my navel to the dip between my breasts. He touches and licks. He explores me as if it's our first time. And in a sense, it is. I've never fully surrendered when we fucked, always holding back a part of me. Not anymore.

Nuzzling my neck, he nips his way to my jaw. I part my lips when he finally reaches that destination, and his tongue slips into my mouth, tangling with mine. The kiss is unlike any we've shared. It's urgent, yet tender. He traces the contour of my lips with his tongue while lifting my arms to pull off my T-shirt. He undoes the front clasp of my bra and sweeps away the cups, freeing my breasts.

"You're perfect," he whispers, lowering his head for another taste.

His mouth is hot on my nipple, his kiss wet and gentle. I arch my back, wanting more, but he keeps the caress soft. His fingers play with my other nipple until every pinch and roll echoes in my clit.

He's as slow in taking off my clothes as he was in undressing himself. I'm panting by the time he's removed my jeans and underwear. When he buries his head between my legs, it's as much as I can take. At the third lap of his tongue, I come. The release is brutal. It tears through me with emotions in its wake that shake me to my core—a need to belong, an infinite well of painful love, a futile will to live. When he positions his hips and enters me, the fragmented feelings come together. They fuse with the warm glow in my body, and for the first time in my life, I'm complete.

"Minochka." He frames my face between broad

hands and starts pumping. His rhythm is leisurely. "This is everything."

I grab his shoulders and hold his gaze, needing him like nothing before. "Perfect."

"Yes." A drop of sweat rolls over his temple. "Like you."

I'm far from perfect. My life is stained with blood. My body is dying. But we have this moment, and I cling to it with everything I've got.

He thrusts slowly, savoring me. I'm tight around him, the aftershocks from my orgasm still making my inner muscles clench.

"Sweet mother of..." he groans as another spasm hits.

Sitting back on his heels, he drapes my thighs over his. One hand wraps around my neck, while the other slips between our bodies. The hold is possessive and dominant. He's careful not to squeeze too hard as he picks up his pace. He hates leaving marks on me. The control etched on his face is stark and raw. He looks like a beautiful, wild animal.

Changing the angle of his penetration, he hits the spot that makes my toes curl. My eyes roll back as he adds pressure to the circles he's drawing on my clit with his thumb. The rhythm of his hips becomes punishing, but it's what I need. My pleasure is already climbing again. The dark lust twisting around my body and stealing my reason demands instant gratification. It unleashes an uncontrollable wildness that makes me lift my hips to take him harder and deeper. It creates a tunnel vision in which nothing exists but him.

I'm close, so close. I chase my release, meeting his every thrust. When he tightens his fingers around my neck, I almost come. I'm drunk on passion, barely registering reality when he pulls out and flips me over.

Before I have time to protest, he's back inside me, taking me with relentless thrusts.

"I want your ass," he says raggedly, folding his hands around my middle and pulling me up on my knees.

Leaning over me, he opens the nightstand drawer and removes a tube. He's better prepared this time. He keeps a warm hand on my back as he unscrews the cap and dribbles cold liquid between my cheeks. The pressure of his cock on my dark entrance stills me.

He kisses my spine. "Tell me if I need to stop."

The words reassure me.

I trust him with this.

I trust him with my life.

He works himself in slowly, and the discomfort is significantly less than the first time, though there's still an extreme feeling of fullness, a sense of being stretched beyond my limits, of being invaded in a strange, unnatural way. But the burn that comes with the stretch only adds to my need, fueling my pleasure, and when he finally starts thrusting, I'm on the verge of coming again.

"Not going to last, princess."

It's been so long since he's called me *princess* that the word jars me from my delirious state. Where he's used the term in a derogative way before, now it's laced with endearment. Pressing my cheek to the mattress, I watch him from over my shoulder. His face is tight with concentration, all his focus on me.

Fastening one hand on my hip and the other on my breast, he orders hoarsely, "Touch yourself."

The moment I do, I know it's over for both of us. My climax is like an electric shock. I'm falling apart and coming together all at once. My lower body tightens, triggering his release, and he plunges deep, then stills with a groan, his cock pulsing inside me. Warmth fills me, and it goes much deeper than flesh. The love I thought I'd never know spreads through my veins, melting the last of the numbing chill in my heart. It should be dirty, this joining of ours, but instead, it's pure and whole. Beautiful.

Surrendering to Yan is the most meaningful act of my life.

We collapse flat onto the bed, his weight pressing me into the mattress. I can hardly breathe, but I want to stay here forever and pretend there are no bars on the windows or defective cells in my body. I want to just lie here and love him, and pretend he loves me back.

"I'm crushing you," he says, kissing my neck.

Too soon, the cocoon in which I'm hiding lifts. And there's no transformation or butterfly, only stark, empty reality.

He pushes up, keeping his weight on his arms. "Take a deep breath." He pulls out when my lungs expand,

leaving an after-burn, but the pain is grounding. "Stay."
A command he loves giving.

He goes into the bathroom and comes back with a
wet washcloth. After cleaning the spillage between my
legs, he turns me over. "Can I get you anything?"

I shake my head.

"Painkiller?"

"I'm good."

He dumps the washcloth on the floor and stretches
out beside me, spooning me from behind. "Sleep."

"I should have a shower."

"Tomorrow. I like the idea of you sleeping with my
cum in your ass."

I swat his arm that lies snugly around my waist.
"You're so filthy."

"I've been accused of worse."

"I thought you're not telling me when to sleep any
longer."

He nips my earlobe and nuzzles my temple. His lips
stretch into a smile against my skin. "This time, you'll
want to obey."

"Oh, yeah? And why's that?"

"Because tomorrow, I'm taking you to see your
grandmother."

29

YAN

*M*ina is in love with me.

I try to wrap my mind around it on the way to Budapest. It's not what I expected, and so much more than I could've hoped for. How can anyone love me, let alone someone as guarded as Mina? At the same time, the attraction makes sense. We're so much alike. We've both seen the uglier side of life, and we can be ruthless. Yet we're both loyal as hell to the family we love. Not to mention, we both need a little more spice in our lives than most people.

Still, we're a world apart. For all the numbing trauma of her past, she feels more, cares more for people than I do. I can see it in the way she interacts with my brother, and even Anton, to some extent. Her hard shell is just that, a shell. Inside, she's vulnerable, fragile. Wounded. And there's a soft side to her, a nurturing and caring part that draws me like a prickly thorn to a lamb's wool.

Even now, as I sit opposite her in the Cessna Anton is piloting, my hand is resting on her knee. The hold may seem casual to an onlooker, but it's a possessive touch, a claiming touch. Now that I know how she feels, I'm more reluctant than ever to let her out of my sight. I'm not blind to how wrong that is. Keeping her against her will is the most fucked-up thing I've done. But I can't let her go. Setting her free would be like chopping out a part of me. She's gotten way deeper than under my skin, and I won't be the same without her.

No, there's no other option. She has to stay. I'm still keeping her forever.

The scale of my feelings has tipped, though. Before, I wanted to own her life and make her pay for her betrayal. Now, a calm acceptance invades my mind. The pressing need for vengeance has shifted to a pressing need to please. To make her happy. Which is why we're on our way to see her grandmother a day before we carry out the hit on Dimitrov. I want to give her everything I can to make up for the love she offers despite the freedom she'll never have.

She's tense, my little soldier. Her body is rigid and her face paler than usual. Disregarding Anton's weight-distribution-impact-on-aerodynamics theory that awarded me the seat facing her, I shift onto the one next to her. I take one of her hands that's clamped between her knees and brush my lips over her knuckles before intertwining our fingers. I wish I could tell her I love her, but I don't know what love means. The feeling I harbor for Ilya is an ingrained duty to protect and take care of him. It's part of my programming. What I feel for Mina is new, hard to define. I only know I can't bear the thought of being apart from her or, God forbid, any harm coming to her.

"Nervous?" I whisper against her ear, sneaking in a kiss. She smells like lemon and honeysuckle. Mouthwateringly delicious.

"What do you think?" she snaps.

"I thought you'd be happy to see your grandmother."

"I'm not happy about *you* coming along."

"Don't fret, princess." I smile. "I'll be on my best behavior."

Snorting, she turns her face toward the window as if I'm not worthy of her sight, which I'm not.

"Not long now." I put her hand on my thigh and massage the knots in her shoulder.

She relaxes marginally, leaning a little toward me. The submission is small, a tiny drop in a vast ocean, but my heart warms as if I've put a blowtorch to it.

A few minutes later, Anton announces our descent. We touch down at the private airport where the same driver from a few nights ago waits.

"Stay in the car," I tell Mina, helping her into the back. And just in case, I nod at the driver, who locks the doors. Love or not, I'm not going to lay temptation at Mina's feet.

With Mina safely locked in, I lead Anton a distance away. I do want Mina to see her grandmother, but I also have an ulterior motive for the trip. Taking out my phone, I pull up the information that arrived last night. Someone took out Mina's assailants, the men my hired team beat and mutilated. I was going to kill them soon, but someone beat me to it. I can only assume it's to make sure they didn't talk.

Perhaps I don't know everything. Perhaps there's more to Mina's attack than I thought.

"What's up?" Anton asks when we're out of earshot.

I show him the media article on my phone. Whoever popped those men has connections in government, high enough to stage the murders as a drug-related gang war.

Anton frowns as he reads. He gives me a speculative look when he's done. "What's this about?"

"Mina."

"Fuck." Lifting his face to the sky, he drags a hand over his beard. "I should've known. This is why we came to Budapest. This is what you've been up to these past weeks."

"Hear me out."

"Do I have a fucking choice?"

"No."

My tone silences him. He sighs and shoves his hands into his pockets. "Spew your poison. I'm listening."

I wasn't going to tell anyone, but the situation has changed. I pull up the photo I haven't been able to look at more than once—not that I need to, as it's burned into my memory—and turn the screen for Anton to see.

"Christ." He pales. "Is that… Mina?"

"This is what they did to her. Ten of them."

"That's why you offed them."

"Not me. I was going to, after letting them live dickless for a couple of weeks while reflecting on their sins, but someone else did the job for me, someone powerful enough to make it look like a drug war."

"Someone must've needed to silence them."

"Exactly."

"What do you want from me?"

"I've tracked them all down, save for one."

"You want me to get information from him."

"I'll owe you."

He grins. "I can live with you owing me. What info do you have?"

"His name is Laszlo Kiss. He went into hiding like the others, but his housekeeper sold the information to one of our informants."

"Must've been an attractive bribe."

"Enough to set her up for life."

"You're investing quite a bit in avenging Mina."

Nothing will be too much. Not all the money in the world. "What's that supposed to mean?"

"You feel for her."

I frown. "Would I have done what I did otherwise?"

"You mean take her?"

I'm not going to answer that.

He watches me quietly. "Ilya is right, you know. You

can't keep her against her will. That's as bad as what those guys did to her."

My anger spikes. In a second, I'm in his face. "It's nothing like that, do you hear me?"

"What is it then, Yan? Is it even about revenge? Fuck, was it ever about revenge? I get that you wanted to make her pay for framing us as terrorists, but look at that." He motions at the phone in my hand. "Look at what they did to her. Don't you think she's been through enough?"

"This is the past," I say harshly, shaking the phone at him. "What happened after has nothing to do with this incident."

"I'm just saying that maybe the girl's had enough shit in her life."

"You don't have a say in this." I take a step closer to him. "She's mine. The only say that matters is *mine.*"

"Fine." He lifts his hands. "But this is going to blow up in your face. Mark my words."

"Just find out what you can from her ex-teammate and let me worry about what will blow up in my face."

"Fine," he says again. "Send the details to my phone. I'll go check it out. I assume this guy is close by?"

"In the northern countryside. After dropping us off at the clinic, the driver can take you. Best be well prepared. I'm sure Kiss expects a visit. He'll be ready, weapons and all. Guards, too."

Anton flashes his teeth, which would've been perfect if not for one slightly crooked canine. "Sounds like my kind of challenge."

"Let me know what you find out the minute you do. We'll meet back here at six. I don't want to get home late. We need a good night's rest for tomorrow."

He salutes. "Gotcha." On the way to the car, he adds, "I can't wait to cash in the favor you'll owe me."

Flipping him off, I get into the backseat next to Mina while Anton retrieves the ammunition we always travel with from the plane. After loading guns and knives in the trunk, he takes the front passenger seat.

"What's going on?" Mina asks.

I take her hand and kiss each of her dainty fingers. "Nothing."

She's quiet until we reach the clinic. She signs in at the gate and stands uneasily until the car pulls away. Interlacing our fingers, I lead her down the path to the entrance. In front of the double doors, she hangs back.

"Yan…"

I can't resist kissing her soft, sweet lips. "Mina?"

"This isn't a good idea."

I narrow my eyes. I want to make this good for her. She better not throw the gesture back in my face. And she better not be ashamed of me, because she's stuck with me. For life.

Pressing a hand firmly on her back, I usher her inside. My brusque manner has the desired effect. She surrenders, allowing me to push her toward the reception area, but the tenseness of her frame doesn't ease.

She announces herself at the front desk. The

receptionist gives us a friendly welcome and tells us to go through to Hanna's room.

Mina's small, slow steps tell me she's not eager for her grandmother to meet me. Tough luck. I want to meet her grandmother.

We go up a flight of stairs and exit on a landing. Mina stops in front of a door, her back so stiff it looks like her vertebrae may snap. After a soft knock, she pushes open the door and enters ahead of me.

I look around the space. Nice. The room is comfortable and tastefully decorated with the focus on practicality. Bars are mounted along the length of the walls for assisted walking while call buttons are strategically placed in case of an emergency. Net curtains in front of a sliding door that gives access to a balcony blow in the breeze.

Mina heads toward the open door. The minute she clears it, her demeanor changes. She becomes loose and relaxed, the very image of calmness and serenity. It's a practiced mask, one she's no doubt mastered for her grandmother's benefit.

A small woman with soft white hair and the same pixie-shaped face as Mina is sitting in a wheelchair in the sun. She's wearing a fashionable red dress with ballerina shoes, her lips a matching shade of red. A book lies open on a score sheet stand that reaches her eyelevel. When she sees Mina, the color in her pale cheeks deepens to pink and her wrinkled eyes turn wide. They have the same color eyes—a magnificent icy blue.

"Mina." She raises shaky arms, the effort it takes not escaping me. "This is a surprise." Her gaze turns on me, sharp and watchful. "And who is this handsome gentleman?"

I let her hug her granddaughter before taking one of her weathered hands in both of mine. "Yan Ivanov. It's a pleasure to meet you, ma'am."

"Call me Hanna." Her evaluation sharpens more. "Ivanov. That's a Russian name."

I nod. "From Moscow."

She switches over to Russian, her accent flawless. "Where are my manners? Please, have a seat."

I draw up two chairs, seating Mina before I take mine.

"Would you like some tea?" Hanna asks.

"We're not staying—" Mina starts, but I cut her short.

"That's very kind, thank you. I'm thirsty." I pin Mina with a look. "As I'm sure Mina is. If you tell me where the kitchen is, I'll get the tea."

Just as Mina's shoulders sag in obvious relief at being rid of me, at least for a short while, Hanna says, "Oh, no. You're our guest." A look of mischief comes over her features. "Mina will get it. She knows her way around."

"But I—" Mina starts again.

"Some biscuits, too," Hanna says with a wink. "And warm milk for my tea." Then to me, "I don't like my tea cooling quickly."

Clever old minx. She's orchestrating it for us to be alone, and I can only imagine why.

"I'll ring for a nurse," Mina offers.

"No, no," Hanna replies with a great show of shock at the suggestion. "They make the tea too weak. Besides, those ladies have better things to do than serve us tea."

Reluctantly, Mina gets to her feet. She looks between her grandmother and me, obviously fighting an internal battle. Remembering my manners, I get up, too. When Mina steps around me, I brush my fingers over hers. It's a slight touch in passing only, as much as I can afford in front of her grandmother, but it's meant to set her at ease. I'm not going to cut Hanna's throat. I'll never harm Hanna, because Mina is going nowhere. She's staying right where she belongs—by my side.

Once we're alone, Hanna scrutinizes me with the kind of insightfulness that speaks of volumes of life experience. "Mr. Ivanov—"

"Yan, please."

"Yan, can you please hand me that blanket over there on the chair?"

I grab the blanket and spread it over her legs. "Better?"

"Thank you. There's always a bite in the air so high up. Beautiful view, though, isn't it?"

I look toward the horizon. The city is spread out beneath. "Indeed. The lights must be pretty at night."

"I'm a lucky lady. I'm lucky to have a grandchild

who provides for me so well. Not that I wouldn't be happy with less."

"Very lucky."

She cocks her head. "Tell me about yourself."

I shrug. "There's not much to tell."

"Have you lived in Russia for all of your life?"

"Mostly."

"Just in Moscow?"

"Yes."

"What about holidays?"

"I didn't travel until I joined the military."

Hanna's brows lift. "Military, huh? I suppose Mina told you she's ex-military, too."

"She told me she was in the Special Forces. Very impressive."

"That girl could read and write at the age of three. She picked up languages like a parrot. Tough too, just like her mother. I won't lie, I was happy when she left the Special Forces. It's not a job for a woman who wants to settle down."

I smile. I doubt Mina will ever want to *settle down.*

"Tell me, Yan, what are your intentions with my Mina?"

I have to smile at that, too. I like her directness. I like that she's protective of Mina. I respect her for grilling me with questions. It's what any loving parent or grandparent should do. It's what I never had, and I'm glad Mina had this feisty woman to look out for her. That she's looking out for her still. "I want to take care of Mina."

"For a short while or longer?"

I don't hesitate. "Forever."

Her lips ease into a curve. "I sense an honesty about you."

"I won't lie." Not about this.

"Then it's serious," she concludes with obvious satisfaction.

"Very."

"I see." She leans forward, gripping the armrests of the wheelchair with trembling hands. "And what do you do for a living?"

"I'm a consultant." Of sorts.

"Where did you and Mina meet?"

"In the bar where she worked."

"What were you doing in Budapest?"

"It was a business trip."

Her gaze softens. "Do you believe in fate, Yan?"

"Should I?"

The expression on her face turns whimsical. "Don't you think some things are meant to be, that sometimes we're in the right place at the right time?"

What do you know? Hanna is a romantic. "I've never thought about it like that."

"Maybe you should."

"I can see the appeal." How much easier our situation would be if we could call it destiny. As it stands now, it's nothing but kidnapping. A sharp prick of guilt nips at a far corner of my mind. It's distant but pesteringly persistent, like a dull headache.

"Are you going to get married?" Hanna asks.

"I don't think Mina believes in that."

Mina's grandmother shrugs. "She's not overly religious, but the reassurance can't hurt, can it?"

"The reassurance?"

"That you're willing to stand by her for life," she says, like I should know. "That you love her."

What am I supposed to say to that?

"A ring won't hurt either." She winks.

Ah. I'm getting lectured for my lack of romanticism by an old lady in a wheelchair. "I'll make sure she gets a ring."

"Good. She likes rubies."

I smile. "I'll remember that."

"What about Mina's job at the bar?"

"She'll come work for me." It's not a lie. I'll have to involve Mina in my future missions. She's not the type who can stay at home without going out of her mind. Judging by how she's behaved since I've taken her, any hint of inactivity makes her depressed.

"In your consulting business?"

"Yes."

Hanna seems satisfied. "I never liked that she worked in that place where men are always drunk so late at night."

Come to think of it, neither did I.

Somberness settles over her features. "Did she tell you about what happened with her parents?"

"Yes, she did."

Her gaze grows more intent. "Did she tell you it may be difficult for her to have children?"

"It doesn't matter to me." I just want *her*. I want her any way I can have her.

Mina's grandmother relaxes again. "Not all men can accept something like that. Not that it's her fault. It happened on a mission. She never told me the details, and I won't ask."

Best not. "You can rest assured I'll do my best to make her happy."

She gives me a broad, tremulous smile. "That's all I want for her, Yan."

"Me, too."

The clinking of cutlery sounds from the door. Mina stands in the frame, a tray in her hands. Getting to my feet quickly, I take the heavy burden and ignore Mina's protest when I start pouring the tea.

"What did you talk about?" Mina asks, looking between us with a frown pleating her pretty brow.

"This and that," Hanna says, smiling at me. "Your Yan seems like a very accomplished man. Quite a catch. Not bad-looking either. Well done, Mina. I think you got yourself a good one."

Mina turns redder than the roses in the vase on the table. "Hanna!" she scolds gently.

"What?" Hanna turns to me. "You don't mind if I'm blunt, do you? I would've made more of an effort to be tactful, but as we grow older and our time shorter, tact sometimes seems like nothing but a roundabout way of saying something."

"No offense taken," I say. "I can get used to your directness, especially if it involves more compliments."

Hanna laughs softly.

"Sugar?" I ask.

"Two. And milk, please."

I add two lumps to the strong black tea and stir in some milk.

"I'll take that," Mina says, reaching for the cup. She blows on the tea before bringing the cup to Hanna's lips.

After taking a sip with much difficulty, Hanna asks, "When are you moving in together?"

"Hanna," Mina exclaims again.

"Actually," I say, "we're already living together."

Hanna beams. "Is that what you came to tell me? I'm so pleased. Where are you staying?"

"For the moment, in Prague," I reply. "After that, we'll see. Our work may require frequent traveling."

"You said you do consulting." Hanna takes a bite of the cookie Mina offers. She chews and swallows before continuing. "What kind of consulting?"

"Human resources," I say.

Mina clears her throat, looking everywhere but at Hanna.

"Since we have a few hours before we need to get back, how about a game of cards?" I suggest.

Hanna's face lights up. "I love cards."

"Careful," Mina says, "she'll clean out your coins."

"Then it's a good thing I have a whole wallet full of them."

"You do?" Mina regards me suspiciously.

"A little bird might've told me to come prepared."
Or the nurses' reports.

Either way, I'm here to please.

FOR THE REST OF THE MORNING, WE PLAY POKER. I LET
Hanna win, but not too obviously. We have lunch
together in the dining hall. Afterward, while Hanna
naps, Mina sits in the chair next to her bed, Hanna's
hand clasped in hers. When she wakes, we take her for
a stroll in the gardens, then come back to the room and
spend the rest of the afternoon sharing more tea and
cake.

Throughout this, Hanna tells me stories of Mina's
childhood, little anecdotes I put away in my mind like
guilty treasures, because I sure as hell don't deserve this
afternoon with its normal airs and the simple yet
profound enjoyment of a family spending time together.
I take it like I took what doesn't belong to me, making it
mine despite the nagging voice in the back of my head
that's questioning my integrity. I've never suffered from
a conscience before, and it's uncomfortable. The doubt
started when Mina told me she's in love with me. It grew
a little when Anton confronted me, and after meeting
Hanna, it's an annoying but impossible-to-ignore notion.

It still doesn't mean I'll let Mina go. It only means I
get to feel bad about it.

Fuck me. I'm developing a moral sense.

While Mina and Hanna are chatting, I remove myself to a corner to give them some time alone and use the opportunity to check my phone for news from Anton. The message is disappointing. Laszlo Kiss had already escaped his weekend residence by the time Anton got there. However, Anton questioned the staff, offering money as an incentive, and he may have a new lead with regards to Kiss's whereabouts.

Our fugitive might have run to his cabin in the Swiss Alps.

This is a nuisance. I need to catch this fucker as soon as possible, before he slips completely through my fingers, and we have the job tomorrow. Perhaps I could spare Anton. He could fly to Switzerland in the morning and be back to fly us to our hideout in Africa by the time our job is finished. He's only supposed to play bodyguard and drive our getaway car. It won't delay us by more than a few seconds if I have to take the wheel.

Decision made, I promise myself to take it up with Anton later.

I'm about to darken the screen when I notice a message from our hackers. Making sure the women are still engrossed in their conversation, I open the encrypted email. It's the classified information I requested on Gergo Nagy, the man who saved Mina from the attack.

I skim through the accolades and go to his military history. Known as The Chameleon, he's a disguise expert, one of the best in the world. And he was in charge of training Mina.

A red flag pops up in my mind, intuition making the follicles in my nape tingle. Heartbeat picking up, I scroll to the attachments and open a photo.

Handsome guy, about my age. Strongly built.

There's something about that mouth, though. It's the way he smiles without actually smiling. It's vaguely familiar, but I can't put my finger on it.

I lift my gaze to stare at Mina. She's talking away, unaware of the cauldron of perturbation in my stomach.

What are you hiding, princess?

Then it hits me, and my heart nearly bursts through my ribcage.

30

YAN

*M*otherfucker.

The realization hits me so hard I have to turn my back on the women lest Mina sees something in my face. My hand shakes as I punch in the code to unlock a file and draw up the images from the clinic's video feed, then zoom in on the face of the man Mina met in these very gardens, the ones we visited a mere hour ago with Hanna. Placing the photo of Mina's companion and Gergo Nagy side by side, I study the image with growing fury.

It's the same man. Well-disguised, but it's him.

Is he her lover, a boyfriend she's been hiding all along? Jealousy burns through my veins, stinging like poison, but before my thoughts can spiral too far down that dark, ugly path, I remember her confession yesterday. It was as sincere as it was unwillingly given. Mina loves *me*, not him, I'm sure of that. Besides, she said I'm the first man she's been with since the attack, and I have no reason to distrust that. That first night in Budapest, she'd been so tight I'd hurt her. Almost virgin tight, which would only make sense if it had been a long time for her.

But if he's not her lover, just her ex-trainer, why did she risk her life to meet with him? That scumbag Tóth said they were good friends, that Nagy saved Mina when he walked in on the near-rape, but still.

Wait a minute.

No.

Fuck.

Suddenly, it all makes sense. The truth thwacks me like a sucker punch in the gut, and a sickening sensation settles in the pit of my stomach. All this time, I blamed Mina. I think back to the dirty shed on Esguerra's property and Mina's small body tied up in there, her pretty face bruised. I think about when we questioned her and how the minutest flicker sparked in her eyes when we showed her the photos of the Delta Force men disguised as us. At the time, I took her reaction for guilt, but I was wrong.

It wasn't guilt. It was surprise. Mina didn't do the disguises. It was Gergo Nagy. She recognized his work but took the blame to protect him.

My heart stutters. Of course, she'd protect him. He saved her from rape, maybe even saved her life.

Motherfucking fuck.

How could I not have seen her innocence before? Was I so desperate to hold her responsible?

A mingled confusion of relief and regret spears

through me. Relief because she didn't frame me. Regret for how this could've—should've—been.

As I digest this further, a wave of filthy self-loathing rolls through me.

I punished her for nothing. She's innocent. That's why she met Nagy here. To warn him. She knew if we found out about his involvement, I'd kill him.

Shit, shit, shit. Every molecule in my body resonates with fury. I want to chase down the motherfucker and strangle the life out of him. But everything is different now. Mina is in love with me, and I don't want to hurt her more than I already have.

Fuck, what do I do?

"Yan?"

Mina's voice comes to me, soft and uncertain. Frightened, even. My name on her lips pierces through the fog of my roiling emotions, pulling me back like a gentle tide.

Pushing everything under the surface, I school my features before facing her. "Mina?"

"Hanna was asking if we're staying for dinner."

There's hope on her face, but also fear. She's still wary of having me around Hanna after my threat. And who can blame her?

"We have a long day ahead tomorrow," I say apologetically, already hating how sad acceptance settles in her blue eyes.

As I speak, I look at her. I look and I look. I can't stop looking.

She's not who I accused her of being. Over the

weeks, I've made my peace with her betrayal. I've come to accept that our one-night stand meant nothing to her beyond the physical. I've congratulated myself for managing to tie her to me with feelings, using sex as a weapon. I've given myself a figurative pat on the back for making her fall in love with me. When her betrayal was my excuse, it wasn't so hard to do. But now, that leverage is gone, and I have to face the fact that maybe our spontaneous sex on the night we met didn't mean that little to her after all.

Fuck. I can no longer use her betrayal as currency. I can no longer take her freedom as payment for a sin she never committed.

Mina turns away to make Hanna comfortable, and I keep staring at her with new eyes. I look and look as one question keeps turning in my mind.

Can I let her go?

The answer sinks into my heart, heavy like a rock, rough with sharp edges.

No.

Fuck, no.

My woman approaches me with a faint smile. "Shall we go?"

It's a smile that nearly kills me.

It's hard for Mina to say goodbye, so much so the air in my lungs constricts with an incontrollable echo of sympathy. The truths I carry in the secret cavities of my chest maul me to a pulp inside. I hold Mina's hand tightly as we get into the car, and I don't let go until we're home.

Ilya is out, chasing women. I wait until Mina is taking her shower before approaching Anton.

"I want you to go after Kiss in Switzerland. This job is too important to trust anyone else with it."

He takes a beer from the fridge and twists off the cap. "When? You do realize after tomorrow, he may already be on the move again, or whoever took out the other guys may shoot him before we get to him."

"That's why I want you to go tomorrow first thing." If he didn't need his sleep, I would've sent him now.

He stills with the bottle tipped to his mouth. "You've got to be kidding me."

My stare tells him there's no joke.

"What about Dimitrov?" he asks.

"We'll manage. Any one of us can drive a car as well as you can."

"What about keeping an eye on the street and exit?"

"I'll get our hackers to tap into the city's street cameras. They can send the feed to my smartwatch."

"It's a risk. Is avenging Mina really more important than not fucking up this job?"

"I'm not going to fuck up this job. We'll take care of Dimitrov. And you'll get your cut, don't worry."

He slams the bottle down on the counter. "It's not just the money. It's our reputation. If we blow this, who's going to hire us in the future?"

"Everything will go as planned."

Planting his hands on his hips, he regards me from under his brows. "I'm going to ask you one last time. Is she worth it?"

Is she worth it? Fucking yes. Ten times over. A thousand times over. Regret weighs heavy on my shoulders, guilt softening my voice as I tell him, "I don't think Mina framed us."

He's quiet for a beat. "What?"

"I think her military trainer did the disguises."

"What the fuck are you talking about? She admitted she'd done it."

"To protect him."

"Who?"

"The Chameleon. Ever heard of him?"

"Yeah. He's legendary." Anton's eyes widen. "Wait. Are you saying he trained her?"

"That photo I showed you, that ordeal? He saved her."

"So," he says slowly, "she owes him her life."

"Exactly."

"Fuck. Have you confronted her?"

"Not yet."

"How did you find out?"

"The hackers. They sent me the info on Gergo Nagy after Tóth mentioned him. That's why Mina went to Budapest. To warn Gergo. I have the security tape of them meeting. He was disguised, but it didn't take much to put two and two together."

"Are you going to take him out?"

"Don't know yet. He obviously means a lot to Mina. Apparently, they're good friends."

"I suppose we can't really hold him accountable.

The guy doesn't know us. If what you say is true, he was just doing a job, same as us."

I sigh deeply, feeling it in my bones. I still have an urge to take him out, but now I owe him for saving my woman. "This complicates matters."

"You don't say."

"I still don't know who's killing Mina's attackers. Or why."

Anton cocks his head. "This Gergo guy, maybe?"

"If he wanted to kill them, he would've done so after Mina's assault. There's something else, something bigger, and I don't have a good feeling about this."

"Fine. I'll go to Switzerland and torture the bastard."

I pat his shoulder. "I knew I could rely on you."

"Just do me a fucking favor and don't screw things up."

I manage a crooked grin. "Not a habit of mine to screw up."

He lifts an eyebrow, leaving the unsaid hanging between us. Yeah, I screwed up royally with Mina.

The water in the bathroom turns off.

It's time to face my princess.

YAN

*A*nton discreetly leaves, claiming he's in the mood for restaurant dining.

I give myself a minute to get my shit together before walking into my—our—room. Mina stands in front of the closet, a towel draped around her body. She's lost weight. The curve of her shoulders is sharper, the bones more pronounced. I push the worry onto the pile the size of Kilimanjaro I already carry in my chest to focus on what needs to be said. She must see from my shaky demeanor that something is off, because wariness creeps into her gaze.

She looks like a doll—porcelain skin, huge blue eyes framed by long lashes, slender limbs, and silky silver-blond hair. She's indefinably gorgeous. There are no words to describe her beauty or value to me.

Crossing the floor, I stop in front of her.

She stares up at me with a frown. "Yan?"

I'm acutely aware of the difference in our sizes, of

her tiny frame and vulnerable bones—not that she'd hesitate to take me on if I were to offer her a fair fight. She's not a princess who favors pink dresses, although with her, I want to play dress-up all the time. She's a rebel in black. An angel in white. A soldier. A woman.

I cup her face. I'm overwhelmed with how small she seems, how my palm easily envelops her cheek and jaw. "Tell me who you met in Budapest."

Every muscle in her body locks. She's so rigid it's a wonder she manages to step away from me. "No one."

I drop my hand. "I know, Mina."

The color drains from her face. "It's not what you think."

"Tell me." It's a plea, not the order it sounds like. I'm bone fucking tired. I can't fight this war of secrets with her any longer. I just want everything to be out in the open, so we can move on. "Please, Mina. I want to hear it from you." I want a clean slate between us.

She swallows. "I swear, he's a friend, nothing more. How did you find out?"

"Security feed. Why did you lie to me?"

She's quiet, ever defiant, ever determined to protect her friend.

"Say it." I can't explain my urge for her to come clean. I only know I need her to tell me like I need to fuck her, and soon. "I already know everything." She doesn't believe me. She thinks I'm bluffing. "Gergo Nagy, right? Your trainer."

"H-How do you know about Gergo?"

"Does Tóth ring a bell?"

"Tóth?" Her voice rises with one decibel of panic. "My superior officer?"

"The fucker sang like a canary before I cut out his tongue." My smile is evil. "After that, not so much. And when I cut off his dick, even less."

She's whiter than the bedsheets. "You said you beat them."

"I may have left out the part about the dick-chopping to spare you."

"So why tell me now?"

"Someone is finishing them off."

Her inhalation is sharp and shallow. "You mean someone is killing them?"

"Yes, and I'm going to find out why." I give her a piercing look, but there's only incomprehension and confusion in her eyes. "Why would someone silence them?"

"I don't know."

I believe her. "There's one person left."

She stares at me, and I can practically see her mind working, flipping through all the photos she's seen so far. "Laszlo Kiss," she says after a moment, and I nod.

"Anton is going after him in the hope of getting information that'll throw a light on what the hell is happening."

"He's going to kill him."

My smile is cold. "Obviously."

"Please, Yan." In a second, she switches gears. She goes from standing there like a salt pillar to frantic, grabbing hold of my arms. "Please don't hurt him." For a moment, I think she means Kiss, but then she says, "Please don't hurt Gergo."

"When those men attacked you, he rescued you. Am I right?"

"Yes," she says with a soft whisper of defeat.

"That's why you owe him."

"My life." She doesn't look me in the eyes when she says, "And more."

Gripping her chin, I tilt her head for our gazes to meet. "He taught you the art of disguise."

She searches my face, probably trying to guess if I also know about the other lie. "It was part of our training."

"So, you took the fall for him when Sokolov questioned you about the disguises."

Surprise—not the good kind—makes a stark tableau of her face. It's both a stunning and disturbingly moving canvas of truth. Falling to her knees, she wraps her arms around my legs and stares at me as big drops of tears roll over her cheeks and plop on the towel covering her breasts.

"Please," she says again, "don't hurt him."

Seeing her like this, begging on her knees and crying at my feet, is more than I can take. It shatters me. For the first time in my life, I feel defeated. Utterly beaten. My chest splits open and feelings I've never known slip in, dark and ugly feelings of failure, remorse, guilt, and fear. Fear of losing her.

I can't lose her.

I go down on my haunches, crouching in front of

her. Reaching out, I cup her wet cheek. Her tears keep on spilling, running over my knuckles into the cuff of my shirtsleeve. My every instinct demands I off him, but I force out the words for the woman who means the world and more to me. "If it's so important to you, I'll spare him."

She drags in a breath. It takes a moment before she manages, "Thank you," through sobs and trembling lips.

I don't deserve her thanks. I don't deserve anything from her. I owe her an apology, but I don't know how to apologize. I want her to know I'm keeping her. Regardless. That I'll always take care of her and keep her safe.

"This doesn't change anything, Mina." The half-baked apology sounds more like a fucking threat. My voice is gruff and hard while my insides are shredded and tangled.

Gathering her into my arms, I press my precious charge against my chest. She's supple and warm in the crook of my body. My cock grows hard against her stomach, and the towel is suddenly too much of a barrier between us. I rip it away to bare her skin. Her nipples are pink and hard. Her soft skin makes my hands itch to touch her. I can't keep them off her.

Like a goddamn caveman, I spread her out there and then. The floor is hard, too hard, but my mind is halfway lost to lust already, and my heart demands possession, proof that she's mine. I fasten my lips around a nipple and graze the tip with my teeth. When her back lifts off the floor, I nearly lose what little of my rational mind is left. She threads her fingers through my hair when I kiss and suck the other nipple, leaving marks I promised myself I wouldn't again. But these aren't the imprints of my fingers. They're hickeys. Marks of ownership. Marks that reassure me but don't wipe away the guilt I've pushed to a dark corner of my soul as I kiss my way down to her pussy.

For now, I lose myself between her legs. I bury my face in her heat and honey. Here, in the midst of our pleasure, I can forget about everything else. I can make her forget, even if only for a few moments on a hard floor. Spreading her with my thumbs, I suck on the tender bundle of nerves hidden beneath her folds. I lap up the cream she spills for me. In no time, she surrenders her pleasure. She gives it to me without holding back, just like the last time when she told me she's in love. With *me*.

Ruthlessly, I take everything. I wrench every aftershock from her body until she turns limp. Then I shove my fingers inside her, curling the middle digit to find her secret spot. I pump her spent body until her need climbs again and more cream spills around my fingers. I'm a bastard. I don't give her time to recover, not even enough to catch her breath. I thrust until she throws back her head and veins pop out on her delicate neck from the strain. I don't advance with consideration or caution. I'm way beyond reasonable civilities. I stretch her tight pussy with three fingers and grind the heel of my palm on her clit until she breaks and comes again. The climax looks like torture. Her body contracts as if being hit by an electric charge.

She falls back on the floor, her back hitting the hardwood surface. Like a man obsessed, I unfasten my belt and pants. I barely take the time to shove them over my hips before I grab the root of my cock and push the head against her entrance.

I want her. I need her. Now.

With a tilt of my hips, I part her tight flesh. She cries out in pleasure, maybe a little pain too, but I'm long past breaking point. I can't hold back. Pushing forward, I stuff her full of my cock. Like I've taken everything from her, I make her take all of me. When our groins are flush together, I move.

I lose myself in a desperate rhythm, knowing I won't last. Keeping my weight on one arm, I pin her hip down with the other to prevent the thrusts from shifting her over the floor. I pump until heat explodes at the base of my spine and my cock erupts with scorching-hot pleasure. I empty myself inside her, making her take every drop just because it's so damn intimate. On the most basic of levels, it's the ultimate expression of affection. A woman can't take more than this, and this is everything a man can give.

Breathing heavily, I press our foreheads together. I intertwine our fingers and kiss her mouth, pouring myself and everything I want to give into the kiss. Together, we come down from my frenzy, from whatever the fuck one would call what I just did. It's more than fucking. It's more than making love. It's more sacred. It's darker. There are no words for what I feel.

When my reason somewhat returns, I roll onto my side, bringing Mina with me. I can't make myself pull out. Not yet. Right there, on the floor, I give her the care I owe her, stroking her back, arm, and hair. A week ago, I desperately wanted her confession. Now, I only want her like this. Soft. Content.

I should be at peace, but I'm not. The seed of guilt has grown. It's growing stronger still, turning like a magical bean into a giant stalk. Finally gathering enough willpower to break our contact, I pull away from Mina and get to my feet.

She pushes up on her arms. "Is everything all right?"

No. Nothing is all right. I doubt it'll ever be again. She turned my world upside down, unearthed everything I thought I was. Guilt is like a cancer eating at my gut. I've never hated myself as much as in this moment.

Her eyes are large, vulnerable. Sweet baby-blue. "Yan?"

Clenching my fists, I consider all my wrongs. "I never told you I love you back."

She drags her knees to her chest and wraps her arms around them. "I know."

"If that bothers you—"

"You shouldn't fall in love with me."

The sincerity of the statement knocks me off balance. "Why not?"

"It's not a good idea."

I can't look at her like this, sitting naked on the floor in a puddle of my cum. It only makes the godawful guilt sharper, the pain more acute. Offering her a hand, I pull her to her feet.

"Thank you," she says.

"For what?"

"For taking me to see Hanna."

My smile is weak. "You're welcome."

As she drops my hand and makes to turn, I grip her wrist. "That night in Budapest, did it mean anything? Beyond the physical, I mean."

Her stare is level. "When I told you it's different with you, I meant now as well as then."

For some reason, her words floor me. I come apart a little more. "Then why did you run?"

"You scared me. I was frightened."

"Only frightened?"

"And intrigued."

The chemistry *was* real. It wasn't one-sided. "I wouldn't have hurt you."

"You wanted to keep me."

I can't argue with that.

"Yan," she continues, then pauses. "The job with Henderson... I had no way of knowing you were involved. I should've trusted my instincts—"

I place a thumb on her lips. "I believe you. It's in the past. We're not talking about this again."

She stands quietly, waiting, but when I don't say more, she turns on her heel and walks to the bathroom.

I stare after her. A bruise spreads in my chest as I

watch her frail shape and tiny form. I can never look at her the same way again. I can only see her like I saw her in Hanna's room—a woman wronged, a woman I admire and adore. Her innocence only acts as a magnifying glass to highlight my shortcomings and faults.

Forcing my feet to move, I follow her into the shower, where I take her again, bending her over and entering her from behind. I'm gentler this time. The storm has wreaked its havoc. For now.

Afterward, Mina offers to cook, but she's tired. Tomorrow is a big day. I order pizza, which we eat naked in bed while watching a news broadcast on my laptop. She falls asleep in my arms even before she's brushed her teeth. Carefully shifting out from under her, I close the laptop and gather the empty pizza box and napkins. When I enter the kitchen, still naked, Ilya is leaning with his elbows on the counter, a bottle of beer in front of him.

He looks me up and down with a grin. "Good night?"

I dump the trash in the can. Our sex life has nothing to do with him. Grabbing a clean towel from the tumble dryer, I wrap it around my waist. "Looks like your night went well."

"Splendid. Blonde. Legs from here to heaven. I swear she could wrap them twice around my ass."

I take a beer from the fridge and twist off the cap. "Good for you."

"What's eating you?"

"Why would something be eating me?"

He chuckles. "You're talking to your twin."

I glance at the closed door of my bedroom.

He follows my gaze. "Trouble in paradise?"

Leaning on the counter and crossing my ankles, I take a sip of my beer. "It's never been paradise. Hell, maybe."

"I thought you were happy. Why else would you fight me so hard over Mina?"

"I fucked up."

He brushes a hand over his head, regarding me with caution. "What did you do?"

"Mina didn't do it."

"Do what?"

"The disguises. It was someone else."

He straightens. "What are you talking about?"

I tell him everything I've told Anton. He doesn't interrupt me as I talk, and to his credit, he doesn't say I'm the worst asshole alive.

When I've finished the grim tale, he comes over and pats me on the shoulder. "It's settled, then. She didn't do it. Shouldn't that make you feel better? I sure as hell feel better."

"In a fucked-up way, I feel worse. I treated her pretty badly."

"Apologize. She lied. You couldn't know."

"Don't you see?" I rake a hand through my hair. "I used the betrayal as an excuse for keeping her."

He shrugs. "Then let her go."

I slide down to sit on the floor with my back against

the cupboard. Swirling the bottle, I digest his words. It's not as if I haven't considered it. At least a hundred times since I learned the truth. And every time I think about cutting her loose, I come up against the same wall. "I don't think I can do it."

Ilya sits down next to me, his arms on his knees. "Why not?"

"I can't live without her." I clasp my head in my hands, the cold bottle pressed against my temple. "I won't know how to."

"You love her," he says in wonder. "Fuck me. I never thought I'd see the day."

Shaking my head, I lean it back against the cupboard and close my eyes. "I don't think I'm capable of love."

"I think you're not giving yourself enough credit."

I tear one eye open and peer at my brother.

"You've changed," he continues. "Now that you mention how you feel about Mina, it makes sense."

"Changed how?"

"You refused to share her."

I crack the other eye open and give him a hard look, ready to launch into the same tired old battle, but he's smiling.

"I thought you were pushing me away." He slams a palm on his forehead. "Meanwhile, you were falling in love."

"I wasn't pushing you away. Mina isn't someone I can share."

"You see? You *do* love her."

"I wouldn't recognize love if you waved it with a flag labeled LOVE in front of my face. Besides, I don't think Mina wants my love."

"Why do you say that?"

"She just said as much. Said it was better I don't fall in love with her."

He scratches his head. "Yeah, well, after how you treated her…"

"What a big fucking mess." At least I now understand why she couldn't trust me and why she didn't confide in me about meeting Gergo.

"The way I look at it, there's only one way to find out if I'm right."

"Right about what?"

"That you love her."

"What way is that?"

He meets my gaze. "If you love her, you'll let her go."

His words gut me. Because he's right. Keeping her is selfish. Keeping her is for me. If I care about her more than I care about myself, I will do it. I will show her the door and set her free. I will let her walk through it and risk never seeing her again.

I never knew a thought could hurt more than a knife in a kidney, but it does. The idea of losing her strangles me until I can't drag in any air. And yet, I've known this all along. It's what's been eating at me since I forced Mina to admit her feelings and declare her love. It's what's been nipping at me, feeding on my newfound conscience. Mina accomplished what no one else has succeeded in doing. She made a human being out of me.

A man.

A man who loves a woman.

The realization knocks me sideways. It kills me. Because in this moment, I know what I'm going to do.

Ilya, so often in tune with my misery, grips my shoulder. "I'm sorry, bro." He forces optimism into his tone. "She may come back. Maybe she'll even stay."

After everything that's happened? I doubt that very much. Only a fool would hope for the impossible.

"She did say she was in love with you," Ilya says. "That counts for something."

"Yeah." My heart isn't in the word, though. My love is dark. It's not a fairy-tale kind of love, the kind women dream of in their fantasies.

Even women like my Mina.

"When will you do it?" Ilya asks, correctly assuming my decision is made.

"After the job." My heart fucking shatters. She won't come back, I know it. "That'll be best."

"Yes," he agrees solemnly. "Better not rock the boat before. We need our ducks in a row."

We sit together in the low light on the floor like the brothers we were before. Like during the many cold, hungry nights when I consoled Ilya with a stolen loaf of bread or a not-so-funny joke, he sits with me through my darkest hour.

I dread tomorrow like no other day.

Tomorrow, I'm setting Mina free.

32

MINA

I wake up tense, the nightmare about my parents still fresh in my mind. The sun is breaking through the window in Yan's room with a soft glow. Normally, the ordinary scene would've settled me, but nothing about this day is ordinary.

It's the day we're taking out Dimitrov.

I don't take anything for granted, not the familiarity of the warm light nor the snugness of the cozy covers. Every minute is precious. Every second counts. Yet I can't find peace in the moment. I can't appreciate the warmth of Yan's body that's pressed against mine or the pretty way dust particles dance in the wedges of sunlight. Unease stirs in my belly, something indefinable poking at my nerves. This is odd. I'm usually calm before a job. The men's edginess must be rubbing off on me.

Yan's breathing is rhythmic, his nose buried in my

neck, but he's awake. I don't need to see his face to know. I'm always in tune with him these days.

"Sleep well?" he whispers against my ear, scraping his stubble down my neck.

I shiver at the delicious friction. "Like a baby." I feel good this morning, and I say a silent prayer of gratitude for the mercy. I need my strength and wits today.

Turning me onto my back, Yan stretches out over me. The heat of his naked skin makes my body come alive, the hardness of his erection nudging between my thighs lighting an instant fire in my veins. He holds my gaze as he grips my wrists and lifts them above my head. Drinking in my expression, he rubs the head of his cock through my slickness before pushing all the way inside. My breath catches from the thrill of the sudden stretch, and goosebumps break out over my skin, the follicles contracting with intense pleasure and a strange, soothing kind of pain.

"Good?" His voice is lazy and still gravelly from sleep, but his eyes are alert and observant, watching my expression as he pulls out almost all the way and slides back to the hilt.

Biting my lip, I throw back my head. The only answer I can manage is a blink.

He kisses my neck, sucking on the skin beneath my ear. "That's my girl."

The approval in his tone makes me melt. The unease drifts away on a wave of passion as he starts to move with an easy pace while lifting his head to study me once more. The way he stares at me with naked hunger, willing me to open myself up and submit to my feelings, is as potent as a physical touch. The way he devours me with a simple regard evokes a pleasure as intense as the stroking of his cock over the sensitive nerve endings inside me.

Being held down like this, taken with his body and eyes, has me responding to him in no time. Despite his leisurely movement, my pleasure builds fast. I'm drowning in need underneath his muscular weight. He's testing his power over me, how hard he can make my body bow, how long he can hold me on the edge before I lose all sense of time and place. All the while, he scrutinizes me with those jewel-green eyes, reveling in my reaction, reverently observing every gasp and moan.

When I reach my limit, that dark, dangerous place where hearts are stolen and minds are lost, he rewards me with relief. Rolling his hips, he applies just the right amount of pressure on my clit to allow me an escape from the maddening prison of need he's trapped me in. He unlocks the chains and permits my heart to take flight on a peak of pleasure. The ecstasy is so severe I'm barely cognizant of my name. How easily he takes my reason.

He lets me finish completely before he comes, filling my body with his seed. He pumps until he's empty, and then thrusts some more. He moves with the feverish determination of a man trying to spill his mark and possession into me. It's no different from every other time we've fucked, and yet, it's not the same. As he rests his forehead against mine, squeezing my wrists, we're completely aligned. The last disharmonious note has fallen in tune. Our coupling is perfect. Complete. Our breaths pant the same melody, our hearts hammering the same erratic beat. We're two instruments resonating in harmony. It feels like...

Love.

The thought is sweet. Bitter. Sobering. Only yesterday, I worried that he'd never reciprocate my feelings, but now, my fear is the opposite. He shouldn't love me. He can't. It's better if my love remains one-sided. I love him too much to hurt him like that. But our hearts have already merged, and the man staring down at me isn't the man who abducted me in a dark alley.

He's the man who loves me.

I reel at the realization. The thought knocks my heart askew in my chest. I'm still battling to come to grips with the uninvited insight when he pulls out, leaving a wet puddle between my legs and a disconcerting coldness in my soul. I'm trying to reconcile that frosty distance with the heat of the knowledge burning in my mind, but then he presses our mouths together in a kiss that consumes me from the inside out. A barrier drifts between us even as that kiss forges our bodies and souls closer together. It's a kiss like no other, a kiss that spells love and goodbye in the same breath. It's push and pull, a force that has equal power to fuse or wreck.

I'm hovering in that confusing space when he tears his lips from mine to press a chaste kiss on my cheek.

"We better have a shower," he says.

Throwing back the covers, he takes my hand to lead me to the bathroom, but the distance between us grows until the atmosphere becomes stiff like cardboard, and my throat throbs with a knot of unshed tears.

When Yan gets out of the shower and hands me a towel, I can't hold my tongue any longer. "Is everything all right?"

He meets my gaze squarely as he dries off. "Why wouldn't it be?"

"You're different."

"Now's not the time for amateur psychoanalysis," he says sharply.

The rebuke is like the prick of a needle in my heart. After what we've just shared, it's bewildering, but I school my features. "You're right. We should focus on the job."

He pulls me to him and kisses the top of my head. "Get dressed. I'll prepare breakfast."

Pushing the nagging worry aside, I focus on the tasks that take priority. While the men get ready, I attach the body pads, apply a bronzing lotion, and work on my cheekbone fillers and makeup while the tanning lotion dries. I secure a hairnet with pins and carefully fit the wig. Then I get dressed. The dangling earrings, bangles, and cluster ring add the finishing touches.

When I'm done, I study my full-length reflection in

the mirror. The result is good. Great, actually. No one will be able to tell I'm not the real Natasha Petrova, not even from close-up. Not unless one's met her in person, and Dimitrov has never met her.

Yan and Ilya are in the lounge when I step out of the room, dressed in their transport company overalls and caps. Ilya gives me an approving nod. Yan runs his gaze over me, but there's no acknowledgement in his eyes. No approbation or disapproval. They're just… blank.

"Yan?" I walk over and try to take his hand, but he pulls away.

He tilts his head toward the table that's laid with cold cuts, cheese, toast, and orange juice. "Better eat something. You'll need your strength."

"Can I get you some tea?" Ilya asks, weirdly sympathetic.

I look between the twins. "What's going on?"

"Nothing," Yan replies curtly. "We're leaving in fifteen minutes. Make sure you're ready."

"Where's Anton?" I ask.

Yan packs some of my neatly folded clothes into an expensive overnight bag for the sake of appearances at the hotel. "Taking care of Kiss."

What? Today of all days? "Couldn't it wait?"

"No." He adds a pair of shoes to the bag without looking at me. "By tomorrow, Kiss could be gone again or dead, and I want answers."

"What about my bodyguard?"

"You'll tell Dimitrov something came up." He shrugs. "It happens."

I gape at him. "Are you serious?"

"Don't worry." Ilya gives my shoulder a squeeze. "We'll manage fine without Anton."

Ignoring Ilya, I keep my attention focused on Yan. "Why didn't you tell me?"

"I don't need to tell you anything," Yan snaps. "You just have to do your job."

I flinch at the outburst.

"It's all right," Ilya says softly. "It's just nerves. The job, you know." He shoots Yan a nasty look.

"Eat," Yan says. "You have ten minutes."

I'm not hungry, but Yan is right. We'll need our strength.

After a light breakfast, I apply lipstick and put on the heels we'd gotten for the occasion. Yan and Ilya test wireless ear mics that are connected to their smartwatches. It allows them effortless and discreet hands-free communication. As I'll be searched, I'm not wearing a mic. I'll only have the phone Yan gives me, which I slip into my bag. It's the secure number Dimitrov used to contact me, in case his guards decide to check. Yan's hackers have uploaded Natasha Petrova's contacts and apps to the phone, complete with mirrors of her social media accounts. One never knows how thoroughly Dimitrov will be checking me out.

We load the crated painting, the case with disguise material, and the overnight bag in the van. As I'm about to get in, Yan curls his fingers around my wrist, and for a moment, the fiercely passionate man of this morning breaks through the surface of icy detachment.

"Be careful," he says.

"You, too."

He kisses me on the forehead, so as not to spoil my lipstick, before helping me into the passenger side. Ilya gets into the back and Yan drives. We make a stop at the hotel a few blocks away from the Hotel Paris, where the two security guards already wait in the room we rented. I take care of their disguises, turning them into Yan and Ilya's doppelgängers, before they walk to the Hotel Paris via the back alleys. We wipe away our traces and fingerprints, check out, store the disguise bag in the van, and it's showtime.

As previewed, we park in a side alley next to the hotel. If Dimitrov's men are watching, our arrival must appear inconspicuous. Petrova would respect secrecy. Flipping oversized sunglasses over my eyes, I slip into my role. My shoulders are squared and my breasts pushed out when I get out of the van. My steps are long, my legs not faltering in the high heels. I nod at the doorman waiting at a service entrance like I'm the Queen of Sheba and proceed ahead of the transporters who are carrying the crate and my bag. We enter via the kitchen and take the service elevator that only runs to the first floor, where the conference room is situated.

I step out on the first floor, the men following behind. From behind my dark glasses, I keep a watchful eye. Nothing seems out of the ordinary. There are no suspicious men lurking around, only some of Dimitrov's regular guards hovering in front of the conference room, pretending to help themselves to coffee from a carafe that stands on a table in the hallway. I recognize them from the photos in the file I studied during our preparations.

The manager is on the floor. He makes a big show of greeting me and wishing me a good stay, then flicks his fingers at a bellboy, who comes running to take my bag from Yan. The manager offers to walk me to my suite, but I decline in my Natasha Petrova voice, stating I don't wish to be disturbed. He hands me the keycard before bowing and kissing my hand, assuring me of his loyal service. I sway my hips as I cross the hallway while the guards drool after me, their eyes fixed on the impressive size of my fake boobs.

It's a good show, a convincing one.

I enter the regular elevator ahead of the bellboy. Yan and Ilya follow, balancing the crate between them, their caps with the transportation company logo pulled down low over their eyes. The bellboy pushes the button for the fourth floor. We ride in silence. I exit on the landing, casting an eye around for surprise elements, but all is quiet. Opening the door to the Klimt suite, I study the space with a critical eye for the bellboy's sake, who isn't in on our plot.

"Everything to your satisfaction, ma'am?" he asks.

"This will do." I take a hundred from my purse and slip it into his hand.

"Why, thank you, ma'am."

"Please put the Do Not Disturb sign on the door on your way out," I order.

"Yes, ma'am."

When the door closes behind the bellboy, Yan and Ilya work fast. They use the hammers in their tool belts to crack open the crate while I inspect the suite. There's no one hiding inside and no cameras I can detect. I take the handheld scanner Yan has zipped up under his jacket to check for bugs and transmitting devices. By the time I'm done, the twins have leaned the painting on the wall in the living room and discarded the crate on the balcony, making sure they've left the sliding door unlocked.

"It's clean," I say when the scanner light comes up green.

"We're out of here," Ilya announces, moving to the door.

Yan grips my hip, hesitating. "Take off the glasses," he says in a strained voice. "I want to see your eyes."

The request unbalances me. It throws me out of my role, and when I remove the sunglasses and place them on the coffee table, I'm Mina. I'm Yan's. For a moment, we simply stare at each other, an instinctive knowledge of belonging passing between us.

Checking his watch, Ilya says, "We have to go."

There's nothing Yan can say without jinxing the operation, certainly nothing like, "It'll be fine," or, "I love you." Love was never part of the plan. My heart aches knowing I'm inevitably going to hurt him, but it's a new love, a young love. He'll get over it. He'll carry on, maybe find someone less damaged to care about. And yes, I want that for him. I want him to be happy. God knows, he had little enough of happiness growing up.

With a squeeze, Yan lets go. Ilya smiles at me before exiting into the hallway. Yan follows in his brother's steps, but stops in the frame.

"Go." I wave him out. There's no time for second thoughts. Timing is everything. The hotel security will already be waiting in the elevator.

He gives me one last look laced with something like longing and uncertainty, and then he's gone. The door closes with a click, locking me into silence.

Right away, my body tingles with energy, like it always does on a mission. It's the adrenaline. Yet despite the physical high, I'm calm and focused. The job makes me feel like I have a purpose other than being Yan's sexual distraction. I didn't realize how badly I needed to get back into action until now.

It only takes me a moment to assume my role again. I straighten my dress and check my lipstick in the mirror. I'm pushing a curl behind my ear when the knock I expect sounds on the door. Donning my sultry face, I open the door to an entourage of men in dark suits. Dimitrov stands in the center, flanked by two bodyguards with earpieces and holstered guns. A short man with gold-rimmed glasses and mousy hair hovers on his left. With his willowy frame and pinstriped suit, he stands out from the rest of the muscled, black-clad clan.

He must be the art expert.

"Right on time." I hold out a hand. "I appreciate a punctual man."

Dimitrov's murky-brown eyes zoom in on me like I'm the piece of art up for auction. "Miss Petrova." He kisses my hand, sneaking some tongue into it. "I'm ecstatic that my manners please you."

The wetness of his slimy tongue sends an internal shiver of repulsion through me, but I hide it behind a smile. "I can't wait for us to do business."

The hunger on his face is savage and blatant. "Then I have to offer my excuse for making a lady like yourself wait while my men sweep the room."

I step aside. "Please tell your men to go ahead."

As agreed, two guards enter the suite to check for bugs, wires, and weapons. A third pats me down after Dimitrov apologizes for the disrespectful but necessary treatment. I hold my breath as the guard sweeps his palms over the body pads on my hips and around my thighs, but they're good quality. The porous material is designed to absorb body heat. Through clothes, they feel as warm to the touch as skin. The guards return from searching the bedroom and bathroom, giving Dimitrov a nod.

"The painting is there," one of the men says on his way out.

My tone is seductive. "My turn." I twirl a finger to indicate Dimitrov should turn around.

"Where is your bodyguard, Miss Petrova?" Dimitrov asks with a raised brow.

"Indisposed. And please, call me Natasha. If I may call you Casmir?"

"By all means, Natasha." He lifts his arms with a mocking smile. "Feel free to search me thoroughly."

I don't hesitate to pat him down. Natasha wouldn't be shy to touch him. On the contrary. I linger near his groin. The touch almost makes me gag, but I do a good job of hiding it. He's muscled. In good shape. His regard is sharp, his mind fast. He'd make a dangerous opponent in any combat.

"My expert," Dimitrov says when the ordeal is finally over, extending an arm toward the mousy man in the blue suit. "For obvious reasons, he prefers to remain anonymous."

I repeat the search with the expert, minus the groin lingering.

When both Dimitrov and I are satisfied that neither party carries a weapon, I invite him and his expert in, closing the door behind them and turning the lock.

"This way," I say, leading them to the lounge.

Dimitrov gasps and theatrically places a hand on his heart when he sees the painting. Flicking his fingers at the mousy man, he says, "Please."

The expert steps closer, squinting as he removes his glasses to clean them on a handkerchief he pulls from his jacket pocket.

Making my way to the bedroom, I throw back over my shoulder, "Champagne?"

"Most fitting," Dimitrov mumbles with a deviant glint in his eyes.

Everything about the man makes my skin crawl, but I blow him a kiss. "I'll be right back."

I move unhurriedly, sashaying my hips. I only walk faster when I'm out of view, and faster still when I pass the table on which a bottle of Dom Pérignon is cooling in an ice bucket. My heels are quiet on the thick carpet.

Five more steps to the bathroom.

I count the seconds. In three, Dimitrov is dead.

One.

Two.

Just as I grip the doorknob, a strong arm locks around my waist.

"Going somewhere, Natasha?" Dimitrov's tone is low and menacing as he shoves his tongue into my ear.

33

YAN

*E*verything is going according to plan, but I can't shake the discord in my gut. This morning nearly killed me. Making love to Mina while knowing I'm going to lose her today shredded me up inside. The space I tried to put between us after our intense lovemaking was the hardest thing I've done after leaving her alone in that suite to meet with a scumbag like Dimitrov.

Ilya and I get into the elevator. The two hotel security men are already stripped to their shirts and underwear. Their jackets and pants are bundled into a bag that stands on the floor. They use a keycard to block the elevator, ensuring it doesn't stop on any floor.

When the doors close, Ilya and I quickly pull off our heavy-duty boots before peeling off the overalls. We're wearing T-shirts and cargo pants underneath. We keep on the cotton gloves we used for transporting and handling the painting. The real purpose of them isn't protecting a precious piece of art, but not leaving fingerprints. The government isn't going to let their police force pursue us for a hit they ordered, not unless we get caught red-handed, but you never know. I don't like leaving unnecessary traces. Our connection will sweep the room clean of Mina's prints before letting the feds in on the scene.

As I shove my feet back into my boots, my mind goes to Mina. Will she be all right?

Goddamn. My focus isn't where it should be. Probably sensing my volatile feelings, Ilya gives me a sidelong glance as he hands his overall to one of the men.

The men pull on the overalls and our caps, and I hand over the keys for the van. No one speaks. We ride down to the lobby in strained silence. Once they've exited and we're on our way up again, Ilya pins me with a stare.

"What?" I snap, feeling like hitting something.

"You've got to get your shit together, man."

"Who says I don't?"

"You're not here." He points at the floor. "You're fucking miles away."

He's right. I'm not the only one with plenty to lose. My brother's life is on the line, too.

"It's Mina," I admit with a defeated sigh. "I'm concerned." No, that's putting it way too mildly. "I'm fucking going out of my mind with worry."

"Hey." He grips my shoulder and dips his head to

catch my eyes. "She's done plenty of jobs without you. She knows what she's doing."

"Still." She's a woman, and a tiny, delicate one at that. And she'll be locked in a hotel room with a dangerous criminal in—I check my watch—seven minutes. Fuck. I grip my head between my hands. Just thinking about it makes me sweat. Every part of me wants to go back and pull her out of there.

"Focus," Ilya says, giving me a shake. "In a few minutes, it'll be over."

It'll be over. Mina and I will be over. Everything will be over. My life will lose all meaning when she walks out on me.

"Don't think about it," Ilya says, correctly guessing what's going through my mind. "You can get drunk later and break all the tables and chairs in the bar."

"It's just..." The fourth floor lights up. The Klimt suite floor. The floor where Mina is, waiting for Dimitrov. "I wish I could lock her up and keep her safe from harm."

"She's not the kind of woman you can wrap in cotton wool. Locking her up will slowly kill her. You saw how bad she got those first few days after you took her. Mina needs this. I bet she's fucking good at it, too."

Pride swells in my chest. Yeah, she'll be good. The best. But still, this is hard. My protective instinct demands I keep her far away from dangerous situations. Then again, until yesterday, my possessiveness demanded I keep her all to myself. Forever. And if I could change my very nature for her, enough to set her free, I can bend my protectiveness to give her my trust.

"You good?" Ilya asks, searching my eyes.

"Yeah." I fucking appreciate the butthead right now.

The elevator pings as it reaches the sixth floor.

Grabbing the bag with the security men's clothes, Ilya says, "Time to play."

We get out on the top floor. I check the image from the city camera in the street below that feeds to my smartwatch, courtesy of our hackers. Two SUVs with darkened windows park in the street just as the hotel security men pull off in our van. Dimitrov and his men get out of the vehicles. There are five guards and a thin man without an earpiece, who I assume to be the arty dude. Dimitrov walks to a city car parked on the curb. The window on the driver's side rolls down. He leans inside and exchanges a few words with the driver. Just as I expected, Dimitrov had us watched. It's a good thing our arrival was well staged. Dimitrov nods. He straightens and pats the roof of the car, then crosses the street with his men. They enter the hotel just as we take the fire escape, making our way to the rooftop.

An ornate wall running around the perimeter protects us from view. We crouch behind it next to the bag with the rifles. Dimitrov should be at the suite now. His men will be searching the room, and Mina will be searching him even as Ilya and I exchange the cotton gloves for thin leather ones.

As I'm zipping the bag with our weapons open, the

ringtone of my phone sounds in my ear. I check the caller ID on my watch.

It's Anton.

A sliver of premonition runs down my spine. He wouldn't be calling now if it weren't urgent. He knows we have exactly three minutes before abseiling over the edge of the building to the balcony of the Klimt suite.

Ilya, who's connected to my smartwatch via our shared communication system, gives me a worried look. I tap the mic once to take the call, checking that my weapon is correctly loaded even as I answer, "Anton?"

"Get Mina out of there!"

My body turns to ice, my veins freezing over.

He continues in a rushed tone. "It's a trap."

34

MINA

The arm around my waist squeezes so hard I can't breathe. Effortlessly, Dimitrov lifts me off my feet.

Fuck. I break out in a sweat. He wasn't supposed to follow me to the room. How far am I willing to take the seduction game? How long before his expert realizes I tricked them? Surely, if he's truly an expert, by now he should know the painting is a replica.

I should let Dimitrov feel me up. I'll catch him by surprise before the mousy man can alert him. We can still pull this off. I can take out both men or at least hold them off until Yan and Ilya arrive.

Trapped between Dimitrov's body and the bathroom door, I keep still, allowing him to lick the inside of my ear as shivers of revulsion run over me.

"Answer me, Natasha," he says, hurting me with his tight hold. "Or shall I call you Mink?"

Fuck!

Shock slams into me. *It's a setup.*

I don't think why. I don't think how. I only think survival.

My seduction plan is useless now. It's going to be a fight.

Constraining me like this, Dimitrov has the upper hand. I have to break free and fast. I'm in a vulnerable position. He can crush my ribs or snap my neck.

My training takes over. I go into an automatic fighting mode. Slamming back my head, I target the most sensitive part of his body within my reach. A crunch sounds as I hit his nose. The impact has the desired effect.

Letting go, he stumbles back a step. "Fucking bitch!"

I use the opportunity to spin around.

Never give an opponent your back.

Blood streams from his nose. He's clutching the broken cartilage between his hands, his eyes ablaze with furious hatred. There's another crunching sound as he sets his nose straight with an evil grin.

Tough bastard.

I bring my leg up fast, aiming for his crotch, but he's not letting me catch him off-guard again. He jumps back, avoiding the kick. At the same time, he pulls back an arm and swings a fist at me.

But I'm fast, too. I duck before the blow connects, using the momentum to make a sideway roll and smoothly push to my feet a short distance away. It's an agile dance that comes easy, one that was drilled into me until it became second nature. I'm now in the narrow space between the bed and the wall, and the nightstand is at my back.

He advances quickly. "You think you can double-cross me?"

I act trapped, letting him believe he's going to get his filthy paws on me. As he reaches for me with the speed of a striking snake, I hop onto the bed and grip the horizontal bar of the four-poster frame. With a powerful push, I swing through the air, opening my legs. Surprise registers on his face as I catch him around the neck in the vise of my thighs, crossing my ankles to secure the death grip.

Smothering his face in my crotch, I squeeze my legs and twist my hips at the same time. A less experienced man would've died from a broken neck in seconds, but Dimitrov isn't any man. He's a hardened criminal used to fighting dirty. He bends with the movement before falling to his knees, almost ripping my hands from the bar. I have no choice but to let him go or fall on the floor right in front of him.

I recover quickly. Before he can get to his feet, I swing back and kick out with my legs, hitting him full in the chest with the sharp heels of my shoes.

The kick hurts. It does enough damage to fold him backward and knock out his breath. Clutching a fistful of his shirt, he looks down at the red spots of blood seeping through the fabric where my heels have broken his skin.

"You're going to pay for this," he hisses, climbing to his feet.

I don't hesitate. I slam a heel onto his hand where he's grabbing the edge of the bed for support.

The unmistakable splintering of bone sounds, and blood pools around the hole my heel has left. Clasping his hand to his chest, he goes back down and utters a cry that's bound to alarm the expert.

By now, Ilya and Yan should be on the balcony. At the sound of trouble, the expert will let Dimitrov's guards in. The priority is stopping him from unlocking the door. I'll deal with Dimitrov after. For the moment, Dimitrov is hurting enough to be out of action, even if just for a short while.

Using the strength in my arms, I swing myself over the bed to the other side while Dimitrov catches his breath on the floor with blood pumping from his hand. I barely feel the burn in my muscles or the jarring impact on my legs as I land on my feet in the heels. I'm about to make a beeline for the door when the mousy man appears in the frame. Taken aback, I stop dead. The man closes the door and locks it before leaning a shoulder against the wall in a confusingly casual stance.

A shot rings out from the other room. Even with the silencer, the sound resonates through me like a brass bell in a church tower.

Another shot is fired in answer.

Shit. Too late. The man let the guards in. Yan and Ilya are caught in a crossfire, and they're outnumbered by three.

My body flashes hot and cold. A setup was the last thing we expected. We don't have a backup plan, not for the war playing out in the other room. Our order to the hotel manager was clear. We didn't want anyone on this floor until the job was done. The whole fourth floor was evacuated and closed for a so-called routine fumigation. With the silencers, it may take a while before someone realizes there's a shootout happening on the floor. And if a guest or employee does catch on to what's going down and calls the police, we're still fucked. If captured, they'll torture us for information on our alliances and clients before locking us up so deep and far away we'll rot before anyone finds us. The government won't come to our aid. They can't admit they ordered the hit on Dimitrov. They, too, were clear with their order.

If caught, we're on our own. We can't rely on help.

My heart and mind race when I think about Yan and what's happening behind that locked door, but I have to trust him to fight his battle. And I have to take care of mine.

I turn my attention to the mousy man, who probably escaped in here to protect himself and Dimitrov from the bullets flying around next door. "Go into the bathroom and stay there. You don't need to get hurt."

Shoving his hands into his pockets, he addresses Dimitrov. "There are two men fighting off five. They don't stand a chance. I'm sure your team can spare a man. Shall I get one of the guards?"

"No," Dimitrov grits out, stumbling to his feet. "The bitch is mine. I'm going to kill her with my bare hands and fuck her while I do it."

So the setup goes this far. The mousy man was never an art expert. Whatever he is, his carelessly spoken words incite me to fury. He doesn't know Yan and Ilya. They do stand a chance.

They have to.

The man shrugs. "As you wish."

The expert or whatever the hell he is doesn't budge. He doesn't come for me. Which is good, as Dimitrov is back on his feet.

Spinning, I turn sideways so I have both men in my sight as I assess the situation. Dimitrov plunges his injured hand into the ice bucket, probably to stop the bleeding and dull the pain somewhat. Then he grabs the bottle of Dom Pérignon in his good hand. Bringing the bottle down hard, he smashes it on the edge of the table. Champagne boils over the broken shards and spills onto the carpet.

I reach behind me for the cord of the lamp on the nightstand, twisting it once around my wrist as I taunt, "Now that's a waste of good champagne."

Holding the broken bottle like a knife in front of him, Dimitrov charges. I jerk up my wrist, pulling the plug from the socket. The cord serves as a lasso and the lamp as a heavy weapon. I swirl the lamp through the air once before lancing it at Dimitrov.

The metal stand hits him on the wrist, and the bulb explodes, paper-thin fragments of glass raining down on the carpet. They crunch under his shoes as he hops around on them, dropping the broken bottle and shaking his wrist with an ugly curse.

"One for Mink," the mousy man says. "Zero for Casmir."

"Shut the fuck up," Dimitrov shouts, baring his teeth as if he wants to rip me apart with his canines.

I lash out again, this time hitting him on the side of his head with the lamp.

Now he's a wounded, fuming bull. His fury takes over, and he no longer fights cleverly. He acts on angry instinct. Sadly predictable. When he charges, his head bent to hit me in the stomach with the full force of his body, I whack him on the back of the neck with the wrought-iron lamp base. The blow is hard enough to make his legs cave. The moment his knees hit the carpet, I tear the cord from the lamp, wind it around his neck, and twist.

He makes a nasty gurgling sound, frantically reaching for my ankles, but I'm already darting around him and jumping onto his back. He swats at me uselessly. His arms don't reach far or effectively behind his back. He goes for my hair, but I duck back easily enough, having predicted the move. Realizing he's not going to pry me off with his hands, he thrashes like a madman, but I'm light and hold on without much effort. Finally, he gives up and tries to wiggle his fingers under the cord. I twist three more times, enough for the cord to cut into the thick flesh of his neck.

The shooting continues, but I force myself not to think about it. I fight Dimitrov with all my might while keeping one eye on the mousy man. The strange little man is still leaning motionless on the wall like some weird sociopath.

"Admit it, Casmir," the man says. "You're getting beaten by a girl."

Dimitrov slams his bloody hand on the carpet. He twists his head and lifts his eyes to the man with a plea for help. The man doesn't move.

What's up with the mousy man's strange attitude? I don't know what his stand is, but I better finish Dimitrov off quickly so I can deal with him.

Unfortunately, Dimitrov is a fighter. The bastard refuses to give up. With an inhuman burst of strength, he rolls onto his side and on top of me. I end up flat on my back, trapped under his body with him facing the ceiling. Before I can ward off the blow, he plants an elbow in my stomach.

The punch takes my breath. Wheezing, I fight for air. My grip on the cord slackens. In a wink, Dimitrov is on his feet, ripping the cord from my hand and cutting my palm with the force. The same cord I used to strangle Dimitrov is wound around my neck. I kick and get in a few punches of my own, but Dimitrov is fueled by his anger. He half-drags, half-carries me to the bed, hauling me up onto the mattress.

Pop! Pop!

The fighting next door escalates. I imagine Yan and Ilya taking shelter behind furniture and wrecking the suite as I struggle for my life. Maybe the guards are keeping them away from the door on Dimitrov's order. Maybe Dimitrov told them my life was his. It makes sense. A man like Dimitrov won't allow anyone else to kill a traitor with whom he has a personal vendetta. And I did deceive him in the most humiliating way, not only using his own lust as a weapon against him, but also making him look like a fool.

My vision turns hazy, but I refuse to give up.

I wrestle harder underneath Dimitrov, scratching wherever my nails find purchase, but his suit jacket hampers my efforts. I go for his face. He leans back far enough that I barely scrape his jaw.

Abandoning the cord, he folds his hands around my neck. His injured hand is functioning poorly, but even so, his force is frightening, the kind fueled by hatred and a blind will to survive. "I'll fucking kill you slowly."

I try to throw him off by bucking my hips, but he's dead weight. A frantic glance at the door assures me the mousy man is still standing there, observing the spectacle with obvious glee. Does he get off on watching people getting killed?

A string of gunshots rings out from closer, maybe just behind the door, but they're faint sounds compared to the buzzing in my ears as Dimitrov continues to choke me. My lungs protest and panic surfaces.

Calling on all my training, I stop fighting his hold, forcing myself to think.

"Not so brave now that you're on the receiving end," Dimitrov mutters.

He pins my neck to the bed with his injured hand while reaching for his buckle with the other, giving me just enough oxygen so I wouldn't pass out. So I'd be conscious for what he has planned for me.

"Are you just going to stand there?" he asks the mousy man. "Or do you want a taste of the traitor's cunt?"

"I'll let you go first," the man replies.

Fuck him. Fuck them.

A loud crack comes from the lounge. It's followed by the sound of splintering wood.

Dimitrov is occupied with his frantic fumbling, pushing down his pants before wedging his hips between my legs. Blood from his broken nose drips onto my face, and drops of saliva splatter over my lips as he snarls, "I'm going to fuck every hole in your body. Then I'm going to watch my men do it. Then, before I kill you, I'm going to fuck you with that broken bottle."

I want to spit in his face. I want to sink my teeth into his tongue and rip it from his mouth, but I tamp down the instinctive urge to fight back with anger. I suppress the impulse to go blindly into the battle. I have to fight with my brain, not my body, like Gergo taught me.

The thought of my friend calms me, and the knowledge that Yan is on the other side of that door gives me strength.

When Dimitrov's cock falls on my thigh, I push off the wig and grip one of the hairpins keeping the net in place. Slipping the curved end around my middle finger, I secure the sharp points between my fingers and make a fist while Dimitrov is shoving up my dress, groping for my underwear. When the bastard grins at me, I stab him in the eye.

His scream is chilling. He tries to jerk away, but I grab his hair in my free hand and hold his face to me. He swats wildly, mostly hitting air. I don't stop. I stab him in the eye and cheek, everywhere my hand happens to fall. He throws back his head and yowls, stilling a fraction of a second in his strain to escape the assault. It's enough to take aim. Putting all my force into it, I jab the long, sharp wire of the hairpin deep into his ear.

The piercing cry of a man pushed beyond the threshold of pain rips through the room. It's not a scream but a thin wail, a sound that goes hand in hand with torture. Nothing hurts like a ruptured eardrum. Nothing makes a person go crazier than a needle in the inner ear.

I pull out my weapon. He lets go of me to slam a palm over his ear. A rivulet of blood oozes through his fingers. It's the longer pause I need to locate the jugular vein in his neck. The prick from the pin in a vein is nothing compared to the pain in an eye or ear, but his good eye grows large while the bleeding one bulges as the hairpin sinks into his neck. Like all animals, he knows instinctively when the end has arrived. Defeat is written on his face, but like all overconfident men, he battles to believe it. He stares at me in shock. The fight has gone out of him completely. He doesn't approach death gracefully.

He greets it screaming and crying.

Shoving a slobbering Dimitrov onto his side, I crawl out from underneath his semi-naked body. He'll bleed out. With Dimitrov eliminated, the mousy sociopath is now my biggest immediate threat. I aim for the door, ready to jump like a tiger, but the man is gone.

Pop! Pop!

I have to get to Yan. I have to help him and Ilya.

My ribs protest when I move. Dimitrov must've cracked one or two with his punches. Ignoring the pain, I hobble away from the bed, but stop as something hard presses against my temple and the unmistakable click of a safety being cocked sounds in my ear.

"Not so fast, Mink," the mousy man says. "You're not going anywhere."

Several questions run simultaneously through my mind. Why didn't he help Dimitrov? Who the hell is he? Why isn't he shooting me already?

I'm contemplating the answers, trying to piece together a puzzle while searching for a way out of this new dilemma, when my gaze falls on the broken bottle on the floor. I can knock the gun out of his hand and stab him with the bottle before he knows what's happening.

Another gunshot.

Lifting my hands, I play for time. "Don't shoot. I'll do what you want."

He chuckles. "I doubt that."

My muscles tense and my body draws tight, preparing to attack. I'm about to move when the wood around the doorknob explodes and the door falls into the room.

A tall figure appears in the frame, and everything inside me goes still, the earth seeming to stop moving. Even time itself stops as Yan stands there with a cold, fierce look on his face. He's covered in blood and aiming a pistol at the man, perhaps one he took from the guards.

My heart at a standstill, I shift my gaze from Yan to the mousy man and the gun in his hand. His finger is curled around the trigger.

The trigger indents the slightest fraction. The spring being pushed back is amplified in the silence that rings in my head. Maybe it's imaginary, but what's real is the bullet in the barrel.

My world starts turning again when Yan speaks.

"Let her go." His gaze sharpens, his eyes tightening. I recognize the intent in those jade-colored pools as he calmly keeps his aim and says, "Now."

The man snickers. "I don't think so. Throw down your weapon or she's dead."

"You're not going to shoot her." Yan pulls his lips into a thin smile. "She's your only ticket out of here."

Yan doesn't look at me, nor at the now-quiet-and-still Dimitrov, who's lying on the bed half-naked, his flaccid cock exposed. All of Yan's attention is focused on the man pressing a gun against my head.

"Let her go," Yan says again, "and I'll kill you fast."

The man laughs. "You're making premature assumptions. I'm not dying today, and I'm not letting her go. As you said, she's my ticket out of here."

Yan's smile turns condescending. "Do you always hide behind a woman's skirt?"

The man folds his fingers around my upper arm, holding me in a tight grip. "She doesn't count for a regular skirt. I've seen her in action."

It's then that Yan looks at me, and what I see in his eyes chills me to the bone. He's going to shoot the man.

The message passes between us. It's an unspoken language only two people who are as in tune with each other as we are can understand. There's the slightest flicker of a smile in Yan's eyes, a smile that's meant just for me. With that single look, Yan tells me everything he showed me this morning. The sum of my life is condensed in that look. Everything I've ever wanted is distilled into this single moment.

Now.

Moving fast, I shoulder the man hard before ducking. He loses his footing, taking a step to the side. The barrel of the gun swings up into the air as he lets me go and tries to find his balance with flailing arms. The shot goes off, the stray bullet hitting the ceiling. Bits of plaster sift like snowflakes to the ground. Before he finds his equilibrium, Yan fires.

Click.

A blank.

I stare at Yan in incomprehension while horror transforms his face. Cold realization settles in my stomach. The chamber is empty. The man registers the knowledge at the same time. A mocking grin splays across his face as he takes aim again, this time pointing the gun at Yan.

Yan's body tightens. He's like a wound-up coil, ready to lunge, but no man is faster than a bullet.

I don't think. I pounce. I grab the man's arm and try to wrestle the gun from him. Yan's voice calling my name reaches me as if from under water. The sound is muddled, distorted. I want to tell him it's all right, to call for help, to get Ilya, but another shot goes off.

For a moment, I'm utterly confused. I'm not sure why a raw, savage cry tears from Yan's chest. I'm not sure why the man's head explodes and his brain splatters over the carpet. Vaguely, I'm aware of Ilya rushing into the room with a shotgun in his hand and sirens blaring in the distance. I'm aware of Yan catching me, easing my body to the floor. I'm aware of his strong hands and the inconsolable sound he makes as he kneels over me. I'm aware of his anguish as he presses his hands on my side and roars, "No. Fucking no. No, no, no."

Following his gaze, I see the red that stains his hands. I see the damage and I know the truth.

He loves me. My flaws and sins, my twisted self, Yan loves me for who I am.

Cupping his face, I whisper, "I know."

"Mina," he says harshly, "stay with me. Stay with me, damn you."

Already, the sirens are fading. But I do stay with him. I stay with him even when the light bleeds out.

35

YAN

"*M*ina," I shout as the life runs out of her eyes right in front of me.

No! Not this. Anything else.

I'll let her go a thousand times over before I let her die.

Panic like I've never known seizes my mind. My emotions wreak havoc in my heart. Fear, anger, remorse, guilt, and more fear assault me. It's more than I can handle. I'm on the brink of falling apart, but I've got to keep it together.

Fuck! I need to think.

I've got to get Mina to a hospital. But where? With a gunshot wound, there will be questions. The government won't stick its neck out for her. The clusterfuck of violence that took place in this suite is already pushing it too far.

Shoving my feelings aside, I act fast. I prioritize actions as a plan forms in my mind.

I search for Ilya. My brother stands next to me, stunned to silence. His gaze is fixed on the blood seeping from Mina's side through my gloved fingers.

My voice is harsh, commanding. "Ilya."

His eyes snap to mine.

"Pillow," I say, holding out a hand.

He grabs a pillow from the bed and shoves it into my hand.

I press the pillow to Mina's wound. "Call our government connection." Making quick work of removing my belt, I fasten it around Mina's waist to keep the pillow in place. It should help to stop or at least slow down the bleeding. "Tell him we need a cleanup."

Lifting Mina into my arms, I rush to the door and almost bump into the manager who enters as I'm about to exit.

"What the hell is going on?" he yells. "One of the maids heard gunshots. What in the name of…" He trails off as he takes in the destruction and corpses. His face goes white.

"We've been set up," I say, shoving him aside.

He glances at Mina's still form. "You can't leave," he says in a shaky voice. "You have to stay here and deal with this."

Coming out of the bedroom, Ilya says, "A team from the government is on the way." He slips his phone into his pocket. His tone is clipped, his manner rushed. "They'll make it look like part of the drug war happening all around the country at the moment."

"But—" The manager gags as he looks at one of the bodies. "My hotel."

"Keep the floor locked down until our connection gets here," I call from over my shoulder, running for the fire escape. We can't risk taking the elevator. No one must see us leave the building.

Ilya runs ahead to get the door. I dial Anton on the satphone via voice command as I make my way down the stairs as fast as I can without risking a fall.

"I'm on my way," Anton says over the drone of an engine. He's in the plane.

"How long?" I ask.

"Twenty minutes."

"Do you have enough fuel to take us to Budapest?"

He doesn't ask what happened or why Budapest. He knows the questions can come later. "I'll refuel at the hangar."

"We'll meet you there."

Ilya opens the service door and scans the alley. The exit is only used for deliveries and putting out trash. No one is about. We're in a blind spot where the city cameras don't reach. The getaway car is parked next to the trashcans. Ilya fishes the key from my pocket and unlocks the doors. We've left Mina's bag with the phone and our weapons behind, but our connection will get rid of those before letting the feds in on the murder scene. We're out of ammo anyway. The time to collect the rifles would've only slowed us down.

I shift into the backseat, carefully keeping an unconscious Mina in my lap. I pull the safety belt around both of us and secure the clasp. It's going to be a fast drive.

Ilya takes the wheel. He's a competent driver. I trust him to get us there safely. He sticks to the speed limit until we're out of the busy city center and then pushes down on the accelerator. The airfield is a forty-minute drive away, but we make it in just over twenty.

Anton waits outside the hangar. He takes one look at Mina before running ahead of us to the plane. He pats the wing. "She's ready."

We scramble inside, me in the back with Mina in my arms and Ilya in the front next to Anton. Questions burn in my mind. What happened? Who the fuck betrayed us? Ripping off my gloves, I check Mina's pulse. It's faint, but it's there.

Hold on, Minochka. Hold on for me.

Anton hands me earphones with an integrated mic. I yank out the ear-fitted ones to fit the headset. He passes a similar set to Ilya so we can talk over the noise.

When we're airborne, I ask, "Any problems with landing clearance?"

"Sorted," Anton replies tersely. "It's going to cost us another fifty grand, though."

I don't give a fuck about money. All that matters is Mina. "Weapons?"

Anton tilts his head toward the back. "AK-47 and two Glocks."

Good.

Ilya turns in his seat to look at Mina. His broad face is uncharacteristically pale. He cares about her, too.

"She should be in a hospital. Fuck! We should've taken her to the closest one in Prague."

"And get her arrested?" I say. "Get ourselves detained? How would we have been able to help her then?"

Sweat beads on Ilya's forehead. "Why Budapest?"

"Mina has a doctor friend at the clinic where her grandmother stays."

"Who says this doctor will help us?" Ilya asks.

I'll hold a gun to the doctor's head if I have to, but I have a feeling she won't deny us medical assistance. I've done my homework. The good doctor and clinic director, Lena Adami, was Mina's late mother's best friend. She's like a godmother to Mina. The substantial donation I recently made to the clinic in Hanna's name can't hurt our chances either.

"He did the right thing," Anton says to Ilya. "Mina isn't safe anywhere in public."

My back goes more rigid than it already is, a muscle pinching between my shoulder blades. "What are you talking about?"

Anton's voice is strained. "There's a price on her head."

I barely manage to tamp down my explosive anger. "What?"

"She's a free-for-all," Anton continues. "Five million. Every hitman from here to Antarctica is hunting for her."

I instinctively tighten my hold on her. "Who? How?"

"That fucker I tortured spilled all the beans." Anton glances at me from over his shoulder. "You're not going to like it."

"I already don't fucking like it."

"I cornered Laszlo Kiss in his cozy little cabin," Anton says. "At first, he didn't give me anything, not until the third finger. Things only got more and more interesting with every finger after that."

"Just spit it out," I snap, dragging a hand over Mina's clammy brow.

"Kiss said they were paid to rough Mina up, all eleven of them."

I sit up straighter. "What?"

"Shut up and listen," Anton says. "The men got paid for the job, and they did the job well. They already resented Mina, anyway. They didn't want a woman on their team, especially not a woman who made them eat her dust. It was humiliating. Their egos were bruised. When the offer came, they didn't have to think about it for long. It was quick money. No consequences. The superior officer would make sure everything was swept under the carpet. Nice and easy. Nothing more to it. They'd carry on with their lives and have a fat bonus in their bank accounts with the added benefit of Mina quitting the team."

I can't believe my fucking ears. "It was a ploy to get rid of her?" From what her superior had said right before I cut out his tongue, the fact that he wanted Mina gone shouldn't come as a surprise, but I can't get my head around the fact that they were willing to go that far just to make her leave.

"That's what Kiss said. After what I did to him, I can guarantee you he wasn't lying." Anton grimaces. "Mina didn't want to quit on her own, so they reckoned she needed a little nudge."

"A little fucking nudge?" Mina was almost beaten to death. There's a chance she may never have children. It's a fucking heavy price to make someone pay just to get her to leave. I'm glad those motherfuckers are dead. I'm glad I made them suffer before someone else killed them.

"According to Kiss," Anton continues, "they got carried away. They were supposed to hurt Mina a bit and scare her shitless, but once the violence started, their bloodlust took over."

"Who was it?" Ilya asks, the fury I feel in my bones etched on his face. "Who paid them? Tell me you have a name."

"Of course I do." Anton adjusts a dial on the control panel. "You're not going to believe this." He glances at me again. "It was Gergo Nagy, her training officer."

Motherfucker. The suppressed anger turns into a wave of rage that rolls through my body until every molecule burns with a white-hot need to kill. The things I imagine doing to that *ublyudok* will make even a hardened killer like Ilya wince.

I'm going to catch Nagy. I'm going to catch him and make him pay.

My voice doesn't carry my fury. It's cold and cruel,

a giveaway that I'm at my most dangerous. "Mina and Nagy were supposed to be friends. Why would Nagy do something like that?" To have orchestrated such a brutal attack, there must've been more to his motivation than sexist discrimination.

Anton rubs his neck. "Apparently, Nagy wanted Mina to work for him, but she didn't bite."

"Doing what?" I grit out.

"Killing."

Snap. The pieces fall into place. Nagy was going rogue. He saw Mina's potential and the money that went with that potential.

"Kiss said Nagy knew Mina needed money for her grandmother's care," Anton says. "The medical bills were piling up. Nagy planted the seed, suggesting they could earn more by working for themselves. Mina declined Nagy's offer. No matter how hard he tried, his arguments couldn't sway her."

"But a vicious enough attack could." The violent vows I'm making in Mina's name seethe under the thin layer of my control. "Nagy arranged the assault and pretended to save her, making her believe she owed him her life."

"That motherfucker," Ilya growls, his lip curling up in disgust.

"Exactly," Anton says. "The experience was traumatic enough to ensure Mina left the military. After all, she'd run into the same trouble in any other team. Her superior officer made sure she understood that. The rest is predictable. Needing a shitload of money to pay for her grandmother's care in some fancy clinic, Mina joined Nagy as an assassin. He sent her job referrals, taking kickbacks Mina didn't know about."

I run my fingers through my girl's soft hair, wishing I could take away what she suffered. Wishing it was me who took that bullet.

Wishing we were in Budapest already.

"How did Kiss know all this?" Ilya asks.

"Nagy and Kiss shared a few drunken nights in brothels around the time Nagy left the military. Nagy bragged about his scheme to Kiss one night after a bottle of vodka. Kiss was an accomplice in the attack, so Nagy didn't consider him a threat."

More puzzle pieces click together. Slowly, the ugly, nasty picture takes shape. "When I went after Mina's attackers, Nagy got nervous."

"He was worried the men would eventually break under the torture and talk," Anton says.

"So Nagy took them out," Ilya concludes.

"Correct," Anton says. "Kiss wasn't hiding only from us. He was hiding from Nagy as well."

Something else is eating at me like acid. "What about the price on Mina's head?"

"Kiss heard from an ex-military connection that it was Nagy himself who put up the bounty."

The fucker. "Nagy saw us together at the station in Budapest," I say. "He knew Mina had taken the blame for the job of framing us as terrorists. He must've been worried she'd eventually tell me the truth, and we'd come after him."

"So he made sure every assassin went after her in the hope that someone would eventually succeed." Ilya spits on the floor next to his seat. *"Ublyudok."* In our business, a man who stabs one of his own in the back is the worst kind of scum. "Who set us up?"

I have a damn good idea, but I want Anton to say it. I want to hear the traitor's name. I want the syllables of that name to sink into my heart and brain. I want the filthy sound of those dirty consonants and vowels to smolder in my thoughts and feelings until I can smother the hatred with the violence I'll commit with my bare hands.

Anton gives Ilya a level look. "Who do you think?"

"Nagy," Ilya says with undisguised hatred.

"After slitting Kiss's sorry throat, I told our hackers to see if there was anything new on Nagy," Anton says. "They thought it was most interesting that Nagy had met with Dimitrov only yesterday at his home in Prague. They managed to get a satellite recording with audio. Nagy, that fucker, casually relayed our plans over a cup of tea, lounging on Dimitrov's pool deck." Anton clenches the yoke as if he imagines it to be Nagy's neck. "I called you the minute I got the info."

Fuck. Mina must've confided in Nagy when she met him in Budapest. There's no other explanation. Nagy sold us out to Dimitrov, knowing we'd be outnumbered and believing Dimitrov's men would take Mina, my team, and me out—a whole lot of birds with one stone—thereby eliminating the problems that would've followed if Mina or her last remaining assailant were to expose Nagy. His bad.

"He's dead." My voice is ice, even as fire consumes my veins. "Ilya, put out word that I'm doubling Nagy's price. It's on his head now, but I want him alive."

Ilya's features soften marginally as he looks at Mina. "You better hope someone finds him before I do."

Not if I get to him first.

Nagy's greed almost cost Mina her life. He arranged her brutal assault and posed as her savior. He pretended to provide her with a means of earning money while taking kickbacks behind her back. He let her take the blame for a job he did. He set her up while posing as her friend. No matter how desperately I long to tear Nagy apart and rip out his intestines, he's Mina's to kill. That doesn't mean I can't make him suffer before I hand him over.

I swear on Mina's life I'll find Nagy. I'll deliver him to Mina if it's the last thing I do.

"How's she holding up?" Ilya asks, his face pulled into a mask of concern.

My gut clenches. Emotions threaten to erupt, but I push them under the surface. If I give my feelings free rein, I'll go stark raving mad, and that's not going to help Mina. "She's tough. She'll pull through."

She has to.

"Buckle up," Anton says. "We're lucky we had the wind behind us. We're touching down in five minutes."

Thank fuck. The hour-long flight felt like an eternity. My nerves are raw, my emotions all over the place. On the outside, I'm acting with the efficient rationality of a man with military training. On the inside, I'm a mess. Mina's injury—an injury that could very well turn out to be fatal—is jeopardizing my sanity, while the information Anton shared is making me boil with rage.

As I hold Mina's motionless body, I take a silent oath to make all the wrongs right. I'll give her the freedom I intended. I'll give her anything in my power. If I believed in God, I'd pray. I'm desperate enough to pray anyway. I'll do anything, anything at all. I'll become a goddamn priest if that's the bargain I have to make.

A vehicle has been delivered to the hangar. Anton, bless his efficient soul, called the rental agency while he was waiting for us in Prague. Ilya grabs the two Glocks to bring with us. Armed with the AK-47, Anton stays behind, using the hangar as a workstation to tap into our satellite and check the area around the clinic for suspicious activities or persons. One can never be safe enough. Ilya gets behind the wheel and drives.

Cradling Mina with one arm against my chest in the backseat, I use my secure cellphone to dial the clinic and ask for Dr. Adami. I didn't want to call while we were in the air and find a team of feds waiting for us at the airfield when we landed. I doubt she'll alarm the authorities, but I prefer to be on the safe side.

She takes my call jovially, presumably because of

that big donation, or maybe she's truly glad Mina finally found someone. I know Hanna talked to her about me, because I planted bugs while we visited Hanna. I'm more grateful than I care to admit that Mina's grandmother approves of me, likes me even.

"Mr. Ivanov, what a nice surprise," Adami says in fluent Russian. "What can I do for you?"

There's no time to beat around the bush. "Mina needs help."

Alarm replaces the warmth in her tone. "What's wrong?"

"She's injured."

"What kind of injury?"

"Gunshot."

Her breath catches. "Where are you?"

"On our way."

"If it's a gunshot wound, she needs surgery."

"That's why we're coming to you."

"Is she in trouble?"

"Yes," I say honestly. "I wouldn't be asking you otherwise."

"I'm no longer an ER surgeon."

"But you were for years." I learned that as part of my research on the clinic. "Please. Mina is out of options. You're her only hope."

"I see." There's a short, strained silence. "Then I hope to God I can help her."

I know what she means. If Mina doesn't make it, both of us will feel responsible for not saving her. But

I'm not going to think like that. If I want Mina to fight, I have to fight right beside her.

"You *will* help her." I'll threaten, torture, and kill to make it happen.

Her voice comes stronger, as if her mind's made up. "There's a staff entrance on the east side of the building."

Closing my eyes briefly, I swallow a relieved exhale. "We'll be there in ten."

At the clinic, the guard waves us through the gates. Adami must've warned him about our arrival.

As promised, Adami is waiting at the eastern entrance. Her face is drawn, her cheeks colorless. "Bring her through. We'll go via the basement. There's less chance of running into someone."

Ilya and I follow her down a flight of stairs and through a maze of underground hallways before surfacing on one of the upper floors. Adami leads us a short distance to a private consultation room. Thankfully, we don't come across anyone. Once inside, she locks the door and closes the blinds on the window.

"What happened?" she asks as I carefully lower Mina onto the examination bed.

"She took a bullet in the side."

"I haven't done surgery in years," the doctor reminds me.

"You're all she's got."

She contemplates me for a moment before saying,

"You better get rid of those bloody clothes and wash up. I'm going to need some help."

"Ilya." I motion at the door, indicating he should stand guard. At least his clothes aren't covered in blood.

Leaving the Glock within reach on the counter, I strip down to my underwear and dump my stained clothes and boots in a trashcan labeled "Biomedical Waste."

"You can scrub yourself over here." Adami shows me a basin and shoves antiseptic soap and a clean towel into my hands.

I clean up as fast and well as I can while she unbuckles the pillow from Mina's side, takes off Mina's shoes, and cuts off the dress.

"My God," she exclaims when she sees Mina's bruises. "What happened to her?"

"I can't tell you that."

Glancing at my briefs, she says, "There's an overcoat on a hook behind the door. I think you'll find a pair of Crocs in the closet."

I pull on the overcoat and shoes as Adami takes Mina's vitals.

"Weak pulse and rapid heart rate," she says, hurriedly gathering hermetically sealed instruments. "She lost some blood, but I don't think she needs a transfusion." She bites her lip. "I'll only know for sure after an ultrasound. She should really be where she can be better monitored."

"If I take her to another hospital, she's dead."

She briefly pinches her eyes shut before giving me a tight nod. "I'll do my best. Turn her on her side and keep her like that."

After washing the wound with soapy water, she examines it. "It's a flesh wound. Mina was lucky. The bullet went straight through her side without hitting any vital organs. There don't seem to be severed arteries or bullet fragments, and I don't see any other obvious damage." She presses around a purple bruise on Mina's stomach. "We'll have to do an ultrasound to ensure she doesn't have internal bleeding. Either way, it'll take her some time to recover. She'll be weak, especially from the blood loss."

"Can you keep her here?"

"You mean in secret."

"Yes."

She hesitates, then nods. "Okay."

I hold Mina's cold body as the doctor gets to work, stitching her up. Thankfully, Mina remains unconscious. Adami works quickly, disinfecting the wound and securing a bandage over the stitches.

When the doctor moves to the basin, I catch her wrist. "Will she be all right?"

"Her chances of recovering from the gunshot are good unless infection sets in."

"She'll live," I say, needing the doctor to confirm it. I need her to say those words.

She gives me a strange look. "For now."

"For now?" The prognosis throws my heartbeat into overdrive. "What do you mean *for now*?"

Her expression is oddly sympathetic. "She hasn't told you."

"Told me what?"

"Hanna said you and Mina are getting married. Is it true?"

Married. Fleeting shards of memories involving rubies and a ring and forever run through my head, but it's hard to focus on anything when the doctor hasn't given me the verdict I need. "What does that have to do with anything?"

"I need to know what your relation to Mina is."

"We're..." What are we? Kidnapper and captive? Boyfriend and girlfriend? Lovers? I can't answer that question. I only know it's not enough. Not nearly. I settle for, "Everything. She's everything."

"I'm sorry. I shouldn't have made that comment. This whole situation..." She waves at Mina. "It caught me off-guard. Mina is very special to me."

I fight the urge to grab the woman and shake her until her teeth rattle in her skull. "What aren't you telling me?"

"I can't divulge personal information to anyone who isn't family. Mina didn't even want Hanna to know. It's best Mina tells you herself, if that's what she decides."

A thousand alarm bells go off in my mind. Something is wrong. Something is terribly wrong. From the pitying way Adami regards me, I suddenly get the feeling a bullet wound is the least of my concerns.

I grip her arm hard. "You don't understand. Mina is *everything*. Without her, hell isn't a strong enough word to describe what my existence will become."

The fever in my soul must be showing on my face, because her shoulders drop in a gesture of tired surrender. "I can see she means a lot to you. I think you mean a lot to her, too. Hanna spoke very highly of you."

Hanna. Fuck. In my panic, I didn't think. I'll have to break the news to her, but right now, I have greater worries on my mind.

"Tell me," I beg. "Please. I'll fix whatever's wrong."

Adami's gaze softens. "I'm afraid this is the one thing you can't fix, Mr. Ivanov."

"I'll do whatever it takes." I'll give my life, my very soul.

She stares at me for a few long moments, then sighs. "All right. Knowing how you feel about Mina, and after this"—she glances at Mina's unconscious body again —"I guess you have a right to know." Tilting her head, she gives me a sorrowful smile. "I'm sorry you have to find out like this. Mina has cancer. Leukemia."

36

MINA

I peel open my eyelids and fight the fog that obscures my mind. It's difficult. I feel groggy and heavy, like I'm bogged down by gravity. Slowly, my blurry vision comes into focus. The room is strange yet familiar. The white walls and contemporary paintings remind me of Hanna's room. The clinic.

I'm at the clinic?

Memories rush back, flooding my thoughts. *Yan!* My pulse quickens. Turning my face to the side, I scan the room in a bout of panic, but then I relax. Yan is sitting in a chair next to the bed, elbows on his knees and head between his hands. As if pulled by an invisible thread of awareness, he lifts his head. The state of him makes my heart ache. More than a couple of days' worth of stubble darkens his chiseled jaw. Under the dark rings that mar his eyes, his cheeks are sunken and hollow. He's wearing a gray T-shirt and sweatpants with the clinic logo, and Crocs on his feet.

Those white Crocs, so uncharacteristic for Yan, put a smile on my face, but the effort cracks my lips.

He jumps up and grabs my hand. "You're awake."

I try to swallow away the dryness in my mouth. "Unless I'm dreaming."

Closing his eyes briefly, he kisses my knuckles and keeps my hand pressed to his lips for a long moment. "Are you in pain?" He touches my forehead. "Cold?"

"Thirsty."

"Water. Yes." He looks around in consternation even though a carafe and a glass with a straw stand on the nightstand. "Ice? Maybe you prefer juice?"

I nod at the carafe. "That will do."

He fills the glass and holds the straw to my lips. "Small sips. Don't drink too fast."

Mindful of my cracked lips, I keep my smile slight. "I know the drill."

"Do you have pain?" he asks again.

"I don't even feel my legs."

"Dr. Adami gave you morphine."

"Adami?" I *am* at the clinic, as the room and Yan's borrowed clothes indicate.

He puts the glass on the nightstand and dabs my lips with a paper napkin. "We couldn't risk taking you anywhere else."

Of course not. It makes sense. "Clever. Thank you."

"Thank you?" In contrast to his drawn features, the green of his eyes is darker and brighter, reflecting a frantic light. "You took a bullet for me and I..." He grips his hair and stares at me like a man on the verge of madness. "What the fuck was I supposed to do if that bullet had been fatal?"

I try for humor. "Be grateful to be alive?"

"Never again, do you hear me? You will never again put your life on the line. Not for me. Not for fucking anyone. Promise me."

I reach for his hand. "I can't make that promise. I acted automatically. If the situation is repeated, I'll do it again."

He grabs my fingers in his large palm, squeezing too hard. "*Never again.* Or..."

"Or what?"

He regards me with helpless desperation, but he doesn't make manipulative threats. He doesn't hold Hanna's life over my head or say he'll go after my only friend.

Wow. I stare at him in wonder. This is huge. It's the first time he's truly treated me like an equal and not his prisoner, the first time he's not forcing me to bend to his will. He may not like my declaration, but he's not telling me what to do or how to behave. In his own way, he's just given me freedom.

The ultimate freedom.

Choice.

The moment is enormous. Tears well up in my eyes. They're tears of joy for not having lost the man I love and tears of relief for being alive, but they're also tears of gratitude for this place in our warped relationship, a place I never thought we'd reach. After the way we started out, it's more than I ever could've hoped for, yet I wouldn't want it any other way. We are what we are. We came together like our natures dictated: in violence and forced submission, in hatred and retribution. What we have now, though, is all the stronger for the obstacles we've overcome.

Yan once said the attraction was always there. He was right. And the kernel of love was always a part of it. We fought for this moment, for what we have between us. It didn't come easily, and I'm not going to deny or waste it.

I'm going to grab it with both hands for as long as I have left.

"Don't cry," he whispers, wiping away my tears with a thumb. "I love you, Minochka, more than you can ever know."

Taking his wrist, I kiss his palm. "I do know."

His eyes glitter like jade stones. "I should've told you." His voice sounds tormented. "Fuck. You could've…"

Died without knowing. I know what he's thinking. I know how his mind works.

"Clever girls know the unsaid is sometimes more important than what's said," I say, repeating the words he'd spoken once upon a time in a stuffy wooden shed. It already seems like a lifetime ago.

He presses our foreheads together, his warm breath bathing my face. "Goddamn, Mina." His anguish is so palpable I can feel it seeping through my skin.

"It's over," I whisper. "I'm all right." A stark image of Ilya with a shotgun in his hands suddenly invades my memory. "How about Ilya? He wasn't hurt, was he?"

He pulls away and smiles. "The butthead is right outside, anxious as fuck to see you."

"Tell me what happened first." I still have too many questions.

His expression becomes closed-off. "There's plenty to tell, but you should get better first."

I raise an eyebrow. "Really?"

"Really what?"

"You're going to treat me like a fragile girl who faints at the mention of guns and blood?"

Sighing, he shakes his head. "What am I going to do with you?"

"Hopefully lots, when I can get my legs to cooperate again."

His eyes darken with lust. "You have no idea. The things I want to do…" Catching himself, he only shakes his head again.

"Hanna?"

"Don't worry. She's already been to see you. I told her you'd been shot by someone who held a vendetta against you from your military days."

"Did she believe you?"

He grins. "I'm not sure. I thought I'd let you handle it how you see fit."

"What about Lena?"

"She's been very supportive." A shadow passes over

his face. "She's letting us stay here until you've recovered fully."

I try to sit up, but it hurts like a bitch.

"Easy." Yan darts forward, helping me into a more comfortable position. "Adami did an ultrasound. You don't have any internal damage, but you've got to be careful not to tear your stitches."

"Are they all dead?"

"Yes." Hatred makes the sharp angles of his face look harder. "Every last one of them."

"Tell me." He won't deny me twice.

His strained voice betrays how difficult it is to relive the event. "When we realized it was a trap, Ilya and I split up. I went over the roof as planned while he took the stairs to go back via the hallway. That way, I could go to your aid, and he could ward off an attack in case they decided to come after us on the roof. Best-case scenario, we could trap them between us in the suite with me coming in from the balcony and Ilya from the hallway. The fuckers were overconfident. They thought having us outnumbered was enough." He sneers. "They were waiting for us inside. I shot one as I came down from the roof. At the same time, Ilya broke down the door. That's when they realized we had them trapped between us with no way out. They took cover, we took cover, and a big shootout followed. We might've been outnumbered, but they had the disadvantage of having to defend their fronts and backs." More tension invades his big body. "In the meantime, you were locked in the bedroom with Dimitrov and his art guy."

"I don't think he was an art expert."

"Whatever he was," Yan says icily, "it's a good thing Ilya killed him before I got my hands on him. It took us long enough to take out the five guards. I was going out of my mind by the time I could finally get to you." If fury could be condensed into a color, it would be the brilliant jade-green of his eyes. Reaching over, he clasps my hand in a gentle hold. "Did that fucker Dimitrov touch you?"

"He tried, but I gave him a good run for his money."

Yan's hold on me tightens. "Fuck, Mina, I always knew you were dangerous, but I never could've guessed how much until I saw it with my own eyes."

"Did Ilya shoot the man who shot me? Things became a bit blurry at the end."

Yan inhales deeply, releasing my hand. Nostrils flaring, he says, "Ilya took a shotgun off one of the guards. He blew the bastard's head off."

One question burns in the forefront of my mind. "Who gave us away?"

Yan stills. Just when I think he's not going to reply, he answers my question with another question. "Who did you tell about our plans?"

My whole body jerks, my skin going cold. It can't be. I only told one person, and I trust him with my life. It's impossible. But the longer Yan and I look at each other, the more I'm forced to face the answer. If Yan,

Ilya, and Anton didn't tell anyone, and I only told Gergo...

"The hotel manager, our connection..." I say, grabbing at straws.

"Who did you tell, Mina?"

"The disguise vendor or copy artist could've leaked the information. Maybe your apartment was bugged or my call to Dimitrov tapped."

"My place is clean and our phones weren't tapped. We scan them on a daily basis. It wasn't the disguise man or your artist contact." The determined set of his jaw tells me he's not going to let me hide from the truth. "Who did you tell?"

Covering my face with my hands, I admit the horrific truth not only to Yan, but also to myself. "Gergo. Gergo Nagy."

"When you warned him." He pulls my hands away. "Look at me, Mina. When you warned him that day here at this very clinic."

"No." I swallow. "Not here. He followed us to Prague. He slipped into the changing booth at the boutique where we bought the dress for my Petrova disguise."

Yan looks like he's about to explode. "He did what?"

"You were engrossed in your work." I stare at my hands, unable to meet Yan's harsh gaze. "He said he wanted to help me escape. I was worried he'd kill you. I said I needed the money from the Dimitrov job, but he wouldn't let it go, so I gave him just enough to set him at ease. I never thought he'd betray me." My mind is a hurting mass of confusion. "Why? Why would he do something like that? I don't understand."

"Why didn't you let him help you get away?" Yan grips my chin and tilts my face back to his. "Why didn't you let him shoot me?"

"I already had feelings for you," I admit with a tremulous exhale. "I swear I didn't mean to betray your trust. All I could think about was the gun in Gergo's hand and how distracted you were, how easy a target in that moment." Holding his gaze, I bite the inside of my cheek. "Do you hate me?"

"No," he replies softly. "I can never hate you. No matter what."

"How did you know it was a setup?"

He releases me. "Kiss."

"Anton found him?"

"Yes." He scoffs. "We found out a lot more than what we bargained for."

"Such as?"

"That Gergo had a meeting with Dimitrov the day before the mission and told him about our plan."

Hurt slices through my heart. "Why would he do that to me? What can justify that kind of betrayal? Money?"

"It's a lot more complicated than that."

He's stalling. "If you're trying to spare me, you're wasting your time. I can handle the truth."

His gaze is doubtful. But it's the sympathy that scares me.

"Yan? What's going on?"

He takes my hand again in the gentle way people do when they're about to share bad news. "Gergo paid the men who beat you." He gives a moment for the information to sink in. "He staged the assault."

"What?" I jerk my fingers from his. "That's not true."

"You didn't want to quit the military and freelance with him. He found a convincing way of changing your mind."

I start shaking. "He's my friend."

"He pretended to save you," Yan carries on relentlessly, "knowing you'd pledge not only your loyalty but also your life to him."

"But why?" I ask raggedly. "Whatever could he gain from making me leave the team?"

"Why do men do the cruel things they do?"

"Money?"

"He got kickbacks from the jobs he referred to you."

I don't want to admit it, but my mind is already racing toward the logical conclusions. My reason is already embracing the truth, even if my heart is having a hard time. "Gergo knew I had feelings for you. I told him as much that day in the boutique. He was worried I'd tell you the truth."

"Namely, that he was the one who framed us as terrorists."

"And because I was falling for you, I became a liability."

Yan's mouth tightens. "He thought setting us up against Dimitrov would kill two birds with one stone, getting rid of both you and my team."

More insights hit me. "He killed my attackers. He killed them to make sure they couldn't talk when your hired team went after them."

Yan nods. "Kiss knew about Gergo's scheme. He confessed everything before Anton killed him."

Tangled emotions sprout from my trampled trust and broken heart. It's the anger I hold on to. The disappointment is too hurtful, too powerful. If I let it, it will destroy me.

When I speak again, my voice is level, my feelings pushed under the surface. "Is he dead?"

"Not yet. But I'll find him. I promise you."

A knock falls on the door. Before either of us can reply, it opens to Ilya peering around the frame. A huge grin stretches his cheeks. "There you are," he says as if he's been looking for me for years.

His genuine happiness at seeing me wipes away the ugliness that has infiltrated my heart. The devastating truth almost seems inconsequential as he bustles into the room and extends his arms to take me into a hug. God knows, I can do with one of his bear hugs right now.

Yan catches him before he can put his arms around me. "Careful. She's still hurting." For once, jealousy isn't his motivation. There's no animosity in Yan's comportment when Ilya presses a kiss on my forehead instead.

"You deserve a spanking," Ilya declares solemnly, crossing his bulging arms.

"Delivered by me," Yan clarifies quickly. His eyes say, *and only me.*

"You had us worried to death," Ilya says.

I look him over. "Are you all right?"

"Not a scratch," he says proudly. "The question is, how are *you* holding up?"

It's impossible not to smile. "It seems Lena did a good job."

"If you need anything," Ilya says, "you only have to ask. Anything at all."

"She's sorted," Yan says a tad forcefully.

Inwardly, my smile grows even broader. I guess Ilya shouldn't push Yan's newfound tolerance too far.

Ilya turns to Yan. "I came to tell you I just got a call from our connection. All's handled. They've cleaned up. The shootout was staged as the last bloody battle of the drug war. They've identified the man who shot Mina."

"Who *was* that creep?" I ask.

"Stjepan Filipović, Dimitrov's second-in-command. Rumor has it, they'd been clashing horns over territory and money for the last couple of years. Filipović wanted bigger cuts and a say in how the business was managed. His connection to Dimitrov could never be proven until his corpse happened to be found in the same room as Dimitrov's. The feds got a search warrant for his house and questioned his staff. One of them talked in exchange for immunity." Ilya looks between us. "Guess what? He was plotting against Dimitrov, turning their drug suppliers against him with bribes. The idea was to force Dimitrov's early retirement with a bullet in his brain. The meeting at the Hotel Paris came as a golden opportunity. It was Filipović's chance to get rid of Dimitrov. Three of the five guards had been bought. The minute we were dead, they were to kill Dimitrov and the remaining two guards. The informant didn't say anything about the painting being fake; he only knew Filipović wanted to blame the killings on a deal gone wrong. Mina was a bonus. Filipović was hoping to cash in on the five mill on her head."

"What?" I gasp.

Yan smacks Ilya upside the head. "She doesn't know about that part yet."

"Oh." Ilya offers me an apologetic smile.

"Five million?" I utter. "Someone put five million on my head?"

"Gergo. Don't worry," Yan says with menace. "I've doubled it on *his* head."

Oh, my God. I'm a walking target. "I'm putting you in danger. Hanna, Lena, all of you."

"Nobody save for us, Lena, and Hanna knows you're here," Yan says. "We're safe."

"Anton is using the storeroom as a base to monitor our surroundings," Ilya says. "You don't have to worry about anything except getting better. Speaking of which, I'm going to help Anton carry some of the heavier stuff." He winks at me. "I'll catch you later, *malyshka*."

"All the loose ends are tied up," I say when Ilya is

gone, "with the exception of Gergo." I never thought betrayal could feel like a physical burn in your stomach.

"Not for long," Yan says darkly. He turns sideways to the window, staring at the gardens with tense shoulders and a clenched jaw.

"What's wrong?"

A heartbeat passes before he speaks. "Lena told me."

"Told you what?"

He looks back at me. The pain splayed over his face is so raw it rips my chest open. "That you have cancer."

Shit. No. This isn't how I wanted him to find out.

"That you'd been in remission for sixteen months," he continues. "You didn't cut off your hair when you left the military. It fell out after your chemo treatment. You must've barely recovered the night I abducted you in Budapest. And now it's back."

"Yan," I say achingly. I should've told him the minute I came to, but I desperately wanted to pretend we were just another regular couple, at least for a short while.

"That's why you got the hummingbird tattoo—a symbol of life, survival."

"Yes."

"Is that why you came here when you ran away? For Lena to run tests?"

I avert my gaze. "I suspected when the nose bleeds and the bruising started."

"Why didn't you tell me?"

I dare to meet his eyes again. "Things were... different between us."

"You were my prisoner." His tone is thick with self-loathing. "How could you trust me?"

I know what his uncharacteristic bout of guilt is about. It's about grief. It's about losing someone when you've only just discovered you love that person. "It's not your fault."

A muscle ticks in his jaw. "Why didn't you tell me when things *were* different?"

"I wanted to finish the Dimitrov job. I needed the money for Hanna, and I didn't think you'd let me if you knew the truth."

"Damn right," he says savagely. "Still, you should've confided in me. I took care of it."

"Took care of what?"

"I made a donation in Hanna's name, enough to secure her stay and cover the bills for the rest of her life."

My chest squeezes tight with a mixture of joy and relief. "Yan. Why would you do that?"

"Why do you think?"

Because he loves me. Despite the ordeal of the last twenty-four hours and what's yet to come, my heart soars with the knowledge. This is the purest portion of my entire life.

"You should've told me, Mina. Fuck, how could you keep this from me?"

"You've kept things from me, too," I point out gently. "You didn't tell me you'd made a donation."

He scrubs a hand over his face. "There've been too many fucking secrets between us. No more, do you hear me?"

"I can live with that."

He walks to the bed and grabs my hand between both of his. "I never knew what I was looking for until I found you. You're everything I never had and will never have again. Please, Mina, I beg you, fight for us."

My stomach knots. "It's not that simple." I try to pull away, but he holds fast.

"I know, Minochka, I know. Hanna told me. She told me how sick you were, how you lost all your hair and vomited until you were so weak you couldn't even make it to the bathroom." He inhales sharply, as if the mental image is torture. "I know it's been tougher than I can ever imagine, but this time, I'll be here for you."

I cup his cheek, trying to soften the blow. "The survival rate is low. Treatment may only prolong the suffering."

His eyes take on a feverish light. "I've done my homework. There's a new treatment. It's still experimental, but the results are extremely promising."

"The previous treatment *was* experimental. I paid a small mountain of gold for it, and here I am."

"This is different. It's more than stem cell transplants and blood transfusions and alternative healing and Reiki and whatever else you've tried. It's revolutionary. Yes, it will involve some chemotherapy, but not as much as you've had before. The researcher who's developing it is a genius. He's not just doing research and clinical trials. He's using volunteers. That's why he's making such big progress so fast. Please do it, Mina. I beg you. Do it for us. *Fight* for us."

Tears blur my vision. "Yan, please... I don't want you to go through the disappointment if it doesn't work. When I told you not to fall in love with me, it was to protect you. Please don't fall any deeper than you already have."

He grips my shoulders. "Fuck that. I'm already going through it, and there's nothing you can do to change that. I can never love you more than I already do. Nobody can." His fierce gaze is bright with his own unshed tears, his hold almost too tight. "No matter how much distance you try to force between us, I'm going to hurt. I *am* hurting. I'll take whatever I can get. A month. A day. A few minutes. I'll give my life for just a moment with you."

His hands fall away as if that speech has taken every last bit of his energy. The man facing me is crestfallen, crushed, lost. It's as much as I can take.

Drawing in a breath, I hold out my arms like an invitation. When he bends down within my reach, I fold my arms around him and hold him close to my chest, my heart splitting open as I feel the tremors wracking his big, hard body. And as his tears wet my neck, I caress his stubble-roughened face, giving him comfort and reassurance the only way I can.

"Shh." I kiss the top of his head, inhaling his strong, virile male scent. "Even if I'm not here, I'll still be with you. That's my promise. Always remember it."

"Don't talk like that," he says in a thick voice.

"No more secrets, remember? We have to be honest. We have to accept death is a possibility, a very strong one."

Yan pulls away to look at me, his handsome features desolate. "Marry me."

"What?"

"Marry me," he says with heated certainty. "Tomorrow. Here."

I swallow past the lump in my throat. "I'm touched, but…"

"But what?"

"I don't want to make you a widower."

"Maybe you won't. I could die long before you. I could get killed on a job."

"Don't say that!"

"Don't you see? What matters is now. I want you in every way. I want you to carry my name for however long we have. Time isn't what matters. A year or fifty isn't what counts." He takes my palm and places it over his heart. "It's what's in here. It's not how long. It's how much."

I try to blink my own tears away as more pureness and unequalled beauty, much more than I deserve, fill my heart, my soul, and all the hours left of my life.

"We'll always belong to each other," he says. "Now. Tomorrow. Until we're both gone."

My tears flow so fast I can't control them any longer. I can only look at him as my heart bursts with love. The numbness I carried for decades is gone, washed away in the tsunami of emotions assailing my mind. With one touch, he made my body come alive. With his words, he did the same to my soul. Instead of being cold and empty, I feel.

He makes me feel so much.

"What do you say?" he asks, hope breaking through the darkness in his eyes to shine like a light on our bleak situation.

"Yes." I smile through my tears. "Yes, I want to be Mina Ivanova."

Forgetting about my injury, he takes me into his arms and squeezes until it hurts, but I don't mind the pain, because he's cut the string that tied down my heart, letting it float up like a red balloon in a bleak sky. But not all of it is bleak.

Mortality makes it bleak.

Love makes it miraculous.

YAN

*T*hanks to Dr. Adami's thoughtfulness, a bed was brought to Mina's room for me. Mina naps frequently due to her pain medication. It's also her body's natural way of recovering. She needs her rest. I like that I'm able to sleep next to her, even if our twin beds put a small distance between us. I can't bear not to be at her side, not even for a second, but there's much to do. When she falls asleep after breakfast, I make my way to the basement where Anton and Ilya are working. They're not only keeping an eye on our surroundings, but also taking care of something else. Something extremely important.

"Any news?" I ask as I push open the door.

The room, one of the bigger storage spaces, is fitted with metal shelves stacked with linens and cleaning products. Despite the bare concrete floor and walls, it's warm, courtesy of the electrical heater Adami provided.

Anton is sitting behind the desk he's dragged inside, studying his laptop monitor. Ilya is poised on the edge of the desk with a packet of potato chips clutched in his hand.

"Nothing yet," Anton says. "Our virus is piggybacking on Interpol software. If Nagy shows up at an airport or train station, we'll know about it." He scratches his head. "The problem, of course, is that he's a disguise genius. He may be right in front of us, and we won't know it."

A problem that irks me to no end.

"He'll come for us eventually." Ilya stuffs a handful of chips into his mouth. "We just have to be ready."

Not a chance I like to take. By now, Nagy knows that Kiss, as well as Dimitrov and his team, is dead. He knows we know the extent of his deceit. He knows he'll never be safe again. No man wants to look over his shoulder for the rest of his life. He may run until the dust settles, but Ilya is right. At some point, he'll come for us. That's what any assassin would do, especially one who knows we have a score to settle—and whose life is worth ten million. The only way he can cancel that price on his head is by killing us.

"What about friends and family?" I ask.

Anton leans back in his chair and stretches out his legs. "He's pretty much a loner." He regards me thoughtfully. "We could draw him out."

"How?"

His grin is all cream. "How do you catch a mouse?"

"No." Absolutely fucking not. "We're not setting a trap. I'm not risking Mina."

"What if it's far away from Mina?" Ilya asks.

"I'm not leaving her on her own. It's too dangerous."

"No," Anton says, "we shouldn't leave Mina, at least not all of us—and especially not now. But we can make him believe she's somewhere else."

I rub the back of my neck. I don't like using Mina as bait, whether she's actually there or not, but it could take years before we nail Nagy and I'm not prepared to wait that long. Every day is another twenty-four hours too long, another twenty-four hours Mina's life hangs in the balance. "Explain."

Anton interlaces his fingers over his stomach. "We get our connection to issue death certificates for us and put Mina up in a safe house."

"Let me get this straight," Ilya says with a full mouth. "We pretend to be dead and let Nagy believe Mina made a deal in exchange for immunity."

"Exactly," Anton says. "We put the safe house address in the system where Nagy will be able to hack it. Not too easily, mind you; otherwise, he'll smell a rat."

"So," I clarify, "we lead him to a safe house and ambush him there."

"You stay to protect Mina." Anton's eyes glitter with cruel excitement. "Ilya and I catch the rat in our trap and bring him back here."

"For Mina to finish the bastard off," Ilya adds with heated enthusiasm.

"No." We can't bring trouble to Adami's doorstep. "You catch the fucker, and I bring Mina there."

"Done." Anton sits up and pulls his laptop closer. "I'll get to work."

"Keep me updated. I want to be informed of everything to the tiniest detail." I turn to my brother. "I need you to go into town."

He hops from the desk. "What do you need?"

"A ring. The biggest ruby you can find. And the three of us need suits."

He gapes at me. "Seriously? What the fuck, Yan?"

"Get a cake," I continue. "Something white and fancy. And Mina will need a dress. Size zero. While you're at it, get me a priest, too."

"No fucking kidding," Anton says laughingly. "Congratulations, man."

"Damn, Yan." Ilya bumps shoulders with me and slaps my back. "Congrats, bro. You're fucking getting married. I can't believe it."

Neither can I. Who would've thought? Until a few weeks ago, I'd never have believed a woman half my size would bring me to my knees.

"Aren't you worried Peter will find out about this?" Anton asks. "It's one thing to keep her, another to marry her."

I give him a hard look. "Sokolov doesn't want me for an enemy, and if he does, we'll cross that bridge when we get there."

"When's the big event?" Ilya asks with a ten-megawatt smile, clearly eager to return to a less stressful topic.

"Today."

Anton looks at me as if I've lost my marbles. "What?"

The dark cloud always hovering at the back of my mind threatens to cast a shadow over our happiness, but I shove it away. I'm not going to wallow in sorrow or negativity and waste the precious time I have with Mina.

"There's something you should know," I start carefully.

From my drawn expression, they must be sensing what's to follow isn't good. Their faces turn serious, all signs of joviality wiped away.

"Mina..." No matter that I've made peace with the diagnosis, it doesn't make it easier to say. "She's got cancer. Leukemia."

"Shit." Anton's olive-toned face goes pale. "Man, I'm sorry."

"Fuck." Ilya drags a hand over his shaven head, looking shell-shocked.

"I don't want you to feel sorry for her," I say in a stern voice. "The last thing she needs is pity."

Anton takes a deep breath. "Yeah, sure."

"She's going to fight." I say it more for my own benefit than theirs.

Ilya grips my shoulder. "I'm here for you, for both of you."

I nod. "Good to know. Get to work. I want to go check on Mina, see if she's awake."

"Great idea." Ilya all but pushes me to the door. "Your place is with her. Go. We've got this covered."

Stopping in the doorway, I look back at my team, the men who've always had my back. "Thanks."

They know I'm not only saying thank-you for dealing with shit so I can be with my woman. I'm grateful that they're here for me, for us. I need them as much for this as for a job, if not more.

Anton nods.

Ilya says, "Don't mention it."

When I get back to the room, Hanna is visiting with Mina, her wrinkled cheeks streaked with tears.

"She just told me," Hanna says, not bothering to wipe away the drops running nonstop down her jaw and chin. Considerately, even at a time like this, she addresses me in Russian.

Mina pats her grandmother's shaking hand. "I didn't want to worry you. I knew you'd try to persuade me to go for the treatment."

"Thanks for convincing her," Hanna says to me.

I hand her a tissue from the nightstand. "Mina is a fighter. We'll get through this."

"Yes," Hanna agrees readily. "You have to believe it, Mina darling."

She's struggling to lift her hand, so I take the tissue from her and carefully wipe her eyes. "In fact, Mina and I have some happy news to share, too."

She looks between us. "You're getting married?"

"Today." I give her an apologetic smile. "I know it seems sudden—"

"No, no," Hanna says. "You're doing the right thing. You shouldn't waste a minute. Not a second."

"I want you to be a part of the day," Mina says.

And doing it here allows that. I catch Mina's gaze to measure how much she's told Hanna. A small shake of her head tells me Hanna doesn't know about the rest, about Mina's job or that a threat bigger than a disease hangs over her head.

"You must have lots to discuss," Hanna says. "I'll leave you to it."

"I'll take you back to your room," I offer.

After making Hanna comfortable in the sun on her balcony, I come back downstairs to tell Mina about our plan.

"You know Nagy better than anyone," I say when I've relayed what Anton, Ilya, and I discussed. "Do you think he'll fall for it?"

She reflects for a moment. "I'm a loose end. If he believes I ratted on him in exchange for immunity, he'll want revenge. He'll come for me, no matter where I am or how high the stakes are. But he's not a fool. He'll watch the safe house, at least via surveillance if not personally, to make sure I'm really there."

"I thought about that. We'll have to make it appear like you're not leaving the house. We must make him believe you're scared with us out of the picture and you all alone. We could stage a conversation with our connection on a phone Nagy can tap."

"If I'm not to leave the house and he can't visually confirm my presence for himself, we'll have to plant convincing evidence that I'm there."

"We'll send a nurse once a day. He'll believe she's treating your wound. Pizza and grocery deliveries. Medical supplies. Anton and Ilya will be waiting there, so there will be signs of life."

"He'll probably find a way to check the delivery invoices."

"You can make the lists, all the things you'd normally buy."

She smiles at me. "I think it could work."

I kiss the top of her head. "I don't want you to worry about anything other than getting well. I'll handle the rest."

Her pretty blue gaze is open and trusting. "I know."

For the first time since I took her, she's giving me her full trust outside the bedroom. She's looking at me like I've always wanted her to—like she's no longer keeping anything from me, not her feelings, not her fears, not her secrets. And it's a stunning thing, to have a woman's intimate trust, to own her respect.

To be the man she trusts with her heart.

I'll never let her down. I'll protect her heart and her truths. I'll give her a safe place to be herself, a place where she'll never have to doubt her desirability or value. She already had my devotion and admiration, and now I'll also give her the freedom I promised. The freedom to be herself.

Above all, I'll always love her. Unconditionally. With everything I've got.

"I was going to set you free, you know," I say, caressing her hair. "After the job." I want her to understand my distance on that morning. I don't want her to ever doubt my love.

She smiles. "You have."

Yes, I have. "The tracker," I say reluctantly. "We can have it removed."

"It doesn't matter. It no longer serves the same purpose."

I hide a relieved exhale. The possessive, overprotective part of me is glad I'll still be able to trace her. In our business, that can only be a plus. Leaning in, I kiss her lips. "I'm going to see Adami about this afternoon. Anything in particular you'd like? I've organized a priest and a cake. What have I forgotten?"

Her smile turns broader. "Looks like you have it covered."

"Okay then." Cupping her head, I sneak in another kiss, this time lingering to part her lips with my tongue. Fuck, she tastes good. All honey and cream. My cock grows hard. I want her so much I ache, but it's way too soon.

I force myself to pull away. Her bow-shaped lips are a pretty cherry pink from my kiss. Soon. Soon I'll kiss every inch of her body. As soon as she's able to walk.

Though the way things are now, *I'll* have a hard time walking.

With a last look at her sitting so small and delicate in the white hospital bed, I close the door behind me and return to the basement to tell Anton we need to arrange a nurse and credible deliveries with authentic invoices. He's bent over his computer, sending an encrypted message to our connection. Ilya has left to take care of the wedding shopping.

I grin to myself, thinking about that. Ilya hates shopping. And for all the grief he's given me over Mina, it serves him right. Then I grimace. He doesn't have the best taste. For all I know, he's at one of those cheap places, renting seventies-style suits with frilly shirts. I shudder at the thought.

Leaving Anton to deal with the logistics, I go in search of Adami to inform her of our wedding plans. It's her clinic, after all. On the way to her office, I spot a nurse coming in from outside. She catches my attention because she's unusually tall, almost my height. Her blond hair is twisted into a neat bun and her makeup is done tastefully. Her white pants and tunic are tighter than the other nurses', deliberately showing off her curves. My mind immediately jumps to Ilya. She's exactly his type, the type we both used to go for before I found Mina.

Automatically, I nod in greeting when she nears, and offer a stiff smile. She doesn't shy away or blush like the other nurses here do when they see me.

"Smoke break," she says in a husky voice, giving me a conspiratorial wink and an answering smile.

I check her nametag. Mariska Molnár. She seems

friendly enough. I'll mention her to Ilya. Maybe he'd like to take her out on a date.

For some reason, that smile sticks with me, even when I round the corner and enter Adami's office. The way Mariska Molnár looked at me bothers me. She wasn't flirting. Her manner was rather haughty, like I'm beneath her. Perhaps it's not such a good idea to play matchmaker.

Adami looks up from her desk. "Can I help you, Yan?"

That smile. It's familiar, like I've seen it before. There's something else too, something I can't put a finger on that doesn't sit right with me. Then I stop dead. She said she'd sneaked in from a smoke break, but there wasn't a hint of cigarette smoke on her.

Fuck!

Spinning on my heel, I sprint down the hallway. There's no time to stop and take out my phone to dial Anton. I run for my life.

For Mina's life.

As I round the corner, I slip on the shiny floor, barely managing to right myself. Yanking the gun from the back of my waistband, I point the barrel in front of me as I race toward our room. From the end of the hallway, I call at the top of my voice, "Mina!"

The door to our room is closed. My senses sharpen. Fear is a monster breathing down my neck as I close the distance.

A loud crash sounds, like metal hitting tiles.

No!

I increase my pace, my lungs burning with the exertion. Two nurses, alarmed by my cry, come running but stop when they see the gun.

"Stay down! Keep the hallway clear."

My mind is a frenzy of madness when I finally reach the door and grip the handle.

Locked.

I don't hesitate. I jump back, charge, and kick it down.

What I see isn't what I expected. The nightstand is overturned, the nurse lying next to it. Mina stands over her, clutching a gun in one hand and her injured side with the other. A red blotch is growing on the hospital gown under Mina's fingers.

"Mina!"

Gun aimed, I rush into the room. Mina doesn't look at me, all her attention on the woman on the floor. I follow her gaze. The nurse is writhing like a snake, a hypodermic needle sticking from her neck.

On closer look, I see I was right. It's a good disguise. Brilliant. But that smile gave him away. It's the same smile he had on his face that day at the station when he looked at Mina and me before averting his eyes. The same arrogant smile I recognized in his photograph.

Nagy seems helpless, harmless, but still. I keep my gun trained on him. "What the fuck happened?"

"Poison," Mina says, not taking her eyes off Nagy.

I fix my attention on the needle in his neck. "What poison?"

"Strychnine."

I'm battling to digest the information. "Where did you get it?" I should've left a weapon with her, for fuck's sake. An oversight I'm not going to forgive myself for.

"Adami."

"You knew he'd come looking for you here," I say as the knowledge sinks in.

"I didn't know, but I wanted to be prepared."

Nagy gurgles, his eyes rolling back in his head. I know what strychnine does. It acts on the nerves that control muscle contraction, mainly those in the spinal cord. It causes agonizing muscle spasms and affects breathing. Death follows from cardiac arrest, respiratory failure, or brain damage.

I touch the hand in which Mina is gripping the gun to pull her attention to me. "Do you want to finish him off?"

Her voice is calm. "No."

I respect that. Nagy convulses. He curls into a ball, snaps straight, and curls up again. His fingers twitch. His body goes still. Finally, his eyes turn dull.

"It's over." I reach for the gun in her hand. "His?"

"Yes."

I put the gun aside and slip mine back into my waistband. "How did you manage to take it off him?"

"I pretended to be asleep. He was going to smother me with a pillow. I stabbed him in the neck with the syringe before he could see it coming. We wrestled. He reached for the gun in his thigh holster, but the poison took effect before he could get a good grip. The gun fell when he stumbled and knocked over the nightstand. That gave me enough time to get out of bed and grab it."

"You're bleeding." I lift up her gown. "Let me see."

"It's nothing."

I unwrap her bandage with unsteady fingers and inspect the wound underneath. "It's not nothing. You tore a few stitches. Come here." Pulling her small body to me, I hold her tight, feeling her warmth, her fragility, her *aliveness*. I still haven't recovered from nearly losing her at the Hotel Paris, and now this. If Nagy had succeeded... I tighten my hold on her, refusing to think of that possibility, pushing the knowledge of her illness deep inside. "I should've given you a gun," I say, my voice strained as I pull back to meet her gaze. "That was a fucking stupid mistake."

"I slept with the syringe under my pillow, just in case."

"Why didn't you tell me?"

"I didn't think it was important."

Yes. To her, it wouldn't seem important. It's simple insurance, something people like us take for granted. I take a breath and remind myself that she's like me. Tough. Capable. Merciless, when she needs to be. Still, my heart feels like it's about to explode each time I picture her in danger. "I want to know these things in the future," I say, my tone hard. I search her eyes. "Even the mundane things you think don't matter."

"Okay," she says easily, still calm as fuck, but the

tremors I'm starting to feel in her body tell a different story.

"It's over," I murmur, cupping her delicate jaw. "He can't hurt you anymore." Recalling her wound, I force myself to let her go. "We better let Adami look at those stitches. I'll call for cleanup."

"Who are you going to call?'

"Our government connection will be happy to know he's rid of Nagy."

"He must still be upset about the war that played out in the hotel."

"He got not only Dimitrov, but also Filipović. He's happy enough."

I'm about to go get Adami, but Mina steps up, wraps her arms around my waist, and buries her face in my chest. "I want to get away from all of this. Just for a while."

Folding my arms around her, I gently stroke her hair. "How does Mozambique sound? The weather is warm year-round, and one can buy an island for next to nothing."

"That sounds good," she whispers.

"What about a Robinson Crusoe style house? On pillars on the water."

"Sounds like paradise."

"I'll get you a nurse, and one for Hanna, too. I already checked with the researcher running the clinical trial. We'll be able to do your treatment at home, as long as we check in at his lab in Europe once a month. I'm having everything prepared as we speak."

"You planned it in advance," she accuses, lifting her head to gaze up at me.

"Not adding on a lab that's practically a small clinic. On stilts." I smile down at her. "That part only happened yesterday."

"Sun, sea, Hanna, you, and me. Yes, that sounds infinitely good."

I kiss her lips. "Let's clean this up, shall we?"

I want to wipe everything clean. I may not be able to take away what she's suffered, but I'm going to damn well make it better.

"Oh, come on," Ilya says, trying not to look guilty. "Admit it. I did a good job."

Anton, Ilya, and I are standing in their room, wearing the shirts, ties, and suits my brother bought. The fit isn't bad. Neither is the style. But when I look down at my borrowed Crocs—white, no less, with a black fucking suit—I want to slap Ilya on the head.

"It would've been almost all right if you hadn't forgotten the shoes." At least he and Anton get to wear their boots.

"You didn't say anything about shoes," Ilya complains.

Anton tries hard to smother his laughter. "It's not so bad."

"Yeah." I adjust my shirt cuffs with a yank. "Right."

"The cake is a winner." Anton gives up and erupts in a fit of snort-laughter.

"Hey." Ilya places a hand on his heart, his face pulled into an expression of indignation. "Yan said something white and fancy. That's fancy and white, right?"

I glare at the cake, which is a marzipan square decorated with big-eyed bunnies climbing all over the sides. The fucking Lapin Cretin and his whole Raving Rabbids family.

"It's white," Ilya says defensively. "It's all the bakery had in white."

"If we pull off the rabbits," Anton says, "it might not be so bad."

A knock falls on the door. Adami pops her head around the frame. "It's time."

An attack of nerves like I've never had, not even on a job, tightens my gut.

"Here." Ilya hands me the ring. "We better go. You don't want Mina to arrive before us."

I slip the ring into my pocket. At least this is the one thing Ilya got right. It's a beautiful stone, deep red and perfectly cut, set in rose-gold and surrounded by smaller rubies.

My heart stampedes like a runaway bull as we make our way to the small chapel where visitors and patients go to pray. The chapel was Adami's idea. I was adamant about bringing Mina there in a wheelchair, but my girl didn't want to hear about it. She insisted on walking in by herself, gunshot wound or not. She's a tough princess.

Hanna and the priest are already there. Hanna hugs me when I kiss her cheek. Since neither Ilya nor I had thought about flowers, Anton picked some in the garden—cornflowers and white violets tied with a blue ribbon one of the nurses provided.

I take my place at the small altar with Anton and Ilya flanking me. When Adami opens the door, I turn to face my bride.

Dressed in a short, white, A-line dress with a whimsical boa feather collar, Mina looks like a vision, the sum of my dreams come true. She's perfect, down to her white clinic slippers. My throat goes dry, my chest feeling like it's about to burst from the emotions inside. Ilya wouldn't let me see the dress before this. I have to admit, he did great. Even if he forgot shoes for Mina, too. Not that it matters what she wears. A potato sack would've been perfect.

Anton rushes forward and hands Mina the makeshift bouquet before offering his arm to lead her down the aisle. As she walks toward me, straight and proud despite her injury, my past and future fall away. All that has been and will be turns inconsequential in the enormity of the moment, the moment in which she freely chooses to become mine.

I give up on containing my emotions. What I feel is too much for any man to conceal. I let it flow, let her smile light up my life and give meaning to my existence. I let her invade my soul and take my heart prisoner. She's sublime. Beautiful. Sheer perfection.

The priest says what priests say at wedding

ceremonies, but I hardly hear the words. I'm too aware of Mina's small body and how good it feels where our sides touch. I'm too aware of her smell and the warmth of her skin when I grip her delicate hand and slide the ring over her finger. The ruby is red like the blood she shed for me, red like my love for her.

"I do," she says, and my world turns just right.

She's mine.

For the rest of our lives.

EPILOGUE: MINA

PRAGUE, 3 YEARS LATER

*T*he view over Prague is magnificent. The restaurant is on the hill next to the castle, showcasing the domed copper rooftops that dominate the cityscape like a scene straight from a fairy tale. The only sight more beautiful than the one below is the man sitting across from me.

Yan brushes back his dark hair with a big, masculine hand. The gesture is innocent, but when I remember what those hands are capable of, a spark lights in my belly. The way his jacket fits his broad shoulders kindles that spark into a flame. His eyes are alight with the knowledge of what he does to me, and the fire in those jade-green depths is a promise of what will happen later at our apartment.

I appreciate that he kept the place. It holds memories for me. Fond ones.

When the waiter has poured the champagne, Yan clinks his glass against mine. "To three years."

"Three years," I echo.

Three years in remission. It hasn't always been easy, but true to his word, Yan was there for me. He told me I was strong when I was physically weak. He told me I was beautiful when I lost all my hair. He fed and bathed me. He held and comforted me. We celebrated the small milestones together. Then the bigger ones. He fought and rejoiced with me. He held me when I had my nightmares. He still does, although these days they're less frequent. He didn't spare any expenses with the medical care at our Mozambican home. He hired a whole team to take care of Hanna and me, to cook and clean and nurse us. He never left my side. Not once. He was my rock when Hanna quietly passed away in her sleep last year. The hole her absence left still hurts, but sharing my grief with Yan makes it more bearable.

Leaning over the table, he grips a lock of my shoulder-length hair and lets it slide through his fingers. It's a seductive touch, one that makes me press my knees together under the table to still the ache between my legs.

"I like the dress," he says in a low voice, brushing a finger along the curve of my neck to my shoulder. Goosebumps follow in the wake of his touch.

He should like it. He bought it. The dress is very feminine, a lace-over-silk creation that falls mid-thigh.

I give him a heated look. "I like us."

"Do you now?" His timbre is rough, lustful.

"We said we were going sightseeing this afternoon," I remind him with a smile. So far, we haven't seen much more than the inside of his bedroom. *Our* bedroom.

My phone vibrates on the tabletop. I glance at the screen. Unlisted number. A second later, Yan's phone vibrates.

Holding each other's eyes, we sip our champagne. This is supposed to be a sentimental holiday to celebrate my third year of being healthy. We're not supposed to work. But I see the temptation in his gaze.

I narrow my eyes in a dare. Kicking off a shoe, I trail my toes up his leg. He stiffens, swallows visibly, and catches my foot before I reach my destination. Placing my foot in his lap, he massages it gently even as his attention sharpens. He's watching me like a hawk, calling the bluff of my failed distraction.

Another moment of silent challenge passes.

When I reach for my phone, lightning fast, he moves too. We're both unlocking our screens, our fingers tapping fast.

I hit send. "It's mine."

He drags a heated gaze over me. "Not if I beat you to it."

"You won't dare."

He raises a brow. "Is that a challenge?"

"You did the job in Poland."

"You did the one in Angola."

My smile is seductive. "Ladies first."

"Oh, but my princess is only a lady when it suits her." He strokes a thumb over the arch of my foot. "We could do the job together, split it fifty-fifty."

"Three million each?" I pout. "I had my heart set on six."

"What's mine is yours anyway, Minochka." His smile is pure sex.

"If you put it like that, how can I resist?"

He checks his watch. "If we hurry, we can catch a flight and make it to the meeting point in time."

"Should we get the check?"

Pushing to his feet, he pulls out my chair. "Only if we go Dutch."

Holding hands, we hurry outside into the magnificent sunlight that bounces off the Vltava River. The sound of our shoes falls on the cobblestone street, a happy rhythm that echoes in the beat of my heart. My breathing spikes with the excitement that always comes with a job.

I feel the pull of danger.

I feel alive.

Yan tugs on my hand, changing direction toward an alley. "Shortcut."

Laughing, high on life and happiness, I follow him down the narrow, shadowed passage. The breath leaves my body when Yan grabs me around the waist and pushes my back against the rough wall.

He cages me in between his arms, trapping me with the weight of his hips. "I think we can spare a minute."

"We're going to miss the flight," I say, already reaching for his belt.

He slides a palm up the inside of my leg, over the

thigh holster with my knife and pistol, instantly making me wet. "We'll take our own plane."

"In that case…" Taking the pistol from the back of his waistband, I drop to my knees and carefully lay the weapon at his feet.

"Fuck, Mina." He catches my head between his hands, his eyes ablaze with need and love. "I can't get over you. Ever."

Unzipping his pants, I stare up at his face. "Then don't."

He threads his fingers through my hair, pulling just enough to make my feminine parts clench. "You're fucking dangerous."

I am. And so is he. My need for him is all-consuming. Complete. I don't care where we are or what time it is.

"Do it," he says through gritted teeth, already impatient.

So I do. I give him what he wants, and he lets me. He lets me disarm him. He lets me make him vulnerable. He lets me conquer him before spinning us around and conquering me right back.

Together, we find light within the darkness, and warmth in the cold pastures of our hearts.

The End

SNEAK PEEKS

Thank you for reading! If you would consider leaving a review, it would be greatly appreciated.

To be notified about our next books, sign up for our newsletters at annazaires.com and charmainepauls.com, and be sure to check out our books in audio!

Dark & Contemporary Romance by Anna Zaires:

- *The Twist Me Trilogy* – Nora & Julian's dark, twisted love story
- *The Capture Me Trilogy* – Lucas & Yulia's breathtaking enemies-to-lovers romance
- *The Tormentor Mine Series* – Peter & Sara's intense captive romance, where we first meet Yan & his crew

- ***Wall Street Titan*** – a sizzling contemporary romcom featuring a billionaire and a cat lady

Dark & Contemporary Romance by Charmaine Pauls:

- ***Beauty in the Broken*** – a dark forced marriage romance about revenge and salvation
- ***The Loan Shark Duet*** – a dark mafia romance with a *Beauty and The Beast* theme
- ***The Age Between Us Duet*** – an older-woman/younger-man romance that will melt your e-reader
- ***Catch Me Twice*** — a heartbreaking second chance romance about betrayal and redemption

Sci-Fi Romance by Anna Zaires:

- ***The Mia & Korum Trilogy*** – an epic sci-fi romance with the ultimate alpha male
- ***The Krinar Captive*** – Emily & Zaron's captive romance, set just before the Krinar Invasion
- ***The Krinar Exposé*** – Anna's scorching hot collaboration with Hettie Ivers, featuring Amy & Vair—and their sex club games
- ***The Krinar World stories*** – Sci-fi romance

stories by other authors, set in the Krinar world

Sci-Fi Romance by Charmaine Pauls:

- *The Krinar Experiment* – alpha alien kidnapping at its hottest, set in Anna Zaires's Krinar world
- *The Krinar's Informant* – an alpha alien captive romance, set in Anna Zaires's Krinar world

Sci-fi and Fantasy Collaborations by Anna Zaires and her husband, Dima Zales:

- *The Girl Who Sees* – the thrilling tale of Sasha Urban, a stage illusionist who discovers unexpected secret powers
- *Mind Dimensions* – the action-packed urban fantasy adventures of Darren, who can stop time and read minds
- *Upgrade* – the mind-blowing technothriller featuring venture capitalist Mike Cohen, whose Brainocyte technology will forever change the world
- *The Last Humans* – the futuristic sci-fi/dystopian story of Theo, who lives in a world where nothing is as it seems
- *The Sorcery Code* – the epic fantasy

adventures of sorcerer Blaise and his
creation, the beautiful and powerful Gala

And now, please turn the page for a little taste of
Dubious by Charmaine Pauls and *Tormentor Mine* by
Anna Zaires.

EXCERPT FROM DUBIOUS BY
CHARMAINE PAULS

I'm a loan shark. Breaking people is in my blood. The Haynes's were supposed to be a straightforward job. Go in and pull the trigger twice. One bullet for Charlie, one for his sister. But when I saw Valentina, I wanted her. Only, in our world, those who owe us don't get second chances. No way in hell will my mother let her live. So I devised a plan to keep her.

It's depraved.
It's immoral.
It's dubious.

It's perfect.
Just like her.

The knock on the door startles me, even if I expected

it. I can't move. I should've taken Charlie and run last night. No, they would've found us. Then it would've been worse. You can't outrun The Breaker.

Another knock falls, harder this time. The sound is hollow on the false wood.

"Stand up straight." Don't show your fear, I want to say, but Charlie won't understand.

No third knock comes.

The door breaks inward, pressed wood splintering with a dry, brittle sound. Three men file through the frame to make my worst nightmare come true. They're carrying guns. Dark complexions, Portuguese, except for the one in the middle. He's South African. He moves with a limp, his right leg stiff. Gabriel is even uglier up close. In the daylight, the blue of his eyes look frozen. They hold the warmth of an iceberg as his gaze does a merry-go-round of the room, gauging the situation to the minutest details with a single glance.

He knows we're unprotected. He knows we're frightened, and he likes it. He feeds off it. His chest swells, stretching the jacket over his broad shoulders. He taps the gun against his thigh while his free hand closes and opens around empty air.

Tap, tap. Tap, tap.

Those hands. My God, they're enormous. The skin is dark and rough with strong veins and a light coat of black hair. Those are hands not afraid of getting dirty. They're hands that can wrap around a neck and crush a windpipe with a squeeze.

I swallow and lift my gaze to his face. He's no

longer taking stock of the room. He's assessing me. His eyes run over my body as if he's looking for sins in my soul. It feels as if he cuts me open and lets my secrets pour out. He makes me feel exposed. Vulnerable. His presence is so intense, we're communicating with the energy alone that vibrates around us. His stare reaches deep inside of me and filters through my private thoughts to see the truth, that his cruel self-assurance stirs both hate and awe. It's the awe he takes, as if it's his right to explore my intimate feelings, but he does so probingly, tenderly almost, executing the invasive act with respect.

Then he loses interest. As soon as he's sucked me dry, I cease to exist. I'm the carpet he wipes his feet on. His expression turns bored as he fixes his attention on Charlie.

Taking back some power, I say, "What do you want?"

His lips twitch. He knows I'm bluffing. "You know why I'm here."

His voice is deep. The rasp of that dark tone resonates with authority and something more disturbing--sensuality. He speaks evenly, articulating every word. Somehow, the musical quality and controlled volume of his voice make the statement sound ten times more threatening than if he'd shouted it. Under different circumstances I would've been enchanted by the rich timbre. All I feel now is fear, and it's reflected on Charlie's face. I hate that I can't take it away for him.

"I'll only ask you once," Gabriel says, "and I want a simply yes or no answer." *Tap, tap. Tap, tap.* "Do you have my money?"

Spatters of words dribble from Charlie's lips. "I–I do–don't li–like them. Not ni–nice me–men."

The man on the left, the one with the lime green eyes, lifts his gun and aims at Charlie's feet. It happens too fast. Before I can charge, his finger tightens on the trigger. The silencer dampens the shot. I wait for the damage, blood to color the white of Charlie's tennis shoe, but instead there's a wail, and Puff falls over.

Oh, no. Please. No. Dear God. No, no, no.

It has to be a horror movie, but the hole between Puff's eyes is very real. So is the blood running onto the linoleum. The lifeless body on the floor unfurls a rage in me. He was only a defenseless animal. The unfairness, the cruelty, and my own helplessness are fuel on my shocked senses.

In a fit of blind fury, I storm the man with the gun. "You sorry excuse of a man!"

He ducks, easily grabbing both my wrists in one hand. When he aims the gun at my head, Gabriel says, his beautiful voice vibrating like a tight-pulled guitar string, "Let her go."

The man obliges, giving me a shove that makes me stumble. The minute I'm free, I go for Gabriel, punching my fists in his stomach and on his chest. The more he stands there and takes my hammering, my assault having no effect on him, the closer I come to tears.

Gabriel lets me carry on, to make a fool of myself, no doubt, but I can't help it. I go on until my energy is spent, and I have to stop in painful defeat. Going down on my knees, I feel Puff's tiny chest. His heartbeat is gone. I want to hug him to my body, but Charlie is huddled in the corner, ripping at his hair.

Ignoring the men, I straighten and cup Charlie's hands, pulling them away from his head. "Remember what I said about being brave?"

"Bra–brave."

So much hatred for Gabriel and his cronies fills me that my heart is as black as a burnt-out volcano. There's no space for anything good in there. I know I shouldn't give in to the darkness of the sensations coursing through my soul, but it's as if the blackness is an ink stain that bleeds over the edges of a page. I embrace the anger. If I don't, fear will consume me.

Gabriel gives me a strangely compassionate look. "You owe me an answer."

"Look around you." I motion at our flat. "Does it look like we can afford that kind of money? You're a twisted man for giving a mentally disabled person a loan."

His eyes narrow and crinkle in the corners. "You have no idea how twisted I'm willing to get." Gabriel grasps Charlie by the collar of his T-shirt, dragging him closer. "For the record, if you didn't want your brother to make debt, you should've declared him incompetent and revoked his financial signing power."

"Leave him alone!"

I grab Gabriel's arm and hang on it with my full weight, but it makes no difference. I'm dangling on him like a piece of washing on a line. He swats me away, sending me flying to the ground, and presses the barrel of his pistol against my brother's soft temple where a vein pulses with an innocent life not yet lived.

"Va–Val!"

He cocks the safety. "Yes or no?"

"Yes!" Using the wall at my back for support, I scramble to my feet. "I'll pay it."

Charlie cries softly. Gabriel looks at me as if he notices nothing else. His eyes pin me to the spot. Under his gaze, I'm a frog splayed and nailed to a board, and he holds the scalpel in his hand.

He doesn't lower the gun. "Do you know how much?"

"Yes." My voice doesn't waver.

"Say it."

"Four hundred thousand."

"Where's the money?"

The ghost of a smile is back on his face. Behind the scarred mask is a man who knows how to hurt people to get what he wants, but for now he's entertained. The bastard finds the situation amusing.

"I'll pay it off."

He tilts his head. "You'll pay it off." He makes it sound as if I'm mad.

"With interest."

"Miss Haynes, I assume." Despite his declared assumption, he says it like it's a fact. Everything about him shouts confidence and arrogance. "Tell me your name."

"You know my name." Men like him know the names of all the family members before they move in for the kill.

"I want to hear you say it."

I wet my dry lips. "Valentina."

He seems to digest the sound like a person would taste wine on his tongue. "How much do you earn, Valentina?"

I refuse to cower. "Sixty thousand."

He lowers the gun. It's a game to him now. "Per month?"

"Per year."

He laughs softly. "What do you do?"

"I'm an assistant." I don't offer more. It's enough that he already knows my name.

He regards me with his arms hanging loosely at his sides. "Nine years."

It sounds ridiculous, but the quick calculation I do in my head assures me it's not. That's almost five thousand per month, including thirty percent interest on the lump sum. I can't call him unfair. Loan sharks in this neighborhood ask anything between fifty to a hundred and fifty percent interest.

"Nine years if you pay it back with the lowest of interests," he continues, confirming my calculation.

Of course, I'm not planning on staying a vet assistant forever. It's only until I qualify as a vet in four more years. By then, I'll be earning more. "I'll pay it off faster when I get a better job."

He closes the two steps between us with an uneven gait. He's standing so near I can smell the detergent of his shirt and the faint, spicy fragrance of his skin.

"You misunderstood my offer." His eyes drill into mine. "You'll work for *me* for nine years."

My breath catches. "For you?"

He just looks at me.

"Doing what?" I ask on a whisper.

The intensity in those iced, blue depths sharpens. "Any duty I see fit. Think carefully, Valentina. If you accept, it'll be a live-in position."

Visit charmainepauls.com to order your copy of *Dubious* today!

EXCERPT FROM TORMENTOR MINE
BY ANNA ZAIRES

He came to me in the night, a cruel, darkly handsome stranger from the most dangerous corners of Russia. He tormented me and destroyed me, ripping apart my world in his quest for vengeance.

Now he's back, but he's no longer after my secrets.

The man who stars in my nightmares wants me.

"Are you going to kill me?"

She's trying—and failing—to keep her voice steady. Still, I admire her attempt at composure. I approached her in public to make her feel safer, but she's too smart to fall for that. If they've told her anything about my background, she must realize I can snap her neck faster than she can scream for help.

"No," I answer, leaning closer as a louder song comes on. "I'm not going to kill you."

"Then what do you want from me?"

She's shaking in my hold, and something about that both intrigues and disturbs me. I don't want her to be afraid of me, but at the same time, I like having her at my mercy. Her fear calls to the predator within me, turning my desire for her into something darker.

She's captured prey, soft and sweet and mine to devour.

Bending my head, I bury my nose in her fragrant hair and murmur into her ear, "Meet me at the Starbucks near your house at noon tomorrow, and we'll talk there. I'll tell you whatever you want to know."

I pull back, and she stares at me, her eyes huge in her pale face. I know what she's thinking, so I lean in again, dipping my head so my mouth is next to her ear.

"If you contact the FBI, they'll try to hide you from me. Just like they tried to hide your husband and the others on my list. They'll uproot you, take you away from your parents and your career, and it will all be for nothing. I'll find you, no matter where you go, Sara... no matter what they do to keep you from me." My lips brush against the rim of her ear, and I feel her breath hitch. "Alternatively, they might want to use you as bait. If that's the case—if they set a trap for me—I'll know, and our next meeting won't be over coffee."

She shudders, and I drag in a deep breath, inhaling her delicate scent one last time before releasing her.

Stepping back, I melt into the crowd and message Anton to get the crew into positions.

I have to make sure she gets home safe and sound, unmolested by anyone but me.

Visit annazaires.com to order your copy of *Tormentor Mine* today!

ABOUT THE AUTHORS

Anna Zaires is a *New York Times, USA Today,* and #1 international bestselling author of sci-fi romance and contemporary dark erotic romance. She fell in love with books at the age of five, when her grandmother taught her to read. Since then, she has always lived partially in a fantasy world where the only limits were those of her imagination. Currently residing in Florida, Anna is happily married to Dima Zales (a science fiction and fantasy author) and closely collaborates with him on all their works. To learn more, please visit annazaires.com.

Charmaine Pauls was born in Bloemfontein, South Africa. She obtained a degree in Communication at the University of Potchestroom, and followed a diverse career path in journalism, public relations, advertising, communications, photography, graphic design, and brand marketing. Her writing has always been an integral part of her professions.

When she is not writing, she likes to travel, read, and rescue cats. Charmaine currently lives in Montpellier with her husband and children. Their household is a linguistic mélange of Afrikaans, English, French and Spanish. To learn more, please visit charmainepauls.com.

Printed in Great Britain
by Amazon